Master of the Banshee

SLEEPER CHRONICLES

Ray Zdan

With the best wishes to Gareth!
Ray Zdan

ISBN: 1999737733
ISBN-13: 978-1-9997377-3-3

My name is Kyle Firestone, and I am a Sleeper.

It wasn't my choice, and I longed for my previous simple life, when my dreams and nightmares were just dreams and nightmares, ending as soon as I woke up. I could easily forget them while brushing my teeth and go on with my life. Everything was different now.

I was happy to lurk in my tiny flat away from society. I had no family and no friends to share my life with, nor had I any desire to do that. The world outside was frightening with all those strange people, and I preferred to spend my evenings alone. I was a humble office worker like thousands of others, doing my job in semi-automation mode. I was happy to hide in the crowd and exist without attracting attention. I needed nobody, and no one needed me. That was until that freak incident on the train. Then everything changed.

Each night my consciousness somehow transferred to Rehen –

an alien world. At first, I wasn't entirely sure if that world was real or simply a product of my swollen imagination. But then I bumped into others living the same cycle with slow realisation freaking me out – this was a permanent curse without the slightest chance of breaking free.

With my consciousness hopping between the two worlds, I was forced to live two separate lives. That wasn't easy.

I was a Prince in Rehen. I even had a small country to rule over, but this role was too frightening for my autistic nature. Back in England, I suffered mental spasms every time somebody in the office laid eyes on my humble person, but I was in the constant spotlight in Rehen. Somehow, I managed to fight my wars and to multiply my enemies. I gained a few friends on the way too.

I was living alone in London without any friends, relatives or family but, on the other plane of reality, in Rehen, I had brothers and sisters who ruled neighbouring kingdoms. Amongst us, there was bitter friction as we vied for the vacant throne of our father. I was unfortunate to find myself in the body of the eldest among them – a clear prime target for whoever wanted to proceed along the line of succession. I did not feel any desire to occupy the seat myself. Life was too complicated even without that grave responsibility. I was advised to trust no one, and I did my best. Still, I wasn't sure if that was the right thing to do.

I had no sympathy for the person who ruled the House of

Chadrack in Rehen – me. I was known as the Bloody Prince, but this notoriety wasn't of my own doing. In fact, I found myself in the body of the Prince on my first day in Rehen – with a blank memory and no clues about my identity. I built my knowledge by picking up bits and pieces, accidentally dropped by others but, when I found out the sickening truth, I began hating the twisted tyrant soul who had occupied the body of Prince Kyleb before me. But since my arrival, no one in Chadrack knew that the soul of the Bloody Prince had changed. Well, almost no one…

I was grateful to my sister, Keely – ruler of the neighbouring Porlok – for unknowingly showing me the Well of Power under my castle – I would never have found the way there myself. I watched her charging her magic Ruby Ring – the Master of Love – in the purple flames of the Well, wondering how vital the role of magic in Rehen was. I was scared by the thought of knowing nothing about that, but I had a similar Sapphire Ring to try.

After Keely left, I was lucky to meet Hawa, the Keeper of the Well – a monstrous creature willing to share a few secrets. I acquired the power, but my blank memory was still the greatest obstacle. I felt like a monkey with a hand grenade or, more precisely, a nuclear button, dealing with a force about which I had no knowledge or skills.

Later, I met my sister Hel. At first, I was freaked by her sobriquet – the Death. She was able to wipe out entire countries with the magic of her Onyx Ring; I was sure about that. I nearly died trying to keep her away from Chadrack, as my own magic skills couldn't even remotely match hers. I was lucky, I didn't get into direct combat with her, but my own fears and clumsiness effectively delivered me into the hands of the Death. I was petrified at first, but later I never felt more alive while drinking tea and eating biscuits with her in the mountains. I wasn't afraid of Death.

I was frightened later when our small party with just a squad of her dark knights in our defence was attacked by an army of ghouls – dreadful cannibals plaguing the land. I saw only a glimpse of her power when Hel ordered me to hide or fall as collateral damage. I was sure she repulsed the attack. I didn't see it.

I ran.

I ran as fast as I could with ghouls chasing me among the rocks and ravens. I was stupid enough to hide in an underground cave and managed to collapse the only exit trying to block the way in for the ghouls. This left me stranded in complete darkness without any food or hope. Nobody would be able to find me there, under the vast mountain range. Nobody would ever look. I was on my own.

My magic Sapphire Ring, the Master of Destiny, was peacefully shining on my finger, nearly wholly exhausted. I needed the Well of Power to make it operational again, but the Well was too far away, unreachable. My Ring was using its remaining energy as a power source for the pitiful piece of a green crystal – the only spark in the otherwise complete darkness of the cave.

All this was in Rehen, in my nightly nightmare.

It was a bright day in London. I was sitting in my tiny flat, looking through the window at the passing planes, sipping my morning coffee and preparing to die.

The weather was cheery outside, but my mood remained dark, with the remnants of hope slowly fading.

My situation was hopeless, I knew that. It was the curse of Rehen – death would be final. If I died in the dream world, then I would never wake up in the real world either. I was stranded in the dark cave without any food or water. The agony could extend into days and weeks, as long as I managed to survive underground. There I would probably starve to death despite being able to buy any bountiful feast I wanted for myself in London. Or I might be lucky enough to break my neck falling into some deep trench in the darkness. That death would be quick. I savoured the thought while stretching my nerves to their limits. There was no easy way to prepare for inevitable. Yes, I was a Sleeper, and I was doomed. I had no one to rely on. I was stuck in the dream world, and only the other Sleeper could make a difference—the other Sleeper whom I trusted.

If that unfortunate turn of events had been a week ago, I could have asked Rick for help. I knew Rick in London, and he was Rhys, my jaeger in Rehen. He could bring a squad of jaegers to clear the path for Prince Kyleb (me) despite any dangers. I trusted him. He knew my weaknesses. He had trained me in sword fighting when I was desperate to fill the shoes of Prince Kyleb, afraid to expose any weaknesses. He was a person I could rely on. He was a friend.

I found him in London by mere chance. Rick happened to be a martial arts trainer. When I was hunted down in London, I decided to book onto self-defence courses. I needed to make my weak body be able to at least to flee if not to fight back. Only when Rick began training me to fight with swords did I slowly realise that he was a Sleeper too. Rick used the same technique, the same approach as Rhys in Rehen, and had the same scar on his face. I had no other way to find out other than to ask him a few silly questions directly.

I was happy to find him. Rick helped me to regain my sanity after that dreadful night when I was kidnapped by John. I thought Hel planned to bring me down and leave my Chadrack defenceless. We had to fight back. We developed a genius plan – to kidnap the kidnapper. The plan was designed to build stronger grounds for Chadrack to be able to deal with my sister, Death. Rick helped me to stalk my giant ginger nemesis across the streets of London. Yes – we kidnapped him! But my sweet sense of revenge quickly died along with hope – my kidnapper wasn't connected to Hel in any way. John was simply a bounty hunter and, as he admitted, had taken me by mistake. I wasn't their target. With Hel at my gates, we failed to gain any points against her that night. The kidnapping of John couldn't help us. But it was an even bigger surprise to find out that he was the husband of my other sister, Keely – she was my ally in Rehen. We had no other option but to release John. Our mission had failed.

Rick helped and supported me through all that turmoil. I was sure he would do everything to save me from death in the underground tunnels, but I couldn't ask him now. Rick had gone missing… His flat was a wreck – I saw it, and Rick had disappeared, leaving traces of blood behind. He was dead.

This was what John had told me when I gathered enough courage to ask him for help. I still was uneasy with the man, and it took all my determination to phone him, but John was the only other Sleeper I knew now that Rick was gone. The image of John – the redheaded giant – stalking me through the streets of London was still fresh in my mind. I couldn't forget the feeling of dread and that night of horror being strapped to the bed, waiting to be killed at any moment. I nearly screamed my lungs out when John pierced my forehead with a knife. I didn't know the meaning of this, nor did I know John then. He was my ginger nemesis, and later that night I cried myself to sleep, sure that I would be dead by morning. I wasn't.

They dumped me in the street – alive but deadly terrified. It wasn't an easy decision to call John with all those fearful memories still live in my mind.

When I finally managed to put my fears on hold, he was kind enough to offer a few opinions and suggestions about missing Rick. *Could I ask him for help again?*

I finished my coffee mulling over this thought.

The situation in Rehen was complicated. Hordes of ghouls might be wandering about in the vicinity. Hel's knights and her Onyx – Master of Death might have considerably thinned them out, but I doubted if entirely. John would need a small army to fight his way to the caves. My sister Hel herself was a substantial threat as well, and only a fool would attempt to approach her when she was using her Onyx against the ghouls.

Would John be willing to help me? Or would he instead celebrate my evanescence and the advance of Keely, his wife, in the line of succession to the throne of the realm? I wasn't sure if I would be keen to rush to help him in a similar situation – it was too risky. I wondered if I would ever become brave enough or desperate enough to ask him.

The ringing phone broke through my intimidating thoughts. It was the receptionist from the sports club where Rick used to work as a martial arts guru.

“Do you have any news about Rick?” I asked after the usual short mandatory pleasantries.

“No, unfortunately... We were wondering ourselves. Would you like to switch to another trainer?”

“No, thank you. I'd better wait for Rick.”

“I understand, Rick is such a wonderful person,” sighed the girl. “By the way, this is very unusual, but we have received a letter for you.”

“A letter for me?” That was indeed very strange.

“Yes. It’s got your name on it, but our address. Do you want me to forward it to your home address?”

“No, I’ll collect it today, don't bother...” I said, then thanked her and hung-up.

Was it a trap? Was it salvation?

Someone had somehow connected Rick with me to that club. It was a small wonder – as if I had been on surveillance. They might have seen us together. But who had done this, if it wasn’t John? I realised that I might have another enemy out there – someone who was hunting Sleepers in general, if not me directly. My heart trembled with fear, but I knew I must find out who had done this.

I slowly washed the cup. An ambulance siren wailed down the street, hysterically flashing blue, and the sound pierced the deadly grip of panic in my brain, setting my body into motion.

Would that letter hold the key to Rick's death? Someone had linked me to Rick but still hadn't found out my home address. Would I be the next person to go missing? Now I had doubts about my hasty decision to go to pick that letter up. I should have asked her to forward it by mail and wait until it arrived a few days later, leaving me plenty of time to drown in self-pity. Should I call her back?

I spent nearly an hour dithering about this then curiosity took the winning hand over rational reason, and I decided to pay a visit to the martial arts club.

It felt strange getting into my camouflage outfit again. The last time I had worn, it was when Rick had helped me to stalk John. I was alone now and didn't know who my enemy was. Not yet.

I adjusted my baseball cap and put on dark sunglasses before slipping out.

The weather was hot. I went out and proceeded cautiously down the hill, taking a few shortcuts. Nobody was following me. At least, I couldn't detect any eyes glancing towards me.

I turned left on Bromley Road. Three women were animatedly chatting at the bus stop, then one of them poked a finger in my direction. They grew silent, and I hunched feeling their gazes piercing me. *Damn!* Was there a trap? Were they waiting for me? I rushed forward, feeling sticky drops of perspiration sliding down my back. A few steps later, a wave of hushed giggle reached me, but I wasn't brave enough to look back.

I almost ran across a few small side streets before slowing down. Nobody had followed me. I painted a broad smile on my grim face and entered the reception of the martial arts club. The girl at the desk readily smiled back, returning my polite greeting.

"Are you sure you don't need another trainer? Just to avoid an interruption?" she asked, flickering her false eyelashes.

"No," I shook my head. "I'll wait... I hope he'll be back soon."

"As you wish," she shrugged, handing me the envelope, and I put it into my pocket, not wasting any time to take a glance at it.

We politely exchanged a few more remarks before I thanked her for her trouble and left, wiping the smile off my face on my way out.

A cloud passed over the sun as I got back to Bromley Road, wrapping me in a gust of chill air. I looked around. The street was empty with a red bus just disappearing around the corner, sliding out of view. It seemed safe, but it didn't feel that way. Hesitantly I turned right into the Inchmery Road, trying to avoid those women at the bus stop.

The green canopy of tree crowns shielded the sky as I passed along the line of orderly red brick houses. Some windows looked at me with clear glass, some were draped with shades, behind which who knows what was hiding.

The street was empty, but the sense of danger was now hidden in my pocket, waiting to be released. The sound of my footsteps reverberated strangely against the red brick walls as if invisible shadows were sneaking after me. Twice I glanced over my shoulder, seeing nothing. The street was empty, but the panic was rising and squeezing my throat in its tight grip. I hunched over hiding behind the useless sunglasses and rushed forward, trying to leave this haunted street as fast as I could.

I almost smiled when I finally turned left onto the South Circular with its usual flow of traffic and headed uphill, leaving the imagined menace behind me. At the same time, the flock of clouds had finally moved away, revealing bright sunshine and making my sunglasses more appropriate again. I ran up the squeaky stairs and stood at the top for a full minute catching my breath, then unlocked the door and went inside.

The mysterious envelope was burning my pocket, but first I discarded the camouflage and washed the sweat off my face before I could turn my full attention to the letter.

The envelope was plain white. It had a stamp but, most likely, it had been hand-delivered; I couldn't find any marks from the post office. My name was written on top of the martial arts club address, but I couldn’t recognise the handwriting. That was very strange and told me nothing about the sender. There was no return address, just as I expected.

I carefully shook the envelope – nothing loose moved inside, but I decided to put on latex gloves just in case it contained something hazardous. It wasn't the first weird package I had inspected in my kitchen.

I spread a few old newspapers on the table, carefully turned the envelope over again, then I took a knife and carefully cut the left side of it. Nothing spilt out, and I opened it wide.

Inside was a folded sheet of paper. I took it out and carefully spread it on the table in front of me.

It was a simple plain white sheet with a clearly printed short message in the middle: "If you value your friend's life and wish to see him again, be in central Vienna, *Graben strasse*, next to *Pestsäule* on Friday, at 1:15 pm. Otherwise, may I humbly suggest to buy a larger mailbox. If you fail to show or attempt to involve the authorities, I'll be sending your friend to you in parts."

Of course, there was no signature.

The message brought a shy smile to my face. Despite the threats, it meant that Rick was alive! He was in danger, that was clear too. For a moment, I even forgot my own miserable position. *John was wrong, halleluiah!* And I was happy about it.

Then my joy faded, overshadowed by grave recollection. I had no idea how long I would be able to survive in the underground caves in Rehen. I knew for sure that my death in the dream would lead to the inevitable end of life here in London too – the two states of my were somehow connected. Rick might be as doomed as me. But maybe I could try to save him before I die? I might still have a few days left.

That thought hushed clouds of misery away, but I needed a plan before rushing headlong to Vienna.

The clock was ticking in my head, and I realised that I had to act quickly. It was already Wednesday. I had nearly full two days to get there.

I brewed another mug of coffee and sipped it, trying to concentrate on the letter again. Whoever wrote that letter didn't specifically mention Rick, but I had no other friend who was missing. There was no other request, except for my presence at an exact moment at the place specified, and I doubted if this was related to any small talk about the weather. The real reason, however, remained a mystery.

The note warned me against involving any authorities. I certainly couldn't go to the police, that was clear, but could I ask somebody for help? I had no idea how to proceed with all this impending sense of danger, the joyful thought of Rick being alive, cautious reasoning and willingness to help him out whirled around my head in a crazy swirl. There was a plain intention to entice me in the note, and it would be plain silly to go there without proper preparation. But the shilly-shallying in my soul could be putting Rick in jeopardy. If he was still alive...

I called John.

He agreed that it looked like a way to trap me.

“I think it’s worth risking it anyway. You’ll never find out what happened to Rick until you get there,” he said after some thought. “It's the only clue, and I could accompany you to Vienna if you don't mind. I am not particularly busy now...”

“I would really appreciate that,” I replied. “I’ll buy the plane tickets and book a hotel.”

“Yes, but book different flights and different hotels for both of us, please, you still may be followed – we shouldn't meet in Vienna or acknowledge our acquaintance. It would be best if we could act independently.”

“That sounds wise, but how will I know you where you are?”

“You will. I’ll follow you, and you’ll see me in the distance, but under no circumstances ever show that you know me. I’ll intervene if anything critical happens, don't worry.”

I agreed. Anyway, it was the best backup I could get.

“Let's meet tomorrow then and plan our actions,” he suggested.

“All right,” I said. “I'll call you tomorrow.”

I still felt uneasy about my role as bait, but at least one man would be guarding me. This thought was reassuring, but I still had no clue how far I could trust John, who, only weeks ago, had been chasing me on the streets of London.

I touched the still tender scar on my forehead left by John’s knife, and even more doubts sneaked into my soul. Was I delivering myself into the hands of dangerous plotters?

I spent nearly an hour meditating over a single cup of coffee. My situation in Rehen was hopeless, and I would probably die anyway – a few days or maybe a week later. I still might have some time to save Rick. He would certainly die if I backed out of this venture, betraying him. I couldn't do that. I had no hope for myself, but I was the only hope Rick had.

John seemed suspiciously keen to offer me help, ready to drop everything and fly with me across Europe. While I appreciated the offer, it raised alarm bells, almost freezing me into inactivity. I did my best to remember my sister's Keely visit to Chadrack, remember every word she had said, every smile and gesture. Was she indeed a friend? Or an involuntary ally? Maybe a stealthy enemy? John was her husband in Rehen. *Could I trust him?*

Hawa, the Keeper of the Well, would die laughing at my thoughts. It had been his first and foremost lesson in Rehen – don't trust anyone, especially relatives. Would I be able to manage this mission alone?

I looked for inspiration from the planes passing outside my window. It was clear: without someone guarding my back, I could easily find myself in some dark dungeon next to Rick, bound, miserable and hopeless, dead in a few days. And Rick would be dead too. I needed John, that was obvious. And I must be extremely cautious, that was obvious also.

The rest of the day was hectic and disorganised. I planned our journey between countless visits to the kitchen, inspecting the contents of my fridge, packing some stuff I might need in Vienna and watching the cars pass down the South Circular. Finally, I booked the evening flight on Thursday for John and the early morning flight on Friday for myself.

Then I spent the afternoon studying maps of central Vienna, trying to memorise streets around the *Pestsäule* and possible ways of retreat. It wasn't necessary, but this kept me busy and my worries at bay. I was tired by the end of the day, sleepy, but glad.

Transfer to the dream was quick and painless.

I knew I was in Rehen already when the distinct odour of dust hit my nostrils. For a few long minutes, I lay still, listening. The waters of the underground stream were quietly running nearby with occasional splashes of droplets from the high ceiling where excessive dew had condensed. Then I heard a strange sound somewhere in the distance. It was a whisper or sigh at first, followed by a barely audible rattle.

A snake?!

I sat up in the complete darkness with my heart racing, and I listened while holding my breath. The rattling repeated a little closer. It had a strange quality as if wooden knuckles were softly beating on a drum, only with very different intervals each time. Whoever was making that noise was much bigger than a snake.

Then a few pebbles rolled along the ground as if someone had stumbled and kicked them.

I reached into my Ring, and it pulsed in the darkness with a barely visible blue hue, but its power was too exhausted for any other task except for lighting the tiny green crystal. I was terrified of the unknown which was approaching me in the darkness but still was reluctant to move. If I risked lighting the crystal now, my position would be revealed.

The rattling was coming closer, and I heard something splash in the water, waves echoing through the apparently sizeable dark grotto. I gasped, still afraid to move.

"Oh!" came a sudden exclamation. "I have a guest! You can stop hiding. I see you..."

The voice was strange – low, dull and crackling as if the speaker had a handful of stones in his throat.

It was no use in hiding any further or maintaining the silence. With a trembling heart, I reached into my Ring and lit the crystal.

"Oh!" another exclamation reached me from the darkness. "You are wearing the Heart of Kjell..."

"Who are you?"

"I am Sluagh," said the voice in the darkness. "I mean no harm to the Heart."

"Show yourself!" I said, stretching out the glowing crystal into the darkness.

"Are you sure you want to see me, dear?" Sluagh still sounded polite.

I wasn't sure as my heart was already drumming an insane

beat in my temples, but the unknown hiding in the impenetrable darkness was even more terrifying.

"Yes, please..."

"Well... "

The rattling resumed, and a huge monster appeared at the edge of my tiny circle of light – only a small part of the monster, in fact. Sluagh was a giant centipede, and the far end of his body was somewhere far away, in the darkness. He bent his head to the right, staring at me with his three pairs of unblinking black eyes.

"Happy now?" asked the creature; its jaws moved to produce that strange rattling sound.

I nearly fainted just looking at those jaws moving a few yards away from my face.

"It's all right with me," I managed to mumble with a wooden-stiff tongue. "And who is Kjell?" I added, preparing for another monster.

"You are wearing the Heart of Kjell and still don't know who Kjell was? The old gryphon must have been feeble-minded to give it to you. It's none of my business, but that seems such a waste! What are you doing here?" Sluagh ended the rant bending its head slightly to the left.

"I am lost," it was almost true. "Is there any way out?"

Sluagh chuckled.

"Of course, there is – you managed to get in here! Why not use the same way out?"

"It was blocked when the ceiling collapsed," I explained. "Is there any *other* way?"

"Then you are unlucky, dear," stated Sluagh flatly. "I am not entirely sure, but there might be only one *other* way if you are brave enough to follow the path by the river of flames. It is extremely dangerous, though, be warned."

"Does that path lead out of these caves?" It was the only concern I had.

"I don't know," Sluagh's voice sounded indifferent. "I have never tried that myself."

"And there's no other way which is safe?"

"Don't pretend to be dumb, dear," Sluagh chuckled again. "Dumb people don't wear the Heart. The only other way has been blocked, as you just said yourself."

I felt utterly hopeless. Death was imminent if I stayed here, and almost certain if I attempted to try the only remaining way out, which anyway may not lead out of caves. And the caves were occupied by that giant insect looming over me which would undoubtedly feast on my body after my death. Or it might become hungry even sooner.

It wasn't difficult to decide with those scary jaws moving over me. The monster looked at me with its three rows of anthracite-black eyes, and I saw no compassion in them.

"Which way is that river of flames?" I asked, not allowing desperation to show in my voice.

"It's not too far, down that tunnel..." said Sluagh pointing with one of its front legs.

"Which tunnel?" there was complete darkness beyond the greenish bubble of light created by the luminous crystal.

"Oh!" the centipede exclaimed impatiently. "How can I tell you when you are blind as a bat?"

Sluagh raised its right front leg and scratched its head with three bright red claws, thinking.

"Could you show me the way?" I asked politely. "Please…"

The monster stopped scratching.

"I am busy," it said at last. "Can't your Heart show you the way?" the monster pointed at my Sapphire with its claw.

"Why do keep calling my Ring the Heart?"

"Because it *is* the Heart of the gryphon!" he extended his red claw and touched my Ring. "Don't you remember Kjell?"

I stared silently at the claw hovering in front of my face.

"Don't pretend you don't know..." the monster took a few steps closer. "You are the One. The Heart will certainly kill you if you are not the One. And, still, you remain so ignorant! How can that be possible?"

I felt like a cripple, not for the first time, with such a lack of knowledge.

"Could you tell me more?" I asked, hoping the creature would not lose its temper.

"What do you want to know?" the giant centipede snapped.

"How is my Ring related to Kjell?"

Sluagh was silent and motionless for too long, and I started to feel nervous.

"The gem in your Ring is a gift," it said at last. "The gryphon sacrifices his heart to the worthy man when he thinks that man is the One, and it is unwavering magic. I knew old Kjell well before you placed his Heart on your finger. He was sagacious and reluctant to choose, but I believe he grew demented with age. He did a stupid thing for giving his heart to the One such ignorant as you. Do I need to explain that the gold around Kjell's Heart is just for holding and has no other purposes?"

"I am aware of that," I nodded quickly, not wanting to risk angering the monster.

"Then use the Heart to guide you out! It is simple. Or don't you know how to use it?" Sluagh's jaws moved just a few inches above me, and I could smell the sickening stench of its throat.

"The Heart is exhausted," I admitted backing off half a step. "This light is all that is left."

"Oh!" Sluagh cocked its head. "One is in trouble then."

An uneasy silence followed this statement. I hunched over a little waiting for those jaws to crush me at any moment, but the monster remained silent and motionless.

"Could you help me?" I braved asking again. "In memory of your friend Kjell…"

"Then you *do* remember Kjell, don't you?"

"No," I shook my head. "Forgive my ignorance. I was poisoned recently. This wiped out a large part of my memory. I didn't mean to insult the memory of your friend."

"Kjell wasn't my friend," said the creature disdainfully. "He was just a stupid old gryphon."

"Why he is so special to you then? There must be plenty of rings like that around. If every heart of a gryphon has these properties, then anybody could make a ring..." I asked recalling the gryphon Rhys had burned outside of the castle.

"Stupid thing! I have told you already! It is the sacrifice that creates magic when gryphon finds the worthy human! If that human is unworthy and takes the gryphon's heart by force, it is an entirely different story."

"Please, don't talk in riddles. What kind of story is that?" I risked upsetting the monster.

"It's not a story. It's nothing," said Sluagh angrily. "If you take it by force and kill a gryphon, it's then just a heart, a worthless piece of meat, dear! You need the will of a gryphon to make it magic."

An uneasy silence fell upon us again as we looked at each

other.

“Forgive me for my ignorance,” I apologised, trying to ease the tension.

Sluagh said nothing.

“Could you show me the way?”

“Very well...” said Sluagh thoughtfully. “I'll show you the way. But the tunnels are narrow, and two of us will not fit side-by-side. You will have to go ahead. Or follow me. Which would you prefer?”

“I'll follow you,” the decision was instant – I couldn't think of turning my unprotected back on its ever-moving jaws.

“Be it as you wish,” said the monster. “I would suggest you have a drink before we go, as there will be no more water on the way...”

“It might be a good idea,” I agreed.

Sluagh began moving as I approached the edge of the underground stream.

“Would you wait for me?” I asked, terrified of being left alone.

“You will have plenty of time to drink,” said the centipede, not stopping.

I seemed like just another riddle. I didn’t feel thirsty but took the advice seriously – I drank my full since no water was ahead, or so it told. Only the river of flames...

Sluagh's body was still moving in front of me when I stood up wiping the last drops from my mouth – he was indeed a *giant* centipede. Countless legs flashed in front of me appearing from the darkness and then disappearing into the darkness again in a somewhat mesmerising display. I stood and waited patiently. The process seemed endless.

Nearly ten minutes had passed until, finally, the shiny black backside of Sluagh with a cluster of bright red claws at the end of the short, thick tail appeared in the faint light of the green crystal. I rushed forward, doing my best not to lose sight of the claws as the centipede continued moving steadily, disappearing into the darkness.

I ran after Sluagh barely able to cast a glance around me at dusty rocks and black, crystal-like structures flashing passed in the gloom of the dim green light. The pace was insane, and soon I was sweating and gasping for air, but forced my body to continue.

I realised that we had left the grotto and had entered a long corridor whose ghostly walls appeared from the dark and were narrowing and expanding randomly without any visible change of direction. The path was uneven, but I managed to keep up without falling flat on my face.

Soon I lost track of time in the monotony. Sluagh moved on, not stopping anywhere and bending all obstacles with his enormously long body.

We passed several other caverns on our way, most likely – I

couldn't be sure with such poor light, but the walls would disappear, and the echo of our footsteps changed, and then the walls reappeared again as we entered another tunnel. Several times the ceiling descended quite low – I could almost touch it with my hand, but much bigger Sluagh didn't seem to have any problems with that. The centipede simply bent its legs without slowing down. The monster knew the way as it proceeded without a moment of hesitation, maintaining the speed and depleting my scarce remaining strength.

My legs began to ache, but I was afraid to let my pace tail off and kept going at the very limit of my physical ability. I was sure I would get lost in no time – who knew how many other passages and side tunnels were hidden in the darkness?

Hours later, I was so exhausted with my legs aching that I began to lean on the nearby walls and once I almost lost my lighting crystal. I yelled to the centipede several times, begging for a break without any success. Sluagh just moved on. Maybe I was too far away from its head to be heard?

We were passing another large grotto when suddenly Sluagh stopped, and I almost bumped into its butt.

"What's happened?!" I asked loudly.

The butt didn't move or answer. I waited, leaning on a large boulder and gratefully taking the opportunity to rest, ready to spring to my feet the instant the marching resumed.

Ten minutes later, Sluagh's head appeared out of the darkness at the right side of its butt. The creature stared silently at me with its black eyes.

"What?" I asked still gasping for air.

"We have arrived," it announced.

It looked like just another spot in the endless darkness.

"Well..." I looked around. "Where is that river of flames?"

"It's just a few paces down that corridor," the monster explained. "I won't go there – it's all yours."

"Thank you," I mumbled looking around, still unable to see anything.

"Don't thank me," observed the creature. "I am sure you will die on your way. And may I remind you – I don't know where that path leads. Maybe you will change your mind?"

I shook my head. Spending the remaining few days of my life without any food and water or eating worms in desperation (if there were any) didn't appeal to me at all. I'd rather die trying to get out.

"Thank you," I repeated. "I'll give it a try..."

"As you wish," said Sluagh. "Good luck!"

Its head passed me and disappeared into the darkness. For some time, I observed the mesmerising movements of its many legs marching away in the dusk then its butt was gone too.

I was left alone in the darkness in the middle of nowhere. Only then I realised that I hadn't asked which way that corridor lay.

"Sluagh!"

The invisible walls of the grotto echoed my voice. I listened, but only grave dusty silence fell around. The monster was probably already speeding down one of the passages.

"Sluagh! Please..."

Nothing... The centipede was gone.

I sat on the rocky floor, almost in tears. I had to find the way on my own. But how? The only option I could think of was to go straight ahead until I bumped into the wall of the grotto and then search the perimeter. I had no idea how many openings I would find in the darkness, how many openings to corridors or side passages were gaping here. I could spend weeks searching all the dead ends and wrong turns! And god-knows-what other dangers lurked in the darkness.

I was already wallowing in a wave of frustration and self-pity when I realised that I needed to take a different approach. I was looking for the river of flames – I might see some reflections of those flames in the darkness if the corridor which led to that river was fairly straight. I jumped to my feet and reached into my Ring, disrupting the link with the crystal. For several long minutes, I stood in complete darkness, allowing my eyes to adapt. It was so quiet I could hear the blood rushing through my veins.

Then I looked around. Sluagh had said it was just a few paces away. The tricky part was that the distance of a few paces for the giant centipede might be much greater for me. I kept on looking with a faint hope that the light wouldn't be blocked by a single sharp corner of the right corridor or by a large boulder in front of the correct entrance.

With hope fading, I cursed my stupidity – not for the first time. At least, I had drunk some water before I attempted that silly chase after the centipede. Now all I had around me was dust and rocks. Death from dehydration might claim my life quicker.

I kept peeking into the darkness until my eyes began to hurt. Tiredness was tightening its deadly grip on me and, still, I had no results. My inflamed brain began producing ghosts and monsters of its own to fill the lack of any visual and auditory stimuli. I was trembling like a mouse looking at the hordes of imaginary creatures lurking in the darkness, at bony hands reaching out for me from the beyond, at crooked fingers trying to rip the heart out of my chest. I felt like I was slowly slipping into an inevitable swamp of insanity.

I was about to give up the whole idea when I suddenly saw a tiny spark or – more precisely – a hint of a spark. I wasn't sure at first if it was a real thing or just another hallucination. I waited, ignoring the imaginary monsters and afraid to turn my head until my neck grew stiff. Then I saw another hint of a flash and one more at the same spot a second later.

I stretched my arm out to indicate the direction and illuminated the crystal in my palm again. Of course, the light was too weak to reach the wall. I had to get closer.

I crawled in the darkness carefully probing the way with my feet and keeping my eyes fixed on that spot where I had seen the sparks. Several times I had to stop, dim the crystal and, waiting for another spark, recheck the direction. I had never realised how large the grotto was – it seemed like an eternity when I finally reached the wall. And there was the entrance to the "a few paces long" corridor gaping open several yards to the left. I was sure now – occasional red reflections danced on the inner walls of the passage even in the faint ghostly-greenish light of the crystal.

I entered the tunnel.

Indeed, what were just a mere few paces for a giant centipede, appeared to be something like a mile for a tired man like me. The temperature was rising as I carefully walked along the corridor. Soon I could turn the crystal off and put it into my pocket. The red glow now was casting enough light to see my way.

But that way was difficult and frightening. Many times, I wanted just to quit, to turn back, let the darkness and self-pity engulf me and wait for my death in some quiet and dusty corner. The air in the corridor grew unbearably hot as I got closer to the opening, which was glowing red ahead of me. It was painful to breathe, but desperation pushed me forward – I had to have a look at that river of flames; it was the only way out!

The last yards were simply scalding. I shaded my eyes and carefully peeked into the enormous cavern, and there was the river – a slowly moving flow of magma forced its way between the steep rocky banks. It appeared from the depths of the mountain on the left and slowly made its way through the grotto, hissing angrily and spitting blue flames.

My heart sank as I looked at the narrow winding path on my right, squeezed between the rocky bank of the magma flow and the wall of the giant cavern. It seemed very uneven, probably with plenty of loose rocks and ravines, and I couldn't even think of what might happen if I should stumble on one of them and fall.

Only a madman could take the risk of walking there. It was almost certain death, but the word "almost" planted a spark of perhaps false hope into my heart. There *was* a dark mouth of the corridor at the far end of the path several hundred yards away, feeding that hope.

The gap was just a narrow slit, barely visible behind the blurring veil of hot air rushing from the flow. Still, it might lead nowhere – the corridor behind it, if there was one, could end in just a few yards, leaving me no other option but to take the burning path back. This thought was frightening, paralysing my will. I wasn't confident that I could make it all the way and reach that slit in the first place. What if I was forced to make it twice?

Suddenly I felt cold despite those waves of heat bursting onto my face, scaring me to death.

I knew I had to try it. I had no other options left. I closed my eyes, trying to envisage that clear underground stream in the darkness where I had drunk my fill for the last time before deciding to attempt this madness. I could have survived weeks there with that water.

But now… I was sure I would never be able to find that stream again without the help of the centipede. And my days were numbered without water. Would it be better just to jump into that fiery flow and end my suffering in a single blow?

I opened my eyes and shook the thought away. My end might be near and miserable, but not yet. I must try it. My life wasn't the only one on a stake – I had to save Rick somehow.

It wasn't difficult to convince myself to postpone this dangerous trek until the next day. I was too tired, already. My running after Sluagh's butt had claimed its price.

I slipped back into the corridor and sheepishly retreated to the calm silence of the darkness. My heart fluttered like that of a frightened mouse but then slowly calmed down with each step I took away from the hellish grotto. I was terrified. I was sure now that Sluagh was right when he had warned me – death here was imminent. I kept repeating this while making my way along the corridor until the painful thought numbed my brain. The fear slowly subsided.

"I must do this!" I cried out aloud with my voice still trembling, and the inner tension was no longer only skin deep. "But not today..."

Slow death in the nameless grotto, starving and thirsty, was waiting for me in the cold darkness. Death in those flames would be painful but instant.

I still had a small spark of hope that I could reach the other side where that dark mouth of the corridor could lead me to safety. I knew that this hope could be false as well, but I just hated to give it up.

I slowly stepped several more yards left from the burning hell behind me with the red reflections of dancing flames lighting my way. My mood was grim, and my thoughts were dark with bestial fear flooding my every single cell. I left the corridor behind slowly creeping along the rocky walls, barely seeing anything around me. A few steps later, I stumbled on a stone and almost fell, suddenly realising that the light from the flames was no longer there.

I went through my pockets, searching for the greenish glowing crystal, and then cursed aloud – it was gone! I had lost it somewhere in the corridor or while peeking at the river of flames. *Damn*!

I stopped.

I could just lay down where I was standing and try to get some rest, but the bloody red aureole at the far end of the corridor kept on squeezing my mind in its deadly grip. I was afraid to stay facing it. It was silly, but I couldn't convince my brain just to take a few hours of rest when the ghostly splashes of molten rock were trying to engulf me in my imagination. I had to get away from it.

I slowly crept down the corridor, leaving those reflections behind, leaning on the walls and probing the way with my feet until I reached the dusty quietness of the grotto where Sluagh had left me to find my own dreadful road to hell. Then I crawled a few feet away from the mouth of the corridor and slumped onto the ground. A nearby stone seemed like the softest pillow when I put my trembling hand under my cheek and cried my self-pity and helplessness out until the wave of tiredness finally took over me.

Life was still. Quiet and completely static. Dark as well.

I couldn't get rid of the deadly fear squeezing my very soul with icy pliers. I felt like a lamb before a butcher with my siblings already lying around me in bloody pools. Hope? Don't even joke about hope. There was none. I must stop lying to myself.

I closed my eyes, forcing the images of that world out of my head. This felt like a grave. But what was waiting for me would not be a grave. That molten rock would burn through my bones, leaving nothing, not even bloody ashes to be scattered across the flowering meadows in Chadrack.

I was doomed. My death was certain, painful and inevitable.

I sipped my bitter black unsweetened coffee trying to drown that overwhelming fear, unsuccessfully. My limbs still felt numb, senses dull, and my will was paralysed.

It was well into the late morning when my phone shrieked sharply calling for my attention. It was John.

"Are we going?" he asked after a few short pleasantries. John sounded friendly, but I still felt chills hearing his voice.

The question shook my brain from its trance. Rick was still in trouble, and we had to do something about it – flights and hotels were booked, and John was ready and willing. It was me who needed a kick to begin moving.

"Yes," I said. "Everything's ready. We just need to go through the details. Can we meet somewhere?"

John was silent for a second only.

"Is the *Black Horse* okay for you?" he asked.

"Yes," I knew the place – it was not too far down the hill. It didn't make any big difference where we met. We just needed a quiet corner for a short chat.

We agreed to meet in half an hour.

I swept my gloomy gaze around the room before setting my body into motion.

I left my dirty mug in the kitchen sink, leaving a few mouthfuls of coffee. Dark thoughts were following me like a shadow as I moved around the flat, collecting my papers and getting dressed. The fear of inevitable death emptied my soul, and I felt like a robotic doll, wearing a meaningless expression and following a preordained program, with all my feelings now numbed to a painful greyness.

It was cloudy and windy outside with sprinkles of damp

pricking my face in complete unison with my mood.

I went down the street, paying no attention to passing cars, buses and people. Everything around seemed irrelevant, and I simply placed my feet one in front of each other, staring into the distance with vacant eyes. Each time my gaze fell on the pavement, I saw the river of flames in my imagination, ready to engulf me, and the drizzle of London was unable to change that.

John was already waiting for me outside the Black Horse. He smiled and shook my hand as we entered and took a side table at the far end of the room.

John ordered a pint of beer. I just asked for a cup of tea.

"You look very distressed," observed John, sipping his beer.

"I am," there was no need to pretend.

"What happened?"

"I am stuck," I said honestly. "Right now, in Rehen I am sleeping in a completely dark cave, deep in the guts of some mountain, and my only possible way out is a narrow path running alongside a river of molten magma. I honestly don't know how to survive that."

"How did you manage to end up there?" asked John putting his ale down with a surprised expression. "Has Death changed her mind and put you in some dungeon?"

I ignored the sobriquet he used for my sister's name and shook my head sadly. It wasn't Hel who had put me underground. It was my own fear and my own poor decisions. The story was long, but we had no reason to hurry. My tea grew cold while I quietly described my last day with Hel, our last meal by the crystal creek when hordes of ghouls emerged from the forest in front of us. I saw the real face of my sister then, I knew why she was called the Death. But she wasn't threatening me. She had turned the mighty power of her magic Onyx Ring against the attackers.

I was vulnerable to that power, I knew. Hel had told me to hide, and I ran. I ran as fast as I could with ghouls sprinting after me. Then I hid underground. And the collapse of the entrance was the final magic act of the Master of Destiny. I had exhausted the power of my Sapphire Ring to protect me from the Onyx when, in fact, there was no need for that protection. I was helpless now, entirely depending on the fleeting fickleness of luck.

John was silent when I had finished the story.

"There is no way to help you, especially when you don't know your location. Even if we could locate the entrance and clear the way, it seems it would be impossible to find you inside the caves," he said finally. "You have gone too far away underground."

I knew he was trying, but my situation was indeed hopeless.

"Is there any water nearby?" he asked.

I shook my head – the underground stream was too far away in the darkness and, if I risked retracing my way back to it without any guidance from the centipede, I would get lost in the first grotto! And I had no light…

"Pity," shrugged John. "I was about to suggest getting a wet cloth and putting it over your nose to breathe through when you walk near that lava flow. It could prevent your airways from burning and might improve your chances of survival."

"I don't know if I still have any chance," my voice was grave as were my thoughts. "The path means almost certain death. Still, it's unclear what I will find on the other side."

"I am sorry…" John whispered, turning the beer tankard in his palms.

I silently sipped my cold tea holding back the tears.

"Do you want to cancel our trip to Vienna?" he suddenly asked.

"No," I shook my head. "We may be the only hope for Rick."

"If he is still alive," observed John dryly. "It may just be a trap for you."

I silently took a few more sips of my tea.

"Well..." said John, halfway through his beer. "Back to more pressing things then – have you booked separate flights and hotels?"

I nodded, producing the printouts from my breast pocket with all the details of his flights and hotel reservation.

"I booked hotels for just three days," I said.

"Sounds like a reasonable time," agreed John. "I would be

surprised if he is alive that we don't get any tangible results in three days."

"I hope you are wrong for the sake of Rick," I passed the printouts to him. "If I don't show up in Vienna, it means I'm dead. In that case, please, try to save him if you can. The meeting is at *Graben strasse*, next to *Pestsäule* on Friday, at 1:15 pm."

He nodded silently, placing his tankard on the table.

"If I don't survive the night, could you take care of my body when you return from Vienna, please?" I passed him a tiny piece of paper with my home address written on it.

"Of course!" he said. "But I certainly hope this won't be necessary."

"Who knows? I must prepare for everything."

He finished his beer and stood up, collecting the papers.

"Well, I'll see you near *Pestsäule* tomorrow," John said. "I'll keep my distance. Don't try to approach me. I'll follow you."

He shook my hand and left. I spent one more hour finishing my tea.

It was raining when I left the Black Horse, but I paid no attention to the nastiness of the weather. All my thoughts were on that narrow path next to the blazing river – would I be able to survive this?

Back home, I absentmindedly gathered some clothing for the trip to Vienna, in case if I managed to survive. I had to set my alarm clock as well since my flight was early. I had to be quick and very careful with timing in Rehen, or the alarm clock could possibly go off as I was midway to safety, pulling my consciousness back to London. That would be deadly under the circumstances, but I couldn't afford to miss the plane.

I spent the rest of the day in bed, waiting. Heads on TV were mumbling something, but I didn't listen.

I had my evening cup of tea with some biscuits and then put my body to rest. Minutes later, I was asleep.

I opened my eyes, but it didn't make any difference – it was as complete darkness as it was with my lids closed. Not a sound reached my ears. I knew I still was in the same grotto – the air was dry and smelled of dust. There was a hint of rotten eggs as well since my flaming nemesis next door was spitting sulphides. I cursed – how could I have missed that yesterday? It was a death trap to stay there for too long – I would be dead by now if the concentration of the gas were even just a little higher.

My Sapphire Ring, the Master of Destiny, was dimly glowing blue, using its final bits of energy to warn me about the danger. I knew all about that without the warning. It was a pity that I had exhausted the power of my Ring on unnecessary earthquakes and avalanches and shielding myself from my sister's magic. Hel had meant me no harm, but it had taken some time for me to realise this. Too late…

The fully charged Ring could significantly enhance my

chances. It could guide me in the darkness and, probably, find another way out without risking death in flames. It could shield me from the hellish heat if there were indeed no other way. But I had stupidly wasted its enormous power, and now the Ring could only warn me of dangerous gas – everything else was down to my basic instincts to survive.

I sat up, brushing away remnants of sleep and dust from my face with the back of my hand. A little light would be helpful…

I went through my pockets, and then cursed aloud, remembering that I had lost my green light emitting crystal somewhere in the tunnel yesterday! *Damn…*

At least, I was sure about the corridor's entrance – occasional spots of a blood red light flashed at the edge of perception straight ahead.

The fear was freezing all my movement, but I had to be fast. My timeframe for action was limited by the alarm clock, which was set for the Vienna flight. I had to move through this nightmare before it started ringing. I would never have a second chance if I failed. I had to reach that slit that seemed to represent safety on the other side of the flaming grotto or else die.

I was sure I would never be ready for this. There was no way around all these troubles. I had to do this. I had to do this. I had to do this… I stood up and cautiously went forward, probing the way with my feet in complete darkness.

My heart was insanely pounding when I approached the black opening, framed only by lonely sparks of redness. My legs felt as if they were made of clay as my very soul trembled and strained to rush out of this place.

I mustered all my willpower and crawled into the tunnel. The floor was more even here so I could move faster, but it was difficult at first without any light.

I was almost halfway into the corridor when, finally, the dimly lit walls appeared in my vision in the faint blood-red light of the flowing molten rock ahead. The temperature was rising too, and I remembered John's advice to cover my face. I took off my jacket to make a clumsy cover for my head. The mask wasn't a design masterpiece, but it was the only protection I had. The only thing lacking was water – what the heck! I pissed onto it. It was the only moisture I had, and I hoped it would help me to last longer.

The gateway to the hell was getting closer. I had to slow down as waves of heat rolled over me with every step, crumbling my confidence into dust, and only the imaginary clock ticking in my ears forced my feet forward.

I took a few more steps and then put on my wet mask just before entering the grotto. Flaming liquid rock flowed the same as yesterday, hissing angrily and spitting blue flames at me. The narrow path on the right was just a few feet wide at the beginning and now looked even more dangerous than it had before.

My soul screamed inside, but I had to ignore it and turned right without further hesitation, resolutely setting my foot down on the bumpy surface.

The grotto was about a mile long and several hundred yards wide, winding its way along with the flaming river. The heat was intense, and I almost choked when I inhaled a mouthful of the hot gas mixed with ammonia. Tears ran down my face and dried before reaching my chin, but I kept on creeping forward, probing my way with one foot before I took another step. The stones weren't slippery, but a single loose rock could cost me my life.

I kept my eyes on the path, trying to spot any dangerous sections before I stepped on them. The mask stank and partially obscured the view, but I did my best to keep on moving.

The way was arduous. I felt like I was in a giant infernal oven. Only a hundred yards further on, I allowed myself a few quick glances at the lava on my left – the river of flames was magnificent in its monstrosity. The current was uneven – I could clearly see the central stream, which was flowing faster and was much brighter too, spitting angry blue flames in all directions. The molten rock closer to the banks glowed with a darker hue, splashing strange shapes above the current which began to solidify and, with the sound of crushed glass, seconds later spattered back into the flow. I moved as far away from the lava as possible, limping down the grotto. Several times I accidentally touched the hot rocky wall with my right shoulder. Now it ached and was, I believed, covered in blisters. My left side was throbbing too, exposed to the flames rising high above the bubbling liquid.

I did my best to move as fast as I could, flinching when I heard any loud hiss of the burning gas. The air was hot to breathe even through the dampened mask, and I could taste acidity in my dry mouth and on my stiff tongue.

The lava flow wound its way along the walls of the grotto and, when it moved away, I slowed down a little conserving my energy. But when the current came closer to my path again, I had to run or risk fainting in the enormous heat. I managed to avoid touching the walls, but my feet were baking alive. The soles of them ached, most likely covered in blisters and soaking in blood. I had no time to check.

I couldn't remember how I managed to cover two-thirds of the way – time was ticking slowly, and it seemed like an eternity had passed. I was tired already but had not given myself the slightest chance for a rest. Not yet.

First, there was a sudden loud bang followed, a split second later, by a giant stalactite detaching itself from the ceiling high above my head and splashing into the lava flow and spattering everything around with myriad drops of liquid rock. I wasn't hit, but now my way was scattered loosely with bright glowing embers almost fifty paces ahead.

I stopped and cursed, wasting my breath. Should I return to the safety of the corridor? But then I would be forced to repeat the whole trek again tomorrow – this thought slashed me like a whip, and I shook it away. Waiting there was certain death – time was ticking, and I had no idea how much longer I would be able to keep on track. My brain was almost fainting and couldn't think of anything better to do than run.

The air burned my throat with every breath as I spurted forward. The path ahead of me was winding, and I did my best to avoid any of the hot splashes of lava as I progressed. I was lucky at first, but before passing the last of the embers and reaching the safer ground, I accidentally stumbled on some loose stones and fell flat, rolling towards the flames. Without thinking, my hands instantly shot forward to grab at the rock and secure my position, balancing on the cliff, which was overhanging the fiery flow. My mask flew off, landing in flames below, and I felt intense heat on my left loin with unbearable pain burning deep into my nerves.

Another stalactite smashed to the ground just in front of the mouth of the corridor where I had entered the grotto. *Was the cave collapsing?*

I choked on the hot air in a desperate attempt to recover. Somehow, I succeeded to regain my balance. Then it took another few minutes to crawl back on the track and stand up, leaving small parts of my smoking clothes and skin adhered to the liquefied rock splashes on the ground. Blood spattered from my wounds, but I did not even have time to curse.

I gathered all my strength and lunged forward again. The rocks under my feet trembled, and I realised that something terribly wrong was happening. I had no time to think as a large part of the track behind me collapsed into the lava stream at the very same instant that I stepped on firmer ground.

I briefly glanced at the piece of the cliff, which was the rocky path that I had laboured along just a few seconds ago. It was now slowly sinking into the flames. I would be standing on it, and burning had I hesitated only a few seconds more.

Then another thing happened, but I didn't see it coming. The lava flow appeared disturbed and hissed more angrily, and I gasped as it began to rise. It didn't pool in the banks, nor did it stop moving. Instead, the flow lifted in the air like the monstrous head of a viper. *Was I hallucinating?*

I screamed – or I thought that I had screamed, since not a sound emerged from my dry throat. I backed away until the scalding hot wall touched my shoulders. Then I screamed again.

My eyes refused to believe what they saw as a gigantic fiery viper emerged from the flames of liquid rock. It was as large as the flow itself, maybe even bigger, since part of its body was still hiding in the lava. The head rose high, almost touching the ceiling of the grotto, then turned to face me sticking out a flaming forked tongue.

A low rumbling sound shook the ground, and I quickly glanced ahead, checking for the tiny slit in the wall, which led to safety. It still was there – a dark gap between the rocks, now not too far away.

When I glanced back, the viper's body was emerging on the other side of the grotto with its head now bowing down over me! Never in my life had I run faster. I felt the ground move, and I was sure that the path behind me was crumbling under the pressure of the monster. I had no time to look back. The enormous heat was already licking my spine when I finally slipped through the slit and into the darkness of the corridor. But still, I wasn't safe. The viper's head smashed the wall behind me but was unable to fit its mass into the narrow passage. It hesitated for a few minutes, with its forked tongue licking the walls with flames. Again, an ear-splitting rumbling sound emanated from its throat as the viper squirmed and twisted in an effort to widen the way.

Then the ground trembled, and I fell, suddenly finding myself in darkness as the entrance finally yielded to the viper's pressure and collapsed with a loud bang.

My heart galloped like a frightened horse as I crawled into the darkness, trying to get deeper into the cold corridor and away from danger.

It was quiet again and, after just a few dozen steps, my strength left me. My body only grew limp and refused to move. I leant on the cold rock, crying without tears. I had made it!

Now, with the entrance to hell buried beneath a pile of rocks, streams of cooling air sneaked in from the other side, slowly filling the corridor and soothing my burning skin.

My strength was sufficient only for a sigh. Then I lost consciousness.

Waves of pain pushed me from the dark sea of suffering, leaving flaming monsters beneath the surface. A loud noise painfully drilled into my ears, firmly anchoring my consciousness on the shores of reality. After a few long moments of confusion, my gaze wandered around until I found the source of the noise. The alarm clock was screeching loudly, trying to wake me up for already the third time.

I slapped the snooze button down and moaned. The most terrible pain squeezed my throat as if I had swallowed pieces of crushed glass for my last meal. I rushed to the kitchen and drank my fill of tap water. It was a quiet early morning outside the window, and I sighed, shaking away the remnants of the nightmare I had just lived through.

I returned to the bedroom, my throat feeling a little easier. It was time to assess the damage.

My face looked tired but had escaped any burns or blisters

thanks to that wet mask. The rest of my whole body had been less successful and ached terribly. There was an infinite number of small blisters on my right shoulder and left calf, and a few ruptured blisters were on the edge of my left palm. The bed was soaked with blood from my burnt side, but the most important thing was that I had been through hell and had survived, still able to move.

I closed my eyes and smiled. The pain felt like a blessing – yes, I was alive! I knew, I was still hopelessly stuck underground, but I had reached ephemeral safety. *Was that a dead-end corridor?* My body stiffened at that thought, but I pushed it away firmly – I clearly remembered feeling the soothing cool air on my skin. It must have come from outside. I must follow that airflow, and it would lead me out, I did not doubt that. If only I had enough strength left to manage it.

My smile slowly faded as I remembered the horrors of the night. What was that thing that had risen from the flaming river and attacked me? I knew I wasn't safe still being that close to the entrance, but it was too late for me to return to Rehen. My plane was waiting for me. I must save Rick.

I took a refreshing shower that which soothed my sores slightly. The cream I found in my bathroom cabinet reduced the pain of my blisters to a bearable level. I then did my best to bandage the most damaged areas, but my shoulder was still too tricky for my shaky hands, and I had to fix the slipping dressing with adhesive tape.

The mirror openly lied to me. My face looked far better than it felt – at least, despite the red eyes, I didn't anticipate having any trouble with the airport security.

I got dressed and booked a taxi.

It was raining lightly. I looked through the window and waited for the cab. My thoughts kept wandering back to Rehen, where my helpless body lay in the gloom and murkiness. *It wasn't safe.* The monster I had managed to escape might still be lurking somewhere close. And I had no idea what other creatures or dangers were waiting for me in those caves ahead.

I had no chance to take proper care of my wounds. My life was slowly leaking away in the darkness through the burst blisters, and I had no way to stop this until I returned to Rehen. Every breath in that dry tunnel also deprived me of moisture. I knew I had not much time left.

I checked my documents, tickets and luggage as the cab arrived. The young Pakistani driver was very keen to help me, which was good, but too talkative, which was bad – I was in no mood to discuss anything, not even the weather.

"Heathrow, terminal three," I said grimly, closing the door. "And, please, drive carefully."

I had had enough of danger.

It was five in the morning, and the streets of London were almost empty. Soon we were crossing countless junctions and stopping at an occasional red light.

The driver continued to annoy me with his questions which I managed to answer in monosyllabic words only. He finally gave up this torment when we passed Battersea Bridge and continued to drive on in silence. We left the Thames behind, and I looked sadly through the window at the passing neat houses of Hammersmith along the still empty streets.

All the way to Heathrow the driver was glancing at me but kept his mouth shut with a look of hurt pride on his face. He silently grimaced as he pulled up in front of the terminal building and got the luggage out without saying a word. I ignored this pantomime, quickly paid, took my bags from his hands and rushed into the terminal. The morning was chilly.

The departure hall was enormous – I reached the middle of it and stopped, unsure where the check-in desk for my flight was. The information boards were plentiful, and I ran my eyes through them several times before the flight I was looking registered finally in my still cloudy brain. A tingling sensation in the back of my head suddenly blew away all traces of fatigue. I was being watched!

This wasn't a particularly unexpected turn of events, but I hadn't anticipated it this early in my journey. John was right, but who was spying on me?

I slowly turned right and went across the hall, pretending to study the billboards. The sensation followed me like a floodlight. I stopped and checked my watch before finally braving a glance towards the entrance from where the source of that strange sensation emanated.

It was a black girl in her twenties clutching a purple suitcase in her right hand. She wore a tight green dress, and her raincoat was folded and hanging over her left forearm. At first glance, it looked as if she was searching for her flight information across the information boards, but her eyes were following me. I checked this by walking a considerable distance to the right and then surreptitiously glancing back. Each time, my gaze met her unblinking black eyes in her expressionless face.

I checked my watch again – I had no time for such games without risking missing my flight. The crowds were too sparse to hide me. I began plotting my way around when the girl unexpectedly collapsed with a short outcry.

I spared just a second to watch people running to help her.

Luggage drop off was quick, and I passed the security controls without any incident despite how terrible look I felt.

I moved slowly amongst crowds, still feeling as lonely and helpless as I had in that fiery underground grotto. The irritating feeling of dust and a sour taste in my mouth persisted despite having brushed my teeth and drunk coffee. And my imagination was still plagued by the menace on the other plane of reality, and it painted images of gigantic flaming vipers outside the terminal building's window.

My body still felt like one enormous sore, so I slipped into a nearby pharmacy looking for some remedies. I bought some painkillers, burn gel and antiseptic liquid, as well as plenty of bandages and stuffed everything into my hand luggage. I took three of the painkillers on the go and put the rest in my pocket.

I circled the waiting hall several times, half expecting that black girl to run after me. People arrived and departed, but she didn't show up again.

I bought a ham and cheese sandwich, a large bottle of still water and a cup of *cortado* coffee and occupied the quietest corner in front of the window. I had to refuel my depleted resources.

Men and women walked in both directions, busy with themselves. I was still waiting for that black girl. I even felt a little concern about her – was she alright after that fit? But she must have passed the surveillance to somebody else. I covertly peeked at the faces passing by in front of me, but the feeling of being watched never returned.

On my way to the gate, I visited the gents and checked my bandages. All looked fine, and my aches had eased a little – the painkillers had already kicked in.

Take off was on time. My seat was next to the window, but I closed my eyes as soon as I sat there, ignoring the safety instructions and all offered snacks. My consciousness was balancing between the two realities, never really fixing on one. At least I was sure that my body was still in that same dark corridor, undisturbed, but I couldn't get it moving. It was still too close to the river of flames which left me feeling uneasy and concerned. I needed a proper nap to be able to crawl further into the corridor, away from the entrance, but the flight was too noisy to allow me to fall asleep.

Touchdown in Vienna brought me out of the trance. I hoped that John was there already, and our attempt to save Rick would be quick, smooth and successful.

Passengers spewed out of the plane, and I followed the herd through arrivals to collect my luggage. Several times I carefully looked around, but nobody seemed to be interested in my humble person.

I was carried along by the enormous stream of people rushing outside to embrace the city, slowly realising that the time I had to spare would be entirely eaten up waiting for a taxi. I gently separated myself from the crowd in the arrival hall and turned right, following the green sign for the city airport train. The platform was full too with people clutching their luggage and nervously glancing at the station clock, but at least we were all were able to fit on the train when it arrived.

I sat next to the greenish window gazing out at a cobweb of pipes as the train passed some sort of chemical factory when my phone rang. It was John.

"How are you?" he asked as soon as I answered.

"Alive and on the move," I muttered. "A few burns, but I've passed the worst part of the way already. I only hope I'm not in a dead-end tunnel."

"That's great news!" sighed John, but I still doubted whether his voice sounded sincere.

I shrugged, but of course, he couldn't see that.

"Let's solve the problems one at a time if possible," said John and casually added after a short pause. "I'm next to *Stephan's* cathedral, near the meeting place already. Don't be late."

"Okay, I'll do my best."

The *Mitte* station arrived sooner than I had expected. I got off the train and followed the crowd into the street. The day was beautiful and warm, but this unknown city was frightening. I spent a few seconds encouraging myself before stepping out of the station. I had arrived. I must save Rick!

From the outside, the station was large, resting its striped body on the massive greenish colonnade. The *Landstraßer* was full of people hurrying about in all directions, and I turned right, where the spire of Stephan's cathedral towered high above the red roofs of the Inner City.

I checked my watch – I still had half an hour until my meeting with Rick's captors, but it was too late to go to the hotel so I was forced to drag my luggage with me which might be an obstacle if I needed to run away in case of any danger. I should have taken a taxi at the airport, but it was now too late for regrets.

I took another dose of painkillers to keep my burns at bay and hurried down the street where the cathedral was just in sight, peaking over the rooftops a few blocks ahead.

Vienna was busy with early afternoon activities – cars, trams, and buses passed by as I crossed the street then a bridge over the shallow river running through the *Stadtpark* on my left. A smiling Turkish gentleman was selling flowers from a stand at the corner of the park. He said something in German, extending a small bouquet of violets out to me, but I shook my head and rushed forward.

I went along the narrow streets of the Inner City, dragging my luggage behind me. I looked back several times, but the street was empty. Any occasional interlopers were more interested in the shop displays than in me. A few steps later, I realised that the buildings had obscured the view of Stephan's cathedral. My steps grew unsure with the loss of this guide. I stopped a few times glancing up, but all I could see was a narrow strip of the sky.

Time was ticking, and I moved forward, feeling more afraid

with every step that I had already gone past the cathedral and was now heading deeper into the Inner City, lost in its narrow streets.

My way ended abruptly at a crossing street. "*Rotenturmstraße,*" said the sign but the name didn't ring any bells. The street was broader and more crowded than the one I had just been on, and I stopped, wondering which way to go.

A Japanese girl was taking photos with her enormous camera just in front of me. She smiled sympathetically, noticing my puzzled look, and I dared to ask her.

"*Stephansplatz?*"

She seriously spoke a few words in Japanese. I wasn't sure if she understood what I was asking.

"*Stephansplatz?*" I shrugged repeating my question.

She just smiled, pointing down the street to the left, then abruptly turned right and followed her laughing friends who carried similar cameras.

The hands my watch were approaching 1 p.m. I only had 15 minutes left, no time for second guessing. I knew Rick's life might depend on this when I turned left on the *Rotenturmstraße* where the girl had indicated.

It was a short walk to the next street, and I decided to turn back if the dome didn't appear around the corner.

Another outburst of laughter caused me to raise my gaze from the cobblestone pavement. No more than twenty paces ahead stood an elegant white bow-fronted double brougham harnessed with two gracious dappled grey horses. A man in a black tailcoat was standing next to it clutching a whip, but it wasn't he who attracted my attention. A tall, sturdy man was standing next to him laughing – I saw only his back, but I couldn't confuse that ginger coiffure with anybody else's. John!

I grinned, but my smile instantly faded when I remembered our conspiracy. I rechecked my watch and walked past John dragging my luggage behind me. I heard a few more giggles as I passed him and entered the *Stephansplatz* with the magnificent cathedral appearing on my left.

Shops and cafés glittered around me, but I had no time to look at them. I had to get through the rambling crowd of wanderers which was being joined by another crowd oozing from the tube and get across the square. The *Grabben* street was just around the corner.

I couldn't check if John had noticed me, but my luggage had been noisy enough to attract his attention. Anyway, he promised to keep an eye on me.

Suddenly I felt scared. What if the kidnappers didn't show up? What if I was unable to spot the person among these hundreds of strange faces all around? What if they missed me?

I slowly went down the *Stephansplatz* ignoring the charms of the city around me. The nervousness and self-doubt, which were flooding me increased with every step. *What if Rick was dead?*

I felt a sudden tremor of the ground and stopped. Nobody else shared the feeling as my startled gaze met smiling unconcerned faces all around me. *What was happening?*

It must be something in Rehen! Was that fiery monster attempting to crumble the walls of the tunnel again? I would perish in a flash of flames if it succeeded in widening the entrance. Or maybe it was just an earthquake. I only hoped that wouldn't collapse the ceiling over my exhausted body sleeping in that dark corridor. It wasn't safe in that tunnel! I must take a nap and crawl away from the entrance, as far away as possible! I looked down at my feet, standing firmly on the pavement while my imagination was painting flames already. I felt a sudden wave of heat passing through my body.

My phone began vibrating in my pocket, and the trance was broken.

"What happened?" asked John. "You've just been staring at the pavement for nearly five minutes. It's about time."

"Something is happening in the dream world," I whispered. "I don't know if I'll be able to hold on any longer. I must take a nap!"

"You can't do that in the middle of the street," John sounded casual – of course, it wasn't his skin that was about to get roasted. "And it is nearly time to meet whoever has captured your friend."

Rick! I glanced at my watch. It was ten minutes past one. I

must hurry. John was right. The nap must wait until I got to the hotel. Rick had no hope if I failed in my mission.

I slipped the phone back into my pocket and turned right onto the *Grabben strasse.*

A white marble tower featuring carvings of clouds, saints and angels dominated the middle of the *Grabben* high above the crowd, and I knew this was the *Pestsäule* where I was supposed to meet somebody in just a few minutes. I rushed towards it, scaring some usually imperturbable pigeons with my haste.

I stopped in front of the monument, breathing heavily and rechecked my watch – it was still a few minutes earlier than the allotted time.

Although the feeling of an earthquake had gone, the tension remained. I had no idea what was happening on the other side of reality, but I was still alive.

My heart raced as I stood my luggage on the pavement next to me and looked around. People were unhurriedly walking in all directions, sitting at the tables of outdoor cafés, chatting and laughing. I looked at their faces trying to spot spying eyes or furtive glances. Everybody was going about their own business, completely ignoring my lonely silhouette standing next to the marble monument.

Had they spotted that I had backup? I had to wipe the expression of worry from my face before looking around again.

John was sitting on the terrace of a nearby café sipping his lager. *Had they spotted him?* Was Rick already doomed?

"Would you like a ticket to the concert?" asked a deep voice belonging to a thin-faced ticket seller, dressed like a Renaissance dandy. "They are performing Mozart."

I shook my head absentmindedly dismissing him and looked at my watch again – it was fourteen minutes past one! I had to get rid of the vendor and do it quickly!

"Are you sure?" the guy squeezed a sticky smile. "Everybody likes music! Don't you like Mozart?"

The guy was irritating and ruthlessly interfering in my mission. I couldn't play his games any longer.

"Give me a ticket! Just be quick!" I gabbled at him fishing my wallet from my pocket.

"Fifty euros," he said with a serene smile. "I will make a special offer and extraordinary discount for you…"

"That is a ridiculous price," I told him hoping that he would go away. "And I only have British pounds."

"That's ok, fifty pounds then," he kept on smiling, making no attempt to hide his clear intention to rip me off.

I handed him a few banknotes.

"Here is your ticket, sir," he said, passing me a tiny piece of paper. "Have a lovely evening!"

I didn't even bother to look at the ticket seller as he left after I had finally freed myself from his sticky grip. A flock of pigeons flapped over me as I spun around with expectant eyes, but no one else seemed to be approaching me. I consulted my watch again. It was 1:20 pm – five minutes past the designated time. I was petrified. What if the person I was to meet had been scared off by that stupid ticket seller? The time indicated in the letter was exact. Had I failed? *Damn!*

I circled the *Pestsäule* expectantly for another fifteen minutes without any success, feeling increasingly frustrated.

Then I noticed a strange woman wearing lavish make-up marching down the street from the *Stephansplatz* with a smile frozen on her face. She held a closed red umbrella in her right hand, pointing it straight upwards. It looked like she had forgotten to open it and had forgotten that it wasn't raining, but her steps were firm, and her gaze was determinedly fixed on the *Pestsäule* behind me.

I expectantly watched as she came closer and stopped a few steps away. Then she abruptly turned around without dropping a word, still holding the red umbrella high above her head. The bidirectional flow of the crowd along the *Pestsäule* was suddenly interrupted by some aimless wanderers abruptly acquiring a focussed direction.

I was forced to take a few steps away as the crowd began to gather around the strange woman, enclosing her in an impenetrable circle.

"Здесь вы видите памятник великой чуме 1679 года, воздвигнутый по приказу императора Леопольда Первого. Здесь вы видите самого Леопольда," she pointed with her umbrella, *"приклонившего колено для молитвы."*

The crowd around her took out phones and cameras and began snapping photos en masse. *Tourists…* The silent curse dropped from my mouth involuntarily, killing all remnants of hope. I backed away from the crowd and took my phone out of my pocket. John answered instantly.

"I don't know what to do next," I complained. "It's well past the stated time, and nobody has approached me."

"I see," said John. "And what sort of note did that carnival guy give you?"

"He sold me a ticket to Mozart."

"Ticket?" John chuckled. "That guy was exactly on time and left the scene immediately afterwards. That's not the usual behaviour of a ticket seller."

I took that small piece of paper out my pocket. It was a pink paper with black letters printed on it: "Tomorrow, 11:30 am in *Schweizerhaus* café, *Prater*." It didn't mention Mozart.

"Does it look like a ticket?" demanded John.

"No," I admitted. "But why did he take that fifty pounds?"

John burst out laughing.

"What does it say?" he asked, still giggling.

"Tomorrow, 11:30 am in *Schweizerhaus* café, *Prater*," I read out in a small voice.

"That's it then! It's another meeting point."

I froze holding the pink sheet of paper in my hand. I had met the kidnapper and hadn't even bothered to memorise his face!

"What do we do next?" I asked John, hoping that he had taken a better look at the guy.

"You've got an invitation for a late breakfast tomorrow, I guess," he said after a short pause. "Use it. We have no other clues at the moment."

"Okay," I agreed. "I hope Rick is still alive."

The daylight suddenly dimmed as I spoke, and again the earth trembled slightly beneath my feet. People around me were laughing and posing for pictures – the earthquake apparently wasn't on their plane of reality. I nearly choked as fear squeezed my throat.

"I must take a nap," I whispered into the phone. "Now!"

"Then hurry," John's voice was calm, but I sensed rising tension behind his words. "Call me this evening when you're ready. I hope everything will be fine with you until then. I'll go have a look at *Prater* right now to help me plan every action for tomorrow."

"I'll be at the hotel," I said and hung up.

For several long seconds, I stood in the middle of the street with my eyes closed, trying to visualise the map of central Vienna I had studied before arriving. There were no shortcuts from this spot. A wave of heat passed over my body again, and I was sure I had not much time left.

I turned around and rushed back to St. Stephan's Cathedral. John was still sipping his lager as I sped past him dragging my luggage on the uneven pavement. His face remained expressionless as he turned the tankard in his fingers and then took another sip. Waves of perspiration cascaded down my back as I turned right into the *Kärntner strasse*. A few blocks later, I spotted a taxi waiting in front of the Opera House and crashed inside it, giving the driver the details of my hotel.

"Quickly, please," my voice beseeched.

"Of course, sir," replied the driver starting the engine. "It's not far away."

The car slipped into the moving line of traffic, and I closed my eyes, trying to relax. Soon… I only needed to get into bed. Something was going on in Rehen. And that unknown "something" was freaking me out.

The driver kept quiet steering the car up and down the unfamiliar city. I kept my eyes closed, feeling strange waves of heat rolling over my body.

"*Scheisse!*" a cry awoke me from my reverie.

The driver slapped the steering wheel, slamming on the brakes as a tall woman dressed in black rushed across the street in front of the car, ignoring the traffic lights. She stopped in front of the taxi, turned her black eyes on me and smiled, and I felt a strange chill in her gaze. *Was it my imagination again?*

"Please," I said, trying to ignore her. "Could we drive faster?"

"Sure…" mumbled the driver squeezing the wheel and watching the black silhouette strolling unhurriedly across in front of the car.

She looked back one more time before stepping onto the pavement. Only then did the car jump forward. I felt the gaze of those black eyes on my left cheek as we moved along. Before long, she was gone.

A few blocks later, the taxi turned left into a cul-de-sac and stopped in front of the hotel entrance. I paid with my card and got out.

The driver opened the boot to get my luggage out, and I glimpsed the outfit of a Renaissance dandy stuffed into a corner. He closed the boot before I could voice any questions.

"Have a nice day," he said, handing me my things and hurried back into his car, avoiding my glance.

The earth trembled again. I grabbed my luggage and rushed inside, not waiting for the taxi to depart. I was running out of time!

A grey haired gentleman in reception greeted me with a smile and booked me in without interrupting his social chat in German with a lady sitting next to the window with her luggage and, apparently, waiting for a taxi. He gave me the room key with a heavy metal keychain which did not fit into my pocket, and politely explained how to get into my room.

I took the lift to the second floor and found my room on the far right-hand side of the corridor. It was clean and neat, facing a small inner yard, away from the noise of the busy street.

I locked the door, put my luggage in a corner and flopped onto the bed without even bothering to take my shoes off – I had no time for that.

My bed trembled slightly under my sweating body as my consciousness slowly drifted away.

First, it was a sound – the distant rumbling hushed by the thick layers of primordial rock beneath me. The dust was tickling my nostrils, and I sneezed before I opened my eyes. This was a mistake.

"You are back," hissed a strange low voice piercing painfully into my brain. "You have returned from your world."

I opened my eyes. The tunnel was dark, and I was unable to locate the source of the ghostly voice, which was still echoing around me. I sat up and silently cursed – my body was aching like a giant wound, and I had no weapon to defend myself against whatever was lurking in the darkness.

An eerie, barely perceptible ruby glow leaked through the rocks piled on my right which barred the entrance. I was still too close to the infernal grotto.

"We need to talk," said the voice, reverberating in the narrow tunnel.

"I don't have time for this," I said, standing up. "It's getting too hot."

"Hot?" the strange voice burst into laughter. "You can't imagine how hot it can get!"

A flame shot from behind the pile of rocks and died as it touched the ceiling. The laughter faded down the tunnel, but the menace remained, sticking my limbs to the ground. I had no idea what was confronting me nor what to expect. My heart fluttered in my chest like a frightened dragonfly trying to break free, and I took a few hesitant steps into the tunnel, away from the ruby glow.

"I can't stay here any longer…" I voiced a weak protest.

"You will," the voice told me firmly.

A few flames flashed ahead in the darkness, blocking my way out. I stopped, slowly realising that I was trapped. More flames appeared from dark holes in the floor of the tunnel, lighting everything around with crystal clarity. I gasped as bright streams of lava followed the flames, suddenly appearing from every corner of the tunnel. A scream froze in my dry throat. Was it indeed, lava?

My legs refused to hold me up any longer, and I collapsed back onto the rocky floor. Tears from my eyes evaporated before they reached my cheeks. I was doomed.

A ring of flames was already surrounding me, rising to two

thirds of the height of the tunnel. It wasn't static. It swirled and moved around me like a gigantic colony of flaming caterpillars. The heat was unbearable, and I tried to shield my eyes.

"Where are you?" my mouth was dry, the words that came out were barely audible, followed by an uncontrollable bout of a cough. "Who are you?"

Heads of vipers rose above the flaming bodies as I moved my eyes around the circle.

"I am right in front of you, silly human," said the same voice. "I am Amykhatapardivamut. Look into my eyes and tremble!"

"Which one are you?" I couldn't hear my own words. "I can't even pronounce your name!"

"I am *many,*" was the answer, which explained nothing. "You may call me Am'ut if that is easier for your tongue."

Sores, blisters and burns on my skin ached like one giant wound, and I flinched in spasms with every wave of heat that came my way. I felt like a mouse sitting in a trap whose captor was now making its mind up how best to fry me.

"What do you want?" I asked with my gaze wandering around the flames, unable to focus on anything.

"I had an agreement with your late father," said one of the vipers.

"I know nothing about that," I said, turning my eyes away, but there was another viper's head wherever my gaze stopped.

"I know this, silly human," hissed the voice disdainfully. "You are not even the son of your father. You are just a mere replacement – I see a spark inside you. But still, you may be of use to me."

Panic raged through my soul like a devastating tornado, swiping all other thoughts and emotions into oblivion. I looked around desperately. There was no way to escape. Am'ut was all around me.

"What is it?" I asked, barely moving my dried lips.

"Your late father had promised me his assistance," hissed Am'ut. "Now it's your turn to fulfil that promise."

"I know nothing about that," I repeated the statement with no doubt in my voice. "I have no idea what you are talking about."

"Of course," several heads of Am'ut agreed in unison. "You are not a King yet. You must become a King to serve your purpose. I have waited patiently, but I will wait no more! You will use your right of birthright, even if that blood does not belong to you. You will lure my enemies in, and I will destroy them!"

I felt a sudden chill in those flames around me. The creature was trying to push me into a quest I had no heart even to think about.

"Why I must fight your wars?" I asked.

All the vipers spoke at once. "Because I ask you!" A wave of heat flashed at my face as they did so. "Serve me or die!"

"Stop! Please..." I raised my hands to protect my eyes. "I've got the message. What do you want me to do?"

"Claim your birthright, stupid!" one of the vipers spat a flame past me and merged back into the circle of flaming moving bodies. "You will send a message to the Road of Gods. You will invite Wayresh and Rhey to your coronation. I will deal with them once they step on the ground."

"Who are they?" I asked without thinking.

"They are your gods, silly human," hissed Am'ut. "They must be destroyed."

"You must be mistaken," I shook my head. "I've seen only the temple of Qu'mun in Chadrack. Nobody has ever mentioned those other names."

"Qu'mun is locked in tungsten, stupid," hissed a viper's head in the circle of flames. "He is weak and not a threat to me. I must destroy those who rule in the Road of Gods. I will deal with Qu'mun when the sea becomes dry. Only then will I be able to reclaim what is rightfully mine!"

"What is that?"

"The world!"

I choked on a mouthful of hot air and bent double in a terrible bout of a cough.

"You are killing me..." I managed to whisper. "I will not be able to help you if I'm dead."

The heat eased a little, and I noticed that the fiery circle had widened slightly.

"We have only two ways to end it right now," observed Am'ut. "You must pledge me your loyalty and trick the gods into descending. Or you will die, and I'll have to find a more cooperative sibling of yours," Am'ut chuckled, adding after a short pause. "Luckily, the late king was quite prolific."

"Suppose, I'll do as you say. You'll succeed in killing those gods, and you will become a god yourself. Would it make you happier if people began chanting prayers in your name? Would you feel better? What will happen then?"

"Then all you folks will die like vermin. You are pitiful pests, this world is not yours," hissed Am'ut maintaining the distance. "But I will let you live if you'll help me."

I looked around at the flaming circle formed by the many tangled bodies of Am'ut which still had no breach. I had no way to escape.

"It doesn't sound like a very good offer," I complained. "It doesn't seem very appealing to have to live a lonely life if you're going to exterminate everyone else. I don't see how anybody with a sane state of mind could ever agree to this."

Complete silence followed for several long minutes. I looked at the many eyes of Am'ut behind the veil of blue flames, and my sense of danger increased with every passing second. I soon felt almost hysterical waiting for an attack.

"I see your point, stupid human" admitted Am'ut finally. "I could perhaps spare a few more lives if that would make your existence happier."

"I'm afraid, that wouldn't be good enough either," I felt petrified before deciding to push a little further. "We need some land to grow crops. We need meadows to feed our cattle. And we need forests to hunt our game."

"I never thought that humans were territorial…"

"We are."

"I think I could leave a piece of land for you intact…" hissed Am'ut with an element of uncertainty. "Humans are indeed strange creatures. Now, will you do as I say?"

"Will I help you to kill the gods?" I paused for a few seconds, gathering all my courage to push it even further. "It's great treason you are asking me to do, and you hope I will be satisfied with a few friends and a nubble of land to dig dirt for all of my remaining life? I am a Prince! I need a kingdom!"

The words surprised me as they came out of my mouth. A wave of heat slashed at me from all sides as Am'ut jumped forward. I flinched, instinctively closing my eyes.

"Don't you dare to disobey me!" flames hissed next to my ear.

There was no time even for a final prayer. I lifted my arm to shield my eyes as only a mere yard now separated me from a painful death in the flames.

Then the vipers stopped advancing.

"How dare you, insolent slug, demand anything? Why should I listen to such a squirt like you? Do you want a kingdom, stupid human? I'll give you a kingdom! I will spare your pitiful Chadrack for you so you can play your potty ruling games. But you will always know that I am your God and the true ruler! I'll leave you a reminder, dirty vermin," Am'ut touched my leg, and I screamed as unbearable pain drilled through my nerves. "But don't you dare to ask for anything else! You will do as I say, or you will die!"

I realised that my consent was no longer required. The heat began to retreat.

"Claim your birthright – I command you!" said Am'ut when I had stopped screaming and finally dared to look at the creature.

"It's not that simple," I managed to whisper catching my breath.

"Why?"

"The Regent enjoys his place on the throne. He will not step down if I just ask politely," I said. "I will need support from my brothers and sisters."

"Then get it!" Am'ut hissed impatiently but maintained the distance between us.

"And I might have to raise an army, a large army to fight the

Regent," this was even more frightening than it sounded. "It will take time..."

"Get it! Get it! Get it! Get it! Get it!" viper bodies chanted, intertwining around me as the hissing flooded me from every direction.

"The realm may descend into civil war," I whispered even more afraid of my words. "Thousands may die..."

"I don't care," one of the vipers stopped moving and looked at me from the flames. "Neither should you. Those pests will die anyway."

Am'ut clearly intended to wipe out the human race from Rehen. Dark menace leaked in these words and, although this holy war and celestial conflicts still sounded absurd, I didn't dare to ask any more. I knew I would have to find another source of information if I managed to get out of this ring of fire alive. I couldn't trust the viper.

"I will fulfil my father's promise," I said, licking my dry lips. I would promise the creature anything just to make those flames disappear. "Just give me sufficient time."

"You'll have your time, human," hissed the viper, and I noticed that this time Am'ut didn't add the usual *silly* or *stupid*. "I will be watching you closely."

For the first time, the ring of fire broke as the vipers began to retreat into holes and trenches in the floor of the tunnel, leaving trails of heated rocks glowing faintly like precious rubies and then slowly fading into blackness. I was left alone.

Only then did I permit myself a quick gasp, instantly leaping to my feet and rushing forward. My thigh that had been touched by Am'ut was throbbing, but my only thought was to get as far away from this place as possible. I fell several times, stumbling on rocks and slipping into shallow trenches, invisible in the dark. My body was utterly exhausted and aching, but I kept on pushing forward until I could no longer. Then I collapsed on the rocks.

I was afraid to close my eyes but could resist the dark wave of oblivion any longer. Moments later, I was sound asleep.

It was early evening in Vienna already. My heart was still racing insanely, and large drops of sweat rolled down my forehead, burning my eyes as they soaked my eyelids. I jumped out of bed, still shaking and downed a few glasses of tap water.

The encounter was the most terrifying, draining my strength and crushing my consciousness into a tiny grey ball of fear. I lowered my aching body onto the bathroom floor, leaning on the pleasantly chilling tiles and squeezing the half empty glass of water. My eyes watered, but it was panic that was ripping my heart apart and paralysing my will. I emptied the glass and placed it on the floor, unable to hold it in my shaking hands any longer.

The soft murmur of city noise outside the window was soothing to my ears, but my terrified brain still refused to calm down. Flaming vipers still danced in front of my eyes, and I had to shake my head to whisk them away. What was that creature?

I had no explanation since my logic tended to shut down when senses of danger and fear overwhelmed me. Now I could barely keep my teeth from chattering.

That holy war sounded like complete nonsense, and I found myself questioning my sanity. Not for the first time.

I tried to recall the names Am'ut had referred to as its enemies – Wayresh? Rhey? I couldn't remember anyone in Chadrack ever mentioning them. Who or what were they? I had no idea. There was only the Temple of Qu'mun standing high on the slopes of the mountain, looming over the capital. The flaming viper had referred to those gods as real beings rather than some mythical fairy-tale. *Were they real?* I felt so confused.

The creature had said that Qu'mun represented no danger for the plan. *Locked in tungsten?* That sounded entirely crazy. I looked around, sensing a shadow of madness looming over me. Had that flaming ring of vipers been a hallucination?

I shook the thought away. My thirst and my blisters were real, leaving no room for doubt. It had indeed happened – my body had encountered heat and flames in Rehen, but my brain still refused to believe. My thigh throbbed like hell, and I carefully slipped my trousers down to have a look.

The wound was half the size of my palm with inflamed redness surrounding a black crater, no larger than a penny. A few drops of amber-coloured liquid were leaking from one edge of the crater and then running down my thigh.

Why? Why me? I nearly wept. It was both painful and pointless, but I had to deal with it. I stripped checking my bandages. Only that crater on my thigh was a new wound – the bandages I had applied before the flight weren't soaked, so I decided not to touch them.

I crawled back to the bedroom and opened my luggage, taking out my scarce medical supplies. I selected a few bottles. Back in the bathroom, I had to bite a towel before pouring antiseptic on the wound. It burned like hell, and I barely held myself from screaming aloud.

Seconds later, the pain eased a little, but the wound was still weeping amber teardrops. I put a thick layer of burn gel on it and then bandaged it, hoping it would heal without infection.

My mind was still clouded by slowly receding panic. I was unable to calm down and a for a few minutes limped around the room, trying to focus. The creature of doom had made its intentions clear – I had to trick those gods into descending to the surface and then Rehen would die in flames. I couldn't let that happen.

But I would die if I simply say no the monster – it would burn me and then turn to my brothers and sisters in Rehen, destroying them one by one until it found a traitor who would fall for its plan. Then the world would perish in the blaze. The flaming vipers held such contempt for humans – I was sure the promise to keep Chadrack intact was an empty one.

It took me almost an hour to suppress the panic, but still, I had no plan. One thing was crystal clear – I must keep away from the throne of the realm as far as possible. It was equally important to keep the seat unoccupied and out of reach of anybody else. The viper would use any opportunity – that was obvious – either with my cooperation or without it. But how long would I be able to stick to this without making Am'ut suspicious? Then I remembered the prophecy Hel had been concerned about. She had spoken about rivers of blood and gold, which would flood Rehen with the new king. I had shrugged it off as absurd then, but it didn't seem quite so absurd anymore.

Am'ut was a great danger to all in Rehen – princes and princesses, town dwellers and rural folk, ordinary people and Sleepers – all would perish in flames. I had not the slightest clue how to fight the monster. I was alone in this fight, not sure how long I would be able to stand my ground. I could trust no one, even John – especially John. I would rather ask advice from my sister Death than trust the redhead who, along with his accomplices, had only recently been stalking me around London. Yes, he was helping me to rescue Rick, and I was grateful for this. Still, there was a small grey worm at the back of my mind which continued to whisper to me that John might be the real kidnapper and his presence in Vienna was for my surveillance only, just to keep my search in the direction which most suited him. I couldn't trust the man, I decided. Not until I found out what his real intentions were.

I might risk asking Hawa, the Keeper of the Well of Power, but first I had to get out of those underground caves alive and return to the capital.

I swallowed another dose of painkillers before dressing and ordering a generous lunch to be brought to my room. I was in no shape to go to eat outside the hotel, and my depleted resources needed restoring.

When the food arrived, I was sitting in the corner with dark thoughts still flooding my brain. At least, death was not today. I ate well, then pushed the trolley outside into the corridor and carefully lay my aching body on the bed.

The TV in front of me was more for background noise rather than anything that captured my attention. My thoughts were far away from there, on another plane of reality. As I thought of my body in the dark tunnel with no light, no water, no food and the flaming monster lurking somewhere close, fear slowly sneaked back into my heart like a homesick stray dog. I had no solution to my problems, but I wasn't prepared to give up without a fight.

I called John later in the evening.

"How was it?" I asked without any preliminaries.

"It will be easy for you, but difficult for me," he complained.

"Why?"

"*Prater* is a carnival place, and on a Saturday morning, it can be crowded. It's easy to mix with the crowd and hide as you would in a labyrinth – anybody could get lost in a horror chamber or any of the many side streets," John wasn't very enthusiastic. "You'll be the primary man of action, I'm afraid…"

"Have you seen the café?"

"I even had my lunch there. The food was good, but the place is not to our advantage. I may not be able to move out of the café at short notice," he sounded discouraging. "I think it would be best if I waited outside. I don't believe that you'll be in any immediate danger in such a crowded place. I only need to spot the man you're talking to, and then I'll be able to follow him. He may lead us to Rick."

"Ok, but how do I to find that café?"

"It's easy," John was casual as always. "You enter the *Prater* through the large gate, then take the walkway past *Madame Tussauds* and keep straight ahead. The café is almost at the end of that walkway."

"Sounds easy."

"It is easy," John chuckled. "You can't miss it. Just don't stay with whoever is there to meet you for too long. Find out their requirements but don't decide anything. If they have taken the trouble to bring Rick here from London, they can wait for a day or two for your decision. We need a plan before we act – just don't sound too anxious when you're talking to them. And ask them to prove that he's still alive – there's no bargaining to be done over a corpse."

"Right!" I said, and the image of my corpse riddled with worms rotting somewhere in the dark tunnel began to haunt my still tired brain. "I'll do my best."

"All right! Let's get some rest. See you tomorrow."

"See you," I said and hung up.

I had my evening dose of painkillers and checked my wounds. The blisters on my right shoulder needed more burn gel, but other sores looked bearable. I was afraid to touch the bandage on my thigh – the pain was tolerable, and the gauze itself was only lightly soaked, so I decided to skip taking a look at it.

Later in the evening, I turned off the TV and let myself drown in the darkness.

I opened my eyes only to meet another darkness, and I couldn't sense the point of transition to another reality. For several long minutes, I lay motionless, listening. Not a sound pierced the silence. The air was cold, but I still could smell the sickening odour of burnt flesh. My flesh.

I braved to raise my head and looked around. Nothing. Not a tiny spark penetrated the darkness, not a hint of that eerie ruby radiance met my eyes. Only the Master of Destiny was faintly glowing blue on my finger. I was alone. The monster was gone but, I was sure, was not too far away. It was hiding somewhere in the deep trenches and watching me.

I had to get out of the caverns. I must find the way.

I attempted to stand, leaning heavily against the wall. My legs were holding. The first steps were a little shaky, but I was moving. Effect of the painkillers was probably felt in Rehen as well, dulling my aches, and I slinked along the tunnel wall, carefully probing the way with my feet. I wasn't entirely sure if I was crawling away from the hellish grotto or towards it. My mind was still confused, but I kept on moving.

My mouth was dry. My tongue felt wooden and barely moved when I tried to lick my lips. I must find some water, or I'd be dead within a few days. I knew I wouldn't last any longer than that.

Damn! A little light would be helpful… I reached into my Ring probing the rocks around, but not a streak of light appeared – the glowing crystals were absent.

I withdrew my will, conserving the remaining charge of the Ring and decided to probe a little further on – in another part of the corridor.

I crawled slowly forward holding my hands against the tunnel walls. The darkness was frightening and, before long, my bored brain began populating it with countless monsters again. Bony fingers were reaching out for me from the walls, creepily covered with dust and cobwebs. I flinched every time my eyes caught imaginary flames at the periphery of my gaze – I was expecting Am'ut to appear and torture me again, but the flames disappeared whenever I looked at them directly. Flocks of bats silently passed me several times rushing down the corridor, stopping just for a few moments to lick my bleeding wounds. I waved my arms, but my fingers passed through the air without hitting anything. I felt worms and spiders crawling on my skin, and I brushed them away, slowly realising that I was going insane.

Several times the bony face of my sister Death appeared hovering in the dark with her shiny white teeth now glistening in a skinless smile.

"Please, Hel. Not today…" I begged her waving my hand. The next moment, the apparition was gone only to appear again minutes later.

A few times I stopped to try to probe for any lighting crystals with my Sapphire Ring, failing every time to spot anything, and then crawled on, shepherded by the distant laughter of invisible ghostly voices in the dark.

The laughter and giggling went insane when I stumbled on a rock and fell, rupturing blisters on my shoulder. I cursed, grinding my teeth in pain but forced my protesting body to raise and start crawling again.

"Leave me alone," I whispered to the ghosts, but no sounds escaped my throat which was aching and as dry as gunpowder already.

I must find water, or I'd die quite soon – this was the only rational thought circling in the madness my brain was creating. The rest were mere hallucinations.

A few more times, I stumbled and fell, and once I ended up in a waist-deep trench. The walls of the trench were cool and damp, and my heart jumped with joy. I felt the floor with a trembling soul trying to find a puddle in anticipation of a few gulps of water. Found none.

I probably spent an hour licking the walls in a desperate attempt to find any tiny droplet of moisture, but the effort only left me even thirstier.

A choir of ghostly voices loudly laughed when I crawled out of the trench. I spent a few more minutes fighting a wave of self-pity before I could carry on again.

I focused on my steps, and the frightening hallucinations backed away, fading into the ink-black darkness. Still, I caught several flashes of blue flames at the periphery of my gaze, but I wasn't entirely sure if they were imaginary or if Am'ut was indeed tracking me down the corridor.

I closed my eyes firmly – it didn't make any difference; anyway, I couldn't see where I was stepping in the dark. Now I was sure that all those lights and monsters were merely the products of my morbid imagination. This eased my tension a little but left me unable to spot any real danger which may flash at me in the dark. There were no flashes when I opened my eyes, and I kept alternating an eyes-open and eyes-shut sequence every fifteen steps I took. It required more concentration but kept the spooks at bay.

I went on, losing track of time and distance completely. The tunnel seemed endless. I became tired and began suspecting that I had crawled out of the wrong side of the trench several hours ago and now was heading back towards the flaming grotto. I stopped a few times, hesitated, wondering whether to turn back but then resumed my slow progression. I wasn't sure if I was doing the right thing. I wasn't sure if I would ever get outside. I just kept moving and trying to keep the creations of my imagination away. The temperature wasn't rising but nor was it dropping either.

Then suddenly I lost the wall I had been leaning against. One moment I was touching the cool surface with the fingertips of my right hand and one step later it was gone!

I took a few more unsure steps. Then I stopped. Maybe I had wandered to the left wall? I extended my hand, but it touched only emptiness.

I cursed out loud, almost crying, feeling helpless and abandoned. I had become used to the wall and was now afraid to take another step without firm assurance at my fingertips. Where was the light when I needed it? The feeling of an invisible abyss being next to me was so intense that I felt paralysed. I carefully lowered myself to the floor. My medications had almost exhausted their limits, and I needed a few minutes of rest anyway. I must calm down and find a solution.

The darkness looked into my eyes and laughed in a distant ghostly voice. I forced my eyelids shut, silently praying for sanity. I knew I was on edge.

But where had the walls disappeared to? I felt around me and picked up a few loose stones. I tossed one where just a few paces ago I had been touching the surface. The stone hit an invisible rock and rolled on the ground a moment later – the wall was still there, but it was something else which now attracted the immediate attention of my swollen brain. It was the echoes that reverberated in the dark. I had to test my suspicions – my slightly shaking hand felt for another pebble, and I tossed it high straight in front of me. It took longer to hit something, but the echoes were clear. The tunnel ended in a grotto!

The sense of joy was brief. I had only one reason for a small smile – I had reached a cavern, and it wasn't in flames. The long hours of confusion and hesitation in the tunnel had ended. I was on the right track!

The smile faded as I listened to the dead silence of the grotto ahead of me. I had not the slightest idea how big the cavern was, what dangers were hiding in the dark or how many tunnel openings – if any – were here. Would they lead anywhere or just leave me stuck in a dead end and, more importantly, would they lead to the world outside?

The task was enormous. I could spend months wandering about there, circling in the darkness. I did not have the luxury of time. I'd be dead in a few days without water.

Water…

I tried to lick my dry lips, but my tongue was as dry and stiff, barely moving. I was slowly dying…

Maybe this grotto had a puddle or even a pool somewhere? Perhaps the water was there just waiting to be discovered? The air was cool, and maybe drops of moisture had accumulated somewhere? I couldn't let my brain slip into fantasies about a refreshing dip – I needed a plan.

Water… Water…

I closed my eyes, savouring the image of a cool droplet growing slowly at the tip of a stalactite somewhere in the dark, swelling until it surrendered to the pull of gravity. Then, it would float down that enormous distance keeping its perfectly round shape until it hit the rocky tip of a stalagmite, streaming down its sides to the crystal clear puddle or – even better – an underground lake.

I almost heard that splash of the droplet. The next moment I was no longer sure if that barely perceptible sound of a falling droplet was real or belonged to the frightening world of hallucinations. I must find out!

I felt the rocks and pebbles around me. I couldn't use my eyes, but my ears still served me faithfully. I grabbed a pebble and tossed it directly in front of me. Then I held my breath listening as it hit a crag in the dark and rolled onto the floor a few seconds later. No splashes…

A grabbed another and tossed it harder, aiming at a steeper angle. Seconds later it hit the ground on the left, still no hint of even the merest puddle.

I spent the next half an hour tossing rocks and pebbles around me. I had to move twice when the ammunition within my reach depleted. Still, the effort did not bring the desired result. I had no idea how far away I was able to toss those pebbles, but each time they ended rolling on a dusty floor. Damn! Maybe I needed bigger ammo?

I carefully selected the next rock which weighed comfortably in my palm. I got back to my feet, trying to get into a more suitable throwing position. As before, the grotto was silent as I swung the rock in my outstretched arm and then threw it forward with all my remaining might. It remained silent for one more second, maybe two. The rock hit something in the dark.

Then something huge detached from the invisible ceiling with the deafening sound of an exploding cannonball. I dropped to the ground, covering my head with my hands as whatever it was crashed with an even louder bang, scattering small pebbles around. The ground beneath me trembled with several fading aftershocks, and then the grotto returned to a standstill again.

I choked in a sickening bout of coughing and sneezing, covered by clouds of dust, spreading from the site of the crash like an invisible avalanche. It took almost the last bit of my strength to rise to my feet again, but the air was cleaner at the height of a few feet above the floor, and it was easier to breathe.

I had no idea how badly I had messed up the passage through the grotto nor where precisely that passage was. I spent another half an hour standing on my shaky legs, clutching the nearest crag and almost praying aloud for it to hold, not to crumble under my grasp. I was afraid to move any further into the unknown. And there was only darkness in front of me – dustier now than before, and again there was no difference whether I opened my eyes or kept them tightly shut.

Or was there?

It looked just like another ghost of my confused imagination – a few faint flashes in the distance on my right. At first, I dismissed it. Then I saw it again in the same spot! It couldn't just be a coincidence. I closed my eyes and patiently waited for a few long minutes, but nothing appeared in the world of hallucinations that existed behind my closed eyelids. It must be real!

I gasped as the flashes began appearing more frequently. Was it Am'ut hunting me down again? *I must hide!*

But I stayed standing in the darkness and staring at the bursts of light that were clearly framing the mouth of the tunnel several hundred yards away. I expected Am'ut to emerge at any moment, but the creature would cast some light in this eternal darkness so I would have a few brief moments to glance at my surroundings and, possibly, even to spot somewhere to shelter or a better hiding place.

Still, no sounds accompanied the flashes, no earthquakes or hissing of flames. That quietness seemed even more terrifying, and I could barely stop myself rushing back to the nearby mouth of the tunnel that I had emerged from maybe an hour ago. Something was holding me still with a trembling heart, waiting for the monster to appear.

I flinched when the flames began appearing from the tunnel at last, but it wasn't Am'ut or terrifying streams of liquid rock.

The light was painful to my eyes, used to complete darkness, but I was afraid to blink, though tears were pooling under my lids and obscured the view. I brushed them away and silently gasped when a flaming torch emerged from the tunnel, held high by someone's hand.

I couldn't clearly see the silhouette of who was holding the torch, but it was a human form – I had no doubts about that. Had my sister Hel sent her knights to search for me?

"Hey!" I attempted to attract attention, but my mouth was too dry and, of course, that person couldn't hear the hushed hissing which escaped my throat.

Desperately I grabbed a random stone and began pounding against the rocky floor. *Please, hear me! Please, don't leave me alone in the dark!*

My efforts didn't go unnoticed. The silhouette stopped, extending the flaming torch in my direction. Of course, whoever stood in the shadows behind that torch couldn't see me. I was in the dark and too far away, but now I had a direction and a definite purpose.

The light was blinding, and I couldn't see who it was I was asking for help from – was it a friend or a deadly enemy? I had nothing to lose – my situation couldn't get more hopeless.

I rushed forward limping on my weak legs, a rock held firmly in my fist, pounding on any hard surface I could find on my way.

"Don't go away, please..." my lips whispered in the dark without making a single sound.

"Who is there?" the voice was female, and it sounded like music to my ears. She apparently couldn't see me.

"It's me!" I tried shouting again with the same mute result. "Wait! Don't leave me here..."

I jumped forward trying to make as much noise as possible, hoping that she would not turn away, frightened by the unknown monster crawling towards her in the darkness. Several steps later, I stumbled on a rock and fell. It didn't create much noise, but the landing was painful, and I lost her from my sight.

I cursed but stood up, limping forward. The torch was still there, and now I could even smell the faint odour of burning tar.

"Who is there?" she repeated her question with slight

impatience in her voice, and I caught a brief reflection of a small dagger in her hand. "I am not afraid. Show yourself!"

Still, I was only a vague noise in the darkness, too far away to be visible. She had no idea what she was confronting – was it an animal, a human or a monster? I admired her courage. I mustn't frighten her. The rock was still in my fist, and I began pounding every hard surface in triplets – I hoped this would reveal me to be a human, still covered by the darkness.

This time I carefully tested my way forward with my feet, with my eyes fixed on the heavenly angel standing at the mouth of the tunnel ahead. I extended my bare hand forward, hoping that the palm wasn't too dirty, and it would be noticed first.

"I am not afraid!" she repeated firmly.

My eyes hurt less as I approached, adapting. I shook the remnants of tears away, trying to get a better view of the woman.

She looked small and fragile, bravely pointing her dagger at me. The flickering of the light from the flaming torch was playing games of shadows on her face, and her features looked sad. I couldn't tell her age from that distance, but her stance was youthful. Her head was loosely covered by a patterned shawl, but the few strands of hair that had slipped out were dark.

I slowly approached, making as much noise as possible, waving my hand in front of me like a flag. She waited. I could clearly see from her face that she was not afraid. She meant what she had said.

Finally, I entered the circle of light, but my legs failed me again, and I collapsed, hitting my left temple. Instantly the light was gone. All hope was gone too.

I don't know how much time I spent drifting in the darkness between the two worlds. When I came back to my senses, someone was touching my cheek.

She withdrew her hand as soon as I opened my eyes, as if guilty. The torch flamed nearby, jammed between three rocks.

“Who are you?” she repeated her question.

I made one more attempt to speak but failed again and, in complete frustration, tears gushed from my eyes.

“Poor mute,” she said and pressed a flask made from dried pumpkin to my lips.

I avidly gulped several mouthfuls of water.

“Thank you so much,” I managed to whisper at last. “I am not mute.”

She smiled and gave me some more water.

“What are you doing here?” she asked.

“I...” I began to clear my throat, which ended in the worst bout of coughing I have ever had.

She pressed her finger to my lips.

“Sh... Don't talk now,” she said. “Save your strength. You can tell me later. Now we must get up and try to get out of here...”

I was already grateful to this angel for saving me. That flickering light of the torch and a few drinks of water had made a huge difference. She had saved my life. I could easily have ended up wandering around those caverns forever without her, and nobody would ever have found my mummified body.

She helped me to stand up, and we slowly moved forward, now in the bright light of the flaming torch, easily avoiding any obstacles. I tried not to lean on her fragile frame too much, but sometimes gravity got victorious over me. Her body seemed strong and grew tense on those occasions, helping me to regain balance, and we resumed our progress a few seconds later.

Several times we had to stop for a brief rest, and she gave me a few more gulps of water. I was grateful but made no more attempts to talk again. I was keen to get out of the underground as soon as possible and didn't want another bout of coughing to hold us back.

I knew I was slowing us down, but my saviour made no objections. She patiently supported me as I struggled down the tunnel, and held the flaming torch in her left hand. The journey was arduous, and I felt almost totally exhausted when, several hours later, we finally emerged into a large and strangely picturesque cave, painted red by the setting sun shining through the large opening.

A crystal clear spring burst from under the mountain to the left side of the cave, accumulating in a pool neatly framed by sleek rocks. A small stream escaped from the pool, running its waters across the cave, disappearing outside with the sound of a distant waterfall.

I slumped next to the stream, burying my face in the cold water and lifting my head only for a short breath. I was finally out! I drank my fill and washed the dust out of my hair. Then I repeated it all until I had had enough of it. She stood next to me, waiting.

I was smiling like a child when I finally lifted my gaze to her.

"Thank you," I whispered, and my throat spasmed again causing a violent cough.

She only shook her head, half smiling.

I stood up on my frail feet when the cough had subsided. I looked around at the clay pots lined up against the wall, dried herbs hung loosely from the ceiling and a fireplace with still red embers by the right wall of the cave, closer to the entrance. A small den was on the left, next to the spring, with dried herbs and straw covered with a cloth.

"What is this place?" I asked as a cough again overwhelmed me.

"Don't talk. You're still too weak," she said seriously and added with some hesitation. "I live here. Be my guest…"

The effects of my painkillers were exhausting, and the sores on my shoulder and left loin increasingly throbbed. The falls in the tunnel had been responsible for the few ruptured blisters, and now my precious bodily fluids were soaking through the remnants of my clothes.

She helped me to the den. I lay my aching body down and watched her busy about, building a small fire and warming up some water in a large kettle.

Then she washed my wounds and dressed them with a clean cloth. She was very serious about that, and once, when I attempted to speak again, she pressed her finger to my lips, silencing me.

"Sh..." she said. "You can tell me everything tomorrow when you feel stronger."

I just lay back and tried to take some rest, forcing everything out of my head and enjoying the blissful feeling of being alive.

Later in the evening, she filled a small pot with hot soup for me, which I gladly accepted. It was almost dark when we prepared to sleep. Only the embers in the fireplace still flickered red.

She came into the den and lay down, spooning me from behind. Deep sleep followed rather quickly, despite the tiredness and pain.

It was the sense of safety, security, completeness and the hushed sounds of the city waking up outside the window that pushed my consciousness ashore from the sea of oblivion. For a few moments, I enjoyed the peaceful existence of a starfish in shallow waters before opening my eyes and brushing away the last remnants of the night's horrors.

I was out. I was alive.

I savoured the thought with a peaceful serenity. Then the tide turned to bring the pain back into my life. I carefully moved my limbs and moaned as I got out of bed. My bandages were soaked from ruptured blisters, and my muscles ached with every movement, the price of the strenuous wandering through the underground tunnels and caverns and taking more tumbles than I could count.

I limped to the bathroom and filled my stomach with tap water, swallowing a mega-dose of painkillers on the way.

I had started the day feeling grumpy, but this was a price I was willing to pay for being alive.

I stripped and carefully removed the bandages. The skin felt sticky with sweat and the liquid that leaked from the ruptured blisters, and I took a long shower to clean everything out. I then spent an hour applying burn gel and new bandages and made a mental note to visit the pharmacy – my medical supplies were depleting too quickly.

The aches and pains began to subside as I finished messing with the wounds and the painkillers finally kicked in.

I washed, brushed my teeth, combed my hair, got dressed and unhurriedly went down to the hotel canteen for breakfast. The background music was softly playing Mozart.

I smiled at the waitress as she poured me my morning cup of coffee. The breakfast was generous. I feasted on scrambled eggs, sausages and cheese. I then took another cup of *melange* and tried some fruit and Viennese desserts.

Back in my room, I called John.

"Glad to hear that," he blandly said when I informed him briefly that I was safe and finally out of the tunnels.

I didn't go deep into detail or mention the young woman sleeping next to me. This wasn't relevant to our mission, and trust still was an issue.

John said he would be in *Prater* in time and, of course, I was supposed to act as if entirely on my own.

"Try to avoid drinking, eating or sniffing anything when you're in the café," he warned me.

"Why?" I asked, realising my ignorance in such matters.

"You might find yourself tied up in some silly basement when you wake up. Remember, we are dealing with the kidnappers," said my former kidnapper, and I believed him. "Please, take this seriously."

With my stomach full of Viennese delights from the hotel canteen I was sure there would be no temptation for me in that café for me other than gathering the required information.

"Good," said John. "See you later."

I felt increasingly anxious. John's warning kept ringing in my ears, bringing a slow realisation of how dangerous the situation was. The euphoric feeling of being alive faded as I collected a few things and slipped a blister pack of painkillers into my pocket – just in case I would need them.

I went out, leaving the key at the reception.

Cheerful sunshine met me as I stepped onto the street. People appeared to be more relaxed, walking around without the usual rush, talking and smiling. I crept downhill towards the city centre like a shadow, limping slightly because of my burnt thigh. I furtively glanced around a few times, but no one appeared to be following me.

I crossed a few side streets before I reached the *Karlsplatz* with the green-roofed domes of the *Karlskirche* hiding behind the tall trees on the right. A few kids were running around with a red ball and shouting loudly while their mothers were too immersed in conversation to notice.

The tube entrance gaped widely slightly to the left. I glanced around one more time before going underground, still feeling uneasy after those few days of darkness in Rehen, but the Viennese tube passages were brightly lit, and there were indeed no any rivers of magma within the vicinity.

I bought a two-day ticket from the vending machine and patiently waited for the train. People gathered around me, but I could spot no obvious threat.

Prater was not too far away. The ride was short, and I got off the tube in the *Praterstern*. A busy street leading to a large square was ahead, just in front of the station. I stopped in confusion, unable to spot the carnival John had mentioned and I didn't dare ask anybody given my limited knowledge of German.

I knew I hadn't got off the train at the wrong station – I had seen the name *Praterstern* on the wall, above the tube map. I just needed to find the carnival.

Hesitantly, I turned left. I still had sufficient time to circle the building, hoping to spot any hint. The *Praterstern* station was big, and I must have taken the wrong exit.

Two ladies pushed prams along the pavement, deeply immersed in an emotional and agitated conversation which I didn't understand. I followed them at first, but then they stopped, occupying almost the entire width of the pavement with their prams and the loud exchange in German became even more heated. I mumbled an apology as I squeezed between them, but they barely noticed me.

Several paces later, a light breeze carried the faint sound of distant music, and I realised I was on the right track. Indeed, it came from a park on the left, behind the station. The expansive, neatly cut green lawn hosted a few families having a picnic in the sunshine. The tall crowns of green-leafed trees framed the place, and I stopped hesitantly, unable to spot the source of the music at first. Kids ran around with candy floss in their hands, shouting and laughing, and I wasn't sure if the music had stopped playing or if the kids yelling had muted it. Then I glimpsed a ferris wheel towering above the distant trees on the right, behind the petrol station. It must be the place…

I crossed the street. There was a broad straight alley just behind the petrol station, framed by tall trees on both sides. The music was playing somewhere down that alley where low two-storey buildings intervened between the quietness of the park and the cacophony of the carnival.

I walked down the alley, passing the stalls of sweet sellers with the crowd steadily growing around me. I joined the flow and stopped only briefly in front of a low bridge between the two buildings, proudly displaying a dark green panel with the word "*Prater*" painted on it in yellow. Like a swollen river, the crowd carried me steadily under the bridge then dispersed in all directions in anticipation of some fun. I was left in a small square next to the gates in front of the bronze statue of a magician. Souvenir shops and cafés circled the perimeter, but it was another café I needed which was at the far end of the *Prater*.

Someone's eyes were watching me, I was sure – I knew that feeling. Small wonder, given the circumstances, but I felt an urge to find out who was spying on me. Brief glances around offered no result. The crowd circled around the bronze magician, mostly families busy with their kids and couples occupied with themselves – nobody looked at me, but the feeling didn't go away. John was nowhere in sight. I checked my watch. I still had enough time for a little investigation.

I painted a bored expression on my face and paid a visit to a few souvenir shops, pretending to look at the fridge magnets, cups and porcelain figurines on display but, in fact, keeping my eyes on the windows. This ruse didn't work. I couldn't spot any spying eyes, but the menacing feeling didn't go away either. Nor was I able to locate John. The danger which was waiting for me in the depths of *Prater* capped the sense of insecurity. I cursed silently, fighting the sudden urge to fish out my phone and call my bodyguard – I would feel much better knowing that ginger-haired was somewhere at my side, but that could compromise our conspiracy.

It was nearly time to find out Rick's fate and stick my own head in the trap. I only hoped that John still was shepherding me.

A cloud had passed over the bright face of the sun when I finally abandoned my amateur surveillance and left a souvenir shop without buying anything. My mood worsened with every step. I crossed the square spending a few minutes meditating in front of the magician's statue then took the path to the left into the depths of *Prater*. It was time.

I made my way amongst the smiling faces like a lost soul getting away from safety at the gates of paradise. I had no idea what kind of hell had been prepared for me in the *Schweizerhaus* and, more importantly, who was the chief devil behind all this.

I went past carousels and catapults, horror rooms and rides, swings and roller coasters, barely noticing any of them. People walked around me like mere shadows with no chance of registering on my mind. I was preparing to enter the unknown.

The noise of the crowd abruptly ended as I walked beneath the green canopy of tree crowns at the other side of *Prater,* leaving the cacophony of the carnival behind. The pleasant aromas of cooking food aromas that hit my nostrils announced that the *Schweizerhaus* was nearby, on the right side of the path.

I entered and was met immediately by a waiter.

"Haben Sie eine Reservierung? Wie ist Ihr Name bitte?" asked the young man.

"Sorry, I don't speak German," I said with a guilty smile.

"Could I have your name, please?" repeated the waiter politely.

"Firestone," I said, and he checked his papers.

"Yes, Mr Firestone, this way please," he led me to a table in the far corner.

He gave me a menu and asked if I would like to order something in advance. I just asked for a glass of water and promised to take a look at the menu.

Whoever picked the table had been very thoughtful about it. The place was large under a transparent roof of glass with several trees standing amid the tables, their branches spreading high above and providing cool shade for the patrons. Privacy was protected by thick greenery around the perimeter, shielding nearly everything from the curious eyes of an outsider. My table was far away from the entrance, with the view of it blocked by a tree trunk, and I now understood why John was so unhappy with the idea of holding the meeting here.

I waited, glancing impatiently at several families at the tables around me, enjoying their meals. No one approached me or even peeked at my side. This was strange. Had they detected our conspiracy?

This was a chilling thought, and I buried my face in the menu pretending to study the prices while I kept covertly scanning my unchanging surroundings and waiting for Rick's kidnapper to make a move.

I received a few questioning glances from the passing waiter, but each time shook my head, remembering John's advice not to drink, eat or smell roses.

The hands of my watch seemed glued in one position as I checked it several times with growing agitation. It was a quarter to twelve already. I furtively scanned the three suspicious looking men who were drinking beer a few tables away to my right, then glimpsed at everyone else – balding men eating with their families. No one even glanced at me. Why had they requested my presence here and then not shown up? *Was Rick dead?*

I turned the menu over in my hands, absentmindedly gazing at the list of delicacies. How much longer should I wait before declaring this to be a failure? Where was John?

I don't remember what I noticed first – the shiny black eyes? Maybe the shy smile framed with crimson red lipstick? Was it the dark blue gown or the intricate coiffure of black hair under a stylish blue hat topped with several peacock feathers? The flamboyant appearance of an attractive woman was hiding her secret glances at me from a table just a few paces away. I looked at her and smiled. She smiled back, maintaining eye contact.

I had no time or desire for adventures and hid behind the menu again, still waiting but still with no result. The hope of saving Rick was evaporating like a drop of ether.

"May I?" suddenly I heard the pleasant low voice of a woman.

I glanced at my watch first – it was half-past twelve. Then I lifted my eyes to follow the voice.

The lady from the nearby table was standing in front of me with a glass of wine in one hand and her mobile phone in another. She indicated the free chair in front of me.

"The problem is," I told her, "that I am waiting for someone."

"And that someone is not showing up..." she smiled, taking the seat without waiting for my permission any longer. "I've seen you waiting here for more than an hour already."

The waiter appeared out of thin air.

"Are you ready to order something?" he asked.

"*Wiener Apfelstrudel* for me," she said. "And it seems His Majesty hasn't made his mind up yet."

Why had she called me that? She put her wine glass on the table and met my questioning glance with a challenging smile, while the flustered waiter disappeared with her order.

"It's not an everyday pleasure for a commoner to meet Prince Kyleb, isn't it?" she added, wiping off her smile.

The situation had become clear at last as the carefully constructed image of the *femme fatale* cracked and crumbled to reveal my enemy.

"Can we get down to business now?" I asked her. "You promised me some news about my friend. Which friend?"

"Yes," she agreed, showing me Rick's photo on her phone, "this friend."

"I still don't know who you are," I observed calmly while feeling the tension rising.

"Not so fast!" she sipped her wine.

"Ok then, what do you want?" I let a hint of irritation slip into my voice.

"Tell me, how dear is that friend of yours to you?" she returned a question with a mysterious smile. "What would you sacrifice for his life and freedom?"

"That's not the right question," I said firmly, "But it seems I am in no position to bargain. So tell me, what do you want?"

Strudel appeared in front of her as if from nowhere. She elegantly probed it a little with a spoon, teasing me and clearly enjoying it.

"Magnificent! You should try it..." she nodded knowingly.

"Maybe next time," I replied dryly.

She ignored my growing anxiety, and I had to wait until she finished her *strudel*, and then calmly asked:

"So, what do you want to trade for his life?"

"One life for another," she whispered, placing her spoon on the plate.

"Could you be more specific?" I asked, feeling a wave of chill.

"I'm not a monster. It will be an easy decision for you to make. I just want what is rightfully mine," she hissed through her teeth almost inaudibly. "I'd like to trade the life of your friend for the life of your pet gryphon."

The statement left me speechless. Instantly I remembered Sluagh's remarks about the Heart of the gryphon. I had no illusions. She was going to kill baby Gwyn in a crazy attempt to make herself a Ring of Power and join the ruling class in Rehen. On the other hand, it was clear that she wasn't one of the rulers or a member of my Rehen family. Was she serving the usurper Regent who now sat on the throne of Rehen after the mysterious death of the king? *Who was this woman?*

"Maybe, you should trade your name first?" I struggled to hide a note of embarrassment in my voice. "I don't know you. You know me already – make it fair."

"You like things to be fair? Then make it fair yourself! You killed the man I loved! You exiled me from my home, and now you are asking me for some stupid fairness?" she hissed like a snake. "I will never forgive you, Kyleb! Don't even bother to ask."

"I still don't recognise you," I said, still wearing my poker face.

"Have you forgotten your poor little sweet creature, darling?" she burst into a bout of hysteric laughter attracting everybody's attention. "How dare you, Kyleb?"

It was a well-calculated move. I blushed red feeling trapped with all eyes suddenly upon me. She must have been close to the ruler of Chadrack long before I occupied his body in my dream. I had no idea what she was talking about, feeling an awkwardness because of my enfeebled memories. Apparently, she wasn't aware of this, though.

"I get your hint but what name do you want me to call you *here*?" I asked when her laughter had faded. I must guard my tongue closely. Her knowledge might be her strength, but I couldn't let her realise my weaknesses.

"Morvarid! Call me Morvarid! In your worst nightmare, in your final dying hour, call me Morvarid!" her eyes flashed with rage as she threw her spoon to the floor with force. "You will never find out my name *here*, Kyleb! Don't even try!"

I sat silently. Her name didn't ring any bells in my head. I had no memories of Morvarid... yet, I made sure my calm expression remained unchanged.

She finally took control of her emotions and waved to the waiter.

"Another *strudel* and a cup of *melange*," she ordered without consulting the menu.

The young man nodded and looked at me, expectantly.

"Do you want anything, *Sir*?"

"Not now. Give me a little more time..."

He disappeared.

Morvarid managed a sleazy smile again.

"It is not a difficult decision for you, Kyleb," she said, resuming her earlier taunting. "Trade some monstrous pet you don't even like for the life of your friend. That creature is disgusting. It's like a flying rat!"

"I will not start trading anything before being sure, that my friend is still alive," I suddenly remembered John's advice. "It would be a very unfair deal to trade the dead body of my friend for a living pet. Or would you prefer that pet dead too?"

I ignored the flashes of irritation showing under her furrowed brow and patiently waited.

Another *strudel* and a cup of coffee appeared in front of her.

"Very well," she said after some visible hesitation. "That sounds fair."

She took her phone out and scrolled through the menus for some time.

"Here!" she showed me the screen with a victorious expression. "See for yourself!"

The phone showed Rick sitting in some dark corner and tiredly blinking in front of the bright light. His left eye was black, and I noticed a few bruises on his left cheek.

"Satisfied?" she stowed the phone away.

"No," I shook my head. "It's not convincing. You could have filmed that a few days ago. I need some solid proof that he is alive right now," I did my best to sound as calm as possible. "He might easily be feeding fish in the Danube as we speak. I won't accept just a photo as proof."

"What do you want me to do?" she asked me angrily. "Cut off his freshly severed finger and send it to you? Which one would you prefer?"

"That wouldn't prove anything either," I observed without losing my calm facade. "I want some sort of live demonstration. No more discussion until then."

Morvarid thought just for a few seconds.

"Fine! You will have your demonstration," she hissed, standing up. "Tomorrow at 10 am. Be outside of the *Donauinsel* tube station. Don't be late!"

"I'll be there, don't worry. Where will we meet next time after that demonstration?" I asked, keeping my eyes on her expression. "I guess we might need further talks to reach an agreement if my friend is still alive. By the way, will you need a live demonstration of the gryphon?"

She stopped.

"Don't be ridiculous, Kyleb. I will find you when I am ready for the next step. Stay in the city. Tomorrow at 10 am. Don't miss your demonstration," said Morvarid before squeezing out another foxy smile. "I know you are tempted to follow me. I warn you – my banshee is protecting me, don't risk your life."

"Banshee?" that sounded utterly insane.

"Don't even try to pretend," she whispered. "You know perfectly well about that. My banshee was carrying the gryphon to me when you intervened. So, in fact, it's my gryphon."

I bit my lip, recalling the glistening mist lifting from the gryphon's body when I had approached it through the crowd. Was she referring to that?

"Are you threatening me?" my tongue spat out without consulting with my brain. "Am I supposed to be trembling now?"

"Don't fool yourself," she laughed viciously, heading to the exit.

Halfway out, she turned back to me with a strange expression on her face, as if remembering something crucial.

"I hope you have sufficient euros to pay for my *strudel*?" her smile was almost angelic before she disappeared into the crowd outside.

I waved to the waiter, but it took almost fifteen minutes for him to prepare my bill. She was gone long before I had paid and left the café. My only hope was John – if she hadn't spotted him. I hadn't.

I fought the instant urge to phone him – he might be busy keeping up with Morvarid, and I did not need to create any distractions. On the other hand, Morvarid might have left someone behind to watch over me. I didn't want to reveal our well-played conspiracy by phoning John.

I quickly glanced around on my way out but couldn't spot any curious eyes following me. It was sunny outside. *Prater* was full of people – children screaming, men enjoying themselves in the sun and showing a certain seriousness and exaggerated importance, women eating ice cream. I walked between the spinning carousels but was unable to spot either Morvarid or John.

I made my way through the *Prater* barely noticing the happy faces, joy and laughter around me. That strange meeting was still playing back in my head, but this only resulted in more questions than I'd had before. That woman – Morvarid – had been deeply hurt by the ruler of Chadrack, the one who had occupied the body of the Bloody Prince before me. She had been bursting with rage, and every cell in her body called for revenge – that was obvious. Only, I had no knowledge what it was for.

The purpose of her request was clear, but I had no idea if she was a lone player or was operating under someone else's control. Who might be controlling her? Mather – the ruthless regent who was sitting on the throne in Rehen? Or maybe she had teamed up with one of my brothers or sisters? I realised that the possibilities were endless, and I wandered around uncertainly like a blind kitten.

I dawdled slowly among snatches of different melodies as each carousel played its own tune. There was something eerie in all this cacophony as if some sinister foreboding hovered above the crowd. A gust of chilly wind swept through my bones, but the menace remained invisible, beyond any perception.

Several screaming kids passed me excitedly waving their candy floss. I jumped aside, watching them running down the road. It was unclear whether they were just fooling around or what the fuss was all about. A dozen paces later they bumped into a little girl and ran away, disappearing behind the corner. The frightened little princess dropped her ice-cream cone on the pavement and began to cry as loud as she could.

I stopped, unsure of how to react. Luckily, my involvement proved unnecessary. A grey-haired man rushed to her, shouting a few German obscenities at the long-gone boys. He took a large handkerchief out of his pocket and clumsily began wiping her tears. The girl pushed his hand away, letting go of an oval silver helium balloon. It soared up to the sky, but its flight was short. A second later, the balloon exploded with a loud bang as it caught on the sharp branch of a tree overhead. The little princess began screaming even louder as if her land of unicorns had suddenly become possessed by evil witches and had disappeared forever.

A few women rushed to help the man, but the distressed cries continued despite the constant flow of words of solace in German, which I didn't understand.

The remnants of the silver balloon landed next to my feet as I stared at the proceedings, still unsure how to react. As the girl continued to cry, the man wiped away her tears, and the women now began to argue among themselves, or so it seemed, gesturing over to me.

I felt helpless. I picked up the remnants of the balloon and extended these to them but was quickly waved away with resentful expressions. One of the women rushed to buy another ice-cream. She went past me without even glancing at the silver patches I was clutching in my hand. Apparently, it was my job to find a litter bin.

I went down the road, the cacophony of carousel melodies and the cries of the distressed child following me. My own dark thoughts and problems now seemed more distant, leaving only the simple task of finding a bin to get rid of the garbage.

The road ended in a small square bearing a star-shaped mosaic on the pavement. Eerily painted mannequins sat on a low bench on the left looking at the house of horrors across the square. The square was empty, and I stopped looking for a bin.

I was about to walk on when a subtle movement at the very edge of my perception caught my eye. It looked like a barely visible wisp of a mist moving from mannequin to mannequin and then slowly drifting beyond the dummy tree where dummy vultures perched and into the house of horrors.

I hesitated for only a second, if at all. If that was Morvarid's protection, I must take a closer look at it. I had seen it twice in Rehen, and both times my dog had scared the creature away. It didn't seem as dangerous as Morvarid had implied.

"Keep the change," I tossed a tenner to the man selling tickets – it was way above the ticket price, but I had no time to wait for the change.

He silently took the banknote and waved me in, pressing the button which sent the low sound of a gong rumbling through the house.

The alarm was intended to wake the ghosts up, but I wasn't seeking any amusement. I had to find that strand of mist.

I went down the dimly lit corridor followed by the creepy music and distant ghostly laughter. The walls were richly stained with fake blood and decorated with artificial cobwebs and plastic spiders. The worst things were the humidifiers hidden in the walls which spewed out streams of vapour, supposed to be scary but, in fact, extremely distracting. The task was nearly impossible – I was looking for one wisp of mist among many other strands of vapour.

I progressed slowly down the corridor, trying to ignore the

plastic skeletons, spiders and headless dolls that appeared before me. More than once, I was tempted to return to the entrance to try to persuade the man to turn the machinery off. But would that raise his suspicion?

I took the squeaky stairs to the upper floor when the music and ghostly cries stopped, and I sighed with relief and then rushed back to the corridor to scan the thinning mist again. Still, I saw nothing suspicious.

A few minutes later, the sound of the gong restarted the whole sequence – either for new visitors or because the ticket seller had decided to give me complete entertainment for my tenner. Clouds of vapour poured out of the walls again, burying my hopes of spotting that strand of mist I sought.

I took the stairs again. It was a little quieter on the top floor and, luckily, no sprinkles! A few dummies eerily painted in red hung from the ceiling wrapped in cobwebs. Two long rows of distorted skeletons guided me to a pedestal carrying a dusty black coffin in the distance where a stocky man wearing the mask of a pig's head was quietly snoring in the corner. The lid began to open as I approached, but I completely ignored the rising plastic Dracula as the mist I was seeking drifted across the corridor just a few paces ahead of me.

I stopped, watching it move slowly from skeleton to skeleton and then disappear into a small dusty form on the floor. I wasn't sure if it was hiding inside that shape or had gone through the floor and was now somewhere below.

I carefully moved the skeleton aside. The shape on the floor was a mummified rat, grinning at me with two long brown teeth. I crouched down to take a closer look just in time to see the glistening tentacle disappear into the rat's mouth.

Whatever that misty creature was – it still was here!

I couldn't bark like my dog, Bysh, and it wasn't my intention to scare that creature away. If Morvarid could handle it, maybe that mist wasn't as dangerous as she hinted at? I had to do something quickly, or it would get away!

The dried corpse looked repulsive, and I hated touching it with my bare hands. So, instead, I placed the ruptured silver balloon on the mummified rat (I had had no time to find a bin earlier) and quickly wrapped up the dry remains of the rodent.

In a brief moment of silence between the ghostly wailing and the eerie laughter of Dracula, I heard footsteps behind me.

"What are you doing here?" demanded an angry male voice.

I turned around to face him – the ticket seller frowned at me, most likely worried by my long absence.

"Err..." I had no idea if that sounded convincing. "That Dracula looked quite scary, and I accidentally dropped some litter behind this skeleton. Sorry about that. I didn't want to leave any mess behind, so I just picked it."

The man only shook his head, looking at the silver remnants in my hand.

"This is not a full day's entertainment," he said. "You better leave..."

I went outside without saying another word, clutching the rat in my pocket. I was glad to get out of that kitsch dungeon, back to the normal world.

The mummified rat wriggled in my fist, and a few times, it felt like it was alive and trying to break free. I took a seat on a bench between the two mannequins and carefully inspected the silver package, wrapping it more tightly and covering even the tiniest of gaps.

Suddenly I felt scared. It was mere coincidence that the mist couldn't penetrate the silver lining of the balloon, but I realised that I was dealing with a force I didn't understand. I'd got hold of the creature – now what? How could this help to save Rick? I had no plan.

John was chasing Morvarid, and I didn't dare interrupt him, but he might be my only source of information. I must wait for him to call me when he had time and news to share. I hoped for some good news since this entire escapade was slowly drifting towards a murky and dangerous swamp I didn't like to think of. I only wanted to free Rick and get back to London, but life usually comes up with its own surprises – here I was, sitting on a bench, clutching the dead rat that held *that* thing in my fist, afraid to let go – the creature could escape through any gap in the wrapping.

A young couple passed in front of me as I sat on the bench. They cast a few curious glances at the silver patches of the balloon wriggling in my fist, and I immediately decided that it would be safer to hold the rat away from prying eyes.

I patiently waited until the couple had turned right and disappeared around the corner then carefully took off my jacket, stuffed the fist holding the package into the pocket of my trousers and hung the folded jacket on it masking the vibrations emanating from the rat.

I turned left and rushed down the road, doing my best to keep my fist still. Several times I had to apologise for bumping into people – I had no time to worry if they thought I was crazy. All I wanted to do was to get back to the hotel and secure the package properly.

I stopped just briefly at the souvenir shop near the exit. The girl behind the counter looked strangely at my arm jerking in my pocket but sold me a roll of adhesive tape without making any comment.

I nearly ran out of *Prater* and down the alley, glancing backwards just a few times – nobody tried to stop me, and nobody followed.

The tube station was almost empty as the crowds gathered in

Prater. I heaved a sigh of relief when the train arrived a few minutes later and took a seat next to the door. Strangely, the creature calmed down too. I even suspected that it had escaped during my frantic run down the escalator, but the silver package was softly humming like a bumblebee when I carefully took it out and listened. It was still safely inside.

I replaced the package in my pocket and looked around. The carriage was almost empty, and I nearly sighed with relief before when my eyes stumbled on two kids whispering something to each other and pointing their fingers at me. Could it be Morvarid's surveillance? That sounded crazy, but I had begun to become accustomed to even the weirdest of things. The possibility might be remote, but I couldn't be sure.

A few more passengers boarded the carriage at the next station, allowing me to take a peek at those kids. They were still whispering something, giggling and pointing at me again – more than once! Their granddad was sitting next to them with his eyes closed, taking a moment out. I flinched when a woman appeared in front of me unexpectedly, putting her massive body in my line of view and obscuring the kids. She didn't look at me and got off at the next station. I went after her – I could swear I heard some giggling behind my back.

I barely glanced at the *Karlsplatz* as I ran out of the tube. The road uphill was almost empty, and I rushed forward without wasting any time looking if somebody followed me. I just paid a quick visit to a nearby store to buy some baking foil.

The eyes of the receptionist looked puzzled, but he gave me the room key without comment. Back in my room, I locked the door. First, I had to deal with the creature without any interruption.

The package was still quietly humming when I took it out of my pocket and wrapped a layer of sticky tape around it without releasing my grip. I had used almost a third of the roll until I was satisfied then I added a generous layer of baking foil and again fixed this with the sticky tape.

The package – the size of a mobile phone – quietly hummed on the table when I had finished and finally got an opportunity to wash my hands. One glance at the mirror explained all those puzzled looks and giggles – a giant cobweb was stuck in my hair, most likely when I brushed past it while trying to pick the dead rat! Luckily there was no spider, and I felt instant relief as I brushed it off and flushed it down the toilet.

I washed my hands several times, but they still didn't feel clean enough. I was interrupted by the phone.

"I've lost that woman," John told me. "She is damn good at knowing this city. Who is she? Have you discovered anything?"

"Yes," I said. "But it's a long story. Can we meet somewhere this evening?"

He was silent for a few long seconds, and I sensed some

hesitation.

"That might compromise our conspiracy," he said finally.

I knew that. Yet I didn't trust him enough to speak about important matters without being able to see his reactions. In all honesty, I would rather have avoided speaking to him at all, but John was my final recourse for information, and I would prefer to look him in the eyes when I asked him certain questions. He might know more about my previous self in Rehen and, possibly, could explain what was driving Morvarid against me. If I could undo some of those wrongdoings, maybe we would have a better chance of negotiating Rick's life and freedom without paving Morvarid's way to the club of power?

"I would prefer to meet in person," I told him firmly.

"Where?" there was obvious disapproval in John's voice.

"I don't know," I shrugged – my knowledge of Vienna was fairly limited. "Somewhere in the park? What about *Karlsplatz*?"

"Okay," John agreed reluctantly. "Let's meet at five."

"All right, see you then..."

Thoughts swarmed through my brain as I restlessly paced the room. I needed answers to many questions, but would it be safe to ask John? Never before I felt more vulnerable. When my consciousness had transferred to Rehen for the first time, I had received a fully grown body with plenty of dark stories riddling its past. My previous self had been cruel, selfish and unscrupulous – I had found this out by putting together the tiniest bits of information people carelessly dropped around me, not too many though. What was the story that hid behind that woman? Was Morvarid's angst also of my doing? I guessed it was – her hatred had bared itself several times, almost physically, during our short conversation.

But all I could do was pace around the hotel room and wonder, occasionally checking my watch.

John was the person who had kidnapped me weeks ago. I still felt chills remembering that night of horror which I had spent tied to a metal bed, expecting to be tortured or killed at any moment. A week later, I had done the same to John. It was a strange way to meet relatives, but we were Sleepers, and that was the only way. I hadn't expected him to be a relative and I couldn't easily forget what he did to me, but then John proved to be married to my sister Keely in Rehen. Now he was helping me to save Rick from that weird woman. Could he know her Rehen identity? Could he know who hid behind the pretty face of Morvarid?

I firmly made my mind to ask him despite all the risks. I must know my enemy.

Then I spent almost an hour on my bed, staring at the ceiling.

When it was time to go, I rechecked the foil wrapped package and put it into my pocket. Maybe John would know how to deal with that creature too?

The weather was warm and pleasant outside, promising a tranquil evening. I walked down the street past Chinese stalls, filling my nostrils with their spicy aromas. The city burst with life around me, but I couldn't get my enemies out of my mind. Somewhere, Rick was being held a prisoner, and I felt guilty as I looked at all the celebrations going on around me.

An impromptu stage was placed under the dark green canopy of treetops in the *Karlsplatz* with loudspeakers spitting out the flaming rhythm of tango. Two couples were circling the dance floor while several dozen others watched and cheered their graceful moves.

I made my way through the crowd looking for John. I found him sitting on a bench under low leafy branches looking at Karl's cathedral. He kept staring at the green domes as I passed in front of his nose and sat down at the far end of a bench, several paces away.

"What have you got?" John whispered a second later. "Who is she?"

"Her name is Morvarid," I told him, keeping my voice low as well. "Does that ring any bells to you?"

"I'm amazed that it doesn't ring any bells to you!" he glanced at me, smiling.

"Why?"

"Well... She used to be your wife before you exiled her..."

"To be honest, John," I said hesitantly, unsure of how to present my true story. "I came into this Sleeper thing only recently, and I have no memory of what happened in Rehen before I got there. I don't know her or why she was exiled."

"I feel sorry for you," replied John after a short silence. "That explains some of the strangeness I've noticed about you."

"Could you enlighten me as to why I divorced Morvarid?"

"The strangest thing is why you married her at all," he smiled. "I always told Keely that the marriage wouldn't last long. You were incompatible, and Morvarid put herself in a dominant position over you which is not the place for a woman who is married to the Prince. You were so overwhelmed by her that you tolerated everything. Well, almost everything."

"What happened?"

"She became bored with you and got herself a lover," he shrugged. "That's when you earned your nickname the Bloody."

I looked at him, but he just gave a nervous cough.

"What happened?" I demanded again.

"You skinned her lover alive and locked Morvarid in the room with his skin on her bed and his dead body placed on a spike in front of her window for three days! I don't know many details, but the rumours were that her wailing and crying was heard in all of Chadrack. She had followers in the capital who raised a riot and demanded justice. Then you ordered the execution of them all

– no less than several hundred men and women – and put their heads on spikes in front of her window as well," he was whispering. "I think she learned her lesson."

John paused and watched the dancers.

"Then you exiled her from Chadrack. You ordered her to be dropped outside the gates stark naked. I still can't believe she survived in the forest. Some of her secret allies must have helped her."

"Did I love her?"

"I don't know. Most likely. Only badly hurt love can be so cruel," he said. "On the other hand, she loved your money, position and power, but not you. And she wasn't the only one like that. You used to have very bizarre relationships, Kyleb."

"What do you mean?"

"You tried to dig out something when there was clearly nothing there. But this can turn into a very long conversation if we continue on the subject," he warned. "Unless you are willing to spend the night here on the bench."

I shrugged. Despite my curiosity, this could wait.

"What else did you got out of her? Why she is holding Rick?" he asked.

I didn't know how far I could trust John, but I had no other choice – we were in this together.

"She wants the heart of the gryphon," I said, waiting for his reaction.

"Your Master of Destiny? She's a complete idiot!" John shook his head. "Doesn't she know that the Ring will kill her at the very first attempt? Or does she want only to strip away your powers?"

"Not *that* heart..."

"How many Rings do you have?" he turned his surprised eyes to me.

I decided not to mention the Diamond Ring yet.

"It's not the ring she wants – she wants the heart of a living gryphon..."

"Do you have one?" now John was even more surprised.

"In fact, I do," I said, inspecting my shoes. "And Rick was taking care of him in Chadrack."

Now John grew silent, trying to understand what I had said.

"I found out that there had been a lengthy sequence of coincidences and I would never have possessed the gryphon on my own," I added. "It was Morvarid's efforts, to begin with, but the creature landed in my yard."

"How had she managed to land a gryphon?" John still couldn't quite believe the story.

"She told me that it was her banshee. And now she wants the gryphon back," I said wryly.

"Banshee?" John asked, his voice rising in horror. "Does she have a banshee?"

"She did have," I muttered under my breath.

John's eyes almost popped out of his head as I told him briefly about how we had found the dead gryphon-mother on my balcony, about the mist separating from the body and baby Gwyn being found when Rick dissected the creature's body just before placing it on a pyre.

"This is very dangerous," he whispered. "Banshees can be very unpredictable. I would never have dared to follow her if I had known about the banshee. Do you believe her? She might be bluffing."

"I was on my way out of *Prater* today," I told him, "when I saw a similar mist drifting nearby."

John gasped, even more frightened.

"A banshee here? In Vienna? How did you manage to escape?"

"I wasn't trying to escape," I told him. "I followed the mist and caught it when it entered a dead rat."

"What? How could you catch a banshee?! It's impossible!"

I showed him the package.

"I reckoned that it wouldn't be able to penetrate even the tiniest layer of metal, so this foil cage has done its job nicely..."

"How did you know that?"

"I didn't. You could call it a happy coincidence."

"Is it still inside?" John asked cautiously.

I listened to the package. It was still humming like a

bumblebee. I nodded.

"Please, take it away, it's making me nervous..."

I put the package back in my pocket.

"Keely will never believe what kind of brother she has," he said after a short pause. "He has a gryphon as a pet, and now he even has a pocket banshee!"

"How should we proceed with freeing Rick under these circumstances?"

"You've caught her banshee. That may give us some advantage. She's now like a black widow spider without its fangs. But are you sure Rick is alive?"

"She promised me a live demonstration tomorrow morning," I said.

"Where? When?"

"Ten o'clock, in front of the *Donauinsel* underground station."

"Ok, I'll be there in advance," said John. "If Rick is still alive, then we must find a way to liberate him. We might get a chance during the demonstration, but he will no doubt be well guarded. It may be difficult. Our other best shot would be to find him in Rehen – he might know more about his whereabouts in Vienna than we do. Are you already out of the tunnels?"

"Yes. But I am still licking my wounds. I'll need a few days to regain my strength before I can travel. And it's about a week-long walk to Chadrack. I have no horse."

"Do you have any idea where Rick is in Rehen?"

"I had ordered him to move out of Chadrack and hide when Hel attacked..."

We grew silent. People in the park were dancing the tango, now more than just a few couples.

"So, the only chance we have is here..." mumbled John finally.

"It looks like it," I agreed. "If Rick is alive, and we can't succeed in freeing him immediately, then I'll have to cancel our flights. We might need more time here."

"We'll need an entirely different method of transport anyway," John shrugged. "How would you be able to get your banshee cage through airport security? It will escape if they will try to unwrap it. And I hate even to think what might happen if by any chance the banshee got loose on a plane!"

"Never thought of that..."

"We could get a train or a bus, or rent a car," said John bending his fingers. "And at Calais, we could take a ferry. The Channel tunnel trains use airport-style security."

"So, in fact, I need to cancel our flights in any case?"

He nodded.

It was already getting dark, but the rhythm of the tango still ignited flames in the hearts of bystanders. A few more pairs had joined the dance floor and circled in the warm light of the many coloured light bulbs.

It was time to return to Rehen. After a quick farewell, I returned to the hotel.

A strange and fragile sense of calm and security lulled me in the dispersing darkness. It couldn't last long, I knew, but I enjoyed the moment with my eyes still closed. It was quiet with only barely audible ripples of flowing water and the soft crackle of burning dry wood disturbing the silence.

I was alone in the den, but my saviour wasn't far away – I heard somebody rustling as the dry logs that crackled in flames offered a sense of comfort in the pleasant warmth. The hay in the den beneath me was soft, smelling of dried thyme and mint, and I smiled before opening my eyes.

The cave was larger than my chambers in Chadrack's castle. Its uneven walls were the colour of rust with small streaks of red, green and blue minerals. A layer of soot high on the ceiling told me that it had been in use for a considerable time. Two large openings gaped – one on the right, dark and silent, and I knew that this led to the underground caverns from which I had managed to escape. The other – on the left – was painted bright by morning sun with a piece of cloudless sky shining through. The distant sound of twittering birds and singing grasshoppers could just be heard above the quietly lapping ripples of the flowing stream.

My saviour was busy at the fireplace. A sooty kettle was already boiling on the stove as she peeled some roots and washed them in the stream.

I watched her working as a disturbing thought sneaked into my soul, spoiling the simple pleasure of being alive. Did she recognise me as the Prince of Chadrack? I doubted that. After all those days and nights spent underground, I was dusty and dirty, far from the image of a high lord. Could I trust her with my true identity? The thought was unsettling and, for a few moments, I battled with my inner demons of doubt.

She had saved me, and that was enough reason to be grateful. Why must I torture myself looking for enemies? But the recent tumultuous events on both planes of reality firmly planted that peculiar mantra in my brain. *Was it safe here?*

We were the only people in the cave, and I couldn't hear the sounds of any other humans outside. Did she live alone? Why would such a young and pretty woman live alone?

Where was the cave? I had had no chance to have a look at the locality, nor would that have been very helpful with my scant geographic knowledge. Was I still in Chadrack? Had I crossed the border while wandering underground? Was it Porlock? Or had I crossed the mountain range underground and emerged on the other side – god knows where?

Was I in a friendly territory? Or hostile? Or some sort of no man's land?

My heart slowly increased its tempo as this vicious swarm of thoughts stormed my brain. I closed my eyes, forcing them out – I would find out everything, only later. The thoughts stubbornly crawled back and again I had to wrestle with them.

I opened my eyes and looked back at the woman who had saved me. She was young with her black hair neatly braided and tied with a narrow leather band. Her face was tanned by the sun, with smooth features and a small mouth. Her almond-shaped eyes were dark brown and had the subtle warm inner glow of midday sunshine. Her dress was clean but faded by the sun – whatever patterns and embroidery it had years ago were now of a uniform brownish-grey colour. A wide brown leather belt was fastened at her waist with a small dagger attached on the right.

I watched her working and forced all doubts out of my head. The feeling of security returned.

She put the washed roots into the kettle and, stirring with a spoon, added a few pinches of dried herbs. Then a crow shrieked unexpectedly somewhere outside the cave mouth. She glanced at the entrance and caught me watching her, then lowered her eyes with a shy smile dancing on her lips.

"I didn't realise you were awake," she said, slowly stirring the brew simmering over the flames. "How do you feel today?"

"Better," I admitted.

"I'm glad..."

I kept on looking, and she kept on smiling.

"What's your name, stranger?" she finally asked in her soft, gentle voice.

"Kyleb," I answered with a slightly unsteady tongue. Her smiling eyes didn't change one bit. "And your name?"

"Shandra..."

"What are you doing here, Shandra?" this time, I managed to ask first. "Alone in the cave?"

The question wiped the smile from her face, and I immediately regretted asking.

"I'm waiting for a prince charming on a white horse to appear from the dark woods down there…" she said with bare irony in her voice as she turned her gaze in the kettle.

My tongue grew numb as I realised that, unknowingly, I had hit a nerve. There was something painful there, something below the surface that still hurt her like a fresh wound, and I felt terrible. She silently accepted my clumsy apology, but her smile didn't return.

I felt terrible. She was a sweet young woman who had helped me out of a desperate situation, and I didn't like to appear ungrateful. I hoped she wouldn't become angry and would let me stay for a day or two to regain my strength before the long and arduous journey back to the capital of Chadrack.

Shandra returned to the den carrying a bowl with a wooden spoon.

"Eat this, please," as she handed it to me. "You need to regain your strength."

The potion tasted strange – a little bitter with a sour aftertaste but was filling and warmed my stomach pleasantly. Shandra watched as I ate.

Later she handed me a large gown.

"I know, this is not the most suitable outfit for a man," it looked as if she felt a little guilty. "But could you change into it? Your clothes need some attention..."

I hesitantly took the gown.

"Don't worry. I'll wait outside. Let me know when you're ready..."

She left.

I stripped, looking closely at my clothes. Would they reveal my identity? They were only plain clothes which, after a few days of struggle underground, were dusty, torn and burnt in several places, looking like a bunch of rags. My heart skipped a beat when suddenly I spotted a monogram with a blue crown embroidered on the breast pocket of my shirt – I hoped she hadn't noticed it. Hastily I tore it off and tossed it into flames. I didn't want to scare her with the evil notoriety of the Bloody Prince.

My bandages looked quite well, only soaked lightly. Shandra had applied them carefully, and I decided to leave them without disturbing my wounds. They were healing fast, and I remembered that I had spent all last evening in Vienna without any painkillers!

The gown Shandra gave me was clean but too big for my frame. I looked like a starving version of priest Kyaal, lacking only a few sparkles on the gown and his pink wig. The thought was disturbing, and I looked around the cave until I found a piece of rope to tether around my waist. Only then did I dare to peek outside.

I stopped, stunned by the view. The cave was high in the mountain, overlooking a valley which stretched towards misty hills just next to the horizon. There was a flowering meadow beyond the cave, dressed in dark green forests as it fell down the slope. Rocky walls framed the field on both sides like the arms of a giant who had turned to stone guarding his gems. And the gems were still there – the green backdrop of the mountain field was richly scattered with blooming yellow-red tulips, white daffodils, scarlet poppies and bright bluebells.

The stream which escaped from the cave mouth continued

down the slope, forming a few waterfalls and several crystal-clear pools on its way. A series of low, dark green shrubs were on the left bank of the stream, glistening like large emeralds, some of them covered by white flowering wild clematis. The right-hand bank was mainly coloured with reds and blues, cascading down to the green wall of the forest, maybe a mile or so below.

The weather was serene, and I stopped just outside the cave mouth to look at the few white fluffy clouds in the deep blue sky. It was bliss after all those dark caves and grottos I had been through.

Shandra was sitting on a flat rock next to the stream and looking at the valley. She smiled at me when I stopped next to her.

"It's so beautiful," I whispered, looking into the distance.

"Yes, indeed it is," she agreed. "I could look at those hills forever. I especially like the mornings when curtains of fog slip down the mountain. Then those hills look like the silhouettes of distant ships, and I pretend that they are waiting for me in the harbour, waiting to take me away."

There was a trace of sadness in her voice, but her lips still smiled. I sat down next to her.

"Where would you go?" I asked, trying to imagine the shapes of ships behind the dark wall of the woods.

"I would go to the Road of Gods if I were brave enough," the smile vanished from her face again. "But I am still just a weak woman, not ready for the journey."

"Why do you want this?" I asked, shocked by the revelation. "You're too young to die."

She shook her head before answering.

"I have lived here for five long years already," she sighed. "Alone, without a single soul coming close. This is killing me slowly, not as surely as a sword would, but I know I'll be ready in a few more years."

There was a chill note in Shandra's words. She sounded like someone who had been sentenced to death, who had already accepted their fate on death row. I looked at my saviour – her face was calm, her gaze fixed somewhere in the distance, but her eyes suddenly became moist.

"I know, I can't hold you here," she added. "But would you stay with me just to heal your wounds before you go? I might never meet another human being in my life."

I carefully chose my words before answering.

"I can't stay long," I didn't dare lie to her. "The life of my friend depends on me. I must go as soon as I can, but I would be grateful if you would let me stay for a day or two until I become stronger for the journey."

Shandra quickly nodded.

"Thank you," she whispered, grabbing my hand. "I wasn't expecting any more than that."

I watched as a cloud hid the bright face of the sun.

"Why don't you go to live in some village or town?" I asked gently squeezing her fingers. "You would be safer there…"

"I can't," she shook her head.

"Why?"

"They've exiled me…" Shandra's voice was barely audible.

"What did you do?" I gasped without thinking.

"A man died because of me," she said firmly withdrawing her hand and standing up. "I'll have a look at your clothes."

"Sorry for rubbing your wounds," I mumbled but wasn't sure if she heard my apology. She had already gone back to the cave.

I felt like an ungrateful swine. Shandra had saved and sheltered me without asking any questions, and I had begun to dig into her past. I had no right to that!

I punched the rock several times. It made my knuckles bleed, but it didn't help to ease the guilt.

An hour later, when Shandra brought my washed robes out of the cave to spread them on a nearby shrub to dry, I was still there – sitting on the same rock and gathering my courage.

"I am sorry, Shandra," I mumbled as she spread my wet shirt over the green branches. "I had no right to cause you pain with my questions. Please, forgive me."

"You have a right to know that you are staying with a killer," she said in a flat voice without looking at me. "It is my burden, and I am not offended. No need to apologise. Would you like something to eat?"

I nodded standing up, glad that the embarrassing moment had passed. Still, I didn't understand her punishment. I couldn't believe this young and pretty woman had done something terrible enough to be expelled her from home and condemned to live as a hermit in some god-forsaken cave. I refused to believe that.

The flames were cheerfully flickering in the fireplace when I went back to the cave. It seemed bleak after all that sunshine outside, but the smell leaking from the kettle on the stove hit my nostrils with a pleasant aroma.

She filled a bowl with her root soup and handed it to me. I silently ate while she watched without interrupting me. The food felt spicy but was strangely filling, and again, I felt grateful for what Shandra was doing for me and sorry for her situation.

She took the empty bowl and washed it in the stream.

"It's very quiet here," I observed as she stood and placed the clean bowl next to the cave's wall where many bunches of herbs and roots were hanging on a rope, drying.

"Yes," Shandra agreed and turned to face me. "Sometimes, too quiet."

"I'm a little confused after all those days underground – am I in Porlok or still in Chadrack?" I asked, just to keep the uncomfortable silence at bay.

"Chadrack," she said. "You'll have to go west if you're running from the Bloody Prince.

"I am not running from anybody," I replied benignly but her statement made my heart sink, and my spine grew numb at the mention of the nickname, but at least this proved that Shandra didn't recognise me. I had no way to explain to her that I had nothing to do with that notoriety and that those atrocities of my predecessor were not of my doing.

"Chadrack is to the east and Porlock is to the west," Shandra gestured. "And we're in the middle of nowhere."

There was a note of sadness in her voice again, which clutched at my heart. She was slowly dying in this cave surrounded by the beautiful flowering meadow and magnificent views. Her loneliness hung in the air and felt almost physical. I wondered what kind of wrongdoing she had done to be punished like this but was afraid to ask any further questions, nor did it really seem important. She wasn't a killer – I could read that in her eyes.

Shandra wrapped a cloth around the kettle's handle and took it off the stove, placing it on the hot rocks which framed the fireplace.

"How had you got underground?" she asked, still working.

"It was an accident," I shrugged. "I went into a cave, and its ceiling collapsed, blocking off the entrance. I had to find another way out."

"It must have been a long journey," she looked at me seriously. "I don't know any other caves in the vicinity."

"It took a few days, I guess," I said. "Time passes differently down there…"

Shandra shrugged and sat down next to the fireplace. She took a charred stick and began burying blazing embers in the hot ashes while I watched.

"Those caves are very dangerous," she said still busy with the ashes. "You were very brave to go there. I heard a loud bang in the tunnel and went to have a look, and it was you waving at me from the dark."

"I nearly died in flames," I sighed. "I'll never tire of thanking you for helping me out."

"Don't say that," she interrupted me. "You'll forget me and everything here as soon as you leave..."

The silence felt awkward, and I had no idea how to fill it. Shandra wasn't complaining or blaming me – she just stated this as a fact, but her eyes failed to look at me.

"I know that grotto with flames," she whispered seconds later. "It's my path to the Road of Gods."

Her words took the breath from me. I looked at the young woman. Her humiliation ran deep, well past the point of acceptance, leaving me gasping only. This was far worse than any dungeon. Shandra was in the middle of this beautiful celebration of life around her, but her alienation was propelling her towards the flames.

It felt wrong.

She had saved my life, and I couldn't just leave her there. I knew this wasn't from obligation alone. I felt strange unrest in my heart, scratching it from the inside, and I was sure it would bleed if I went away leaving those warm, beautiful eyes behind.

Part of my soul would gladly exchange all my lordship in Chadrack for a quiet cave like this, away from all those gossips, politics and confrontations, away from wars and fight. It seemed to be a peaceful harbour in the middle of nowhere.

I forced my eyes shut, and the sad face of Rick appeared, staring at me with the blackened eye as I had seen him with on Morvarid's phone – I must save him. I couldn't abandon him now when I reached solid ground and safety. We hadn't found where Morvarid was hiding him in Vienna, and he was still in great danger while in the hands of that vile woman.

Morvarid had been easily upset just at the mere sight of me. She wouldn't hesitate for a second to harm Rick if she thought that would benefit her somehow. I was sure that my previous complicated marital life was not related to Rick, but would that stop Morvarid? Was she behind those crow attacks on me in Chadrack?

"When are you leaving?" the question was quiet but struck like a whip, ripping my daydreaming apart.

Shandra looked at me, and I suddenly felt the pain of her loneliness which pierced through the healing wounds of her soul like a rusty dagger again and again, not cutting deep, only hurting.

"I don't know," I almost whispered. "In a few days, I guess. My friend is in great danger. I must help him."

Shandra didn't say a word. I traced her glance to the depths of the cave, but there was nothing here, only the black gaping entrance of the underground tunnel. She froze, unblinkingly gazing into the darkness. I felt clumsy and ungrateful, and deep inside me some overstretched chord just snapped, pulling my guard down.

"When people are doing the wrong things for the right reason, Shandra, it hurts most. I don't believe you are a bad person, and I don't believe you deserve a fate like this. Let me do the right thing for the right reason this time," I said, shaking my head. "I must go, but I will not leave you here. I don't have a white horse. In fact, I don't have any horse at all right now. I came from the wrong direction, and I may be the wrong prince... But would you travel with me?"

"Where, Kyleb?" suddenly she looked frightened.

"Chadrack."

Shandra's face froze. Then she jumped to her feet and quickly ran out of the cave without a single word, leaving me speechless.

What had I done wrong now?

I dashed outside and found her collapsed next to the stream.

"Shandra!"

She was limp and silent, and I felt the ground slipping beneath my feet. I felt her pulse. Shandra was breathing, and her heart was racing like a frightened horse, but the beats were strong and regular. Had she fainted? I splashed some water on her face, but it had no effect.

I took her into my arms carefully, like a sleeping child, carried her back into the cave and laid her down on the den.

"Shandra..." a barely visible shudder past her face as I gently brushed a strand of hair away.

Several times she took a deep breath but didn't wake up. Her eyes remained closed, and I could see her eyeballs moving behind her closed lids. The sight was terrifying, and I stared helplessly, afraid to do anything. Was she epileptic?

My heart sank as I had no idea how to deal with seizures. I crawled into the den next to her and carefully embraced her. Several more times, she took a deep breath and quietly moaned. Tears pooled in her eyes and then ran down her cheeks, but I was afraid to wipe them away with my trembling hands.

"Shandra… Please…" I clung to her body as if I was drowning. "Wake up…"

My whisper died in silence. Her eyes continued to move behind the closed lids, and I gasped as a tiny streak of blood leaked from her lips. Was she dying?

This lasted for more than an hour, full of tension, horror and helplessness. I held her in my arms, afraid to let go. Then Shandra slowly opened her eyes. Her gaze wandered and was very vague at first.

"Thank god! Shandra, you frightened me..."

She sat up, covering her face with her hair, but I could still spot a blackened eye. Maybe she had hit her head as she fell?

"Are you all right?" I asked, still holding her hand.

She stood up.

"Yes, I'll be fine, don't worry," she attempted to smile but failed. "I need to wash my face..."

The stream was just a few feet away, but she went outside, and I followed her. I still wasn't sure if her fit was over.

She splashed some water on her face, but I got the impression that it was a mirror she needed more. Then she did her hair, half covering the damaged eye and stood up. I went closer.

"You don't need to hide this from me," I said, gently brushing the hair aside. "You must have hurt yourself when you fell..."

"Most likely..." she agreed.

We didn't speak at all much later that day. Shandra busily prepared some soup for us, and I sat all day next to the stream –

watching her and wondering what I had done wrong. Had I unknowingly triggered the fit? It had at first been a vague intention, but now I felt an obligation to take her back to Chadrack. Maybe a healer could have a look at her illness? She had saved me from certain death, and I must help her, but I was unable to find the right words to convince her. And time was pressing.

We ate our soup in silence.

When night fell, we quietly lay on the den. I embraced her and waited for a dream to take me away.

"Maybe I will go with you, Kyleb," she whispered after some time at the edge of the dream. Or was it just a dream?

My soul felt empty. I knew she was sleeping next to me in the cave, but in Vienna I was alone. I stretched my muscles before getting out of the bed. It didn't help.

I was slowly sliding into melancholy. That was dangerous. I had to stop myself before it began to damage our quest to save Rick.

It was the day for the demonstration that Rick was still alive, and I must be sharply alert with a crystal clear mind – it may be our chance to liberate him.

Cold water on my face brought me back to my senses. I briefly glanced at the sunny weather outside, dressed and rushed to the hotel canteen for my breakfast.

I called John shortly after that.

"I've found out that the *Donauinsel* station is on a bridge, so I think she'll bring Rick on a boat just to make sure you can have a look at him, but that you don't get an opportunity to get any closer. She must be damned smart, much cleverer than I thought," he reported. "I've already rented a boat and will be on the water as well. If the demonstration goes as I think, we might get our chance."

"That's good news!" I told him. "Still, I must be at that station and on that bridge in case she's got surveillance in place. She might cancel the demonstration if I don't show up there."

"We can't risk that…" he agreed.

"I hope Rick is okay," I said. "But I don't know whether he's a good swimmer. Keep him close if your plan involving crashing boats."

"That's an excellent idea!" he chuckled. "I'll grab an extra life vest, just in case. Let's stick to the plan and make Morvarid think that we're playing by her rules. See you there!"

"See you…"

Blasts of adrenaline pumped through my circulation as loud heartbeats filled my ears, my mind cleared, and instincts became sharp and lightning fast – this time, we were hunting, not being hunted.

I decided against leaving the mummified rat in the hotel room. It didn't feel safe enough. I double checked the wrappings and slipped it into my pocket. Just before leaving, I took a dose of painkillers – the wounds weren't bothering me too much, but I didn't know what was waiting ahead. The day promised to be interesting.

I strolled down the street, creating the superficial illusion of a still sleepy tourist. The blood inside me was boiling, but I had no idea where and when Morvarid's surveillance would begin to shepherding me. I didn't want to make them cautious.

I only hoped that our small international operation to rescue Rick would be over today. I had no desire to meet Morvarid again.

Trams and cars passed down the street in a large-city-like solemnity despite the sleepiness of a Sunday morning. I passed the *Karlsplatz,* empty at the early hour, and entered the tube station glancing around, but couldn't spot anybody watching me.

I went down to the platform and leant against the wall waiting for a train. A sleepy girl was standing in front of me next to an elderly black lady with a walking stick. Still, nothing looked suspicious.

Then a young man got off the escalator in a tight t-shirt exposing huge muscles almost entirely covered with tattoos. *Here comes the surveillance,* I thought and caught myself smiling. Luckily, the young man didn't bother to look at me directly. He just leant against the wall several yards away and buried his nose in his mobile phone.

A few minutes later, the train arrived. The doors opened, spitting out several passengers, and then we entered, strangely, all in the same coach.

The old lady and the sleepy girl took their seats. I grabbed the pole next to the door, and the young man leant against the door next to me, still busy with his phone.

He left at the next station without casting a single glance at me – my guess had been wrong. Who else could be Morvarid's aide? The old lady travelled on a little longer but left well before the *Donauinsel*. The sleepy girl was already asleep, most likely travelling to the end of the line.

This was curious – no surveillance? I felt a little disappointed.

The train stopped at the *Donauinsel,* and I got off. There was a broad passage on the right with a view of the river, and that's where I went. Morvarid was clear about that – I must be outside the station. She didn't specify which side of the bridge or where I must wait. John's guess about a boat seemed very likely.

A sweet sense of victory was already hanging in the air. All John had to do was crash the boat, grab Rick, and we could return to London tomorrow.

The waters of the Danube below the bridge looked dark in the bright sunlight. Countless rooftops of the *Innere Stadt* were on the right while a few skyscrapers constructed the skyline on the left, partially obscured by the bridge itself.

I checked my watch – I was fifteen minutes early. Still, I was alone on the bridge. This was a little disappointing, but maybe Morvarid had placed more guards around Rick? That could present more obstacles for John, but I trusted in his strength and hoped that Rick would be able to struggle his way free with a little help.

I leant on the rail and watched. Nothing changed. The dark water glistened in the sun, flat and calm, slowly moving south. Trains rushed behind me, several minutes apart, but no one else appeared on the bridge.

My heart started to race when I spotted a small boat in the distance. I quickly rechecked my watch – it was almost on time!

I felt disappointed again when the boat came closer – it was John sitting at the helm wearing a bright yellow life vest. He looked relaxed, enjoying the views and taking random pictures with his camera. John didn't look at me, but I was sure he had seen me well in advance. He passed slowly under the bridge to the other side.

My team was here. Where was Morvarid? *Where was Rick?!*

I waited, growing more impatient with every passing minute. John circled his boat back and forth around the Danube several times but with less enthusiasm and less picture taking.

An hour later, still nothing. At around half-past eleven, my phone rang. It was John.

"I don't think she's going to show up," he said hesitantly. "Let's face it – either she spotted our trap or Rick is dead."

I was forced to agree with him.

"We need another plan," I told him, still unable to acknowledge the failure. "Let's meet somewhere."

"I have to take the boat back first," he said. "Let's meet around Stephan's Cathedral in about half an hour. Just don't approach me. Follow me at the greatest distance you can manage without losing me. I think we'll be able to find some small café on a side street. Just follow me, and we'll talk inside."

"Okay."

He hung up, and I watched for some time as his boat grew smaller and smaller and then disappeared.

I crossed to the other side of the bridge and returned to the tube station. My mood was grim, feeling an increasing sense of failure. What had happened? Why had Morvarid changed her mind? Had they detected our conspiracy?

Questions buzzed around my head like a swarm of angry wasps. The train arrived, and I got on. The carriage was full of kids, talking loudly and laughing; the noise hurt my ears. I silently cursed, unable to concentrate on my dark thoughts any longer, but nor was their cheerfulness contagious either. I patiently waited until the train arrived at *Stephansplatz* station and got out, welcoming the silence.

Hesitations returned like a pack of stray dogs. I hated to believe John's suggestion that Rick might be dead, but hope was slowly fading and the bright day around began to dim.

Our attempt to liberate Rick had again led to a dead-end and remained entirely dependent upon the goodwill of Morvarid which I doubted we could rely upon.

I navigated my way through the crowds in *Stephansplatz,* walking back and forth around the cathedral but couldn't see any sign of John. I managed to evade the ticket sellers and elegant broughams with horses, whose drivers were hunting around for wandering tourists. I had no time for any even polite chat. My desperation was growing with every minute.

I looked nervously at my watch and prepared to call John when I spotted his ginger head appearing from around the corner. He passed slowly in front of my nose, not stopping and not looking.

I pretended to admire the view, then started to follow John as instructed, several hundred paces behind him. We looked in the windows of several shops then visited a souvenir stand. John bought a fridge magnet and placed it into his pocket. Then he returned to the street, slowly moving away from me and melting into the crowd. Luckily, he was tall enough to see, and his red hair shone like a distant beacon.

I followed him to the end of the *Grabben* street and then nearly lost him when his ginger head turned right unexpectedly, disappearing down one of the side streets. I dashed after him, leaving the crowds behind. The street was quiet and empty with a solitary redheaded figure slowly strolling away. I followed.

We walked several hundred yards. Not a single soul appeared around, and nobody followed – I checked.

Then John slipped left through an open door and disappeared. I passed the spot several times until I was confident that nobody had followed us. Only then did I go through the doorway after him.

It was a café, I entered the narrow lobby, and went down the wooden staircase that led from it. The place was entirely in the basement with massive vaulted ceilings, and I instantly understood why John had chosen to talk there – no windows. The walls were heavily decorated with countless racks of wine bottles, dried garlic and wooden spoons. Quiet music met me downstairs as I looked around. John was sitting in a far corner. He waved to me.

I crossed the entire room, weaving between rows of empty tables. It seemed we were the only customers – it was too early for lunch.

I took a seat next to John with my back to the wall. Now both of us were facing the entrance, but nobody else appeared.

"This situation is bizarre," said John at last. "I can't think of any other reason for it, except for Rick's death. I'm sorry, I understand how unpleasant that sounds…"

We were interrupted by a waitress – a woman in her forties

who smiled too much and indulged in far too friendly backslapping. This drew my suspicion, and I was about to stand up and walk out when John ordered a generous lunch accompanied by a bottle of red wine, coffee and dessert. Was this part of the plan? I was starving after spending that hour on the bridge so added *Schnitzel* to John's order for myself.

"Sadly, you might be right," I agreed with John when the waitress had left us alone. "Still, there might be other reasons. I have no memory at all of Morvarid, but you may know her better. Yesterday she sounded like quite an unreasonable person on more than one occasion. Do you think she could simply have changed her mind?"

"She could. Yes, she was often somewhat unstable," he was serious. "And, I think, at times psychotic… You can expect nearly anything from her. Once she ordered her maid to be hanged just because she handled her spoon wearing gloves of the wrong colour!"

"And I was married to that monster?"

"We all sometimes act like monsters, but yes – you were married to her. Briefly."

The appetisers arrived – something made from cheese and stuffed with marinated vegetables. Then a large plate of German potato salad was placed between us.

"Then Rick might be still alive?" I humbly suggested. "We

can't be sure until we see his body."

"Everything is possible with your unstable ex-wife," agreed John. "But you may never find his body if she decides to kill him. The only hope is to find him in Rehen. You said that you were out of the tunnels already, didn't you?"

I nodded, pouring us some wine, and we began to eat.

"I'll be moving from there in a day or two," I said. "But if I may remind you – it might take me a week to reach the capital. I have no horse. And I have no idea where Rhys went with that gryphon. My only order to him was to protect it from Hel."

"Damn. We're wandering around like blind kittens," John looked frustrated.

"We must wait a few more days before making a final decision. Rick may still be alive, and we can't waste any opportunity to save him." I said firmly.

"We have no opportunities at all at the moment," John shook his head. "All we can do is to wait for your crazy ex-wife to create one."

I shrugged.

"I still don't understand," I said, chewing the potatoes. "How can we possibly reach a deal with someone who can change her mind without warning or for any apparent reason?"

"We knew from the beginning that this was a no-deal situation," said John placing salad on his plate. "We need to find out Rick's fate and, if possible, his whereabouts. Then everything would depend on quick and appropriate action and not on any fragile agreement we might strike with that mad woman. That's the only viable way I can see to deal with your ex-wife."

"But how do we find anything out? She left us no loose ends..."

I sipped some wine. We sat for several minutes silently.

"Everything depends on how desperately she wants whatever she's after. That's the only hope we have, I'm afraid," observed John.

John's roasted pork and my *Schnitzel* arrived with mashed potatoes and salads. We ordered more wine.

"Do you still have that banshee?" he asked suddenly.

I tapped my pocket and nodded. The dead rat still was there.

"Did you bring *that* here?" John's eyes nearly popped out of his head.

"I thought it would be safer to carry it with me rather than just leave it in the hotel room. They might have just simply tossed it in the bin."

"Maybe... Just keep it where it is. I don't want to lose my appetite."

We ate well, washing everything down with glasses of red wine.

"You know," said John chewing. "Maybe we scared her."

"How?"

"You managed to catch her banshee, and so you've left the snake without her poisonous teeth. She tried to achieve everything with her banshee, and now she must be feeling quite terrified and helpless without it. Don't you think?" he winked.

"You might be right. But how could this help us?"

"I don't know yet. But we are now in a stronger position. I think Morvarid will try to contact you and claim back that thing if she's not too scared," John indicated my pocket.

"Well, then we have no other option but to wait…"

He nodded, still chewing. "Let's wait and see…"

My mood fell with the slow realisation that the evil woman had everything firmly back into her own hands. The fact that her banshee was well wrapped up and stashed in my pocket seemed irrelevant. Later, when *strudels* and coffee arrived, I asked, "How long are we going to wait?"

"I think two or three days at the most. She was never a very patient person."

"In other words, if she is going to act, it will be soon?"

"I think so," said John thoughtfully. "As far as I remember her…"

We paid our bill, left a tip and went out separately – John sneaked out first then I followed half an hour later.

The feeling of failure was thick around me. I went down the

street, unable to look at all those smiling faces in the bright sunshine. John's assumption that Rick was dead had hurt me deeply. Rick (or Rhys as I knew him in Rehen) had had no troubles at all until I crossed his path. I blamed myself for his kidnapping, and that sense of guilt shadowed me wherever I went. The day seemed grey despite the clear blue sky and hot sun. Even knowing that a beautiful woman was embracing me on the other side of reality was unable to lift my mood.

I stopped, looking around. Was Morvarid following me? I didn't care. I only wanted to get back to the hotel and sit quietly in a corner until dark.

I saw only the pavement on my way back. Nobody troubled me until I got to the hotel.

I nodded to the receptionist, responded to his greeting, took my room key and turned to the stairs instead of using the lift. The corridor was empty and silent as I walked on the soft carpet, treading as silently as a lost soul. I froze in front of my room. The door was slightly ajar, and this could mean only trouble. My heart slowly sank to my ankles as I stood motionless, trembling.

A good five minutes passed. I listened. Not a sound. Then I cautiously opened the door ready to run off at any moment.

My room was upside down as if a pack of crazy mammoths had stampeded across my room in a blind panic. All the wardrobes and drawers were wide open, and my scant belongings had been tossed on the floor. The sofa and pillows had been ripped apart. The TV set was on the floor, broken. I cautiously checked the wardrobe. All my clothes were on the floor as well, and the safe was gone – luckily, I hadn't put anything more valuable than Morvarid's note inside it.

I immediately almost ran back to the reception.

The smile vanished from the receptionist's face as I tried to describe the terrible condition of my room to him.

"Klaus!" he called through the open door leading to the back room.

A grey-haired gentleman appeared wearing a worried expression on his face and holding a cup of coffee in his right hand. The receptionist uttered a quick phrase in German, and the blood drained from gentleman's face leaving him as white as a ghost. His hand shook as he placed his cup on the reception desk.

The pair of them left a young girl to supervise reception and followed me to my room.

"*Oh, mein Gott!*" one of them whispered behind me when we stepped through the door.

They both stared at all the wreckage with apparent horror.

"Is anything missing?" asked the receptionist at last.

I looked through my belongings scattered around the room and shook my head.

"I didn't put anything of value in the safe," I said, indicating the empty wardrobe.

"We are so sorry," said the receptionist. "We do apologise, and we will certainly investigate this incident. Shall we call the police?"

I froze. I remembered the clear warning that Morvarid had given in her first note about involving the authorities. Would this compromise Rick's situation even further?

"That is not necessary for me," I shrugged. "Nothing's missing. But I'll certainly need another room…"

"Of course, sir, and accept our apologies, please. The room was serviced this morning soon after you left, and everything was fine then. I am very sorry. Nothing like this has ever happened before in this hotel. May we offer you a free room for the rest of your stay?"

"You may," I said, accepting the offer.

"Klaus…" the receptionist nodded, and the grey-haired gentleman left immediately. "Do you need any help with your things?"

"No, I can handle this."

"It is such a terrible thing. We are so sorry…" the receptionist retreated into the corridor and called somebody on his mobile. A short and emotional conversation in German ensued.

I collected my things before Klaus returned and handed me another key. I thanked him and departed, leaving them to deal with the wreck.

My new room was on the fourth floor. I used the lift.

I called John as soon as I had closed the door and tidied my things away. He wasn't surprised to hear the news.

"I think somebody was looking for your rat," he observed calmly. "You made a wise decision to carry it with you despite all the dangers involved."

"I don't like this situation. I may be paranoid, but the staff here might be in league with my ex-wife," I said. "They were too emotional – I don't know if genuinely – and offered me a free room, but do you think it's still safe to stay here?"

"I think it's the safest place in Vienna for you right now," he chuckled. "I doubt if they would risk attempting the same approach again. Luckily, the rat is still with you. It would have been an entirely different and dangerous situation if they'd been successful. Are you sure your banshee is still safely inside?"

I took out the silver package and carefully listened. The bumblebee still hummed inside.

"Yes."

"Great," said John. "Keep it safe. And better stick around the hotel – we don't know how and when Morvarid will attempt to contact you."

"Sure, let's keep up to date by phone."

I hung up after a short goodbye.

Despite John's assurances, I didn't feel safe. I sneaked to the door and pressed my ear against the wood. It was quiet at first, but then I heard footsteps – someone was sauntering down the corridor and dragging something behind them. My heart almost jumped out of my chest when that someone stopped in front of my door. I distinctly heard someone shuffling through a bunch of keys!

Go away! – I screamed silently.

I grabbed at the door chain and secured it before whoever it was touched the door handle. I wasn't going to surrender without a fight!

I jumped when, unexpectedly, something heavy dropped on the floor. My nerves were on edge, and I dashed across the room, grabbed the key and went back to the door. Something was going on beyond it, but I didn't risk peeking outside. Instead, I put the key in the lock and turned it twice, locking the door and leaving the key half-turned in the lock. Now they would have to break the door down to get inside, and I would have enough time to call the police if anything unexpectedly occurred.

Something brushed softly against the door, and I jumped away, looking at the handle. It didn't move.

Then someone sighed in the corridor, and I heard footsteps again – that someone was slowly walking down the hallway, again dragging something behind. The sounds retreated the same way they had come.

I spent some time guarding the door, but the corridor remained quiet.

The silver package was quietly humming on the table when I left the door and went back into the room. The sound was slightly louder than usual and immediately drew my attention. *Was the banshee trying to escape?*

I wrapped a few more layers of foil around it, securing it with sticky tape until the package had almost doubled in size. The bumblebee inside now was now muted, barely audible, still gently vibrating.

I spent the evening migrating between the locked door and the dead rat, but nothing else happened. I was tired when dusk began to flood the room through the window. It was time to go back to Rehen.

I quickly brushed my teeth and slipped into bed.

Shandra was still peacefully sleeping next to me. I watched a barely visible smile play on her lips and listened to the soft ripples of the creek as its waters flowed next to the den before sneaking out of the cave to meet the world beyond. It was one of those rare and fragile moments of completeness that I wished could last forever, but nature called. I made the feeling of joy last as long as possible until I couldn't hold on anymore. I crawled quietly out of the den, trying not to wake her and went outside.

The sun was bright, rising in the deep blue sky above the forest in the east. The valley below was as blissful as before, bursting with the colours of millions of flowering blossoms. A quiet breeze brought refreshing waves of chill from the icecaps of the mountains, still hidden in the fluffy crowns of a few lost clouds.

The air was pure, as I filled my lungs and strolled along the creek following the crystal flow. I could spend a lifetime here – among those flowering meadows with a beautiful woman next to me, and my heart ached in the knowledge of my approaching departure. I must return to Chadrack and find out where Rhys was hiding with the gryphon. If he knew where Morvarid was holding him, John could hatch a plan for his liberation. We didn't have much time with him still being in the hands of my mad ex-wife. A few more days in Vienna, perhaps…

I reached the first of two waterfalls a few hundred yards further on where the stream fell from the height of five or six yards onto a flat rock bed, pooling in the knee-deep hollow before escaping again through a gap on the right. It looked like the perfect shower, and I couldn't resist the temptation.

I stripped and carefully took off the bandages Shandra had applied – my wounds were healing fast with most of the blisters already gone and only redness still marking spots where they had been. Then I entered the stream.

The water was cold, and I suppressed a cry when it touched my skin, afraid to wake up Shandra. A crystal clear bliss cleansed me, washing away dust and ashes and soothing my still irritated skin. I couldn't ask for more.

Once I had had my fill of the chilly delight, I left the shower, slightly shivering and sat naked on a flat rock until the morning sun dried my skin.

I wondered what kind of fit it was that Shandra had yesterday. She hadn't complained, but I was worried about her. I recalled the feeling of helplessness when I held her lifeless body, waiting and praying for her to come back, and a cloud passed the bright sunshine dimming the joy of my day. I must get her to the healer.

I put on my oversized gown and returned to the cave.

"Good morning," Shandra greeted me, busy with the stove and pots.

"Blissful morning," I agreed. "Did you sleep well?"

She sighed.

"The usual nightmares mostly. I can't get rid of them."

"Life hasn't been easy for you, I guess. No wonder it all comes back to you at night in disturbing dreams," I told her.

She stirred the soup silently for a few moments before replying.

"Life is never easy, and that's not just for me, Kyleb. Everybody has their problems, everywhere…"

She handed me a bowl of soup, and we ate in silence.

"Your clothes are dry," she observed after we had finished. "You can get changed if you like."

I wasn't too bothered about how I looked, but Shandra had performed miracles with that bunch of dusty and burnt set of rags which had previously been my robes. I gathered it up and went outside, back to the waterfall to change without embarrassing Shandra.

I folded the gown and stretched my body, enjoying the unspoiled view of the valley when a broken line of dark figures, looking like small bugs from a distance, emerged from the forest almost a mile away. For a full minute, I froze, unable to believe my eyes. The dark silhouettes gathered in groups moving along the forest line, and my heart skipped a few beats when they attacked something, probably a deer – ghouls!

Silently I rushed uphill back to the cave as fast as I could.

"Shandra!"

She froze with a pot in her hand.

"What?"

"We must flee immediately," I gasped, catching my breath.

"What's happened?"

"Ghouls have just come out of the forest. They'll spot the smoke in no time. We're dead if they get to us!"

"Are you sure? There are no ghouls in these lands."

I hastily nodded.

"Come! Hurry!"

She placed the pot down and stood up.

"I guess we have no time to gather anything?"

"No! Leave it!"

"Couldn't we just hide in the tunnel?"

I quickly shook my head.

"It is a dead-end, remember? They might explore it to the very end if they see that somebody has been living here. We must run to the forest. That's the only hope we have!" my voice sounded desperate.

Shandra hesitantly stepped away from the stove with her gaze still wandering over her scant belongings. I grabbed her hand, almost dragging her out of the cave.

Luckily for us, the ghouls were still busy at the same spot where I had seen them stop.

"Please, keep as low as possible," I said running, "and as fast as possible too!"

We jumped across the creek, leaving the field that flamed with scarlet poppies behind. There was less vegetation here, but the occasional shrubs that were scattered around provided light cover as we dashed from one to another, making our way to the steep cliffs on the left. It was the only way and a precarious one. We had to descend the slope along the steep rocky wall and get closer to the place where the ghouls were dismembering their catch before we could reach the safety of the dark green woods at the foot of the mountain.

We dashed out from shrub to shrub, covering the bigger part of that distance. My heart trembled each time we left the fleeting safety of a bush to run through the rocky field in plain sight of the ghouls. They were busy. Blood splashed in every direction as a grim reminder of what fate would wait for us there.

So far, we had been lucky to escape their attention as we leapt from shadow to shadow among the dark green shrubs. Our luck ended a few hundred yards further on when vegetation gave way to a rocky plane.

"What shall we do now?" whispered Shandra hiding in the shade of thin branches.

"We'll wait," I squeezed her hand, keeping my eyes on the feasting ghouls.

Before long, they noticed a strand of smoke escaping from Shandra's cave, and the late morning silence was pierced by their howls. A small group of four rushed up the slope where the cave mouth was, while others left their bloody feast and spread out across the meadow like a pack of overgrown fire ants searching for more meat.

Shandra gasped as a pack of dark creatures jumped across the creek, sniffing the air like wild dogs as they dived into the shrubs several hundred yards away from us.

"Run!" I hissed, releasing her hand and sprinting after Shandra towards where the forest stood, dark and thick.

We had no time to look back, but a victorious howl behind us clearly announced that our escape hadn't gone unnoticed. The shelter of the woods was near, but it would be impossible to find a safe place and hide with all those bloodthirsty pursuers chasing at our heels. Our fate was clear. It was only a matter of time before they would get their hands on us.

We ran for our lives despite the apparent hopelessness of our situation. The howling was closing in.

A large rock whizzed passed me, almost hitting my head. It narrowly missed Shandra too.

"Run! Run!" I gasped without slowing down.

We smashed into the dark wood like two meteors, never hesitating, not even for a single fraction of a second. Running was much more difficult here with slippery moss, thick undergrowth, fallen trees, ravines and trenches barring our way. The roaring of ghouls continued to close in despite all our efforts. They were faster than us.

Suddenly Shandra cried out in pain, falling. I stopped with a quivering heart.

"I've done something to my ankle! I'll be a burden to you," tears of desperation rolled down her cheeks as she whispered, waving me away. "Run, save yourself!"

"I'll never leave you," I whispered, picking her up in my arms and dashing forward between the low branches of dark green firs.

It was hopeless, I knew that.

Shandra cried as I silently said my goodbyes to this world and ran as fast as I could. I knew I'd never wake up in Vienna if I died here – these were the strange rules of Rehen, and this was how Sleepers ended their lives. The police would be puzzled about finding my dismembered body in a hotel room which was barricaded from the inside. It would be one of those murders that remained unsolved – nobody would ever guess that I had been killed on another plane of reality.

My strength drained as I carried Shandra through the dark and silent woods. There was no place to hide, nor did I have weapons to defend us. We were doomed!

Shandra screamed, and I finally braved to glance behind me. A tall, dark figure dressed in black leather decorated with human knucklebones was just behind me, already raising his bludgeon in an attempt to smash my head.

Then suddenly an arrow hissed past me and plunged into the throat of the attacking ghoul. An expression of surprise froze on his distorted face as he slowly collapsed, and dark blood poured from his mouth.

More arrows hissed around us, and more ghouls collapsed, their howling silenced.

I leant against the harsh bark of a nearby tree, shaking and deadly tired. My heart still raced insanely, and my legs refused to hold me up any longer. I sat down on the moss, still holding Shandra in my arms. She was crying.

Seconds later a squad of horsemen emerged from the woods, and I recognised the colours of the royal jaegers of Chadrack. Their crossbows flashed as they reloaded and showered the retreating ghouls with deadly arrows.

One of the jaegers stopped next to us, as the whole squad

rushed forward hunting the fleeing creatures.

"Are you hurt, my Lord?" asked the jaeger dismounting and rushing to help me with Shandra.

"Thank you," I only managed to squeeze out, shaking my head.

"It's a great honour to serve the Prince of Chadrack," said the jaeger.

Shandra let out a short cry and fainted. I was too tired, even to curse. The jaeger helped me to lie her down, and I collapsed on the ground next to her, still gasping for air.

I wasn't sure if this was one of her fits, but she opened her eyes seconds later with her face now as white as freshly fallen snow.

The jaeger stood guarding us with his crossbow ready while the sounds of the battle moved towards the edge of the forest. In fact, it wasn't a battle. The ghouls were running for their lives, but the jaegers were faster on horseback, getting and exterminating them one by one like miserable, dirty vermin.

"These woods are very dangerous, my Lord," said the jaeger looking around. "Did they kill your horse?"

"I had no horse," I admitted. "But we must get back to the castle quickly. My sister Hel has left us in peace, but there are still urgent matters to attend to in the capital."

Shandra stared at me with frightened eyes.

"As you wish, my Lord," said the jaeger and barked a sharp

command to others.

The fight was almost over but, at his orders, the jaegers halted their horses, and the pitiful remnants of the pack of ghouls fled as fast as they could, disappearing into the woods.

"Thank you for saving our lives," I said to the jaeger who helped Shandra to her feet. "What is your name? Who must I be grateful to?"

"I'm Jesper, my Lord. You don't need to thank me," said the jaeger and simply repeated. "It's a great honour to serve the Prince of Chadrack."

Shandra moaned and nearly fell trying to stand on her injured ankle. I rushed to help her.

"Is it bad?" I asked, supporting her.

"Nothing serious, I think. It doesn't appear to be broken," she said coldly. "I can move it, but it hurts."

I looked as jaegers gathered around with their crossbows, remaining on guard. This place was dangerous, as Jesper had said – dark woods sheltered strange creatures and the pack of ghouls they had chased away could shortly be followed by another.

Jesper spoke quickly with his fighters as I stood silently with Shandra. Nobody dared to question my request. They had no spare horses, but Jesper found a solution. Shortly, two horses stood in front of me – their riders had stepped away and mounted other horses in a pair.

I helped Shandra to mount. She said nothing, only looked at me with her eyes wide, still frightened.

"Have you seen Rhys recently?" I asked Jesper before we began our journey.

"Yes, he's in the caves with that strange animal. He was unable to follow Bedwyr as you ordered," he answered.

"Good," I mumbled. "I'll need him."

That was great news, it meant that Rick was still alive, and our struggle in Vienna would soon be over. But I didn't yet permit myself the luxury of even the briefest of smiles.

"Let's go!" I ordered, and we galloped through the woods without a backward glance.

Shandra and I were at the head of the group with three jaegers scouting our way ahead, two guarding our flanks and the rest of the jaegers following us with their crossbows at the ready.

The horses ran along the barely visible path made by wild animals, winding between the strange arches of black rock towering above the treetops. The trees were mainly firs, shielding the daylight, and we galloped like the wind between the grey shadows with pieces of moss and crushed mushrooms scattering away from the hooves.

Shandra looked like a trapped wild animal with her gaze flitting around, not focusing on anything, seeking no escape as her horse ran with the pack. I now thoroughly regretted not taking the time for explanations. I could only imagine what turmoil was in her head – her quiet life had been left behind, a gloomy unknown was waiting for her ahead, and she was afraid to even glance at me, the Bloody Prince.

The dark firs gave way to alders and ash trees, later followed by oaks and pines. The black arches ended with firs, and I was glad to be away from them. Now the forest was lighter with greater spaces between the trees and scarce undergrowth, allowing us to gather more speed. We left several creeks, and flowering meadows behind under the hooves of our horses and sometimes the range of majestic peaks covered with snow emerged on our left.

The journey was fast-paced and arduous. Twice we stopped by crystal streams to allow our horses a few moments of rest, to drink their full and to graze upon some grass. Those stops were even worse than galloping. Shandra was silent, avoiding my gaze every time I laid my eyes on her. My heart bled, but there wasn't much I could do at the moment. I only hoped she would still give me the chance to explain.

Dusk fell when we finally reached a campsite where several groups of jaegers had gathered for the night. The men were quiet, exhausted after fights with the ghouls, but a tangible agitation rippled through the camp as I stopped my horse in the centre and helped Shandra to dismount. A young guy took the horses away, and all eyes were suddenly upon me.

"Are we going to war, my Lord?" someone asked.

The silence was thick with tension as the men held their breath, awaiting my answer. I knew how it looked – our forests were plagued with ghouls, Ikent, our port on the Braaid, had been burned to the ground. I was sure everybody knew about my sister Hel's attack, and it had been met with major dissatisfaction that I had decided to evacuate and abandon the capital and send the army away instead of defending our land.

"No," I said, and a murmur spread around the camp. I wasn't sure if it was one of relief or disapproval.

Shandra was still limping on her injured ankle, and Jesper helped us to find our way to a fire pit where a wild boar was roasting on the flames. We sat down.

Nobody spoke as we waited for the meat to be cooked. It was getting dark when Jesper began cutting the boar, and we were given a few of the best pieces. We ate silently with only a quiet whisper sneaking around the camp. I wasn't sure, but I think I heard the word "witch" repeated several times.

A few yards away from the fire pit was a shaggy shelter, built from dry branches and bales of straw. It was used to store skins and provisions of dry meat and mature cheese. It wasn't a palace, and Jesper apologised as he led us there, but it was the only shelter on the campsite – jaegers were harsh hunters who slept under the sky next to the fire whatever the weather.

The jaegers tossed a few bearskins on the ground to keep us warm, and they framed walls with deer skins to shelter us from the wind. Bags of dry meat hung from the ceiling, but I was so tired that I didn't mind sleeping in the pantry. I helped Shandra into the improvised den, and Jesper placed guards around the shelter.

The jaegers talked quietly around the fireplace as I lay on the skins next to Shandra. She flinched when I tried to embrace her, and this unconscious reaction felt like the thrust of a dagger piercing my heart.

"Don't be afraid," I whispered. "I'll never hurt you."

For some time, we listened to the wind outside the shelter and the soft crackle of burning logs.

"I don't believe you," she muttered a few minutes later. "You should have left me behind."

I was about to protest, but she stopped me.

"Don't say anything," she whispered.

Sadness lulled me into a sleep that night.

Sunshine glanced through my hotel room window, but I had mixed feelings about that. I felt happy that Rick was now within our reach, but the way Shandra had reacted to the Bloody Prince left my heart bleeding. I spent almost half an hour searching for the words to make a proper apology. Nothing felt right.

Then I called John.

"Rick's alive," I told him as soon as he answered.

"Has she called you and given you a demonstration?"

"No. I met my jaegers in Chadrack, and they told me that he's alive," I explained. "He is in the caves with the gryphon, next to the capital."

"Well, I'd say that's the best news – how fast can you reach him?"

"Maybe in a day or two. It's quite a distance, but we're on horseback," I said. "Unless something unexpected happens, of course. The woods are full of danger."

"I know," he replied. "Nothing is the same… so we must wait a little longer unless Morvarid makes the first move."

"What could she do?"

"I don't know, but remember that Rick is still in her hands, and we have no idea where. She may simply kill him if she sees no other solution."

"That's a nasty thought. Let's hope it doesn't happen."

"You can't do anything about it," John was serious. "Let's wait. Just keep me updated."

"Maybe we could meet and make some plans?" I asked, still hoping to find a quicker solution.

"Don't get impatient," he calmed me. "We have no solid ground where we to start. And unless we have something tangible, it's better to keep our conspiracy. You don't want to push Morvarid into doing something crazy in desperation."

"Okay, that sounds reasonable… What would you advise doing next? Visit *Prater* again?"

"I wouldn't bother," he said. "She knows your hotel and where to find you. She might do something without risking to put herself in danger."

"Possibly…"

"I doubt if she's holding Rick in the city. And is your rat safe? I don't know what would be best – to find a secure place to leave it or to just carry it with you."

"I'd rather carry it with me."

"Then pack it thoroughly. You certainly don't want that banshee escaping – I guess, it is rather pissed off right now."

"I'll be careful, don't worry," I promised.

The morning was strange. At first, I wanted to dive back into bed and hide under the pillow, shielding myself from the outer world until I could find a proper apology for Shandra. That was difficult in itself. Our recent escape from the ghouls was still vivid, plaguing my limbs with restlessness. I paced the room several times but found no peace and decided to have breakfast first since an empty stomach was always a lousy adviser under challenging situations.

I checked the package. The mummy was faintly humming – the creature was still inside. I wrapped it in a few more layers of foil and adhesive tape as John had advised. I washed my hands and got dressed before putting the rat into my pocket and heading downstairs to the hotel canteen.

Several guests were already enjoying Viennese delights, and I looked at the offering suddenly feeling ravenous. I downed a generous portion of scrambled eggs, a few pieces of ham, cheese and several roast sausages. After washing everything down with a large cup of coffee, I turned to some fruits and desserts. Then I had a double espresso and returned to my room feeling full but still restless.

I paced the room in circles haunted by the frightened eyes of Shandra. Her whisper – *I don't believe you* – still rang in my ears, and I couldn't find the right words to convince her. I was the Bloody Prince in her eyes, and the keyword was "bloody". How could I prove to her that I wasn't *bloody*? I couldn't just tell her my secret.

I spent hours drowning in frustration, but I still couldn't find the right words, only gave myself a terrible headache. I needed to take a walk in the park, breath in some fresh air and find a different approach.

I dressed, slipped the rat into my pocket and went outside to embrace all that the city had to offer.

The sunshine was cheerful, and I stopped, hesitantly looking at the late Monday morning traffic, unsure which way to go. People rushed by in both directions, and I turned right towards the centre.

I strolled downhill unhurriedly, still frowning from the headache that squeezed my temples. The noise of traffic that rushed down the street didn't help, and I walked on, looking for a quiet and peaceful corner. The shady *Karlsplatz* was on the right, but it was filled with groups of young people from a nearby university. They gave me a few strange looks as I passed them on my quest for quietness.

I crossed the *Friedrichstraße* and walked a few blocks towards the centre, brushing against the crowds of tourists with maps and cameras at the ready and eyes sparkling. I realised that the *Stephansplatz* would be even more crowded and turned left onto the *Opernring*. The morning breeze blew the aroma of roasting coffee beans into my face as I tried to avoid the crowd. I needed to find a tranquil corner to organise my thoughts.

My eyes stumbled upon two men strangely acting when I crossed the street. They followed me, keeping a distance and stopped every time I stopped, talking among themselves in low voices. Several times, I glimpsed them, pointing to the side of my body, and this made me even more suspicious.

I went down the street, feeling increasingly anxious. Several times I stopped, pretending to admire the view and taking photos on my phone while, in fact, furtively glancing at the two men. They kept their distance, still pointing at me. This couldn't be just a coincidence.

I passed the *Heldenplatz* on my right, barely casting a glance at the broughams lined along the street and the bronze *Erzherzog* Karl galloping on his horse on a high pedestal. The men went after me.

My imagination had already painted images of me being dragged into some dark cul-de-sac. I couldn't run off or hide anywhere. I desperately needed a plan.

The solution came in the form of the *Volksgarten* across the street from the Parliament building. I slipped through the gate, dashed between the blooming rose bushes and dropped onto the nearest empty bench, hoping that my pursuers wouldn't dare to attack me in this open public place.

They didn't. One of them even nodded to me and managed a nervous smile as they rushed along the street, still quietly talking. I frowned, following them with my eyes until they were hidden behind the corner on the right. I waited for half an hour, but they never appeared again.

But then I noticed other people acting strangely.

A young couple entered the *Volksgarten* through the gate laughing. Then they stopped abruptly, barely reaching the flowering roses several yards away from me, frowned and turned back, leaving quickly through the same gate.

A woman pushed her pram down the path next to me, talking on the phone, barely noticing the surroundings. I tried to smile at her, but she looked at me with an expression of disapproval, screamed something in German and rushed past me running to the street as if a couple of hellhounds were chasing her.

This was all very strange. Then a gust of wind blew from the East, splashing an explanation at my face. Never had I smelled a fouler odour – it stank as though a ton of dead rats were decomposing in my pocket! Was it the banshee performing some magic on the dead and dried flesh?

I took out the package. The humming was unchanged, and the foil cover seemed intact, but the foul odour grew even stronger than before, and I felt my generous breakfast slowly rebelling against the digestive powers of my stomach. I barely managed to force it down, hiding the rat back into my pocket.

I felt trapped. I couldn't return to the hotel smelling like a zombie. I needed a better-sealed coffin for the mummy. But I couldn't go shopping with that stench in my pocket either.

I fried in the sunshine for nearly an hour, waiting. People came in and out of the *Volksgarten,* avoiding the bench I was sitting on in large circles. I remained patient.

My moment came when the *Volksgarten* was almost deserted with only two ladies pushing their prams out at the far end of the garden. I stood up and unhurriedly walked to the right where I had spotted a few suitable leafy bushes, inspecting the roses on my way... It was difficult to remain calm with a trail of that horrible stench following me, but I did my best to look bored and indifferent.

I buried my nose into the rose blossom, waiting until the women had left the garden and turned away behind the corner. Then I moved the leafy branches aside and quickly dug a hole with my bare hands near the roots of a white rose, placing the shiny package inside.

"Ashes to ashes, dust to dust..." I mumbled covering the

package with dirt.

I then returned to my bench and spent another hour in the sunshine, observing the shrub from a distance. People moved in and out of the garden, but my bench no longer stank so nor was it avoided. The burial place was away from the main walkways, and nobody expressed even remotest interest in the white rose flowering there.

I felt it was safe. I just had to act quickly.

First, I washed my hands in the public toilets near the *Rathaus*. I found a grocery store down one of the side streets and bought an airtight plastic container, big enough to hold the package without leaving too much empty space. Half an hour later, I was back in the *Volksgarten*.

The garden was now full of people enjoying their afternoon, and I had to circle it several times, keeping my eyes on the white rose until I found an empty bench to sit down. The bush with the white blossoms was only a few paces in front of me. I just needed a suitable moment to dig the rat out.

The day was long and pleasant, and I cursed the weather, sweating in the sunshine. More people were gathering in the garden rather than leaving it, and I had to keep on sitting on the bench, clutching the plastic container and patiently waiting for my moment. Soon I knew every leaf and every blossom on that white rose which remained inaccessible behind the moving line of prams, mothers, fathers, grandmothers, grandfathers and couples of all ages.

Dusk was already falling when the place began to become deserted finally. I waited until I was left alone. Only then did I dash towards the white rose. The soil looked undisturbed, and I started digging with extreme caution, afraid of piercing the foil. Minutes passed, leaving me with growing desperation. I forced my fingers deep into the dirt around the roots of the rose, but the fact remained unchanged – the shallow grave was gaping and empty! The silver package was gone!

Suddenly I felt weak at the knees and sat down next to the gaping hole. A giant unknown loomed over me in the evening sky, crushing me with its weight. Why had I left the hotel? Now the banshee was back in the hands of Morvarid! My deadly enemy had recaptured her lethal weapon. There was no other way left but to crawl at her feet and beg her to spare Rick's life, promising her whatever she wanted.

I felt so stupid. I had to warn John.

He was furious, and his sullen silence was more eloquent than any shouting.

"I think you'd better go back to your hotel," John said dryly. "She might send you a message."

"Okay, I'll call you later..."

I felt a chill carry me, like an autumn leaf on a high wind. My heart clenched in fear. Stupid me! How could I have thought of such insanity as to leave the banshee behind? How could I have ignored the danger?

I felt the ghostly features of a triumphant Morvarid and her bodiless creature peek at me from behind every shrub in the *Volksgarten* as I turned left on the street and almost ran back to the hotel. I was scared to death.

Breathless, I grabbed the key and ran to my room.

First, I locked the door and put the door chain on, barring the entrance. That was silly since Morvarid could easily send her banshee through almost any obstacle. Would she dare to kill me?

I fell flat on the bed and covered my head with a pillow. Why was this happening to me? What wrongs had I done in my life to be punished by such a double nightmare existence like this? I didn't ask for Rehen and its dangers, and now my real world was crumbling to pieces too, infested by crazy people and dangerous creatures. Several minutes passed. Nobody answered me, and I felt myself drowning in a wave of self-pity.

The dark shadows of panic slowly crawled out of every corner and gathered in my heart.

We had almost succeeded in defeating Morvarid, but, with the banshee gone, I was afraid to even think about what might happen to Rick.

I spent the rest of the evening in bed, commiserating over the lost possibilities and cursing my own carelessness. The feeling of total disaster kept me locked in one place. I was simply unable to move anywhere. It was dark when I lost consciousness and transferred my mind to Rehen.

I must find Rhys in Chadrack as quickly as possible. That might be our only hope of saving him.

The morning was damp, and it was early. Shandra was still asleep next to me with her cheek pressed to the deerskin. I watched her for a while, feeling lonelier than ever before. My body longed to embrace her, but my mind was afraid to make a move. I knew she feared me too, and that knowledge froze my movement. I had to find out how to melt that fear in both of us.

I quietly left the shack, trying not to wake her. A soft drizzle sprayed from the sky and mixed with the morning fog as I moved my eyes across the field. I could see a small creek in the distance on the right. The mist was thicker there, revealing the dark shapes of our horses grazing on the damp grass.

Jaegers were quietly talking around the still warm fire pit next to the shack. Some were still asleep.

Jesper jumped to his feet as soon as he saw me. He approached me paying his respects on his way.

"Was everything to your liking, my Lord?" he asked.

I nodded, looking at the camp, which was slowly stirring into life.

"I need to get back to the castle quickly," I told him. "Take fewer men, only a small squad sufficient for protection – we're not going to fight a war. Let the others continue dealing with the ghouls."

"As you wish, my Lord," said Jesper.

"I want you to send two or three men ahead of us," I added. "I want them to find Rhys and bring him back to the castle as soon as possible. If Rhys is dead, then bring back the gryphon."

"I'll do as you say, my Lord," nodded Jesper. "They will leave immediately."

I watched him go through the stirring camp, speaking to the jaegers. The men brought the horses closer to the shack, grooming and saddling them amidst the rainy drizzle.

The day began unpleasantly with my mood dropping low. I still blamed my own carelessness with the banshee. It seemed that John had been right – that a relaxed attitude *could* cost lives. I only hoped that those lives wouldn't be mine or Rick's, and I had yet to discover how to deal with Shandra's fear of the Bloody Prince.

I watched the two horsemen disappear into the dark woods without a road. The door of the shack squeaked behind me, and I turned around to have a look, meeting the frightened eyes of Shandra peeking through the gap.

"Are we still in danger?" she whispered fearfully.

"Yes," I said. "We'll be at risk until we reach the castle."

She gasped closing the door, and I wondered if the greater danger in her eyes was ghouls or myself. That felt painful.

"Shandra…" I knocked on the door.

"I'll be out in a minute," she said, shuffling inside.

Now all the jaegers had arisen and were saddling up their horses and preparing their crossbows. A group of ten or twelve crossed the creek and disappeared into the woods heading west, the way we had come yesterday. Others gathered around Jesper, waiting for my command. I waited for Shandra.

She appeared from the shack with her dress now belted using a long string of deerskin with her small dagger attached to it. Her eyes still fearfully darted around, but her demeanour appeared calmer as she stood next to me facing the jaegers.

I helped her to mount. No one talked as three riders disappeared into the woods to the east, scouting our way ahead. We followed them shortly afterwards with almost the same formation as yesterday with Shandra riding on my right and Jesper just behind us. Three riders were in front of us and two more on our flanks with their crossbows at the ready. The rest of the jaegers gathered behind us as our squad flashed through the woods.

There were no roads there, and I wondered how they managed

to find the right way between countless tracks of wild animals with the sky still gloomy and the fog still rising. I would be going round in circles, I was sure, but the jaegers released their horses into a full gallop without a trace of hesitation.

The drizzle stopped an hour later, and the fog slowly began to clear. The woods were still creepy, full of strange shadows shaped like ghouls, haunting my imagination, but I couldn't focus on them as we were moving too fast. Countless trees flashed by in seconds, forest paths and roads in minutes as we passed them all, hurrying as fast as we could. The horses were doing their best.

It was well past noon when the sky began to clear. The forest stepped aside as we stormed out of shadows into a large sun-lit clearing. Jesper called a halt.

"Our horses need a break," he explained his decision. "It's still a long way…"

I nodded silently, running my eyes across the flowering meadow surrounded by a dark green wall of forest. A magnificent range of mountains towered in the distance behind the woods on the left with high peaks hiding in the clouds. Several wooden cabins were scattered on the right, surrounded by fields of crops. I shaded my eyes to have a better look. The cabins were humble with grass-covered roofs and tall chimneys made of dark rocks rather than bricks. The village was silent – I couldn't hear any dogs barking despite the squad of jaegers emerging from the forest nearby. Strangely, I saw no people working in the fields, and not a strand of smoke rose from any of the chimneys.

"What village is that?" I asked Jesper dismounting.

"Blackhead, my Lord," he said. "It's halfway between our campsite and the capital."

"Any people live there? It doesn't look abandoned," I demanded. "But I can't see anyone around…"

"They're ordinary, friendly people. We stopped there only a couple of days ago," Jesper shrugged. "I'll send someone to take a look."

Shandra's hand was trembling when I helped her to dismount. I passed our horses to one of the jaegers, keeping my eyes on the village.

Two men went down the meadow carefully approaching the cabins. They went around a small circular pond and passed a flourishing field of crops before disappearing into one of the houses. We waited.

"I have a very bad feeling," said Jesper. He signalled to his men, and jaegers gathered around us, ready to defend. A few minutes elapsed, like a long, tense intake of breath. Then a man dashed out of the house vomiting.

Jesper barked a command, and three more men ran across the field with their crossbows ready. We waited amongst the flowering bluebells and poppies. Blackhead was silent. Only jaegers went from cabin to cabin, going in, coming out empty-handed.

I looked at Shandra – she was as pale and as frigid as a statue of salt.

"Are you unwell?" I asked, but she didn't answer as her gaze wandered over the cabins.

One of the men ran back to us.

"They all are gone, my Lord," he said, addressing me. "Dead."

Shandra gasped behind me.

"Is it safe?" asked Jesper.

"Not a living soul," nodded the jaeger. "You must come and have a look."

"Any clues who did this?" I asked.

"Ghouls, my Lord," the jaeger's voice was grim with undisguised anger. "Without a shadow of a doubt."

"I'll have a quick look," said Jesper. "We don't have time to investigate."

"I'll come with you," I said, setting my feet in motion.

Shandra dashed after me.

"I am not sure if what's to be seen is suitable for a *lady*," said jaeger grimly.

"I can handle it," murmured Shandra without stopping.

"Take care of the horses," said Jesper told the other jaegers. "We'll leave as soon as possible."

We went through the flowering meadow, where the cabins of Blackhead stared at us with empty windows. The village was small with only one street with no more than a dozen cabins facing each other across it. It had a ghostly feeling – no sound of people talking, no dogs barking, only the growing buzz of flies.

I stopped at the first cabin. There was no need to go inside, the door was open, and one of the jaegers emerged shaking his head.

"Any survivors?" I asked, already knowing the answer.

"No, my Lord."

A bloody trail ran through the door. Then I saw similar trails emerging from other cabins and joining like bloody creeks, running down the street and pooling in the centre of the village where a pile of something was lurked, thick with flies.

"Are these bodies?" I asked, pointing to the pile.

"I don't think so, my Lord," Jesper's voice was as cold as ice. "Knowing ghouls… they don't have a habit of leaving any bodies behind."

Shandra dashed forward and ran down the street past the pile, scaring clouds of flies on her way. I had no chance to stop her, nor could I run after her. The flies circled around only briefly and returned to their feast. Shandra hesitantly stopped in front of one of the cabins, closest to the forest, and then entered through the gaping door.

We went down the street, carefully avoiding the bloody pools and rivers. I stopped in front of the pile, still unsure of what I was looking at. A thick carpet of flies moved over the bloody remnants, but it wasn't bodies.

"What is this?" I whispered, holding my breath.

"Guts, my Lord," said Jesper. "Ghouls leave guts behind, taking only the bodies away."

I turned away feeling spasms rising in my stomach. I looked at the cherry trees flowering among the empty cabins, which helped the churning I felt to calm down a little. Then I noticed barns behind those trees whose doors were wide open and which had similar piles of guts in front of them.

Not long ago, a battle with ghouls had unfolded in Ikent which had been similarly devastated by the creatures. We avenged the dead then but again the horror of pain, suffering and death had crept up from the south-west, sneaking through our forests like irrepressible termites. I was the Lord of this land, and I felt I must do more than just send a handful of jaegers across the vast woods of Chadrack. I'd ask Bedwyr, but I doubted that my general and the army of Chadrack would be very helpful. Again, not for the first time, I thought of strengthening the borders. Should we build a wall?

"Only two days ago they were fine. I talked to them," Jesper shook his head. "Now Blackhead has gone! Vanished!"

"It can't be the same pack that chased me," I said, fighting the rising spasms again. "Ghouls can't move as fast as horses, can they?"

"No, my Lord," Jesper shook his head. "It must be another pack harvesting closer to the capital…"

"We must get moving then," I said, turning my back on the guts. "We don't have time for funerals."

I wasn't even sure if funerals were appropriate for guts when whole bodies were missing.

"Let's move!" Jesper commanded his men, and we went back across the flourishing fields of crops, leaving the horror, guts and flies behind.

Shandra was the last to leave the village. She walked through the flowering meadow without seeing anything – frightened, frigid and humble. I didn't dare to ask what she had found in that cabin, but the Blackhead massacre had crushed her entirely.

The horses were still hot, but we couldn't stay there any longer. At least, the poor animals had had enough time to drink their fill and graze some grass.

"We must avenge those deaths," I said to Jesper. "I'll have Bedwyr rally the forces. Those vermin must be exterminated."

"It will be as you say, my Lord," nodded Jesper, and I thought I caught a note of doubt in his voice. "There must be more than one pack around, I guess. We must travel faster and with greater caution. If we're lucky, we may reach the capital before dusk. I'll warn the other jaegers, with your permission. There's a large hunt waiting for them in the south."

I nodded, and he gave brief orders to his men.

"Are you okay?" I asked Shandra, helping her to mount the horse as two riders rushed past us, heading back to the jaeger campsite.

She nodded silently, still pale as death. I couldn't blame her. The sight of the devastated village haunted my mind too. I still could hear flies buzzing, and those bloody trails and piles of guts were vivid in my eyes. I mounted my horse and looked back at the cabins. My eyes widened as I saw indistinct shadows moving in the woods, unsure if these were tricks played by the wind or my imagination or if they were real ghouls leering at us.

"Let's go," my command came as a whisper, but everybody heard it clearly. "Fast!"

It didn't feel safe, even with the jaegers protecting me. I guessed nobody felt safe. Those lands were dangerous. We were just lucky to have avoided any ambushes so far.

The dark, hungry mouth of the woods engulfed us again as we once more pushed our horses into a gallop. Our group was small, and we stood no chance if a large pack of ghouls lurked somewhere on our way ahead. I was scared but did my best to hide this. Shandra was still pale, riding next to me and clutching the reins of her horse. Her eyes were fixed ahead, never looking back, never casting even the shortest of glimpses at me. I felt sad. She thought she was my prisoner, and I couldn't explain anything to her. Not on galloping horses, not in front of the jaegers.

Jesper sent three horsemen ahead to scout our way and placed more protection around Shandra and me.

The horses galloped down the invisible tracks with trees on both sides merging into endless dark green walls. Several times we scared birds and wild animals, and each time my heart slumped to my ankles expecting the worst when their cries, shrieks and the sound of breaking branches pierced the tremulous silence of the forest. I did my best not to flinch. Nobody spoke.

We took another short break on the shores of a small creek a few hours later, letting our horses catch their breath, drink and graze. I sat down on the soft moss, trying to calm my almost hysterical tension, but failed dismally. The distant shrieks of crows somewhere in the woods only increased my nervousness, and all I could do was just sit and wait until our steaming horses had drunk their fill. Shandra sat a few yards away from me, looking devastated completely, and I had no idea what had hit her most – fleeing from the ghouls, the death of the village or me being the Bloody Prince? My heart bled between shudders of fear, but I knew I could do nothing about that.

The jaegers stayed on guard around us with their crossbows ready.

"Can we get moving?" I asked, unable to bear the tension any longer.

"The horses are still drinking, my lord," Jesper pointed out the obvious. "We can if you so wish."

I looked at the poor animals still struggling to breathe and steaming and slowly shook my head. We waited another half an hour in silence.

Suddenly an arrow hissed a few feet in front of me and disappeared in the dark woods.

"What was that?!" Jesper sprang to his feet at once.

"It was me," one of the jaegers lowered his empty crossbow. "I thought I saw a shadow moving in the woods…"

"Thought?!" Jesper's face grew crimson. "You *must* see what you're aiming at!"

"Let's go," I interrupted him. "We can't stay here any longer."

Moments later, we were back on track. The poor horses had bloody saliva dripping from their mouths, but the image of the desolate village in our minds propelled us forward as fast as we could.

At dusk, we reached the river with a dirt road next to it and turned left. We had to find the bridge which was several miles upstream. We lost a horse before we reached it. The poor animal collapsed on the go with bloody saliva bursting out of its mouth. The rider was luckier, getting away with just a few bruises.

"How far are we from the castle?" I asked Jesper.

"No more than ten miles, my Lord," said Jesper as the jaegers dragged the corpse of the horse off the road.

I lifted my eyes to the sky where the enormous silver globe of Wyrna was taking shape in the dark blue velvet. Three rings sparkled around the globe – three rings richly shone with gold, while the spaces between them glistened white. Shandra gasped as the long howl of a wolf pierced the silence above the woods.

"We must move, my Lord," said Jesper. "Let's not give those wolves too large a feast."

"Let's go," I nodded, setting my horse on a silver lit road between the dark woods.

The wolves howled closer, and the horses gained speed without any urging.

"But not so fast. The horses are on edge," I cried out as we rode so we slowed down a little.

We rode another three or four miles until one more horse collapsed on the go. The rider was unfortunate this time and broke his leg. We had to leave four jaegers behind to help him reach the capital during the night.

The howling stopped a mile later. Most likely the pack of wolves had found the fallen horse. I only hoped that the men we had left behind would be safe.

It was well after midnight when we finally reached the castle. It was empty and, of course, nobody was expecting us.

I left the horses to the jaegers and took Shandra inside. She silently followed me looking crushed and empty but asked no questions. This squeezed my heart, but I hoped that we would have plenty of time on the morrow for explanations. I hoped to find the right words to convince her that I meant no harm. She might need some time to decide if she wanted to share her life with the Bloody Prince. In the meantime, I was glad that at least we were safe.

I left Shandra in one of the guest rooms next to my chambers, and I barely remember how I managed to reach my bed.

The blackout came the instant my head touched the pillow.

It was almost noon in Vienna. I woke up deadly tired and with a terrible headache. I spent nearly half an hour in the safety of my bed trying to calm down after that terrible race among the shadows. But life on this side of reality was no better. I flinched at every sound from behind my closed door, expecting the deadly mist of the banshee to leak through the keyhole and attack me. I hid under the covers allowing my imagination to torture me until I could stand it no longer. My empty stomach began to protest, claiming its rights.

I didn't have too many options on how to satisfy my hunger. The hotel canteen was already was closed. I could either eat somewhere out or buy a few snacks from a nearby grocery.

I made up my mind while I was brushing my teeth – wandering around the city wasn't an option. That could expose me to all sorts of threats and limit the possibilities of my reactions. Without John's immediate backup, I could only rely on visiting the grocery and grabbing a few quick snacks.

I dressed and spent a few minutes standing at the door before I opened it, listening for any sounds from the corridor. It seemed completely calm outside, so I braved to turn the doorknob.

The day was sunny. I turned right and rushed down the street where a grocery store was a few hundred yards away. I didn't look around but was confident that Morvarid had placed surveillance on the hotel and my slipping out would not go unnoticed.

I spent no more than ten minutes in the store, just enough time to buy some ham, cheese, a few packs of biscuits, a few bits of fruit and a bottle of juice. The street was empty when I left the shop, but I didn't feel safe. I hurried uphill back to the hotel, wondering what Morvarid's next move would be.

The receptionist smiled widely, passing me my key along with a white envelope. My heart sank as I took them and thanked him. *That was quick!* I didn't expect to receive a message from Morvarid that quickly. Suddenly I was scared.

Back in my room, I dropped on the bed and inspected the mysterious envelope. It bore my name and my new room number without any other writing. Inside was a neatly printed sheet of paper with apologies for yesterday's unpleasant incident and an invitation to a complimentary dinner in the hotel restaurant this evening. The time wasn't indicated as it had been in her previous notes from Morvarid, and, of course, the note was not signed.

Morvarid wanted to come out to play again? Well... at least, this time, she was paying for it.

I called John.

"That wasn't unexpected," he said. "She has her banshee back, and she can now safely return to her original plan. We're right back at the beginning again."

"I hope it's not too late for Rick," I sighed.

"Only death is final," John said firmly. "Don't forget to insist on a demonstration. She'll have to bring Rick from her secret dungeon, and then we might have a chance."

"Would you be able to provide my backup during this meeting?"

"I don't think you'll be in any danger," his voice was serious. "But yes, I'll stay outside. Maybe this time I'll be more successful in tracking her."

"When should I go?" I asked him. "The invitation doesn't specify a time."

"She's inviting you for dinner, isn't she?" he asked. "Get down at six – it's a bit early for dinner, but you'll have a chance for a little surveillance ahead of her arrival. That might be useful."

"I'll do that," I promised and hung up.

The day had begun unpleasantly and an even more unpleasant evening already lay ahead of me. The imaginary mist of the banshee hovered above my aching head, creating images of apocalyptic destruction whatever I laid my eyes on. I blamed myself for losing the creature, but it had been a stupid idea to carry the rat around in the first place. I should have packed it with a few rocks and sunk it in the middle of the Danube instead. I only hoped that John was right, and the situation had returned to the starting point.

Was Rick still alive? I felt guilty. I was the one to blame for his kidnapping and all the subsequent disasters. Rick's fate was slipping out of my hands, and I blamed myself for that too. I had the determination to liberate him from the claws of my crazy ex-wife, but I lacked the means. Morvarid was sly, and I doubted if she would do something stupid enough to reveal Rick's whereabouts in Vienna, as John was hoping. Our only real hope was Rick himself. I knew I would be able to find this out quite soon when he'll return from the caves. Dead or alive.

I spent all day with every nerve straining, about to explode, sitting in the corner of the red sofa. The TV was on, but I wasn't watching it.

It was a few minutes past six when I finally gathered sufficient courage to start moving. I carefully brushed my teeth, shaved and combed my hair as if preparing for a funeral. I put a new shirt on for the occasion and polished my shoes.

I took the invitation and left my room, putting the key into my pocket. The restaurant was downstairs, and I could reach it through the hotel lobby without the need to go outside. That was useful if someone was watching me from the street.

A neatly dressed grey-haired gentleman met me at the door, and I presented him with my letter. He nodded knowingly.

“Yes, Mr Firestone, this way, please...” he led me to the corner table in the middle of the two large windows.

I froze. I couldn’t imagine a more exposed seat – it was clearly visible from the entire restaurant and, of course, from the street outside. If Morvarid had intended to put me in a spotlight, I was going to spoil her plans.

“Do you have any tables with a little more privacy?” I asked the gentleman.

He stopped hesitantly, his smile vanishing from his face, and then he nodded, painting the smile back on.

“If you wish,” he said. “This way, please...”

This time the table was almost completely separated from the rest of the hall by a wooden wall on the left and a bar on the right. The front view was further blocked by a large flower arrangement while the back wall was decorated with some artificial greenery.

“Is this okay?” asked the gentleman.

“Yes, it's much better,” I even managed to smile back.

“Would you like to order something right now?” he asked.

“I’d like to look at the menu first...”

He nodded and left me with my doubts. I looked around, and a shy victorious smile passed over my lips. The only option for surveillance of me here was by sitting at the bar and facing me. But the bar was still empty. Morvarid would have a hard time playing her secrecy games tonight.

I carelessly looked through the menu as sad thoughts crawled back into my head. I had been dragged into action without any proper preparation. Was John's advice not to drink and eat anything still in force? It felt a bit excessive, especially when the letter had invited me to a "complimentary" dinner. Why bother with some intricate poison when a weapon such as the banshee was available? I still had no knowledge of its capabilities, but the horror and awe in John's eyes when he spoke about the creature had been contagious, and it had planted fear in my heart too.

The waiter approached me several minutes later, and I made up my mind, ordering a lavish dinner with appetisers, traditional Viennese escalope and several desserts including *strudel,* so enjoyed by Morvarid the last time we had met, and some wine.

The restaurant was still almost empty, and I wondered if John was already in position outside on the street. I suppressed my nervously twitching leg and began waiting for Morvarid's appearance. Hidden loudspeakers quietly played waltzes as I cautiously looked around for the floating mist. I almost jumped out of my skin when my phone beeped in my pocket.

"Are you there?" it was a message from John.

"Yes, I'm sitting next to the bar," I answered.

A bottle of wine appeared in front of me, and the waiter filled my glass with a charming ruby liquid. I asked for a glass of water as well. It might be a long evening ahead, and I decided not to rush things.

"I can't see you," complained John. "Any free seats inside? I can't play a beggar on the street without attracting attention."

"I guess so," I replied. "It's not too crowded, and nobody is troubling me."

"Pretend you don't know me," John's instructions were clear.

The *Strauss Waltz* quietly played in the background, creating an exceptional Viennese atmosphere as I tasted the wine. It had a mild flavour of prunes with a very distinct floral aftertaste, and I took a few more sips while waiting for my first course to arrive.

I was finishing my appetiser when John appeared in the doorway. He glanced only briefly in my direction then turned all of his attention to the approaching waiter.

Apparently, all the tables were reserved as the waiter kept shaking his head. John took a seat at the bar and ordered a glass of beer and a few snacks, paying for it all there and then. Although he was directly in front of me, he never cast me a second glance.

The restaurant was slowly filling with people – singles, couples, even bigger parties, but nobody troubled me. Soon John had company at the bar when another, seemingly random pedestrian, decided to have a drink. They were soon talking and laughing like old friends, and the waiter had to ask them to lower their voices.

The *Wiener Schnitzel* arrived with a traditional potato salad, topped with a quarter of a lemon. It was hot and smelled delicious. I washed the meat down with another glass of wine and even began to sway slightly, following the rhythm of the waltz playing in the background. The tension fell away. The banshee was not here. John was guarding me. What could possibly happen?

Later my strudel appeared in front of me, and I stopped the waiter who was taking away my empty plate.

"Can I ask you to find something out?" I inquired and then, encouraged by his nod, enquired, "Who is paying my bill? I was invited to a complimentary dinner, but have no idea who to express my gratitude to..."

"We have been told that it was compensation from the hotel for an incident that happened a few days ago, but maybe you know more about it..." he smiled. "If you would like to express your gratitude, I think anyone on reception would be the right person."

I thanked him, and he went away.

I felt disappointed. All this fuss had, in fact, been unrelated to Morvarid, at least directly.

John's laughter now dwarfed all other sounds in the bar. I had to tell him the news but hated to reveal our well-executed conspiracy. It might still be handy in the future.

I took out my phone and sent him a text. The message was brief – "False alarm".

A few seconds later, John took out his phone and read the message, then typed a reply and carried on sipping his beer, talking with the guy at the bar.

The response was also short – "Let's meet in the *Karlsplatz* in half an hour."

It was time to end the evening. I finished my desserts and downed the last of my wine.

"Anything else?" asked the waiter.

"No. Thank you. Please, pass my compliments to the chef and the person whose idea this was. It was a real pleasure. Now I'd better get some rest in my room..."

"You are welcome..."

I got up and left through the hotel entrance. John stayed at the bar.

Still, the dinner could have just been a distraction for us, and I double-checked my belongings while back in my room. Everything was in place. I didn't have another packed banshee to attract my ex-wife.

The evening was warm. I went outside and strolled down the

street past closing shops and Chinese stalls. The sounds of a tango engulfed the *Karlsplatz* once again, and I quickly spotted John already sitting on a bench in the shade.

I made my way through the crowd of happy smiling faces, mostly watching, and just a few dancing.

"What was that all about?" asked John impatiently. "I realise that nobody showed up, but maybe you should have waited a bit longer. Why did you leave?"

"I found out that the hotel was footing the bill for my dinner as compensation for having my room wrecked and it was their invitation," I explained. "It was no use waiting when nobody was ever likely to show up. And it's getting late. I guess we both have more important things to do in Rehen."

"Well, I hope all is as it seems, and we haven't just lost the only possibility of finding out something solid about Rick," said John bitterly.

"Speaking of Rick," I said. "I'm going to see him in Rehen quite soon. I've managed to get back to the capital already. It's just a matter of a few hours until I'll be able to speak with him."

"That's great news!" John forced a smile. "Please, call me first thing in the morning. If we can find out where he is, we can take action straight away."

"Do you think he might be somewhere nearby?"

"I think he'll be within reach," he smiled.

For a few minutes, we just sat and listened to the tango. One melody ended and, after brief applause, another fiery story of love and hate began to fill the air.

"It's getting late," I said finally. "Let's go... "

We parted after a short farewell. Before long I was in my bed, still wondering how I could ever have fallen in love with Morvarid. Life seemed so cruel and iniquitous, and I drifted into the darkness with this thought.

I felt a presence in my room before I even opened my eyes. A chair squeaked under somebody's weight, and I held my breath, trying to guess who would dare to disturb my sleep. Was it a friend? Shandra? Rick? This thought was comforting, and I gladly opened my eyes.

I gasped. A dark bearded man was sitting in a chair in front of me, scratching his nails with my dagger.

"Who are you?" I demanded.

"That's exactly the question I expected," said the stranger pointing at me with the dagger and smiling. "You don't recognise me, do you, brother?"

I cast a quick glance through the opened door – armed men dressed in black with yellow breastplates across their chests were filling my chambers; unknown men in uniforms I didn't recognise.

"Yes, you are entirely in my hands, brother," the man was

satisfied with his nails at last and put my dagger away.

"Shandra..." I whispered.

"I can assure you – no one has died in the castle of Chadrack yet," the man grinned. "We came in peace."

"It is not in exactly my understanding of peace to wake up to find my chambers full of a foreign army," I said through clenched teeth.

"These are not exactly your chambers, are they?" the man's eyes were calm as the same grin escaped through his thick black beard. "You only see these chambers in your dreams, don't you? And you've never seen me in your dreams, that's why you're wondering who the man cleaning his nails with your dagger is. *Caramba*! I got you, brother!"

The man stood up from his chair. He was tall and heavily built with bulging chest and arm muscles, but he was far from clumsy – his gait was as gracious as that of an attacking panther. And I felt he was as deadly as a panther. I looked around the bedroom, desperately searching for a weapon but found none. The man stood up and closed the door leaving his army behind it and then turned his black eyes back to me.

"Don't worry," he said without a smile. "Your secret will not go beyond this room."

The statement sounded sinister.

"Who are you?" I repeated my question.

"You may call me Seisyll, Kyleb," he said, taking the chair and sitting down again. "I came to talk to you, not to conquer you. But I must admit, that thought was tempting indeed."

My heart skipped a few beats as his eyes drilled into my face, studying my reaction. I felt doomed, and the calmness of Seisyll's voice seemed even more alarming. My sick predecessor had ordered the death of Seisyll's daughter. *Not me*! Was the Prince of Mordak now in my chambers to seek his revenge? A whirlpool of images flashed through my brain – a scar-faced man named Melvyn telling me how he had raped and killed the young Princess then the same man hanging on a cross in the woods, dead. A dark wave of fear washed everything away as I recalled our preparations for a war against Mordak. No further need for war or defence – the ruler of Mordak, Prince Seisyll, was sitting in my bedroom playing with my dagger. All he needed to do was quickly slash my throat.

My silence went on for too long.

"Oh," Seisyll said grinning. "I forgot the proof."

He took a Ring out of his pocket – a golden band, shaped in the form of two gryphons, holding a bright yellow Citrine within their claws – and put it on his finger. For a second, Seisyll's smile seemed almost childlike as he observed my bulging eyes.

"I'm sorry for your daughter," I finally managed to utter with a trembling heart.

"Don't be, Kyleb," this time Seisyll's smile seemed genuine. "I have no daughter. Never have had. It's impractical to have offspring in our position."

"I don't understand…" I shook my head.

"We don't have much time," he cut my speech off, wiping out his smile. "I think I owe you a little explanation so, please, listen without interruptions. It is not a great surprise that I have a few spies in your castle, always have had, as I suppose the real Kyleb has always spied on me in Mordak. I immediately knew what had happened when they told me about your odd and unusual behaviour. I had to test it out. I didn't believe your tale about poisoning, but that poor cook had to die, I suppose. It was a smart decision – my compliments. I sent that drunkard and thief Melvyn to pose as your spy and tell you that silly tale about the Princess. The real Kyleb knew I had no daughters, and you didn't. You bought the story, and I got my proof. The real Kyleb would have killed Melvyn with his own hands the instant he opened his mouth to spit out those lies."

I stared at him, disbelief painted all over my face.

"Who killed Melvyn then?" I asked.

"I did," Seisyll said calmly. "He knew he was a part of my plan, and I couldn't risk keeping him alive. I carved the message for you on his forehead, but you didn't get that either. That's why I had to wait for the right moment to pay you a personal visit.

And here we are! The empty capital of Chadrack and the ruler sleeping in his chambers without any guards – you're a genius, Kyleb! I couldn't have asked for more."

The man was implying that he knew I was a Sleeper. I was sure he was about to kill me. He was just taking his time to enjoy tormenting me.

"I see," I mumbled. "Now that you know my secret, what are you going to do about it?"

It was no use pretending any longer.

"Nothing, *brother*," Seisyll took my Master of Destiny – the magic Sapphire Ring – out of his pocket and tossed it to me. "I've told you already – I come in peace."

I didn't buy his reassurance. Reluctantly, I slipped the Ring on my finger. This was as useless as keeping it on a table. I felt a weak jolt while it connected to my neural systems, but the Ring was exhausted, discharged, unable even to shield me if Seisyll chose to attack. Of course, all magic manipulations were out of the question.

"You tricked me into that elaborate plan. You've won," my voice trembled slightly. "Yes, I am a Sleeper. The Bloody Prince is no longer here. What is it you're after?"

Seisyll chuckled.

"Relax," he smiled. "You'd be dead by now if that was my intention. I thought I'd prefer to help a fellow Sleeper to avoid the ploys played by the family."

The smile vanished from his face.

"Oh! So now you know my secret too," he said seriously. "Either we form a team or only one of us is going to get out of this room alive."

"That sounds like a threat," I observed.

"It is a threat," agreed Seisyll. "Honestly, I wouldn't like to kill a relative, especially an heir to the throne. But I will if I am forced to."

I flinched, virtually sensing a dagger slicing my neck.

"Who else in the family is a Sleeper?" I asked.

"Just the two of us, dear brother. That makes our acquaintance unique," Seisyll grinned. "As I said, I wouldn't like to spoil a good alliance. We can combine our forces and easily get the throne back. I think some of our other brothers and sisters would support your claim although we may need to suppress the ambitions of some of the others. Don't you ever dream of ruling the world, Kyleb? I would happily be the second most important man in the realm and rule in your name. C'mon, brother, it would be fun…"

"I've got the picture," I said grimly.

The man was offering me the role of a marionette. I would prefer to retain my free will proudly but nor was I ready to die either. I could use Seisyll as a guide through the swampy politics of Rehen, but his desire to rule could be deadly for all. And not just because of him. Only a few days ago I made a deal with that flaming viper. In advance I knew I would avoid fulfilling my part of that deal – too many deaths were at stake, and I intended to avoid taking the throne as well as not allowing anybody else to sit on it. This might be a lifetime struggle, but I knew it was the only chance for this world. We were all doomed if I agreed to Seisyll's demands, but maybe I could buy some time to find a way around it? That didn't sound too optimistic – I was sure he would put more than one safeguard in place. This might become damned problematic.

"It's not that difficult a decision, brother," Seisyll nervously rubbed his Ring as my silence stretched into a long minute. "The future is bright! We'll make an excellent team, I know it."

"I'm frightened by that too bright future," I mumbled, "but I'm in. Consider it that we've made a deal. You'll be my right hand man when I get on the throne. Now, are you satisfied?"

"I knew we'd reach an agreement," Seisyll's smile was victorious. "But have no doubt, brother, I have the means for this plan to succeed – with or without your active support. You better stick with me, Kyleb."

I failed to return a smile.

"Now get dressed. And would you please order your men to lower their weapons?" he asked casually. "They've been standing like that for a few hours already, and I'd hate to kill anybody in the backyard of my ally."

I cursed. Only a few moments had passed since I'd accepted the deal, and I was already receiving orders from him! But I didn't want my jaegers to be killed, and the power was obviously on Seisyll's side. I got out of bed, mumbling obscenities and put my pants on. Seisyll watched me with apparent complacency. He stood from his chair only when I had finished dressing.

"Let's go, brother," he opened the door. "Let's surprise the world."

I stepped through and froze. The hall was still full of armed men as I expected, but they were pointing their spears and crossbows at me. It was Seisyll's army. He stopped next to me and suddenly burst into laughter.

"The expression on your face was worth a million, dear brother," he was still grinning. "Sorry, I couldn't resist the pleasure."

He waved to his men, spears were lowered and crossbows disarmed.

We passed amongst them, slowly proceeding to the balcony. I felt like a lamb amid a pack of wolves. Seisyll was clearly enjoying the entertainment and walked next to me with a broad smile shining through his black beard. I heard footsteps behind me, but I wasn't sure if his men were following us or simply regrouping – I was afraid to look.

We passed through the hall. Never had the balcony seemed as big as when we stepped forward and the scene beyond unfolded before us.

The yard was full of armed men – Seisyll's men with yellow breastplates, pointing their spears and crossbows and surrounding a handful of my jaegers led by Jesper. My men were outnumbered several times. Indeed, Seisyll had prepared well for his visit.

"Please, brother," he whispered, standing next to me. "Don't force me to spill blood."

He looked at me expectantly.

"Listen to me!" I raised my hand. "My brother Seisyll came here on a peaceful visit. There is no need to fight. Jesper, order your men to put down their weapons, and Seisyll's men will do the same."

"You heard what my brother just said," Seisyll waved.

"As you wish, my Lord," said Jesper lowering his crossbow.

Other jaegers followed his lead. I looked at Seisyll, askance. He met my glance with a grin.

"Ifan! Put the weapons down. There will be no fighting," he said, pointing at the yard. "Break camp… here! Send a few hunters into the woods – I'd like some roast venison."

Suddenly the yard was on the move like a disturbed anthill. My jaegers stood motionless amid that turmoil.

"Jesper, resume the guard at the gate," I ordered. "Let Seisyll's men in and out freely."

"As you wish, my Lord," repeated Jesper and passed a few commands to other jaegers.

"That was a very wise decision, Kyleb," complimented Seisyll, observing the turmoil.

"Could I have my chambers back?" I asked.

"Yes, brother," Seisyll looked at his men. "We'll just need one more little chat, and I'll order my men to vacate the premises."

"What is it?"

He straightened his shoulders. His facial expression was now serious.

"As I told you before – I have plenty of safeguards in place in this deal," he said, studying my reaction. "I need to install a few more."

I kept a straight face.

"What is it? Do you want me to sign a treaty?" I asked.

"Don't be ridiculous, Kyleb," he said seriously. "Nobody would recognise your signature. It's useless. You're not the Bloody Prince."

Seisyll took a piece of parchment out of his pocket and handed it to me.

"This is my number," he said. "Call me – first thing in the morning on Earth. I'll tell you what to do next to gain my trust."

I took the parchment.

"I guess, trust must be mutual to make things work," I said weakly.

"Don't you trust me, brother?" Seisyll narrowed his eyes, staring directly into mine.

"It's the first rule of the family – trust no one," I shrugged. "Isn't it?"

"You're a fast learner," he smiled. "I like that. We'll talk later about trust, brother. Believe me – we are now only a family of two. We'll have different rules."

"For some reason, I feel like a prisoner in my own home. I can't really understand – why," I let the irony shine through my words. "Do you have any explanation, brother? I think it'll be hard to build any trust on such shaky ground. I'll need something more solid."

"Now you sound like a future King," Seisyll winked. "I like that even better. Let's go and gain some trust!"

He turned around and left the balcony. I had no choice but to follow him.

His fighters still swarmed my chambers, clutching their weapons but at least they were not pointing at me. Seisyll marched across the hall. I merely followed. The men parted, allowing us through until we stopped in front of the hearth.

"Is this some kind of trick?" I asked with growing agitation.

"You know what it is," Seisyll said casually, stepping onto the hearth and stretching his right hand up into the chimney.

The wall parted, revealing a secret passage.

"Let's go, Kyleb," he waved impatiently. "Your Ring is completely exhausted as I can see. You'd never make your way alone."

Seisyll stepped through the gap, and I had no other option but to go after him. The passage was brightly lit with a myriad of green light emitting crystals scattered across the walls and the ceiling indicating that Seisyll's Citrine was fully charged and able to handle much more than illumination only. Only I wasn't sure about its other properties.

The wall closed behind us.

The path was narrow, winding between large rocks, stalactites and stalagmites, and we progressed in silence, slowly stepping down into depths of the mountain. I knew the way, and I knew what waited at the end of it.

Seisyll seemed to be confident in what he was doing, but I wasn't sure if I liked this particular turn of events. I still felt like a flea between his thumbs – I was certain he could crush me any moment and again I couldn't understand why he didn't do just that.

The tunnel ended in a large grotto. Seisyll stopped, beholding the Well of Power, and I stopped next to him. Mesmerising purple shadows moved slowly along the walls of the grotto – cold reflections of the purple flame locked beneath the surface of the Well.

My Sapphire weakly jolted my finger, urging me closer to the source of the Power. A few purple sparks rose from the Well to greet me, but I continued to wait, still unsure why Seisyll had brought me here. I looked around, but Hawa, the Keeper, was nowhere in sight.

"I could watch this forever," whispered Seisyll. "But we have something more important to do."

"What's that?"

"Let's charge the Rings, brother!" he eagerly stepped forward. I followed.

The surface of the Well swelled as if giant purple jellyfish shivered within its depths while two columns of purple sparks rose high above the surface to greet us. Seisyll's Ring shone like a small sun as he extended his hand and touched the shivering ripples. I realised I had to do the same or risk, even greater vulnerability. Fully charged, the Master of Destiny was capable of great things – shielding me from Seisyll at the very least.

I stretched out my hand, feeling the power building around me. An outburst of sparks engulfed my Ring as my fingers touched the surface. Seisyll grinned, looking at me while my Sapphire shone brightly and began pulsing like a beating heart.

Waves of energy rushed through my body, sparks from the Well rose as high as the ceiling of the grotto, and time itself seemed to slow down, become irrelevant, cease to exist.

My mind reduced to a spark and became lost among the other sparks in the dark, primordial depth of the Well. I knew the process, and it didn't frighten me as I joined the flow waiting for the ripples of the Well to take me ashore.

When the journey was over, I found Seisyll sitting on a rock watching me.

"How do you feel?" he asked, and this time his voice sounded friendly.

"Fine," I nodded. "How long have I been away?"

"Half an hour, perhaps," he shrugged. "Let's get back before our people become nervous."

"Give me just a minute," I said, sitting down in front of him. "That won't make a big difference to our people."

I ordered my thoughts and reached into the Sapphire with my mind, bringing the blue sphere of Destiny to the forefront of my mental sight. Seisyll raised an eyebrow but didn't comment when I turned my focus on him. I had to test his story, and this moment was as good as any.

I found an image of Seisyll sitting in my room watching me as I slept. Then I scrolled back through his entire journey to the castle of Chadrack from the Braaid where an elegant three-masted corvette waited for him a few hundred yards from the shore. I crossed the great river with him back to Mordak, where he had begun his journey with several squads of knights.

Seisyll watched me silently. Of course, he was aware what I was doing but patiently waited while I scrolled back through the images of his timeline.

He travelled busily around Mordak. I saw him holding meetings with his generals, giving commands and fighting back ghouls. I saw him training along with his soldiers, mastering swords, spears and knives. I quickly ran through images of him speaking words of love to different women then him making love to them.

I stopped when I found what I was looking for – his hand carving a word TRAITOR on the dead man's forehead, a man who had already been strangled and crucified. I scrolled through a few more images to when the man named Melvyn received a few golden coins as he listened to the story he was to repeat.

Seisyll was telling the truth.

I exited his timeline, and the sphere collapsed.

"Are you satisfied now, brother?" asked Seisyll before standing up.

I silently nodded.

"Let's return…"

We left the grotto the same way. Seisyll led the way, and I

followed shortly behind him. This trip to the Well had only proved that he had truthfully admitted his part in the plot against me and he was guilty of being the cause of some of my problems. Had I gained any trust?

I looked at his muscular back a few steps ahead of me. The answer was still no, and I had to find a way how to navigate through his crazy plan while keeping the throne vacant. I touched the healing scar on my thigh – a reminder of Am'ut – and shuddered. Many lives and the future of this world were at stake. Would Seisyll believe me if I told him the truth? The answer was also no. But I had to buy some time to think my way out of this.

Seisyll opened the exit from the passage, and we were back in the hall, now full of his men.

"All out!" Seisyll waved his hand, urging them away. "Wait in the yard!"

"I'd gladly offer you a glass of wine, Seisyll," I said when we were left alone. "But I've no idea where it's being kept."

He chuckled, taking a seat at the table. I sat down in front of him.

"Don't worry," he grinned. "We'll have plenty of opportunities to feast."

"And how do you plan to proceed with this?" I looked at his dark eyes but could read nothing in them.

"Your part is easy, Kyleb," he said, twirling his Ring. "You need to gain the support of Porlok and Lyme. I'll handle things on my side of the Braaid."

I decided not to mention my alliance with my sister Keely, Princess of Porlok.

"It will just be a matter of formality for you to claim the seat in Wagorn with all or nearly all of the family behind you," he said seriously. "And then the fun will begin. We'll come to an agreement about how to divide the power. I'll stand in your shadow, of course, don't worry. This place is big enough for both of us."

I didn't like the way this sounded but didn't let that show on my face.

"What do you want me to do?" I asked.

"Call me in the morning," he whispered. "We need reliable contact beyond this world."

"I will," I assured him. "Have no doubt."

"The consequences will be grave if you don't, I must warn you," he said seriously. "I'll raise a world against you, and you'll be dead in no time, bearing in mind how easy it is to get to you. I know which strings to pull."

"I'll call you," I said firmly, ignoring his grim reminder.

"We have a lot of vulnerabilities as Sleepers, brother," Seisyll shrugged. "But I'm had more than twenty years in the business. I know how to play. Rely on me, Kyleb, and you'll be the King in no time."

"I'll keep my promise, Seisyll," I repeated for the third time. "I'll call you in the morning."

"Good! I expected that, and that's in your own best interests. Now, I think I'll have my roast venison somewhere in the woods," Seisyll stood up from his chair. "I don't want to make our acquaintance too obvious yet. I'll be waiting for that call. Be smart, brother."

Seisyll left without casting a second glance at me – swiftly and silently like a panther, leaving the door open.

I jumped to my feet, listening to the sound of his footsteps receding down the corridor until they died away into silence. Shandra! Had Seisyll harmed her? I dashed into the hallway. It was empty with no trace of Seisyll or his army. I rushed left and stormed through Shandra's door without knocking.

She was sitting on her bed – fully dressed, with her hands resting on her knees. I stopped at the door, smiling and breathless.

"I only wanted to check if you were unharmed," I gasped. "Sorry for the intrusion."

"I heard some trouble in the yard, *sir*," she said, still sitting.

"My brother Seisyll was visiting," I thought I owed her an explanation, but that didn't really explain anything. I did my best to sound calm and confident but failed. "Thank God you're safe."

"You make it sound like it wasn't a friendly visit, *sir*," she observed.

"It was a strange visit, indeed," I admitted. "Why don't you call me Kyleb, like before?"

Shandra blushed and lowered her gaze.

"I had no idea then that you were a Prince," she whispered. "I still have trouble with that thought."

I crossed the room to her bed.

"Am I a prisoner?" she asked suddenly.

I sat next to her.

"No, of course, not! Why?"

"Am I free to go?"

"Yes, you are free to go wherever and whenever you want," I assured her. "That's your decision, not mine. I am only asking you to stay if you can."

"A man in your position can have any woman he wants. Why me?"

The question seemed of paramount importance to her. I could understand her distrust, but nevertheless, it felt painful. Deep in my heart, I was sure of the answer, but how to express it, how to dress it in the robes of words and let it live aloud? I had known beforehand that any attempt I made would be just a hazy awkward shadow of what really hid in my heart, a poor representation of that feeling of completeness that had filled me the first night in her cave as I listened to her quiet breath in the den or the morning as I watched her gracefully moving around.

"You know nothing about me, sir," Shandra said with tears in her eyes when I failed to respond. "I'm a killer, that's why I was evicted from the village. I was evicted from Blackhead. It doesn't matter now because the village no longer exists – everybody is dead, but the guilt still remains with me."

"I believe you had reasons to do what you did."

"No reasons can change the fact that I'm a killer," tears now rolled down her face. "I'll tell you the story then you could have me taken to Blackhead and dumped in that pile of guts, and that would be the right decision. It was one of your jaegers that I killed. I poisoned him with red dragonroots, and he died horribly. Do you want to know why I did that?"

I failed to answer.

"I had a brother, Cardell, three years younger than me. We lived in Blackhead, and he was keen to become one of your jaegers. He was first everywhere – to help with the crops or to repair a roof damaged by the wind or to sing a song or to dance a dance. Everybody liked him. Cardell was my only family after our parents died when we were kids. He was only fifteen when one of your jaegers agreed to take him on as an apprentice. Cardell's joy was over the roof, but everything ended three days later. That jaeger took him to stalk a deer and raped him in the woods. Cardell hanged himself the next day. His body had been ripped and gnawed at by wild animals when we found him. There wasn't much left for a pyre. I spent that whole summer mourning him."

She paused for a few seconds. I didn't dare interrupt.

"There had already been the first frost of autumn on the fields when the jaegers stopped at Blackhead again. I recognised the man instantly. He smiled and laughed as if nothing had ever happened. I made him a drink, and he thanked me. An hour later, he was screaming as his blood and his life leaked from everywhere. He died too soon. I wanted him to scream and bleed forever. Then they made me build him a pyre, and I was exiled as soon as his ashes grew cold. They hoped that the wild animals would get me, but I survived. You know the rest, *sir*. Now it's up to you to decide if you still want me to stay. I am a killer."

Her story had shaken my very soul, and my heart was breaking. Shandra looked at me like a frightened lamb expecting the strike of a butcher's knife any moment.

"I am sorry about your brother. I don't blame you for what you did. That man was guilty and deserved his brutal punishment. You must stop torturing yourself," I said finally. "You'll always be the angel who saved me, and I'll always remember you lighting your way with a torch in that endless black tunnel. I'm still in that tunnel, Shandra, but I feel safe with you, and I want you to be safe with me. I can't put it into the right words, but I know that I'm doing the right thing."

I took her hand.

"Don't say anything. Don't decide now if you're not sure. Just give me a chance..." I asked her.

"I need your promise then," she said quietly. "A solemn royal promise."

"What kind of a promise?"

"If you ever change your mind about me, you'll let me go before your order to the hangman..." Shandra almost whispered.

"Of course, I promise. You have my word! That is silly, though! You're free to go whenever you want," I told her, holding her hand. "But I'll never change my mind about you."

We sat there in silence. I had no idea what else to say, how better to convince her or what I could add to what I had said. I wasn't very good at being persuasive.

"Could I call you – sir?" she asked, still looking away. "I feel uncomfortable with Kyleb right now..."

"I don't mind if that makes you feel better."

She silently nodded, wiping her tears away. The neigh of a horse pierced the silence, and I jumped to my feet.

"I must see my brother departing," I said. "Please, don't go anywhere. It's safer to stay in your room."

"I'll do as you say, sir," she said.

I returned to my chambers. Although my Sapphire Ring was now fully charged and capable and could provide me with maximum protection, I felt more comfortable with a sword. I peeked over the balcony to check on the Mordakans. The yard was already almost empty with the guards standing silently at the closed gate.

Seisyll must have left without waiting for my farewell. On the left, jaegers were fetching their horses from the stables, Jesper among them.

"Are you leaving?" I asked.

"Yes, my Lord," he answered. "The ghouls are still wandering around..."

"I want you to send a few men to Bedwyr," I ordered. "I want the army back. The citizens can return as well – the danger is over. And stay here with your squad until the army returns. The castle needs protection. I don't want any more surprises."

"I'll do as you say, my Lord," replied Jesper. "Sorry about the Mordakans, my Lord. They just appeared from nowhere. We didn't see them coming."

"Not everybody comes through the front gate," I mumbled. "We'll take care of that later."

I dismissed him. Moments later, I saw Jesper giving orders to his men, and two horsemen immediately departed through the gates. The rest of the jaegers returned their horses to the stables leaving the yard deserted again.

I leaned on the balustrade with my heart now more uneasy

than ever. Prince Seisyll of Mordak thought that he had conquered me without a battle. I would find out about the strings attached quite soon, I was sure, but I wasn't willing to be his puppet, and I couldn't go down the route he was pushing me. *Damn!* This felt as bad as a full-scale war with everything slowly slipping out of my control. *Damned Seisyll!* His deception had tricked me into a panic, and panic is a bad adviser. I had to find a way to regain control. I needed my army back.

My meditation was then interrupted by the sound of the door quietly opening in the hall, followed by a few light footsteps. Who was there? Another Mordakan left behind to spy on me? I turned around quickly, but my eyes were still blinded by the bright sunshine and unable to see clearly in the shadows of the hall. Who was checking my chambers?

The hilt of my sword brushed the balustrade when I turned to take a better look, drawing the weapon out of its sheath. I cursed my clumsiness as the sword crashed to the ground with a loud clatter. *Shit!* Someone rushed out of my chambers, and I heard the door closing.

I picked the sword up and dashed after that intruder. By the time I reached the corridor, it was empty and already deadly quiet – I couldn't hear any retreating footsteps or closing doors. I cursed again silently. Was Shandra all right? Now I regretted leaving her in the room alone.

I approached her door and quietly tapped. Nobody answered. I opened the door and carefully looked inside.

Shandra was still sitting on the bed and looking at the door expectantly.

"It's a very strange morning," I said, sheathing my sword. "I hope it will all return to normal in a matter of days."

Shandra visibly shuddered – apparently, she knew the "normality" of the Bloody Prince too well. Her attempt to smile resulted in an uncertain and sad image of a smile which squeezed my heart with an even greater chill. I clearly understood the magnitude of her fears after finding herself with Kyleb the Bloody Prince. But she wasn't aware of the change of the soul that now occupied the body of the Prince. I had done my best to hide this fact, but it hadn't been enough. Seisyll had proved that a short while ago. But it wasn't me who was cruel in Chadrack, and it was not *my* lousy notoriety! Except Shandra had no way of knowing this.

"Maybe, we should go and try to find something to eat?" I asked her and took her hand in an attempt to hide my worries.

She nodded, standing up, her hand still in my hand. We crossed the room, and she withdrew her hand from mine before we entered the corridor. I didn't dare to object.

We crossed the hall and negotiated a few staircases on our way to the kitchen, meeting no one.

"Why it is so empty here?" asked Shandra.

"I ordered everybody to evacuate."

"Why?"

"We believed that my sister Hel was about to attack us," I explained. "So, I decided it was a good idea to save the lives of the capital's residents. She didn't attack us, by the way…"

"I'd forgotten that Death is your sister…" she looked even more frightened.

"Yes, she is," I had decided not to withhold the obvious.

"I'm sorry," said Shandra. "I am so unfamiliar with your genealogy."

We entered the empty kitchen.

"We'll need to search around here," I said, scratching my head. "I've no idea where anything edible might be found."

"Maybe I'll start by building a fire?" asked Shandra. "Or don't you want some hot food?"

"That would be nice," I said going through cupboards, cabinets and storage rooms, searching.

Shandra built a fire while I collected some smoked ham, cheese, several eggs, cabbage, a few potatoes and a carrot.

"It will take a while, but these will all make us an excellent stew," said Shandra as she inspected my gatherings.

"We have as much time as it takes," I assured her.

I just leant back and watched her moving around as she cut the meat and vegetables and put everything into a pot. I had the feeling that this usual and simple activity helped calm down her own anxiety and gave her a short opportunity to organise her thoughts and feelings.

I was silent. So was Shandra.

I felt ravenous when she finally put a plate of the deliciously smelling stew in front of me and handed me a spoon.

"Thank you," I smiled her, trying the food. "It's very tasty."

"It's nothing special," she said, sitting at the table across from me, putting a plate down for herself.

We ate silently. I wasn't lying. The stew was exceptional.

Then our moment of tranquillity ended abruptly. The door opened without a tap, and I met the surprised gaze from the pale, almost white, eyes of Saqia as the blue woman entered the kitchen.

Saqia was my gift or, more precisely, my curse, which was how I felt about it. My sister Keely had brought her to my court for my pleasures. I never found out what Keely's behest to her was, but Saqia was quite persistent in trying to fulfil her duty. I never touched her but didn't have the stomach to send her back to Keely – she would undoubtedly sell the blue woman to another Prince. This didn't feel right, and I allowed her to live in the castle. I thought she had left during the turmoil of evacuation, but I was wrong, apparently.

"I'm sorry for the interruption, my Lord," she said, stepping closer. "I was looking for something to eat."

"We have enough stew," said Shandra standing up. "Unless you still feel hungry, sir?"

"I'd greatly appreciate that, my Lord," Saqia put a smile on her face.

I shook my head, feeling uneasy, the way Saqia had eyed Shandra hadn't escaped my gaze.

Shandra stood up to search for a clean plate and a spoon, while the blue woman placed her chair next to mine and sat down, waiting.

I did my best to ignore the look in her virtually white eyes, turning my entire attention to my plate. I separated my vegetables, fished for a decent chunk of meat, placed it in my mouth and began chewing thoroughly. The next moment I felt a hand on my left knee, slowly travelling up my thigh. I almost choked.

"I was worried about you, my Lord," whispered Saqia, smiling knowingly.

I caught her hand midway up my thigh and placed it firmly on the table. She was still smiling when Shandra returned with a clean plate and a spoon.

"Are we still in danger, my Lord?" asked Saqia taking the spoon.

I noticed that she was trying to ignore Shandra, turning all her attention to me.

"No," I said calmly. "I've given the order to cancel the evacuation and recall everybody."

"That's a relief," said Saqia as she carefully probed the stew.

We ate silently. The moment of magic was gone.

I caught a few leering glances from Saqia but chose to ignore them, feeling increasingly uneasy. Shandra kept her eyes on her plate, carefully chewing each bite. Too carefully, I thought, wondering how to end this embarrassment.

A short tap on the door ended the silence. I was glad when one of the jaegers appeared and told me that Rhys had returned and was asking to see me.

"I'll meet him in my chambers," I said, and the jaeger left.

I stood up, trying to keep away from Saqia.

"Will you excuse me?" I asked, addressing Shandra. "State affairs…"

She nodded, placing her spoon on the table. Saqia carried on eating.

"If you'll help me to find my room, sir," said Shandra standing up too, "I'll be more comfortable there..."

"Sure!" I gave her a warm smile and led her out of the kitchen, leaving Saqia behind to finish her plate of stew.

We entered the corridor, and I carefully closed the door behind us. Shandra was silent all the way as we navigated the staircases, halls and corridors back to that part of the castle where my chambers were. I guessed she needed some time to adapt. Her back was still stiff and straight, but she now braved to meet my gaze without flinching, and once she even managed a shy smile.

"Please, wait here," I asked, opening the door of her room. "I must speak to this man. He might know how to help my friend."

"I will, sir," she nodded, entering.

I left Shandra in her room, much calmer now.

Bysh, my big dog, yelped like a small puppy when I opened the door. He licked my hands and face before he allowed Gwyn, the baby gryphon, to join in with the excitement. Once the animals had calmed down, I was able to shake Rhys's hand at last.

"I'm delighted to see you alive," I told him. "Have you any idea where you are being held in Vienna?"

"Why do you think I am in Vienna?" he asked puzzled. "I didn't realise I got that far."

"I got a letter demanding a ransom, and that letter led us to Vienna. John is with me," I explained. "I didn't know any other Sleepers who could help me liberate you."

"Do you know who's kidnapped me?"

"We do – it's my ex-wife Morvarid."

"You know so much more than I do!" exclaimed Rhys. "I'm being held in a steel cage in a tented wagon with no views of the outside. My cage is squeezed between the enclosures of a lion and a tiger, and the wagon is always locked. They only open the door slightly at dusk so I can't catch even the tiniest glimpse of the surroundings. The men who feed me and the cats always cover their faces, so I've never seen what they look like. They feed me vegetarian stuff, so it's impossible to make friends with my carnivorous neighbours."

"Have you any idea where you are?"

"No," said Rhys. "Sorry... They beat me unconscious in my flat, and ever since then, I've been either drugged and blindfolded or caged and covered."

Our hopes of tracing him in Vienna crumbled as he spoke. Morvarid was far more cautious and smarter than we had expected. Damn! She had left no loose ends for us to pick up! Despair and a sense of failure flooded me as I looked at Rhys, wondering if we still had any straws to grab at in this turmoil.

"But I'm just an ordinary jaeger – you're the Prince. I don't own anything. What does she want?" shrugged Rhys. "I don't even know her!"

"Haven't they told you?"

He shook his head.

"She wants Gwyn," I said. "To be precise, she wants Gwyn's heart."

"Why?!"

"My crazy ex-wife thinks she could get some magic artefact out of the gryphon's heart."

"Gwyn?" Rhys was petrified. "Is that even possible?"

"On the contrary. It's impossible, but she believes otherwise."

Rhys grew grim, and he lowered his gaze.

"Better let her kill me," he said firmly. "But don't harm Gwyn."

"I would prefer to save both of you," I said firmly. "Let's have a seat. You need to tell me everything, no matter how insignificant that small thing might seem to you. We've lost contact with my ex-wife in Vienna, but it might be possible to glue some pieces of information together? What do you see? What do you hear? What kind of food do you eat?"

We moved to the table and sat.

Rhys thought for some time. I stroked Bysh's head as he laid it on my lap.

"Have you been able to identify the language your kidnappers speak?" I asked him finally.

"No, but I'm certain it is not English or German."

Dead end there then.

"You're asking me about so many things..." he said after some time. "Not sure, but I think I'm in a circus. It's only speculation, but I'm sitting in a wagon with two exotic cats. Sometimes in the evenings, I hear snatches of music in the distance, but they never let either the tiger or lion out."

"That might be something..." I said. "We need to find a circus in Vienna. Is the wagon stationary, or is it moving?"

"Right now, we're moving," Rhys sounded disappointed. "We've been travelling for two days already, but I've no idea of the direction. Sorry..."

"Don't apologise," I said. "There's already a lot to think about. Maybe we'll be able to find some old posters. I don't believe there are many travelling circuses in the city so it might be relatively easy to spot. If we've got the name of it, maybe we could find the direction it's heading?"

Rhys shrugged.

"Maybe it is not that hopeless then. Tell me more about how you traced me to Vienna," he asked.

I briefly described all our adventures to him, starting from the visit to his flat. Rhys listened carefully but, with his limited knowledge, was unable to add anything.

"I think I was drugged when they grabbed me," he said. "I don't remember anything – it's just a blank page in my memory. I don't even remember crossing the Channel."

"I just don't understand why Morvarid took all that trouble to drag you across Europe. Wouldn't it have been better to hold you somewhere in the London suburbs, don't you think?"

"I can't understand that either," said Rhys. "Maybe she had her reasons?"

"John says she's rather eccentric. I have no memories of her at all."

Gwyn was twirling around like an overgrown kitten. He was almost two-thirds of the height of Bysh now but was twice as playful. He was growing fast.

"I must ask you to be extremely attentive. Even the smallest clue could bring us closer to where you are. Look at everything that comes your way. Maybe your cage has some markings, are there any trademarks or inspection labels? Phone numbers? Tags?" I asked Rhys after a small pause. "Maybe the tiger has a collar?"

"No, I haven't noticed anything," said Rhys. "I'll double check all that tonight."

"Be careful," I said. "Don't underestimate those predators, don't get too close."

"Don't worry," he smiled. "I'm a jaeger here. By the way, many thanks for taking the trouble to mount this operation. I honestly never thought that you'd attempt to rescue me. Now I have some hope."

"I think you'd do the same for me," I said seriously. "I had no hesitation as soon as we got the first clue."

"Gwyn, come!" Rhys stretched out his arms and the gryphon jumped onto his lap.

"He'll soon be too big for that," I observed.

Gwyn looked at me with his eagle eyes and produced a harsh cry. Rhys patted his head.

"There's only one thing I'd like to ask you," said Rhys. "Whatever bargains are made, whatever ransoms are agreed, never negotiate on Gwyn; even at the expense of my own life. I think he's far more important to the realm than I am."

"I'll never bargain on any life – yours or Gwyn's," I said. "But we do need to play it safe. Don't get into any trouble, and I'll do my best to bring you home."

Rhys put Gwyn on the ground, and the youngster immediately started running around.

"I want you to stay in the castle – take whichever room you fancy, and come to see me tomorrow, first thing in the morning. I'll need any information you have been able to get."

"Have you resolved your issues with Hel?" he asked.

"I think I have," I shrugged. "For the time being, at least. By the way, the western route to the castle across the mountains is blocked forever."

"What do you mean?"

"It's a waterfall now instead of the staircase, and the bridge has collapsed."

"Sounds like you had quite a battle."

"No, it was out of desperation," I smiled. "All right, go and get yourself comfortable."

Rhys stood up and whistled to his menagerie. Bysh and Gwyn dashed after him fooling about, and Rhys looked at them like a mother hen. He was a friend, and I was firm in my intention to save him, but hope now seemed even more ephemerous than before when we visited his wrecked flat. His body could by now be encaged anywhere in Europe. At least he still was alive. I distinctly recalled the horror and fear of my own kidnapping, and that spine-chilling feeling didn't leave me as I watched Rhys cross the room and disappear through the door, followed by Gwyn and Bysh. He seemed to be quite as normal at a glance, but I could clearly understand what kind of hopelessness hid behind his sad smile.

I listened to his footsteps, fading to the right down the corridor. Then I cried my helpless anger out aloud. We had seemed so close, but now everything was slipping away through my fingers like dry sand.

Circus? Was Morvarid related to a circus? That sounded crazy but not unlikely. I was sure John and I would have to look at that possibility. It might be nothing, but it was all we had.

I left my chambers with a troubled heart. I had another soul to calm and their fears to dissipate. A few seconds later, I stood in front of Shandra's door hesitantly, then I tapped and opened it.

She was sitting on her bed facing the door.

"I'm back," I announced, somewhat unnecessarily.

"Did you find what you were seeking, sir?" Shandra asked, standing up.

"No," I shook my head as I drew closer to her. "Everything is more complicated than I expected. But there's nothing I can do right now so we can go for a walk around and I can show you the castle a little."

"If that's what you wish, sir," Shandra looked at me calmly. "I'm ready."

"Let's go…"

She obediently followed me without asking any questions. I realised that the ice was melting, but still too slow. The true kind Shandra bravely holding a torch in that dark grotto was still far away, hiding behind a wall of fearful thorns. I didn't want to push her and kept my distance, hoping her real self would find a way back to me. I knew I must be patient.

We turned left and went down the corridor, our footsteps echoing between the empty walls. I had no plan where to start our little tour, nor did she take the lead. We just walked on.

The day outside was cheerful, and slivers of sunshine slipped through the narrow windows of the corridor, framed by heavy scarlet curtains. I was a poor guide with my absence of knowledge or memories, but Shandra didn't ask anything, and I was grateful for that.

The corridor ended with a wide staircase leading to the throne room. We took the stairs down, still silent. Shandra stopped at the bottom.

"Is this?" she began to whisper uncertainly, and then let her voice trail off.

"The throne room," I finished for her. "Let's go and have a look."

I took the lead towards the seat carved out of black basalt and covered with a white fur skin. Two large hearths were at either side of the throne, now cold with only traces of tar where flames had licked the rocks.

"As you wish, sir," I heard her whisper behind my back.

We went down the aisle. A cool breeze ruffled the dark purple curtains through the open windows, playing an intricate game of shadows with the flashes of sunshine. Sometimes it seemed like somebody was moving along the wall trying to keep up with us, but, every time I looked, the hall was empty.

I took the steps up the dais and turned back to face Shandra as I leant on the throne.

"Is this the place where you make your decisions and judge your people, sir?" she asked, still standing in the aisle.

She looked humble and uncertain, and my encouraging smile didn't help.

"It's only a seat, Shandra. Don't be afraid," I said, stretching out my hand. "Come closer, please. I'll show you."

She moved forward, hesitation in her every step and doubt painted all over her face.

"Don't be afraid," I repeated. "Come..."

She looked at my throne as if it was the nest of rattling snakes.

"Look!" I slipped my hands into my pockets and sat down. "It's only a seat—nothing to be afraid of. Come closer, Shandra. Have a seat next to me. There's plenty of space here."

"I don't know if it's appropriate, sir," she murmured, approaching the throne.

"Please..." I took her hand. "Have a seat with me."

Shandra carefully sat down with her spine rigid and muscles tense, ready to spring to her feet at any moment and run away. Her reaction saddened me, and I realised that the throne hall wasn't the best place to begin showing her around. We must get out of the castle.

"Let's get outside," I offered standing up. "It would be nice to walk around the capital in such beautiful weather."

Shandra nodded, and I hurried down the aisle, looking at the purple curtains trembling in the light breeze. Only halfway down did I realise that I alone. Shandra was still standing next to the throne clutching something in her hand.

"You've lost something, sir," she said, her eyes wide and her voice trembling.

"What is it?" I returned to the dais.

"Here…" she extended her hand. It was the piece of parchment Seisyll had given to me that morning – it must have slipped out of my pocket when I pulled my hand out of it.

Shandra took the steps down the dais and handed me the parchment.

"Thank you," I put the piece of paper into my breast pocket. "My brother gave this to me earlier, and I nearly lost it. Silly me… Let's go outside."

I took her hand, and we went down the aisle, followed by the moving shadows and flashes of sunshine. Shandra visibly relaxed outside. We crossed the yard and turned left, meeting no one on our way.

The capital stretched ahead of us – magnificent and empty. We went between the inns and bakeries, shops of merchants and forges – all closed and empty. It was an eerie experience. Vacant houses looked at us with hollow eyes of windows, patiently waiting for their owners to return. We carried on through a few cobblestone-paved streets and squares before turning left again and returned to one of the gardens that enclosed the castle.

We sat down in the shade of a large chestnut tree. Shandra was almost back to her former self. For the first time since our return to Chadrack, she called me Kyleb and blushed immediately, lowering her eyes. We talked a lot, laughed a lot and grew sad together as we unwillingly touched on the sores in our souls. But the periods of silence were brief.

All the time, I felt someone's eyes were upon us. On several occasions, I furtively glanced around but was unable to spot anybody spying on us. I didn't want Shandra to become alarmed so continued with all that sweet nonsense talk, joking and laughter, hoping that she wouldn't notice my growing agitation. I was happy to have her real old self back.

Later in the afternoon, we paid a quick visit to the kitchen and filled a basket with smoked meat, vegetables, cheese and apples. I didn't want the annoying presence of Saqia again so led us back to the gardens where we could hide between shrubs and fountains and eat our meal undisturbed.

I continued to sense spying eyes at the back of my head, and we changed our hidden position several times. I did my best to keep my worries concealed.

Later in the evening, I took Shandra back to her room.

"That was a lovely day," she said, standing in the doorway. "Thank you for everything."

I noticed that she omitted the usual "sir".

"Thank you, Shandra," I said sincerely. "Thank you very much for staying."

I kissed her goodnight and left.

Back in my room, I took the piece of parchment out of my breast pocket and carefully spread it on my bed. Nine numbers were scribbled on it, and I meditated over them for nearly fifteen minutes until they were firmly set in my brain. Then I dropped the parchment on the cobblestone floor in the hearth and ignited it using my Ring. Seconds later, it was gone.

I had trouble falling asleep. It had been a long day full of events – Seisyll, Rhys, Shandra. I allowed everything to circle around my head as I slowly drifted away.

Although the morning was grey in Vienna, it wasn't raining. I jumped out of bed and wrote down the numbers on a sheet of paper while they still were fresh in my memory.

I still hadn't made up my mind how to feel about Seisyll's request. A call seemed somewhat unthreatening although I couldn't understand why it was so important to him – important enough to threaten me with a full-scale war against all of Rehen. I suppressed the urge of consulting John. I had no idea how close he was to my sister Keely. Would she share the secrets of the realm with him, her husband? I had no clues. He might be a lousy adviser, and I was reluctant to give him too many of my secrets. I didn't have a clue if I could trust Keely with this either.

Trust no one, especially the family – that was the first advice Hawa the Keeper had given me.

A call, on the other hand, seemed fairly innocent.

I found my phone and keyed in the numbers. I listened to the long beeps for nearly a minute, but nobody answered. Maybe I'd got the numbers wrong? I dialled again. The long beeps drilled into my ear again, and I almost lost patience. Finally, they were interrupted by a click, and a frail male voice answered.

"*Hola*!"

I felt lost. This must be the wrong number…

"Seisyll?" I asked uncertainly.

The voice at the other end was overcome by a long bout of terrible coughing. I waited patiently.

"You must be Kyleb," said the man when his cough had finally subsided. "I've been waiting for your call."

"How can I be sure that you're who you said you were?" I asked.

"I haven't said anything yet," observed the man. "But I like the way you're thinking. It must be in your blood. No, you can't be sure, and neither can I, even if we met face to face. You need a bleeding wound to be carried across, only then can you be sure."

"I'm familiar with the concept of tagging," I said dryly. I wasn't going through any form of flagellation for him, even if he asked for it. About that, I was adamant.

"Very good…" the man chuckled slipping into another bout of coughing. "Then you must be aware that in our current situation it would be useless. We're too far away from each other. The matter of trust will always be an issue for us, Kyleb. Take everything with a pinch of salt. I will do the same."

I fought against my rising anger. The voice on the other end of the line did not fit the image of Seisyll in any way. I couldn't understand what kind of a joke this was. Seisyll had asked me to call this number, and I had. Now this strange man was haranguing me about trust. Who was he? How was he related to Seisyll? I was slowly losing patience.

"What do you want?" I asked when the man had finally finished wasting his breath lecturing me.

"Not too much," he said. "I need a sign from you that you made the call."

"What's that?"

"I am sure you've seen the cliffs towering above the waterfall, haven't you?" the man asked.

"I have."

"Did you notice the piles of oiled firewood on top of them?"

"No…" I admitted. I'd never looked that closely.

"It doesn't matter – they're there," the man hacked before continuing. "I'd like you to light them tomorrow morning."

"And give a sign to somebody I don't know?" I was outraged at the suggestion.

"Yes, it's a sign," the man continued his slow monotonous mumbling. "It's a sign for your army to return to the capital immediately. The messengers you send wouldn't be that quick.

You'll send a sign to your army, and I'll get the proof I need. You're not risking anything."

I grew even more suspicious, but I couldn't simply just ring off.

"Your request is a little complicated," I told him. "I have no access to the waterfall from the capital. And travelling around the plateau will take a few weeks if not longer. I can't see how this can be done any quicker."

The man chuckled and then began coughing again, and I had to wait again until the cough triggered by the chuckle subsided.

"I guess, it won't be too difficult for you to create a bolt of lightning or two with your Ring," he said finally.

"I'll think about it," I promised quickly, making an attempt to silence his frail speech which was already irritating my ear.

"Yes," he said. "Think seriously, please. May I remind you that the family don't like Sleepers?"

That sounded like a threat, not for the first time.

"I've got the message," I said grimly. "I'll think about it."

"Good. Then I'll await your decision."

The man hung without any goodbye.

I didn't genuinely believe he was Seisyll. Or was he? The thought was irrational, contradicting the image of Seisyll I had recently seen in my chambers. That Seisyll couldn't be a fake – he wore a Ring. I knew that the Ring was genuine – it had all the properties. But that frail voice I had heard over the phone just didn't fit. What kind of game was this?

Could I ask John? Maybe...but I wasn't willing to reveal this out before giving it a proper thought. There was a part of the story that was still missing, and I decided to postpone the chat until those missing pieces became clearer. I had more pressing things to discuss with John than to wade through the muddy waters of assumptions.

I washed my face and brushed my teeth before calling John.

"Any news?" he asked at once.

"Not as much as I expected," I sighed.

"Have you met Rick, at least?" he demanded.

"Yes, but he's no idea of his whereabouts. His best guess is that he's being held in a travelling circus in some van between the cages of a lion and a tiger," I said. "And he feels they've been on the move for two days now but in an unknown direction."

"Shit! She's fled the city! But you have a firm proof that Rick is still alive. Not too much..." John agreed. "We may have to do our own research on these bits of information until we get something more useful."

"Could we have a look to see if some old posters are still hanging around?" I suggested. "If it is a circus, they should have given some performances, shouldn't they?"

"I was about to suggest the same," said John. "Let's start looking around *Prater*. It seems like the right place for a circus."

"Agreed," I nodded. "Let's meet at the gates."

"Okay. When?"

"10 o'clock? I need breakfast."

"Sharp. See you then…"

I quickly checked my watch. It was nearly nine. *Hurry! Hurry!*

I quickly dressed and paid a quick trip to the canteen to build my energy with coffee, scrambled eggs and sausages. While I ate, I kept wondering about the request from that strange man. He wanted a signal to be sent across Chadrack. What kind of a sign? Was it supposed to represent a distress call? Indeed, it looked like this. But I didn't trust the man.

I was vulnerable, a sitting duck in the castle without any protection. Seisyll had proved this perfectly. But why had he given me the number of that man?

I had no time for a lengthy deliberation. The clock was ticking, and every passing minute took Rick away from Vienna in an unknown direction. I topped up my breakfast with a double espresso and ran out, leaving my key at reception.

I joined the flow of people down the street who were reading newspapers, drinking coffee or having their breakfast snacks on the way.

The tube station was busy, and I quickly bought a ticket from the ticket machine and took the escalator. The train arrived in no time, fully packed, and I had considerable trouble squeezing on but chose not to wait for the next one – time was pressing. A few stations later, I was carried out with the crowd, but it was my stop anyway.

The street in front of the tube station was very different from that of the Viennese weekend elegance – cars, buses and trams were racing in all directions in the weekday morning traffic. Trains rumbled on the bridge above the station as I turned left and followed the route to *Prater*.

I crossed the street and rushed through the now empty alley. John was waiting for me at the gate.

"So, Rick has no idea where he is?" John's first question was obvious.

"No, unfortunately. This is bad for us," I mumbled following him through the gate. "It's all based on assumptions. He is caged between the two big cats, and occasionally he has heard snatches of music. That's all we have right now. Sorry, no other clues. They even only feed him at night, making sure he cannot take the slightest glimpse of any surroundings."

"But then he might even be outside Austria by now..." John was as optimistic as always.

"Yes, by now..." I trailed off, suddenly realising the full difficulty of our task. "They began moving several days ago, just about before that failed demonstration when Morvarid disappeared, and they've been on the go since then."

"Well..." John stopped. "The whole thing is crystal clear now – if we succeed in finding the name of that circus, maybe we could work out which way they are going and the estimated time and place of their next show. If Rick is there, we may have an opportunity to get him."

"Too many ifs in our plan..." I sighed.

"Anyway, we have no other," he said firmly.

"I think we should split up," I said, stopping in front of the magician statue. "We'll be able to cover a bigger area."

"Good idea," said John. "Which street do you want to choose – right or left?"

"Left..."

"Ok. Call me when you spot the first poster," John turned around, heading right.

I walked away from the magician. The grey clouds hung low, and gusts of chilly wind swept me along the way as I turned into the street, leaving *Madame Tussauds* on my left.

The *Prater* was empty and quiet on a workday morning. I made my way past the stationary carousels, water rides and still closed cafés, feeling like a ghost in a motionless land of painted happiness. Nothing moved – the lights were out, and no music played. I knew that the banshee had gone away with Morvarid, but still I felt some eerie presence pervading the air, and I carried on, hunched over. I had no idea what it was. It just didn't feel right.

I carried on, peering along every sidewalk but didn't spot any posters. The traditional merry-go-round, the spaceships and the teapot rides were lifeless and empty. I could find no hint of a travelling circus performing anywhere – there were no adverts or posters of any kind to be found.

My phone was silent too. Seemingly, John had had no results either.

A few yawning men were chatting in the distance, most likely they lived in the *Prater* – I had spotted a few surprisingly ordinary looking houses (who would want to live in a carnival?). I gathered my courage to ask them about travelling circuses, but they hurried away before I could get any closer.

An old lady was hanging her laundry to dry in the wind in front of one of those houses, and she looked at me and smiled. I returned her smile.

"*Wonach suchst du, junger Mann?*" she demanded.

"Excuse me," I put a polite, silly smile on my face. "I am looking for a circus for my children. Do you know of any travelling circus nearby?"

A hint of surprise passed her face as she measured me with her gaze. Did I look too young to have kids?

"Sorry, I not speak English good," she said with a terrible German accent and obvious difficulty. "No circus in *Prater*. Was circus last week in *Meiereistrasse,* now gone. Will be another in two weeks."

"Pity," I said. "Do you know the name of that circus, the one that was in the *Meiereistrasse*?"

"Not sure," old lady shook her head, trying to remember.

I waited patiently.

"The Black Forest or the Dark Forest, I don't remember," she said finally and added, "Who pays attention to those travelling circuses..."

"*Vielen Dank,*" I managed to thank her in German.

She nodded at me and returned to her laundry. Still, I could feel her gaze on me as I walked away.

I slowly went around the corner before I fished my phone from my pocket. John answered immediately.

"Any luck?" he was quick to ask.

"No posters so far, but I met a nice old lady who told me that last week there was a circus called the Black Forest or the Dark Forest. She wasn't sure. Do you think it's worth beginning to explore using those names?"

"With all due respect to your old lady, she may be too old to be reliable. It might have been a circus that was here last month or even last year," he didn't sound too encouraging. "You can't rely on her old memory."

"Have you found anything yet?" I asked, hopefully.

"No... There are no posters of any kind. I think I'll try some streets outside of the *Prater*."

"Ok, keep on looking. I'll go back to the hotel and try to find out how good that lady's memory is. Anyway, we've nothing more substantial..."

"Fine. Let's keep in touch!"

I put the phone back and hurried from the *Prater*. The place was giving me the creeps, and I was glad to leave it entirely to John.

The tube was slightly less crowded on my way back. I squeezed into a corner, patiently waiting for my station, looking at no one. The fate of Rick was at stake, I knew this, but the frail voice I had heard over the phone continued to haunt my ears. What kind of a game was Seisyll playing? Who was that man I had called this morning? Where was he? And what hidden meaning was behind his request? The feeling was terrible, but I still hadn't decided what was worse – to follow the lead Seisyll was offering or to face the odium of the family be despised by all the people. And I was running out of time to make that decision.

I left the tube at the *Karlsplatz* and hurried uphill without paying attention to anyone. A chilly wind pushed at my back, and I was glad to close the door and leave it behind. My room had already been serviced. I turned on the TV to keep me company in the background and began to ponder in front of my tablet, struggling with the hotel's incredibly slow Wi-Fi.

Both names – the Black Forest and the Dark Forest – were in use. The memory of the old lady proved to be not as bad as John had anticipated, and I wished her every blessing as I dug deeper into the world wide web.

I rejected the Black Forest quite quickly since this circus had given performances in French Toulouse only two days ago. They couldn't be our guys.

The Dark Forest seemed much more complicated. The circus had no web page, and I had to dig deep into local social groups and internet portals, which was even further complicated by my limited knowledge of German. That was tricky despite the help of online translation services.

All this time my phone remained silent. Apparently, John's meanderings around the *Prater* hadn't brought any success.

Finally, I managed to trace the Dark Forest in Zurich, Vaduz and then later in Linz between the kidnapping of Rick in London and our arrival in Vienna. It seemed they were in a hurry and desperate for money, giving only one performance at each location despite fully sold-out tickets, perfect feedback and requests from the public for more performances. That was strange for a circus. They had rushed to Vienna but weren't performing there – that's why we couldn't find any posters. I wondered which grapevine that old lady had used to find out about the Dark

Forest. I was sure I wouldn't ever be able to find that out.

I had a strong feeling that this circus was indeed related to Morvarid, but I didn't find any mention of performances featuring a lion or tiger. Then I remembered Rick saying that the cats never left their cages. I phoned John.

"Any luck?" I demanded as soon as he answered.

"No," his voice was quiet and grim, trying to hide his disappointment. "What about you?"

"I've stopped searching for the Black Forest. They performed in Toulouse two days ago, so I don't think they're our guys. The other circus was really hard to trace, but I've been able to follow part of their route across Europe through Switzerland and Lichtenstein to Austria. The Dark Forest has given just one performance at each stop despite requests from the public, and they've not performed in Vienna at all. That's why we couldn't find any posters."

"That's very interesting," said John. "Your old lady wasn't as useless as I thought then..."

"It's strange for a travelling circus to stay in Vienna but not give a performance, don't you think?"

"Really... Unless they had more important things to do here than to perform!"

"Exactly!" I exclaimed. "That's why I think they're our guys."

"Where are they going next?"

"It's a bit vague. They've advertised a show in Zakopane next week."

"Zakopane? Where's that?"

"Poland, just across the Tatra Mountains."

"I don't carry a map in my head," said John. "Are there many ways to reach Zakopane?"

"You can always go round in circles, but the direct route is quite clear," I shrugged. "The distance isn't great, only around two hundred and fifty miles – I've checked. We'd be able to come back any moment if the lead proved to be false or Rick gets something more specific about his whereabouts."

John was silent for a few moments.

"Do you think it's time for us to go?" he asked.

"I think so," I said. "It's the only lead we have..."

"Okay, let's give it a go," agreed John. "Start packing your things and check out of the hotel. I'll rent a car, grab my stuff and meet you downstairs."

"Very well, I'll meet you there..."

I packed my scant belongings in no more than twenty minutes. I stood in the middle of the room with my luggage in one hand looking around to make sure I had collected everything when my phone rang, displaying those nine numbers I had keyed earlier that morning.

I put the luggage on the floor.

"Hello?" I answered with some irritation. "I'm a little busy right now. What is it?"

"I won't take up too much of your time, Kyleb," the frail voice said at the other end.

"You've already told me about the firewood," I interrupted him. "I've taken that into consideration. What else do you want?"

"I want to remind you about the consequences of not lighting it," said the man.

"You'll tell everyone that I am a Sleeper," I caught myself sounding rude but couldn't help with it – the man was just too bothersome. "I've got it."

"There would be a war, Kyleb," he calmly said after I had finished my tirade. "I'd have to kill you and place brother Shane in Wagorn since he is the next in the line of succession. Do you know brother Shane, Kyleb?"

Of course, I hadn't the slightest idea what he was talking about.

"You may not value your own life, Kyleb," he continued after I failed to answer his question. "But I'll tell you about brother Shane. He calls himself the King of the Plains of Cobu and the wastelands of Wurgh. It's a huge piece of land in the East, Kyleb, a very big area with the savage tribes of Hayli roaming it back and forth. Hayli respect nothing but brutal force, and that's the way brother Shane is ruling them. The hordes of Genghis Khan would pale into insignificance if Hayli emerged out of the wastelands."

"What's to stop them from doing that right now?" I asked when he stopped to catch his breath.

"Only two natural obstacles, Kyleb," the frail voice trembled. "Patna and its lava flows and the Bloody Sea. With your death, I would have enough ships to get Hayli to Wagorn. The ghouls will seem no more threatening than annoying mosquitos if Hayli gets loose. And they will do so if brother Shane claims his right after your death. Have you heard the prophecy?"

"Which one?" I asked. "About the rivers of gold and blood that will flood the realm with the new King?"

"Yes," the man paused before continuing. "I think it's about brother Shane. That seems very likely if events evolved down that route."

"That wouldn't be my problem if you'd already killed me," I reminded him.

"That's true," chuckled the frail voice. "But it would be a disaster for your people, for the souls you care for or love. Go to the yard tomorrow morning and look at your capital, Kyleb. It's been empty since you moved your people to safety. You care for them. There will be no safety if tribes of Hayli come out of the wastelands. And there would be rivers of blood running down the streets of your capital. Are you ready to let that happen, Kyleb?"

The question hit me unprepared.

"Why should I believe you?" I asked.

"Because I'm telling you the truth," said the man. "You'll have plenty of opportunities to check the story, but now let's build some trust. Kyleb, light that damned firewood in the morning, and let's pave the way to glory. Remember that my men are closer than your army if you choose to do the opposite. You and your men will be dead by nightfall."

"That's a strange way to build trust," I observed.

"You may find a lot of strange things in Rehen," chuckled the frail voice. "I hope you'll choose wisely now because you know the consequences, Kyleb. You've said that you're in a hurry. I won't hold you up any longer. I'll wait for your sign in the morning."

He hung up, and I angrily tossed the phone onto the bed, but I barely had time to drown in doubt before it started ringing again. It was John.

"Are you ready?" he asked. "I'm waiting downstairs."

"Just give me a second," I grabbed the luggage and rushed out.

I considered my guesses and assumptions again while waiting for the lift. If I was wrong about the Dark Forest, it might cost Rick's life. If I was right, it might cost both mine and John's life as well. I doubted if Morvarid, who had made so much effort and taken so much trouble to capture Rick and insanely taken him across Europe, would ever leave him unguarded. If those guards were armed, we might have a serious problem.

I decided not to mention the phone calls to John – they weren't related to our quest in any way, and I still couldn't make my mind up about the role of my sister Keely in my problems. Her gift – Saqia, was too persistent, too pushy. Was this her own initiative or as ordered by Keely? I couldn't be sure.

I checked out of the hotel. John was sitting in a grey economy sedan just suitable for our purpose – not too big and not too shiny.

"Jump in!" he said, opening the door.

I dropped my luggage in the trunk and closed the door, ready to go.

"Which way?" asked John starting the engine. "How do you spell that Zakopane?"

I checked my tablet and spelt it out to him. John weaved some magic on the GPS navigator, and a pleasant female voice began giving us directions for the nearest route in perfect English.

We turned right at the *Karlsplatz,* moving slowly with the flow of traffic. A soft drizzle began to spray from the low grey clouds as I looked at the passing crowds, now blotchy with colourful umbrellas.

"You look worried," observed John turning right in front of the *Stadtpark.*

"I am worried," I acknowledged. "I've just realised how risky this business is. There are only two of us, and we have no idea how many men Morvarid has. We might fail to return. They might kill us."

"Don't panic," John did his best to sound encouraging. "We'll do it safely. I hate to rush without reconnaissance, and we'll keep a distance until an opportunity arises. We can still call the police if the situation does become hopeless. We'll do everything safely. Or would you prefer to abandon the search and leave Rick to her mercy?"

"No, of course, not!" I shook my head. The suggestion was ridiculous. "Only remember that I have no experience in such things."

John did have the experience, I was sure. He was a bounty hunter who kidnapped Sleepers, and I guessed he had been in a situation or two that required military combat behind him.

"Trust me," he assured me. "We'll liberate your friend if he's there."

I nodded, but the word "if" in his statement created another cascade of doubts. What if I was wrong? What if we were leaving Rick somewhere in Vienna, cutting off any possibility for Morvarid to contact me. I looked at John. His face was calm; his frowning only slightly as he negotiated the traffic.

The drizzle stopped as we left the centre. Charming and elegant central Vienna streets gradually changed into the suburban, with lovely one-storey buildings and green gardens. Later these were left behind too. Endless fields of crops stretched away on both sides of the road.

"How are things in Chadrack?" John asked after some time. "Never had a proper chance to ask."

"The capital's empty right now," I responded, stirring from my gloomy thoughts. "I ordered an evacuation when Hel approached. Nobody's come back yet..."

"It must feel lonely..."

"It does," I admitted thinking about Shandra sleeping in her room.

I wondered if the jaegers had already reached Bedwyr. How many days would it take for the army to return? Seisyll was still waiting somewhere nearby. I recalled the threats of the frail voice, but I still had no idea how that man was related to Seisyll.

"How's Keely?" I asked.

"She's doing fine," John smiled, keeping his eyes on the road.

"Have you ever met Seisyll?" I risked asking.

"Yes," he said. "Why are you asking?"

"I'm just curious," I lied. "It's always good to know your neighbours, and I have no one else to ask."

"Seisyll wears the Citrine, the Master of Wealth, and you could call him the god of merchants," said John. "He could easily talk his way into Wagorn and sit on the throne, but Seisyll is the youngest in the family, and the rules of succession are quite strict."

"So, he's a liar?" I demanded. I knew I couldn't trust him.

"On the contrary," John shook his head. "He never tells lies, especially while he's wearing the Ring. His strength is in negotiations, but he always tells the truth. It might be not the truth you want to hear, or he might withhold some part of it, but if the words have left his mouth, you should believe them. His power seems to be more like a curse, I think. Even Keely has stronger magic than him. But nobody can outdo Seisyll if a deal needs to be done. His Ring guides him safely through all the dangerous currents under the surface. Has he offered something to you?"

The question was a tricky one. My sister Keely was his wife and the head of the neighbouring kingdom of Porlok in Rehen. She was keen to build an alliance with me, and more than once, she had suggested leaving Seisyll out of it. I hadn't asked why. It seemed to be a slippery slope to speak with John about Seisyll any further. He might tell his wife everything, and I wouldn't like to upset Keely.

"No!" I shook my head a little too vigorously. I hoped he hadn't noticed that as he looked at the road ahead.

John didn't comment.

I watched the vast fields passing by on my right with countless wind power stations mesmerising my gaze with the random movements of the wind blades and grew silent. John glanced at me a couple of time and decided not to disturb my moment of meditation.

Dark clouds rose on the eastern horizon when we reached the bridge across the Danube.

"Should we stay here?" asked John looking at the red roofs of Bratislava stretching out on the other side.

"No," I told him. "We're two days behind already. Let's go as far towards the mountains as we can. We'll look for a place to sleep there."

"As you wish," he shrugged. "I hope we'll be able to find a motel."

"We'll see…" I mumbled as we travelled across the bridge.

We stopped only briefly on our way to fill up at a petrol station and buy some groceries then we rushed across the city, leaving its boundary half an hour later.

The dusk began to spread its grey wings quite early because of the clouds above.

"We can't drive through the night, you know," John mumbled. "We have to find a place where we can rest."

"I know," I said earnestly. "We'll stop if we find a motel on our way or we could sleep in the car..."

"A motel would be a better option for us," observed John. "Sleeping in a car is dangerous. You never know what or who might wake you up in the middle of the night and more than likely it wouldn't correspond with any convenient circumstances in Rehen."

"Guess you are right. Let's start looking..."

We drove into the broken foot of the mountain range, which was mainly woods and meadows rather than bare rocks. The landscape changed quickly, but we had no time to look at the view.

The satnav led us from the main road through some unnamed narrow serpentine, as we crossed the first range of the mountains.

We passed through several small villages scattered randomly on both sides of the road but found no sign of a motel or any other type of accommodation. It was getting dark.

"I can't stand it any longer," said John turning right onto a dirt road and going a little deeper into the forest. "Let's sleep here."

We crossed the woods and John parked in a small meadow, slightly off the road. We depleted our grocery reserve almost immediately as we attacked it like two hungry wolves.

John went out to answer the call of nature while I stashed the garbage away and reclined the seats.

"There's a stream nearby," he announced on return. "But it's too dark to get closer."

"We'll have a look tomorrow," I told him stretching my legs in my seat.

John got in and locked the doors. He was a big man, and his knees were resting against the steering wheel, but he didn't complain.

"Bearable," he murmured, putting his folded jacket under his head in place of a pillow.

The statement required no comment.

Soon the loud snoring of John filled the car. I turned over several times, trying to find a more comfortable position. Then at some point, I slipped into the darkness.

My mind still was wandering in the shadows somewhere between the two worlds when a quiet tap on my door brought it back to focus. I did not attempt to resist. There was a prolonged period of silence. I could already feel my body and move my muscles, still listening to the silence. Then the barely audible tap on my door repeated. It couldn't be Seisyll! He hadn't been that polite last time. Was it Shandra?

I quickly jumped into my trousers pants and put my shirt on.

"Come in!"

Rhys squeezed through the door.

"Sorry to disturb you at such an early hour..." he began to apologise.

"What's happened?" I interrupted him. It must be serious if he was prepared to risk waking up another Sleeper. Luckily, the time was appropriate.

"You asked me to tell you if something happened. I don't know how to explain this," he said, closing the door. "We didn't move anywhere today. I heard a few strange cries in the early morning, but there was only silence after that. Nobody showed up to in the evening to feed the cats or me. And we haven't moved."

"That's very strange," I said, scratching my head. "Are you in a city somewhere or out in the countryside?"

"It's too quiet for a city. I could hear some birds twittering, but no people talking, no music, nothing…"

"Any sounds of cars moving?"

"Somewhere in the distance. Rarely."

"Indeed, that's very strange," I murmured looking at him.

Damn! It would be much more difficult to find them hiding somewhere in the woods. I cursed in my mind, keeping my face straight – there was no need to place additional stress on Rhys; he was already too worried. It seemed that Morvarid was winning, but I couldn't give up that easily.

"We're coming after you, don't worry. I can't tell you exactly how far away we are, but we will be getting closer to you tomorrow," my voice was calm, and my face was straight as I said this. "Just stay in the middle of your cage where the cats can't reach you through the bars."

"I know," Rhys nodded. "The bars are holding, and I think they will hold."

"Just stay alive. We'll find you."

"Thank you," he said, looking humbly at me. "I don't know how I'll ever be able to repay you for this."

"I think you'd do the same for me if required. I hope we manage to reach you in time."

He shrugged and smiled sadly then turned back towards the door.

"Rhys!" I exclaimed.

He stopped.

"Try to nap as much as you can during the day – I know this sounds odd, but I want you to listen while you're on Earth carefully. If you hear anything other than birds twittering, please let me know at once," I said seriously.

"Ok. I'll do that. I never thought it was possible to cross the barrier during the daytime..."

"You've never tried."

"That's true..."

He left.

The news Rhys had brought were unsettling. What had happened? Were they hiding? It was one thing to trace a travelling circus following posters around a city, but it was an entirely different thing to spot a few tented lorries somewhere in the wild woods on quite a big mountain range. I could understand why Morvarid was hiding. But why they weren't feeding their animals then? Short of supplies?

I was pacing my chambers with dark thoughts plaguing my mind when a quiet tap on the door brought me back to reality. Rhys again?

"Come in!"

The door opened, and Carwyn appeared in the doorway carrying the usual bowl of water and fresh towels.

"Good morning, Carwyn!" I was glad to see the old butler.

"Good morning, my Lord!" he bowed. "It's great to see you at home..."

He put the water and towels down in the usual place.

"Is Bedwyr back as well?" I asked. "I'd like to speak with him at once."

"No, my Lord," Carwyn shook his head. "It's a two-day journey to the Braaid. I met the jaegers in the forest yesterday, and they told me it's safe to return. I had been staying in the cabin of my late parents, not too far from the capital. I came back at once to get everything ready for your return, but you were quicker than me, my Lord."

"I'm glad you are back, Carwyn," I smiled at the old butler.

"There's been a lot of changes here, my Lord," he smiled back.

"What do you mean?"

"You destroyed the bridge, and the waterfall looks different. You've built a great defence for Chadrack, my Lord!" Carwyn nodded happily.

I didn't share his enthusiasm.

"But there's been one more change, Carwyn, that you may not be aware of," I told him seriously. "Lady Shandra is in the guest room just next door. Please, make sure she is treated the same way as you treat me."

"Yes, my Lord! With great pleasure," he nodded, still smiling. "It will be as you wish. Would you like me to serve her? Or do you think it would be more appropriate for my wife to do that?"

"It might be a good idea," I agreed. "Maybe she'd feel more comfortable with a woman..."

"My wife will do it, my Lord. I'll tell her immediately."

"Good..." I thanked him. "It's so good to have you back..."

Carwyn bowed.

"Where would you like to have your breakfast, my Lord?"

"The dining room will be appropriate, I think..."

"Will Lady Shandra be joining you there?"

"I hope she will..."

"It will be ready as soon as possible, my Lord!"

"Thank you, Carwyn."

He bowed again before leaving.

I knew it was time to make the decision which I could postpone no longer. I wasn't ready. Seisyll had asked me to call the frail man. The frail man had asked me to light the firewood and give a signal to my army. He made it clear that another army was waiting nearby, and my failure to comply would bring death to everybody in the capital – not so many though if we were to rely on numbers, only we were not dull statistics. The list included Jesper and his jaegers, Carwyn and his wife, Shandra and me. The frail man hadn't explained why he needed the fire lit, but I wasn't ready to sacrifice lives because of that lack of knowledge. It was a leap of faith, and I felt I must make it. If Seisyll wanted me dead, he had had more than one chance to slit my throat. It was something else that he was after, and I was running out of time to find it out what that was.

I went to the balcony and looked out over rooftops of the city, running uphill from the castle to the distant temple of Qu'mun, halfway up the slope of the mountain. A few chimneys were spitting smoke into the morning sky – some of the citizens were already at home preparing something for breakfast, and I realised that the list of casualties might be much longer if I failed to comply.

I reached into my Ring and brought out the blue sphere of Destiny in front of me. The castle obscured my view of the waterfall and the cliffs towering at its sides, but I didn't need to see them directly. The firewood was visible in the sphere.

The piles were large enough to serve as pyres, but I waved away that disturbing thought. I searched for ways to ignite them. The frail man had suggested a bolt of lightning would do the job. I looked closer. The firewood was piled over a pool of black oil carved into the rock and shielded with cloth from the rain. It was held in place by five metal rods anchored into the cliff, and it seemed that lightning was indeed a perfect solution. Still, the sphere warned me as I scrolled the timelines of probability – a random strike could blast the rock and destroy the cliffs without lighting the wood, without sending a signal to my army. Was that the expected outcome of my clumsiness?

I cursed. Indeed, it felt like a trick. Seisyll hadn't told me enough for me to trust him. I must find another solution.

I expanded the view of gathering clouds around the capital at the same time. I might have no army in the city, but I had the Ring! Seisyll had made a big mistake in helping me to charge it. I knew what powers I could unleash.

I waited a few more minutes. The sky grew dark, with thick clouds swirling above the capital. I had no idea where Seisyll and his men were hiding, but he said they would be near. The Master of Destiny couldn't find him for me – I had to act blindly.

It was an eerie sight watching the giant storm swirling slowly in complete silence. I moved its epicentre a little to the south and unleashed all the static electricity it had on the forest. It was a blind shot, but I tried to cover as wide an area as possible.

The cloudburst was deafening as countless thunderbolts hit the woods with the tallest trees bursting into splinters. I had to shield my eyes from the bright flashes but didn't drop the blue sphere – I wasn't done with this yet. Hurricane winds followed, battering what remained of the woods after the thunderstorm had ceased. I raised a few twisters to scout the area, levelling the forest to the ground. Seisyll's men were gone if they had been there. I might have killed returning Chadrackans as well if they had been sheltering in those woods. I hoped they hadn't stayed outside the city when they were that close to home. Nobody could have survived that storm if I had by chance hit anybody with all that power. Then I dropped the sphere. The silence was abrupt and deafening.

Seisyll had asked for lightning, and now he had it! But not the way he had wanted it. I wouldn't let him catch me off guard again.

I looked at the storm slowly dissipating in front of me. The clouds were thinning without dropping a single drop of rain. The flashes of lightning had ceased long before this. The centennial trees outside the castle lay flat with smokes and flames still rising here and there where the lightning bolts had managed to ignite the wood.

Only now did I notice jaegers gathering in the yard below the balcony. Some of them had crossbows at the ready, pointing at the gate.

"Are we under attack again, my Lord?" asked Jesper.

"Not yet," I told him. "Close all the gates, and I want them guarded. I don't want any more Mordakans in my yard!"

"It will be as you wish, my Lord," said Jesper and began directing his men.

I looked at the chaos in the yard. We had too few men to act as a fully-fledged garrison, but our walls would help us, and the Mordakans could no longer enjoy any further advantage of surprise. The tall forest on the left bank of the river, which had served them as a good cover last time, was lying in piles of smoking debris. This would make for an arduous approach for the Mordakans, and anyone on the walls would easily spot them. No more surprises there. The jaegers could hold the defence, and I could organise another similar lightning storm to repel the attack. Seisyll had made a mistake. We would be able to maintain the defence until Bedwyr brought the army of Chadrack back.

I only hoped the Mordakans would be wise enough not to return, but I was ready if Seisyll chose to do so.

I passed my gaze across the empty capital when thousands of crows unexpectedly streamed out of every corner of the city walls. The black streaks of shiny wings joined into a monstrous whirlpool south of the capital, slowly circling clockwise above the debris in complete silence.

I froze only for a second – my mysterious menace was back! Was it Seisyll's doing? My previous encounters with the crows had been unsettling but seemed more like a challenge rather than a real threat. Were they building an attack this time?

I quickly scanned the rooftops of the empty capital – a stream of the jet black birds was steadily flowing down the streets, rising into the sky and joining the thousands of others circling slowly outside the walls.

For a few minutes, I stood clutching the railings of the balcony and looked at the avian gathering. Had it been caused by my thunderstorm? Had I hit someone responsible for the crows? I must find out!

The crows circled in the sky, but the centre of the silent black tornado slowly moved to a spot just outside the wall. Suddenly the birds dispersed and melted away, completely gone in the blink of an eye.

Something was going on outside the castle gates! I didn't think twice before rushing to the corridor, buckling the sword to my belt as I went.

The yard was empty, and I passed through the gate, with a dismissing wave to the guard. I crossed the road that wound south next to the river and stopped – the stone bridge had gone and, as far as I could see from this side of the river, the staircase, which had once been carved in the rock face of the mountain, had also gone, hidden under the powerful and noisy current of a new riverbed. A few trees lay broken with their leafy branches peeking from the muddy water. The large boulder which had smashed the bridge rested a few hundred yards downstream on my side of the river bank.

I looked around, my hand resting on my sword hilt, ready. The ravens had gone, and it looked like just another peaceful morning, except for the rubble on the left. But nothing and nobody moved there either. I was about to relax when a hint of a motion sneaked into my perception from the other side of the river. Something big was there. The silhouette was ghostly white and constantly shifting its shape like splashes of running water. It was behind the thin shrubs on the other shore, looking at me with its rainbow eyes.

I was hit by a wave of chill despite the full sunshine, as a mob of imaginary ants started to march down my back. The eyes of the creature were focused on me, and some primordial, almost devout fear filled my feet with lead firmly fixing my soles on the riverbank.

I was sure that it would be impossible to cross the raging river. The rapids were moving loose rocks down the stream, deadly even for a creature of that size. Was I safe? I guess I wasn't…

For more than ten minutes, I looked at the creature behind the shrubs, unable even to barely breathe. Then it moved.

The white head of the serpent emerged slowly from behind the shrubs, glaring at me with unblinking eyes, the colour of a rainbow. A sparkling crest, unusual for a reptile, crowned its vertex, giving the creature remote resemblance to a peacock. The crest shone white in the light of the morning sun, hurting my eyes and blurring my vision.

I managed to step back a few paces as the serpent's head still rose several more feet above the vegetation, and a part of the reptile's body slid through the bush. It appeared to be shiny white and soft, covered with fluffy silverfish feathers. Then a pair of mighty wings appeared, sparkling like slivers of glass in the sun. The protection I'd imagined that the impenetrable river could provide was instantly crushed to dust. The creature could easily reach me if it had such a desire and my sword, I guessed, would be no bigger an obstacle for the creature than a toothpick.

I felt completely paralysed, unable to move, unable to blink, unable even to think.

The winged serpent tilted its head trying to catch a better view of me, sticking out its double tongue twice, as if tasting the air. The raging river between me and those unblinking rainbow eyes seemed to cease to exist for a moment, and all the colours of the world faded away in the sight of this blinding white body.

It was like being in a trance, and I completely lost track of time – what seemed like an eternity could easily be just mere seconds.

Then the serpent raised its body high above the river, now resembling a pillar of shining light. The mighty wings spread far away out to the sides, above the low shrubs of the riverbank. It cast one more glance of its rainbow eyes on me, then slowly wafted its wings as if testing the morning breeze.

I didn't notice the exact moment when it rose into the air. The rainbow eyes released their grip on me and fixed on the sky instead as the creature gracefully bent a few tree crowns and flew away downstream of the raging river. The shifting image soon reduced to a shiny white cloud and then disappeared behind the riverbank vegetation.

My senses returned slowly. I wiped the drops of perspiration from my forehead. My right hand was still clutching the sword, but my heart had slowed down its gallop. I retreated carefully, glancing over my shoulder, expecting the ghostly apparition to reappear at any second. The guards opened the gate as soon as I banged on it.

"Did you see that?" I asked them, pointing to the sky, where the shining serpent had hovered just minutes before.

"What, my Lord?"

"The white serpent with wings?" I asked, hoping that I was not going insane.

Both guards shook their heads.

I left them wondering, but I didn't care. I had been scared by this unexpected experience. The serpent seemed flawless, stronger than a sword despite the fluffy appearance of its coat. I felt it was even stronger than my Ring, though I would never dare to test this theory.

Back in my room, I dropped on my bed, still drenched by awe and bestial fear. What had I just seen? Was it just a weird local animal? After already having come across the gryphon, a giant spider with a human head, a talking centipede and a flaming viper, I knew I could expect almost anything in Rehen. Still, the flying serpent was in an entirely different league. I only hoped it wasn't an enemy, but if the creature was behind those crow attacks, I might be doomed.

This thought pinched my heart with fear again, and as I lay on the bed, my soul soaked in self-pity. My torture was interrupted half an hour later when Carwyn told me that the breakfast was ready. I spent a few more minutes adjusting my appearance and brushing the grim thoughts away while he patiently waited.

We left my chambers, and I followed him to the dining room with barely suppressed impatience. Shandra was already there dressed in a lovely light blue gown embroidered with small white flowers. Her hair was neatly combed and pinned with a blue clip.

"Good morning, Shandra!" I greeted her.

"Good morning, sir" she lowered her head.

"Did you sleep well?"

"Oh, yes," she smiled. "But that strange storm woke me up this morning, and I was even more surprised by the other things as well. Fortunately, Melvis was very understanding."

"Have you been treated well?"

"Yes, but it wasn't necessary," suddenly she was serious. "I don't want to sound ungrateful, sir, but I'm used to taking care of myself."

"It's fine, Shandra," I took her hand and gently led her to the table. "Let's have some breakfast."

That morning Carwyn spoiled us with roast pork, fish, salad, cheese and fruit. The wine was red.

We enjoyed our breakfast unhurriedly while the stupor caused by this morning's encounter slowly melted. Good food, good wine, the excellent company did the job. We ate, talked, even joked and laughed.

I just wanted to relax and forget all the tension of the last few weeks when I had rushed from one disaster to another. Shandra seemed to be enjoying the moment as well.

I did my best to smile a lot and told her several very dated English jokes that I tried to adapt and tailor to Rehen. My efforts weren't in vain. Her ice seemed to be melting. She constantly forgot to add that awkward "sir". Sometimes she even called me Kyleb.

We took a long walk around the empty castle, meeting no one on our way. I was visiting a large part of the castle for the first time myself too since I'd never braved to take that long tour on my own. We sat in the magnificent gardens enjoying the shade of the apple trees, listening to the birds twittering in the leafy branches and the grasshoppers playing their melodies in the neatly trimmed grass. Sometimes we talked, sometimes we subsided into silence, but each time we simply felt the presence of each other.

After lunch, I interrupted my welcome break and briefly visited Rhys.

He was lying on his bed, but not sleeping. Gwyn the gryphon was sitting next to him with a very concerned look, occasionally putting his head under Rhys's arm as if trying to hide in his armpit.

"Sorry to disturb you," I said as the gryphon rushed to greet me. "Any news?"

"No," Rhys shook his head. "I've had several naps, but all I could hear was the normal nightly noises of a forest – silence, an occasional breeze and the random hoots of owls, rarely the sound of cars passing in the distance."

"Anything else?"

Rhys shook his head hesitantly.

"Ok, keep on napping, please, maybe something will show up," I said, turning away towards the door.

"Wait!" Rhys exclaimed, and I stopped midway. "I'm not entirely sure, but I think there's a river nearby. I think I could hear water running through a rocky bed when the wind dropped. But it's on the very edge of my perception, and it could also just be an illusion."

"So, we have a forest, a river and a road nearby..." I said slowly. "It might be something. I'll need a very detailed map of the area... At least, it's somewhere to start."

"I'll try harder," promised Rhys.

I sincerely hoped that John and I had chased after him in the right direction. But Morvarid could easily have tricked us by putting a false lead on the internet. She could have taken her travelling circus to the Tyrolean Alps, and our quest to find the caravan in the Tatra Mountains could become as useful as trying to chase a will-o'-the-wisp.

"By the way," I asked him, still half-afraid of seeming insane. "Have you ever encountered a white flying snake in our neighbourhood?"

"Flying… What?" Rhys looked puzzled.

"A giant feathered white snake with huge wings – have you ever seen it?" my attempt to explain myself seemed clumsy.

"I've only heard a legend when I was a child. A creature like that visits people at some critical point just before a huge disaster, war or epidemic. Have you seen one?"

"I did. Today…"

"I hate to tell this, but it is believed to be a dreadful omen. I can't explain; maybe you could find somebody who knows more about it?"

"I'll try. And Rhys, please, keep this secret."

"As you wish," he said without adding the usual "my Lord".

Rhys closed his eyes, preparing for another nap as I left the room. I stopped in the corridor. His words were unsettling, and I wondered if the creature had been attracted by the thunderstorm that I had created. Was it related to my brother somehow? What kind of disaster was the snake heralding?

A terrible sense of fear grasped me, and I gritted my teeth, waving it away. I guessed that I had angered Seisyll and maybe even killed some of his men during that thunderstorm, but I couldn't play by his rules, I couldn't be his puppet. It would be dangerous for everybody if I claimed my right to the throne of the realm. Was that creature Seisyll's? Chadrack was already vulnerable but could this lead to more disasters?

I was about to return to Shandra and hated to frighten her again when her fears for the Bloody Prince were just beginning to wane. I took a few deep breaths and shook my head, forcing the worries out of my head. I couldn't allow Shandra to see them.

I looked out of the window – it was calm outside with a lazy breeze barely stirring the green leaves on the trees in the midday sunshine. If any menace was looming over Chadrack, it wasn't yet here.

I found Shandra where I had left her – in the inner garden on the south-eastern side of the castle. She was sitting in the shade of a flowering linden tree and watching bees visiting the fragrant blossoms on the lower branches. She smiled, spotting me in the distance, but her smile faded as I approached.

"You look worried, Kyleb," she observed, and I saw a shadow of concern cross her face too.

"It's probably nothing," I mumbled sitting down next to her with face failing to echo those words.

"Still, you're tense and unable to hide it," she said thoughtfully.

"The capital is empty, and I am worried about the safe return of the citizens," I attempted an innocent little lie.

"The capital was empty earlier this morning too, but you weren't that worried then," she observed in her soft voice.

I was a poor liar when I was with her.

"I saw an animal today," my voice was low, close to a whisper. "It was a bizarre creature, and my friend has told me it might herald a disaster."

"What kind of an animal?" she gasped.

I told her about the white snake. Shandra listened without interrupting me, and her face remained calm and serious.

"Did it fly away?" she asked when I finished.

"Yes," I nodded. "It flew south along the river, towards the

Braaid."

"I've never heard anything about a white flying snake or any disasters it may bring. Not even in a legend or fairy-tale. The monster is no longer here, Kyleb," she looked at the bees again. "Maybe now it's a Mordokan problem already since it flew to the south. Or maybe it's not a problem at all. I can't advise you, Kyleb. I'm just a silly woman."

"You're right, Shandra," I risked a cautious smile. "No need to worry when nothing has happened. Let's go for a walk."

Shandra took my hand and stood up, and I led her to the left on a cobblestone path winding slightly between the thick dark green shrubs covered in countless fragrant blue blossoms. The eastern wing of the castle stood silently on our left, looking out at the garden with a series of narrow windows. Just once I glimpsed the blue face of Saqia peeking at us from the third floor. The face disappeared the next instant, but I immediately chose to leave the garden and stay away from her white eyes.

We took an alley heading slightly uphill and walked in the shade of tall poplars. A soft breeze played among the shivering leaves casting vibrant shadows at our feet. I led us through the gardens, alleys and passages around the castle. A couple of times I again glimpsed Saqia looking at us through the windows but did my best to strike the blue woman from my mind. Shandra looked relaxed and happy at last. We carried on, talking and laughing and later, just before lunch, we became lovers.

I had asked Carwyn to pack our lunch in a basket, and we went into the empty capital to have a picnic in the park. Shandra didn't ever mention my worries again, and I was grateful for that. We ate lamb and cheese and drank wine sitting on the grass. Life felt complete, and I did my best to forget everything, merely enjoying the moment.

Shandra and I were sitting on the edge of the large fountain in the empty square with our feet splashing in the water, enjoying the sunshine. This moment of bliss was suddenly interrupted by angry shouts and cries in a nearby street. I stood up, shading my eyes, still holding Shandra's hand.

Several men and women appeared from around the corner, shouting angrily and punching the youngster in front of them. He was a boy in his early teens with long blond hair, barely covering his bruised face. The youngster's wrists were tied behind him, and he was sobbing loudly.

I got out of the fountain and approached them, Shandra followed me a few steps behind. The shouts stopped as soon as they noticed us.

"What's happened?" I asked.

"We've caught a marauder, my Lord!" explained one of the women still short of breath from her strident shouting.

"Where are you taking him?" This might have been a strange

question for the Lord to ask, but I couldn't just let it go.

"To the temple of Qu'mun, of course!" the woman was still breathless. "He needs to stand trial."

I felt anger rising as I instantly recalled Milo – the youth I had saved from torture and death in the temple. I could never forget his gaze – helpless and full of pain – as Kyaal, the priest, carved the words of a psalm on his back. Images of rotting bodies and bones in the Grave of the Silent flooded my mind. I knew beforehand what the verdict from Kyaal would be for this youngster and I couldn't allow this to happen.

"No need to take him to the temple," I told them. "I will judge him right here."

The group exchanged a few surprised looks, but nobody dared to object. The youngster dropped to his knees and began to cry even louder. I knew I was heading into direct confrontation with the temple and, probably, with some of my previous orders as well, but I didn't care. The temple has caused too much suffering already. It must change, and I blamed myself for not having done that sooner.

"Tell me, what happened?" I asked, addressing no one in particular.

They began talking all at once, raising a loud cacophony, followed by the sobs of the youngster. I couldn't make out a word they were saying.

"Silence!" I hushed the noise and pointed to one of the men. "You talk."

He took a hesitant step forward, glancing back at the breathless woman.

"We were away from the city as you ordered, my Lord," said the man. "And we returned when we were told to return."

Everybody nodded their heads except for the sobbing youngster.

"You're still alive, thanks to that order," I reminded him.

"We are very grateful, my Lord," nodded the man. "But we found him sleeping in our house when we returned. He'd broken in through the window!"

"What other damage have you found, apart from the broken window?" I asked.

"The house was empty," said the man. "We'd taken all our valuables with us."

"Correct me, if I am wrong," I said, taking a few more steps closer. "You found him inside, but the only damage was the broken window?"

"Yes, my Lord," the man nodded. "We seized him and were on the way to deliver him to the temple when we met you."

"I won't allow any more trials in the temple!" my outrage surprised even me, but I managed to calm it down. "Does anybody have anything to add to this man's speech? More damage? Anything was stolen?"

They fell silent, shaking their heads.

"Very well," I said. "Let's hear the other side. What's your name, young man?"

The youngster stopped sobbing, but his eyes remained fixed on the ground.

"Byward," he whispered, then added after a short pause, "my Lord."

"Tell us your story, Byward," I stood in front of the youngster and kept my voice calm, but he was still afraid to raise his eyes and face me – was I worse than Kyaal?

Byward was silent for some time. I didn't press him.

"I was at the market with my father – we are farmers, my Lord," he said. "Our farm is on the shore of the Braaid, quite far from here. When everybody started to move out of the city, we became separated in a rush, and I got lost."

He started to sob again. I patiently waited until he calmed down.

"What happened next?" I asked.

"I had nowhere to go," he said. "The night was cold, and I tried several doors – all of them were locked. Then I took a stone and forced myself in through the window. I didn't mean any harm, but I had nowhere to sleep – our farm is too far away, and I didn't know the way."

"Have you done any other damage, apart from the window?" I asked him. "Tell me the truth, Byward."

Byward raised his eyes for the first time and looked at me.

"I did," he whispered. "I ate a piece of the smoked ham I found in the store. I was cold and hungry."

The breathless woman gasped, but I paid no attention.

"I've heard enough," I announced. "As a sovereign of this land, I find you, Byward, guilty of breaking the window and stealing the smoked ham."

I allowed a small pause before looking at the sobbing boy.

"I am sentencing you to work for one week in the kitchen of the castle without any payment," I said, and the sobbing stopped. "You'll have enough food to eat and a place to sleep."

A murmur passed through the group. Only Byward remained silent.

"You will find Carwyn in the castle," I continued pointing to the man who had given his testimony. "He'll reimburse you the cost of replacing that broken window and the ham. This is my order."

"As you wish, my Lord," said one of the men. "What do you want us to do with this kid?"

"Leave him with me," I dismissed them. "I'll take care of him."

Everybody paid their respects and left. Byward still knelt in front of me. I felt a gentle hand on my shoulder.

"You did great," Shandra whispered in my ear. "I felt so sorry for the kid. But why you didn't you let them take him to the temple for trial? You have too many responsibilities here already…"

"There is no justice in the temple, believe me," I told her approaching Byward. "Stand up, kid."

He rose to his feet reluctantly. I produced my dagger with the golden handle and, ignoring his gasps, cut the ties loose.

"You're not to run away," I told him. "You still owe me a week's work in the kitchen, and I believe your father will show up looking for you by then."

"Thank you, my Lord!" he whispered gratefully. "I'll do exactly as you say."

"Then you'll follow us, Byward," I said, taking Shandra's hand. "We'll take you to Carwyn."

We passed a large square and several winding streets on our way back to the castle. Byward followed us dutifully several paces behind, now calm and silent, carrying the basket with the leftovers and crockery from our picnic.

On the way, I told Shandra the whole story of poor Milo.

"That's terrible," she exclaimed when I had finished.

"Now, do you understand why I did what I did?" I asked.

She nodded silently, her beautiful eyes full of tears.

"Sorry," she whispered, clenching my hand. "I just

remembered my brother."

Carwyn found us in the back garden of the castle and informed us, with his usual formality, that the dinner was ready. I briefly told him about the trial and delivered Byward to him.

"Thank you, my Lord," said Carwyn. "I'd greatly appreciate some help."

He took the boy to the kitchen.

"Why you are so kind to me?" asked Shandra on our way to the dining room.

"You saved me, remember?"

"Is that the only reason? Then you could toss me a coin and forget me. Why bother?"

"Because I like you much," I confessed, more for myself than for her.

"Only that?" she asked. "Then you'll forget me the next time a pretty new face appears in the neighbourhood."

"That won't happen," I said seriously. "But I would like to refrain from the word *love* for a while until we get to know each other a little better. This is going to be serious, I know, but I don't like to rush things."

"As you wish, my Lord," she smiled, touching my cheek.

Then we had dinner.

We parted at dusk when I led Shandra to her room.

Jesper was waiting in front of my chambers with a serious

expression on his face. I waved him inside – I didn't want us to be overheard by anybody and for panic to spread.

"There's too few of us to defend the whole city, my Lord," said Jesper as soon as he had closed the door. "I've put guards on all the gates, but they will be of little use if the Mordakans should decide to sneak in. A few arrows could take the guards out without raising any alarm."

I had been expecting him to say that. It wasn't a complaint, Jesper was only stating facts.

"Gather your men in the castle then," I ordered. "Leave the gates shut but unguarded, we'll check on them in the morning. Could your men hold the castle through the night if there was an attack?"

Jesper was silent for just a few moments.

"Yes, my Lord," he nodded. "We'll barricade the doors and wait for them in the galleries. We'll be outnumbered if it's the same squad, but they won't be able to take us by surprise. We have sufficient arrows."

I dismissed him silently with an uneasy heart. I hoped Seisyll wouldn't dare to return intending to cut my throat. My Ring was capable of throwing a few nasty cataclysms on the Mordakans – I hoped they had become scared by the demonstration I had performed that morning. But, as a Sleeper, I was vulnerable at night – I couldn't stay awake and wait for Seisyll. John and I were on a mission to liberate Rick. This was risky by itself, and all I could do in Chadrack was to put my safety in the hands of the jaegers. If Seisyll decided to punish me for my defiance, we might need to survive a few nights under siege until Bedwyr was able to get the army back to the capital. Then it would be Seisyll's problem to think about his own throat. A squad of Mordakans would stand no chance against the army of Chadrack. If only we could manage to survive those few nights.

I went to my lonely bedroom, but a soft tap on the door stopped me before I had the chance to undress. It was Rhys.

"It's undoubtedly a river," he announced. "I clearly heard water splashing!"

"Good news," I told him. "I think we'll be able to get on the right track faster now."

"That would be great," Rhys said. "It's the second day without food and drink, and I fear I am starting to look very appetising to my neighbours."

"We'll do our best, don't worry," I shrugged.

"And I heard a train in the distance," said Rhys seriously. "I have no doubts about that."

"That's something!" I couldn't help a cry of joy. "It'll certainly narrow our search. Just be patient and, please, don't do anything heroic."

"I won't," promised Rhys. "Hope to see you soon!"

"I hope so too..."

He left, I undressed quickly and got into bed. The night was falling.

The morning was foggy and grey. John was still asleep as I quietly got out of the car to stretch my legs. Long strands of white fog flowed down the slopes of a nearby mountain and gathered in the narrow valley. A touch of chill shivered the last remnants of the night's sleep away as I looked around. It had already been dark when we stopped here last evening, but neither was too much visible now because of the fog. I heard water splashing on the right and followed the sound until I found a crystal-clear stream squeezed between rocky banks under the shade of leafy shrubs.

I washed my face. The water was painfully cold, but the light numbness it left felt pleasant. I even risked rinsing my teeth.

It was very quiet with only the occasional sounds of falling rocks somewhere in the distance, most likely disturbed by an unseen animal. I returned to the car, sat down on a large rock and patiently waited for John to wake up. I knew from my own experience how dangerous it was to disturb a Sleeper – you never know what is happening on the other side of reality. It was always better to wait until the Sleeper returned on his own.

As I sat surrounded by strands of thinning fog, I felt calm and peace slowly sneaking back into my soul. The scent of approaching success was dizzying, but I deliberately fought this feeling. Our venture was not yet over.

Rick's leads might be quite substantial if we were on the right track after him. I needed a map. I fished the phone out of my pocket and cursed – the battery was flat, so I put the useless device back. Damn! John was still asleep, and I had nothing else to do but wait.

The silence was unsettling, and I did my best to keep my brain busy, preventing my imagination from populating the thick wall of fog with monsters. I kept wondering what Seisyll would do next, would my scarce defenders be able to stand their ground? The frail man had threatened to kill me and everybody else in the castle by the end of the day if I contravened his wishes. I was still alive. Had that been merely an empty threat? I supposed I would never be sure.

It was chilly, and I wrapped my jacket tightly around me, remembering the warm sunny day with Shandra. I knew she was sleeping only a few yards away in Rehen, but I felt lonely and abandoned, sitting on a cold rock in the middle of a foggy nowhere. I passed my gaze over the dark grey silhouettes of trees circling the glade from the south and the hint of peaks behind them. The strands of fog barely moved, and I closed my eyes, remembering Shandra and our little picnic in the park.

My meditation was interrupted by the sound of a car door opening. John crawled out, yawning.

"How are things going?" he demanded, stretching his neck up.

"Good morning to you too," I smiled. "Everything seems okay. We've got several clues, but the area still seems to be enormous."

"What kind of clues?"

"Rick's kidnappers haven't moved – that's good for us, but he can't pick up on his location, and he's had no food or drink since they stopped nor has he seen anyone. His feline companions haven't been fed either, and he's afraid of looking too appetising."

"That sounds interesting," John yawned, "and disturbing. Something's happening, but I'm afraid we won't be able to find out what until we reach them. Is he already in that city you mentioned?"

"No," I said firmly. "It seems like they're stuck somewhere in the mountains."

"That's strange..." he shook his head. "Why aren't they feeding the animals?"

"I can't figure out that either..."

"If he were in the city," said John, "it would be easy to find the circus by following posters. How can we possibly find him in a whole mountain range?"

"It will be difficult," I agreed. "But I collected some clues overnight. Rick says there is a forest, river, road and train track nearby."

"The combination of those four things might narrow our search, indeed. Have you looked at the map?"

"No..." I sighed. "My phone's dead, and I've got no charger."

"I think you should start keeping one with you," he smiled, reaching out his own phone to me. "I'll stretch a bit more, and we still have a bit of food left."

"There's a mountain creek nearby if you want to splash your face with water."

He grinned widely.

"Of course, I will..."

I drilled into maps on his phone.

"Where do you think we should start looking?" I asked.

"Look along all the way to that Polish city," he said. "I don't think you'll find too many spots with all four criteria, but we'll have to visit each possibility, I'm afraid."

He went to the stream, and for some time, I heard him mumbling something behind the thinning strands of fog. I studied the map.

"Shit! Damn! Shit!" I jumped at John's sudden outburst.

"What?" I asked, putting the phone away.

"Have you seen that shit?" his silhouette behind the veil of fog was pointing at something.

"I haven't seen anything. What is it?"

John kept on pointing his finger to something upstream. I went closer.

"Have you seen this?" he asked again.

It was a dead moose partially submerged in the shallow water.

"And I've just washed my hands in there!" he looked wretched.

"I hadn't seen it," I said, deciding not to mention that I'd washed my mouth here out too.

John returned to the car cursing and mumbling. I stood there still looking at the corpse and couldn't believe my eyes. It must have been hidden by the fog before or I would undoubtedly have seen it.

The creek was a little swollen just upstream from the dead body, and the water bubbled around the obstacle. I gasped as one strand of fog began to rise from the moose glistening like distant starlight. Instinctively I raised my hand covering my eyes when the Master of Destiny on my finger emitted several blue sparks. They remained in front of me, hovering in mid-air.

"I'll be damned..." I heard John's whisper behind me.

The banshee rose from the corpse in the shape of an attacking

king cobra but suddenly froze as it met the sparks. The confrontation lasted just a fraction of a second. Then the creature dashed away, intertwining with the real fog.

"I nearly pissed my pants," said John seriously when it was over. "You guys have mighty Rings, but I never thought they were capable of transferring here or doing any of their magic on Earth..."

"Neither did I…" I sat down, still trembling a little.

Tension drifted away with the mountain stream and slowly, my ability to think returned.

"Are you okay?" asked John, a note of concern in his voice.

"Yes, I am," I confirmed.

"Let's get out of here," John helped me to my feet. "And as fast as we can..."

We almost ran back to the car. John started the engine, and the car instantly jumped forward onto the empty road.

"Have you looked at that damned map?" he asked a few minutes later when we were finally able to focus on our primary task.

"Yes," I said. "That was an easy thing to do, but the search for Rick won't be so easy, unfortunately. This road is in the middle of a valley along with the river and railroad and with mountain ranges on both sides. There will be many places that satisfy all four criteria. In fact, we'll have to check every side roads with any forest alongside it on our way, I'm afraid."

"That's encouraging," a portion of irony leaked through John's words. "Here comes the first!"

"Let's check it!"

We turned down the narrow side road which ended abruptly a few hundred yards later. The wrong one! We checked five more dirt roads with the same result before we reached a small village where we bought some food at a local shop to keep our protesting stomachs happy.

A few more exhausting hours of trials and errors followed. We visited every side road on our way.

The sky had cleared, and the weather was great, but I had a dreadful fear that Rhys may end up severely dehydrated in his enclosed wagon, frying somewhere in the sunshine.

We had a quick lunch on the go and carried on searching. Sometimes we tried our luck by asking local people, but nobody seemed to know anything.

John's face darkened with each mile we travelled. Keeping spirits up when faced with constant failure was difficult. Our progress was slow; each dirt road was narrow and winding, sometimes difficult to pass. Some of the roads led to cabins, mostly empty, but most of them led nowhere, and I realised that we might need a week to cross the Polish border. I guessed that Morvarid wouldn't wait a week, but there was no way to speed the process up. All roads looked the same, and we had no clue as to which ones were safe to ignore, so we had to check each one.

We passed through several more village and two larger towns looking for any forested wild areas. John was completely exhausted. I was silent, and an uneasy feeling of failure filled the air – just another dirt road, another few miles up the foot of the mountain and just another "nothing" again.

It was already late afternoon when just another dirt road emerged on the left across the rail tracks with thick forest on both sides. John dutifully turned left, and we crawled almost a mile uphill, seeing nothing but the dark woods around us.

"Let's rest a little," complained John. "My eyes are aching, and my bladder's going to burst in the next five minutes."

"Okay."

John stopped at once and dashed to the nearby shrubs, undoing his zip on the way. I got out as well, taking the opportunity to stretch my aching muscles and move around a little after the long ride.

Then I heard it.

The deep growling was almost at the edge of perception. Then again – this time louder.

"Did you hear that?" I whispered to John.

"Yes," he said, appearing from behind the shrubs. "Are you thinking what I'm thinking?"

"It might be the lion or the tiger... It's certainly not a dog!"

"Jump in! Let's check it out!"

We drove uphill as quickly as possible then we saw it – the vast clearance within an abandoned quarry at the far end.

Several trucks and wagons stood at a distance of several hundred yards away, painted with smiling clowns and monkeys, dogs and lions.

"We've found it!" I exclaimed.

John hit the brakes, then quickly reversed the car and parked it on the right side of the road, keeping a thick shrub between us and the clearance.

I was about jumping out already when he stopped me.

"Wait. Let's observe for a while. It might be a trap!"

My heart froze. He was right. We knew nothing of what was waiting for us here.

"I am so glad we've found him at last," I smiled widely.

"Me too," said John seriously. "But let's remain careful. Last time we nearly bumped into a banshee, remember?"

For the next hour, we sat in the car like a pair of frightened rabbits in a hole, ready to flee any moment. Nothing happened – the wagons and trailers looked abandoned and lifeless.

"Do you think it's time to act?" I asked John.

"Are you sure the banshee is not guarding them?" he replied with another question.

I was becoming a little irritated by his issues with banshees. I felt protected by my Sapphire and was already frustrated with waiting while our friend was drying out in the sunlight just across the field.

"I'm going," I told him and opened the door. "Are you with me?"

"Yes, yes, I'm coming... Let's just keep quiet."

We crawled out of the car, leaving the doors slightly ajar and avoiding making any noise but that was unnecessary – the lion began to roar again, and I could easily have danced a haka in the middle of the field without being heard.

"Let's keep close to the forest," whispered John.

I silently nodded. It may be overcautious, but at least two deadly dangerous animals were here. We knew they were caged, but how could we possibly be sure that no one else was running free?

Our progress was slow. The lion kept roaring angrily – easy to understand if he had had no food for three days. Everything else seemed still and lifeless.

Then we found a clown – fully dressed and in some weird makeup. He was lying in the middle of the flowering meadow with his head unnaturally turned to the left. We waited, but he remained motionless with a bloody knife in his right hand. His belly had been widely torn apart, exposing guts. The grass around the body was undisturbed, revealing no sign of a fight. The clown's empty eye sockets seemed to be looking at the road as creepy maggots moved within them.

"It's the banshee..." whispered John.

"He did that himself?"

"The banshee did that in his body," explained John. "He could only watch and die..."

The clown was still clutching my silver foil package in his left hand – torn apart, exposing the mummified remains of the rodent.

"He found the rat," I pointed whispering.

"And freed the banshee only to meet his death," John whispered back.

We left the corpse undisturbed and moved on. Several paces ahead remnants of a small white dog lay in the grass. The tiny body had been twisted and brutally torn into two pieces.

The lion's roar continued to fill the entire quarry with primordial fear as we slowly moved closer.

We found a young girl dressed like a ballerina next to a brightly painted green wagon decorated with giant red poppies. Her hands were gracefully raised above her head as if for a dance, but her bloody torso had been twirled around several times as if by a mighty tornado.

"They were rehearsing something," said John looking at the body. "Until the clown decided to open that damned package."

“Looks like they’re all are dead,” I observed. “That's why they haven’t fed the animals.”

“Have you seen Rick recently?” asked John suddenly. “He might be dead too...”

I stopped.

“I saw him just a few hours ago before I went to sleep. Do you think he might be?” I felt a sudden wave of frustration.

“Let's check the lion – you said Rick was next to him?” suggested John.

Spotting which wagon held the cages was easy with the almost constant roaring. We found several more bodies on our way in the most unnatural poses, torn into pieces and already infested by maggots. The smell was awful, but we kept going. A half-naked man with huge bulging muscles hung like a rag doll on the open door of the lorry where the lion was caged. His eyes had popped out of their sockets and hung on nerves like a macabre chandelier.

John produced his Swiss army knife from a pocket and started to cut through the painted canvas covering the trailer. The lion’s roar stopped immediately.

“Rick, are you here?” I asked from behind John.

“Yes, I'm here,” came the slow reply. “You’ve found me!”

The voice was harsh and low but clearly audible. We both smiled, and then laughed. John pressed harder with his knife cutting a large hole in the canvas.

Soon the piece of canvas dropped off, exposing a narrow passage between the metal cages. The hungry eyes of the lion were on the right, and I could spot the pale face of Rick at the back of the cage on the left. The lion flashed a paw through the iron bars directly into John's face but hit only air as the red-haired man jumped to the left, avoiding the strike.

"This might be tricky," he mumbled. "We must feed the lion."

"How?"

"There's plenty of meat around here, just put anything on a stick," John said plunging his knife into the canvas again as the door of Rick's cage appeared to be closer to the tiger. The paws of the lion appeared in front of his face several more times, and each time he jumped away.

Finding a stick in the woods was easy. It was crooked but served the purpose. I was hesitant about where to start.

I couldn't even think of touching any human remains, but the dog seemed suitable, so I put the rear part of it on the stick. John was in the middle of his second cut into the canvas away from the lion when I returned.

"When do you want me to feed him?" I asked.

"You can start now," said John without looking. "I'm tired of jumping around already."

The lion grabbed the offered meat and leapt to the back of his cage, gnawing.

"How are you?" I asked Rick.

"Thirsty. Would be grateful for some water," he replied. "Had they abandoned us?"

"No," I said. "All are dead."

"Dead? What happened?"

"Looks like the banshee..." said John, still working on the canvas.

"I'll be right back," I said, leaving John to deliver the explanations.

I returned to the car and collected a few pieces of cheese and ham from our grocery supplies, two wheat buns and a bottle of water. Rick hadn't had any food or drink for several days. We had to address that too.

Back at the cage, I pushed everything through the bars trying to avoid the roaring beast on the right.

"What happened to the tiger?" I asked. "I can't see or hear him..."

Rick delayed his answer until he had drunk the entire contents of the bottle.

"That's better," he sighed. "I don't know what happened to him. He just stopped moving."

"When?" asked John halting his activities.

"Yesterday... Does it matter?" Rick started to chew the buns and cheese.

"Yes, it does," said John. "If it was yesterday then the banshee isn't here."

"What makes you so confident?" asked Rick.

"We saw it this morning quite away from here," John responded, finishing with the canvas.

Now part of the tiger's cage was also exposed. The striped frame was at the far end of the cage with its hind legs protruding through the iron bars as if it had been trying to escape. The body was intact, and only the fixed gaze of the clouded eyes gave a clue that the big cat was dead.

"If it was the banshee," said Rick chewing. "Why am I still alive? And why is the lion still alive? Aren't we supposed to be dead too?"

"The metal bars of the cage prevented the banshee from getting into you," I said. "The tiger's paws are sticking outside – that's how it was able to enter and leave the body. You've just been lucky."

"Why is that?" now John was curious.

"I think the metal bars act as a barrier to the energy-based creature," I said. "That's why I succeeded in capturing the banshee in a foil."

"Jeeze! I would never have thought of that!" exclaimed John.

"Have you captured the banshee?" Rick stopped in the middle of a bite.

“I was just lucky,” I wasn't keen to exaggerate that. “Maybe I’ll tell you some other time...”

“Now we have another problem,” announced John grimly.

“What?” I asked.

John silently pointed at the massive lock hanging on Rick's cage door.

“We need to find the key,” I said. “Who fed you and the cats? Or who did you see last?”

“I don't know," said Rick. “He kept his face covered.”

“He?” John turned back to me. “Obviously, it wasn't the ballerina. Let's check the others’ pockets first.”

The idea was repulsive, but we had no other choice. I left the hanging strongman to John and headed to the clown’s corpse. The stench was sickening with thick clouds of flies buzzing around and bunches of maggots crawling around the exposed gut. I felt his pockets – nothing; felt around his belt – nothing, and then felt his breast pockets – nothing.

“Empty!” I announced.

“Empty!” responded John.

We searched the other terribly disfigured and torn apart bodies. Empty, empty, empty, empty and empty!

“What next?” I asked John when we had finished with the corpses.

“Let's try the wagons, and we better hurry – night is falling, and I'd hate to sleep here," said John.

John took the ballerina's carriage. I went to the wagon of the magician.

It wasn't easy. Lots of strange things were there – countless ornamental boxes, hats, weird equipment, shiny crystal balls, stacks of cards, magic wands, colourful fans and artificial flowers.

"Empty!" John cried outside, heading to another wagon.

I still was stuck here. Naturally, I skipped the crystal balls. But the boxes almost drove me crazy. I picked up every single box, listened shaking and then put it back. Nothing... I looked around before leaving the wagon when a big pink fan with gorgeous ostrich feathers on the right side of the door drew my attention because it had an odd bulge in the middle. I touched the feathers and suddenly felt cold metal behind them. I pushed the feathers aside, and there it was – a big bunch of keys hanging on the wall. I grabbed them and ran out of the wagon.

"Found something!" I cried.

John popped his head out of the strongman's carriage.

"Excellent! Try them – I'll keep on searching, in case you've got the wrong set of keys!" he replied, disappearing inside again.

I rushed to Rick and reached for the lock, narrowly missing being caught by the lion's paws. Rick helped me from the other side of the cage. A quick look through the keys quickly eliminated most of them – they were just the wrong type.

Then I started to try the remaining few. A sudden roar from the lion took me by surprise, and I dropped everything on the ground. I had to search in the grass, collect the keys and start again from the beginning.

"What are you doing here?" a very calm male voice came from behind me.

I turned around.

Several men in dark uniforms with the white word "POLÍCIA" on their left breasts stood in the middle of the field watching me.

"What are you doing here?" one of them, apparently senior, calmly repeated his question in broken English with a strong Eastern European accent.

I cast a few glances around, but the man shook his head and placed a hand on his gun, and I instantly rejected all thought of trying to escape. I couldn't leave John and Rick behind either. I looked at the dead bodies scattered across the field and decided to start with the truth.

"We're trying to save our friend who was kidnapped over a week ago in London," I said, trying to sound as calm as he had been.

"Is that your explanation for the murders as well?" he gestured around the field.

Rick gasped behind me, and I felt weak at the knees at the implication.

"We have had nothing to do with these killings," I said firmly. "They were dead long before we got here."

"Interesting..." the man pointed to the clown's corpse. "Are you trying to suggest that this man cut himself open? Or did you help him?"

I decided to play ignorant rather than try to explain the entire banshee thing.

"I don't know how they died," I said, keeping my voice calm. "I didn't see it happen. They were already riddled with maggots when we got there. Luckily, our friend is still alive."

The officer came closer, keeping his palm on the gun.

"I see..." he drawled. "So why is he still in the cage?"

The question was interrupted by a roar from the lion.

"We haven't been able to find the key yet," I explained.

The lion jerked his paws through the bars again in a desperate attempt to reach the officer. However, not a muscle twitched in the man's face as he regarded the hungry predator.

"Any luck?" John asked, emerging from the strong man's wagon with a large bunch of keys.

He noticed the police and stopped midway.

"Oh, another crew member," observed the officer.

He waved to his subordinates, and John was hand-cuffed in no time.

"Killing people is a serious offence," he said to me shaking his head. "Let's assume that you're telling the truth – why haven't you reported this to the authorities?"

My gaze wandered between Rick, still-caged, John already hand-cuffed and the smirking face of the officer.

"We've had no time for that; we're trying to help our friend…" I humbly tried to explain. "He's been in this cage for several days without any food or water. We decided to take care of him first. Our next step would certainly have been a phone call to the police."

"That's not true," said the officer. "We observed you sitting in your car for quite a long time and, apparently, making plans on how to get rid of the corpses. Why didn't you rush to call the police then?"

"We were afraid…"

"Afraid? Why not call authorities then?" he was still smiling, and a slow realisation emerged in my mind that indeed Rick was only bait – the real fish here was me. I just wondered why they hadn't tightened their grip sooner; they'd had an opportunity or two in Vienna, I was sure.

I started to retreat slowly.

"You're not the real police, are you?" I asked.

The officer was still smiling as he waved his hand.

"You're very clever…" he told me watching as his comrades knocked me over and put handcuffs on me too.

"Why are you doing this?" my voice was breaking in desperation.

The man only smiled, producing a key from his breast pocket and shouted a few short commands in an unknown language.

His comrades opened Rick's cage and quickly pushed me and John inside.

The officer smiled again, locking us in and putting the key back in his pocket.

"I've never seen greater foolishness than a loyal friendship," he said, still smiling. "This is bad for you and lucky for us."

"So, as we're already locked in, could you take the cuffs off?" I asked, having no hope of this happening, but surprisingly he nodded.

"Why not? You'll be able to scratch your lice!" he laughed. "Pity, the tiger is dead. It would have been more fun."

The handcuffs were taken off. He stood in front of us, grinning widely.

"Who ordered you to capture us?" I asked.

"Be patient," he said. "You'll find out in no time. I think the boss will be very happy with the catch."

Suddenly his smile moved to the left side of his face, and his head began to turn around in unnatural jerky motions with his eyes popping out of their orbits and red streaks of blood rushing down his chin from a bitten tongue. His body was still erect swaying on limping limbs. His aides rushed to support him.

"What just happened?" asked Rick.

"I'm not sure," I whispered. "Stay in the centre of the cage and don't touch the bars."

The creepy pantomime continued. Now another man was trembling like a tree in a high wind which blew off his hair, face, and limbs. Bloody remnants rolled over and dropped on the grass next to the clown.

"It's the banshee…" whispered John.

Cries of panic mixed with the loud roar of the lion. Grown men were flung around like a bunch of autumn leaves caught in a twister. But this was no wind. The macabre picture unfolded in slow-motion resembling a low budget horror movie, except all this terror was happening in the real world in front of our astonished eyes. I could clearly hear the cracking of bones and gurgling in their throats even from a distance, as streaks of blood painted the green grass scarlet.

Half an hour later, the banshee became bored, and the bodies began to drop to the ground one by one. The sparkling mist slowly rose above the grass in the falling dusk, and I realised that it was now our turn.

Hoping that the Master of Destiny would give me some protection, I placed John and Rick behind me and watched as the misty creature approached. The banshee hadn't been scary when it invaded the dead rat, but now it was confronting us with its full power, immediately after the eerie demonstration that had left the field scattered with human flesh, brains and blood.

It hovered like a giant crystal ball at eye level, a few yards away from the cage. I stood in front of it, shaking with fear, but still full of determination. My Sapphire dimly glowed on my fist.

John cursed loudly behind me as several tiny tentacles appeared from the wisp of mist, hesitantly extending towards the cage, but the strife lasted a few seconds only. The banshee retreated and faded away without even attempting to approach us any closer.

The night fell fast in the mountains. Soon it was too dark to see anything beyond the distance of an outstretched arm. A mournful wailing echoed from high peaks in the darkness, making it clear that we may have won the battle but the war with the banshee still lay ahead.

"Guys," I turned back to Rick and John. "We must remain on guard, or we'll be dead like that tiger before dawn."

"I'll only need a short nap," said John. "I'll be able to arrange a safe place for myself in Rehen in no time."

"If you could get somebody to look after Gwyn, I could stay on guard," said Rick. "Bysh can take care of himself."

"That's no problem," I promised. "I'll do that. As for me, I need a full night's sleep. There's a dangerous friend I need to visit, and that can't wait. Our lives may depend on it."

"You folks are full of dark secrets," complained John, but agreed to guard me along with Rick.

"Just stay away from the bars," I warned them again. "We're more or less safe if we stay in the middle."

"You two take your time," said Rick. "I'll guard us."

"I'll be back in half an hour," said John lying down on the floor.

I placed myself next to him.

"Don't lean on the cage bars, Rhys," I whispered before drifting into the darkness.

It was early morning in Chadrack. The birds quietly twittered outside my window, but it seemed too quiet. I sat up, listening. My room was empty, and I couldn't hear any sounds of disorder from either inside or outside the castle. Had there been an attack by the Mordakans during the night? I was still alive.

I quickly dressed and buckled my sword to the belt. The hall was empty, and I passed through it listening carefully. There were no sounds of a battle, no screams…

I carefully opened the door and smiled with relief to find Carwyn standing in the corridor with the usual bowl of warm water and towels.

"Good morning, my Lord," he bowed.

"Good morning, Carwyn," I greeted him.

He entered my chambers, put the bowl on a table as usual and placed the fresh towels and garments on a chair nearby.

"Do you have any particular requests for breakfast, my Lord?"

he asked, turning back to me.

"No, Carwyn. Just the usual," I replied, getting dressed.

"Will Lady Shandra be joining you?" he asked.

"I hope so," I said sincerely.

I owed her a brief explanation. My current complicated position in the cage could end at any moment and in an unexpected way. I didn't want to frighten her.

Carwyn was already heading out when I stopped him.

"Carwyn!"

He turned back.

"Yes, my Lord?"

"I have two more essential tasks for you this morning," I told him washing my face and wiping away the remnants of moisture from my face with a towel.

He said nothing but waited patiently.

"First thing – I want you to have a look at Rhys and take Bysh and Gwyn out of his room without waking him up. Take good care of them, especially Gwyn. Don't wake Rhys up, let him rest all day long undisturbed," I requested as casually as I could. "Place a guard at his door. This is crucial."

"I understand, my Lord," said Carwyn. "It will be as you wish. We usually have no problems with Bysh. I hope the gryphon will simply follow him."

"Good," I said, combing my hair.

He stood in front of me, waiting for my second request.

"And I'll need a lamb, immediately after breakfast," I said, finishing my hair.

"Dead or alive?"

"Dead, of course."

"I will do my best, my Lord," he said. "It will be as you wish."

He bowed, which was utterly unnecessary.

"May I ask you a question, my Lord?" he began hesitantly.

"Go ahead."

"Is Rhys under arrest? Have he done something inappropriate?"

"No. Why do you ask?"

"He's my distant relative," explained Carwyn. "I took the trouble to make him a good jaeger in your service, and I would be greatly disappointed if he had failed you."

"No, he's done nothing wrong, but he'll need his full strength for the task I am preparing him for. I'd like him to be fully rested."

"I understand, my Lord," he bowed again. "Please, forgive my impudence."

"It's all right, Carwyn."

"I'll let you know as soon as everything is ready for breakfast," he said.

"Thank you, Carwyn."

He bowed one more time and left. I slowly finished dressing, thinking about our miserable situation. It all seemed to be hopeless. We were locked in the cage, and even if we somehow manage to get out, the place was still haunted by that almost invisible beast, tearing every living creature into pieces. It couldn't get inside the cage, but we nor could we sit in the cage forever – without food and water, fried by the sun or chilled by night fogs.

It seemed that my Sapphire Ring was the only sound protection we had, capable of whisking the banshee away, but I had no idea of its "capacity". The Ring may already be exhausted after the colossal storm I had created yesterday. I must get it fully charged again and keep it ready to repel any attack by the banshee.

A lamb was promised to Hawa. It was a while ago when Rhys and I had needed a quiet place where we could sleep all day long while interrogating John in London. I thought that the tunnels next to the Well were safe enough, but they were only safe for a Prince or a Princess. Rhys wasn't a Prince, and I had had to beg for his life. Hawa, the Keeper, had agreed to spare it for a lamb. Promises are meant to be kept, especially important ones, especially when I needed more advice from Hawa. I had to kill the banshee. Hawa might know how to do this.

I wasn't going to sit in the cage and wait for our captor to show up. I had no desire to meet Morvarid again. A person who tossed away the lives of several dozen people and who had designed such an intricate plan to capture me was hardly a friend. Maybe I could try some manipulation of destiny once my Sapphire was fully charged? I thought I could organise a landslide despite the mountains not being very high. I just couldn't see how this would help us.

Absentmindedly, I paced around my chambers with fragments of facts and assumptions mixing with fear and clouding my reasoning. I must find a way out of that cage, out of those fields of death and out of those mountains. Only I didn't know how to stop that killing machine.

I wandered onto the balcony and stopped, clutching the railing and looking at the day slowly breaking above the still empty capital of Chadrack. A few smoking chimneys indicated that people were returning, and that life was slowly getting back to normal. Only my restless soul fluttered with uncertainty. I must survive, but I had no idea how.

Someone closed the door behind me, and I heard quick steps coming through the hall. I turned around quickly to face whoever was approaching me, placing my hand on my dagger as I did so. But soon a broad smile sneaked into my face. The silhouette emerging onto the balcony took the form of Shandra. She smiled back at me.

"I couldn't wait to see you," she whispered.

I held her silently in my arms, and my worries and troubles

shrank and distanced themselves, not too far away though, just around the corner.

"I was desperate to see you as well. I just thought you were still asleep," I told her. "I am not sure if I'll be around later in the day, but I'm yours for breakfast."

"Are you leaving?" she stared at me, frightened.

"Well, I must," I told her hesitantly. "I won't be too far away, but I'll be quite busy."

"Is it because of me?" she asked seriously.

"No, silly," I kissed her. "I can't explain it now, maybe later, but this is very important for me to do."

"State affairs?"

I smiled. Of course! It was state affairs if it was related to the ruler. And I was the ruler in Chadrack.

"Yes, you may call it that. Someday I'll explain, I promise."

"Don't make any promises if you're not going to keep them," she said. "I'll wait, and I don't need any explanations."

"I *will* explain," I replied. "It's a long story, and I just don't have enough time for that right now."

"I believe you," she kissed me.

"I'll be back really soon," I promised.

We stood embracing on the balcony, and it seemed like an eternity passed.

"Breakfast is ready, my Lord and Lady Shandra," announced

Carwyn from the doorway.

"Let's go," I took her elbow and led her inside.

We passed through my chambers and the corridor. The dining room greeted us with pleasant aromas. The breakfast was more than generous this time with roast pork, fish, vegetables, salads, fruit and nuts. The sweet smell of freshly baked bread was especially inviting.

I seated Shandra and took my place on the opposite side of the table. We ate in silence. Shandra barely looked at me, and I didn't want to disturb her. Then I noticed a crystal-clear teardrop travelling down her cheek.

"What's happened?" I asked her softly. "Why are you crying?"

"I've suddenly thought that you might not return," she said after some time. "Can I come with you?"

"I will return to you, Shandra, don't worry," but somehow my assurances didn't sound very comforting. "No, you can't come with me; it's too dangerous for you. I'll return as soon as I can."

I didn't add – if I would stay alive. I wasn't afraid of Hawa. Monstrous as he was, I was sure he meant me no harm. I feared the angry ethereal creature raging outside of the cage, just next to my sleeping body, which could kill me at any moment in my sleep.

"I feel danger," she whispered. "I don't know what's going to happen, but you are involved in some perilous game, Kyleb.

Please, promise me you will be careful. I'm afraid to lose you."

"I promise, Shandra," I was sincere. "Whatever I do, I'll do my best to stay in one piece and return to you as soon as I can."

She was right in every aspect. I was in a deadly situation, and god only knows how I would be able to handle it. She sensed the danger even if the danger was far away on the other plane of reality. I hoped I would succeed, but these could very easily just be empty hopes.

"I hope it will be as you say…" she whispered.

I sat in front of her, not knowing what else to add, then hesitantly put my wine on the table unfinished.

"I must go," I said, standing up.

She kept her head down, saying nothing. I went closer and kissed her hair. She didn't move.

"I must go…" I said again quietly.

"Go…" she whispered back. "I'll wait for you…"

I met Carwyn in the corridor as I left the room.

"Everything has been arranged as you requested, my Lord," he assured me. "Anything else I can do for you?"

"No, Carwyn. Thank you."

The lamb had been neatly placed in a basket, conveniently just in front of the hearth – I couldn't ask for more. I took the basket and opened the hidden passage.

I stretched my hand out into the opening, and the Sapphire

flashed blue connecting to the thousands of green-light-emitting crystals scattered on the walls of the tunnel as I stepped inside. The light was dim but sufficient, and I hurried forward, carrying the lamb on my back. The walls closed behind me.

The path meandered between the black monolith rocks and giant stalactites with clusters of amethyst crystals glistening on them, but I paid no attention to the sparkles as I hastened forward until the purple shadows of the Well appeared before my eyes.

"Hawa!" I placed the basket on the ground.

"I'm here," I heard a familiar voice followed by the familiar chuckle. "Why are you here this time?"

A giant spider with a grotesquely melted human head crawled from the shadows.

"I've brought you a lamb," I gestured at the basket.

"A lamb?" Hawa crawled closer. "Oh! You're keeping your promises..."

"Here!" I moved the basket in front of him.

"Oh!" his purple eyes grew brighter in the ghostly light of the Well. "Young and fresh. It will be a feast!"

He carefully inspected the white body of the lamb, gently touching the white skin with his claws and then put the basket away.

"What is it you're after this time?" he asked, turning his eyes to me. "You never appear with offerings without asking for something in return."

"My Ring needs the Well," I shrugged.

"Didn't you charge it recently when you shared the Well with Seisyll? How did you manage to exhaust it so soon? Go ahead. The Well is yours as long as you're sitting on the throne here," he chuckled. "You don't need my permission for that."

"And it's always good to visit a friend," I added, ignoring Hawa's mentioning of Seisyll.

"I am no one's friend," said the Keeper instantly. "Don't fool yourself."

I shrugged and stepped closer to the Well. The purple surface swirled and bubbled as I extended my arm.

The Master of Destiny flashed blue as the purple wave rose from the Well like a liquid tower and engulfed my arm. Slight shocks like those from a naked electric wire ran through my skin. I lowered my arm and sat on the edge of the Well. I looked at the columns of sparks, and purple thunderbolts hitting my Ring and felt a tremendous power building around the Sapphire – enough to split the ground and move mountains. This could shield us from the banshee, but was it able to kill the creature?

"Feels good, doesn't it?" asked the Keeper.

"Yes," I replied. "It's an extraordinary sense of power."

"You have survived an encounter with the Onyx. Were you successful with your magic?" he asked.

"Well... it was rather an intense period," I explained. "I had to create a few avalanches and landslides, a small earthquake, not to mention constantly shielding myself from the Onyx for a few days..."

"You need to tell me more," Hawa's eyes sparkled with curiosity as he crawled closer.

"I would gladly do that, but it's quite a long story, and I still have some urgent matters awaiting me..."

"Take your time, Kyleb. I am not rushing things," hissed the Keeper. "But I still insist on hearing the story."

I gave him a short and strongly edited version of what had happened since I had met Hel at the waterfall. He listened without any reaction.

"You have been busy, indeed," he observed when I had finished. "I told you – you'll remember everything. I am glad your memory has come back."

"Still, not completely, I'm afraid," I said withdrawing my palm from the Well.

The Sapphire glowed with intense blue light which gradually subsided as the Well grew still again. I noticed that the crystals in the ceiling of the grotto grew brighter.

Hawa came closer. He looked far more ghostly in the greenish light.

"Do you know anything about banshees?" I decided to turn to

more pressing questions.

"I do," he said. "Why are you so interested in these harmless creatures?"

"Harmless? Have you seen any recently? They're like killing machines!"

"Are we speaking about the same banshees, dear Prince?" asked the Keeper calmly. "They are harmless ethereal creatures. Just don't rile them. I think even such a divine beauty as this innocent lamb could kill under certain circumstances."

That image of a harmless banshee didn't quite fit with the images in my head as I still saw a whirlpool of flying blood and body parts. The deepest animal fear was already rooted in my heart, and I was powerless to suppress it.

"Are there any ethereal creatures other than your harmless banshees?" I asked. "The one I saw was simply monstrous, killing everyone in its way. I wouldn't call that harmless."

"Raging banshees can become awful creatures like any other angry wild animal," Hawa continued his lecture. "But if you feed them, be nice to them – you can have a faithful pet. Every creature needs a little love."

"Feed them? How?" the thought was so absurd I almost laughed.

"Don't pretend you don't know," the Keeper chuckled again. "I'm sure you've done it before."

"I don't remember," I said. "What could I use as a carrot for the banshee?"

"Ethereal entities feed on energy, it's simple," said Keeper. "And you have plenty of that in your Ring."

"But they *are* dangerous!" I felt my hackles rise just by thinking of it.

"Dogs can be dangerous too if you keep teasing them," observed the Keeper. "Banshees are lovely if you handle them right."

That was very hard to believe. On the other hand, I knew that Morvarid had managed to handle the banshee somehow, even without a Ring. Or had she just fed me lies and fantasies?

"Is there any way to kill a banshee?" I was reluctant to try befriending the invisible monster and rather keen to finish it off in one go.

"I doubt that," said Hawa laughing. "Let me know if you can figure that one out. But I still don't understand why you need to kill it? Where did you find the creature?"

"In the woods, next to the waterfall," it was a half-truth.

"Strange," the Keeper raised one of his legs and gently scratched the head. "They've never showed up in the vicinity of the Well before. They must be desperate. Be gentle, if you meet it again, no sharp moves and no aggression. Love makes miracles."

I hated to go any further into explanations of our hopeless

situation within the cage with that lovable ethereal beast raging around and killing people. It was clear that I would have to find out any workable solution for myself.

"Don't get me wrong," said Hawa. "I think you should try an easy way first."

"Do you know what the hard way is?" I asked.

"No," said the Keeper. "I can't think of any. With a banshee, you are either its best friend and master..."

"Or?" the implication was chilling.

"Or you're dead," he chuckled. "It's better not to deal with them. Better to stay away..."

It was a wise piece of advice, but also too late. If only I had known that before… I wondered how things would have turned out differently if I had left the banshee to float away in the *Prater* and stayed away from it. It was me who had wrapped it in the foil and most likely scared and angered the ghostly mist to boiling point. It was entirely my fault that the creature was now massacring everybody in its way. But it was too late for regrets. Would it calm down in time? The banshee I had encountered was too far from the image Hawa had painted as well as being too scary.

It was time to go, so I stood up and said my goodbyes. Hawa followed me silently with his glowing eyes until I disappeared into the tunnel. I heard shuffling in the basket from a distance and the sound of breaking bones as he started his feast on the lamb. I didn't turn back to take a look.

Back in my chambers, I faced my fears again. Hawa had told me nothing useful. I still had no idea how to fight or how to kill the banshee. At least, my Ring was now fully charged – I hoped it could protect us for a while.

I needed a quiet place to sit alone and to think. The banshee situation was scaring me to death. I wasn't sure what was happening in the cage with Rhys and John, but the simple fact that I was still breathing assured me that the invisible killer monster had stayed away from them. For now.

It was around noon in Chadrack and midnight in Slovak Tatras by my estimation. Time was pressing. I must gather all my courage for the inevitable confrontation tomorrow, but my chambers didn't feel like the right place for this. I quietly sneaked into the corridor and bumped into Shandra, who was pacing back and forth just outside of my door.

"I was waiting for you," she said with a concerned look on her face.

"I'm glad you were," I smiled. "Did anything serious happen?"

"No," she shook her head. "I just missed you. But how did you get in? I thought this was the only door…"

The smile froze on my face. I wasn't ready to reveal the truth about the Well just yet.

"This castle still has its secrets," I said vaguely. "I sometimes stumble upon them myself. How was your morning?"

She didn't press the matter any further, simply shrugged as we began to move away from my door.

Our light chatter slowly eased my tension and pushed my fears away, as we slowly walked through the corridors and galleries of the castle, heading nowhere in particular and seeing nobody. It was like the last ray of sunshine just before the storm cloud broke. At the back of my mind, the thunderstorm already fretted, searching for ways to defeat the shapeless enemy while my face enjoyed the warmth of Shandra's smile.

"You're not listening," she complained when we entered one of the gardens through a tall arch.

"I am listening," I protested, making my way to the fountain and sitting down on edge.

"I can see you're worried," she stated this as a fact. "You're talking to me, but your mind keeps wandering somewhere else. It seems like you are back in that tunnel where I found you, helpless. Am I interrupting some important state-related matter?"

"You're not interrupting anything," I assured her. "I have some problems, but I need to solve them myself. You can't help me with this."

"Try me!" she smiled teasingly.

"It is too complicated to explain just like that," I said seriously.

"Let's just pretend it's not the case and enjoy what we have right now..."

"As you wish," Shandra sat down on the edge of the fountain next to me.

We spent the next half an hour talking about the pleasant weather and the beautiful garden surrounding us. Then Carwyn approached us with a concerned look on his face.

"What's happened?" I asked before he had an opportunity to open his mouth.

"I'm sorry to disturb you, my Lord," said the old butler. "But there are some matters which require your attention."

"I'll go so you can talk privately," said Shandra, standing up.

"That's not necessary," I objected and turned back to Carwyn. "What is it?"

"You expressed a wish to withdraw all trials from the temple and conduct them yourself," he said. "There is one waiting."

There could not be a less opportune time for this! I was able to forget my worries when I was chatting with Shandra. I needed to organise my thoughts, preparing for the night ahead, but the trial... I wasn't ready for this now.

"Bring them to the throne hall in a half an hour," I said sighing. "I'll be there by then."

Carwyn bowed and left.

"Shit!" I quietly cursed as he left and then immediately

apologised to Shandra. "Maybe *you* could help me to hold the trial? You have the perfect sense of justice for that."

"You did it well last time, Kyleb," she said. "Everything was sensible and just. I don't think I'm in a position to try anybody. I am a nobody who just happens to stand next to the Prince. I don't have any authority. Why can't you perform your justice again?"

"I have a challenging and complicated matter waiting for me…" I began vaguely. "I've told you about this before. I don't want anybody else to be aware of that. I'm not ready to deliver any justice this time, but I would be grateful if you can give me a helping hand, Shandra. You've said you're willing to help."

"I'm not sure I'll be able to manage this," she said.

"I'll help you," I took her hand as we turned back to the castle. "Just listen to what they tell you, and then listen to your heart. I will be there with you and will make sure that everything will be as you say."

"I don't know…" she began, then paused. "I'll do as you wish."

"I'll need your help in executing justice when I'm not around the castle," I continued the persuasion. "I don't want to give it back to the priest and the temple – remember that poor lad Milo?"

"Yes, you told me," she sighed. "I'll do my best."

"Don't be afraid," I put my arms around her shoulders as we moved on. "You'll be fine."

As we walked back through the silent galleries and corridors, the path seemed endless. I wondered how Carwyn had managed to find us.

Murmuring greeted us as we entered the throne hall. Not too many were there, and their voices fell silent as we passed. I looked around but still couldn't make out who was the guilty party or who was the victim.

I seated Shandra next to me and sat down on the throne. Everybody stood in silence in front of us, looking at me expectantly.

I took my time to look at the face of each of those standing in front of me.

"Lady Shandra will hold the trial in my name," I announced finally. "It will be as she says."

A wave of hushed murmur spread through the hall as Shandra stood up.

"Let's hear from the victim," she said in a loud voice.

A ripple passed through the front row as the crowd spat forward a pale young girl in her teens. She looked around with frightened eyes, confused and chaotic, and then began to sob.

"Calm down, child," said Shandra still standing firm in her place. "Nobody is going to hurt you. What's your name?"

"Myrna..." her voice was very quiet, barely audible.

"Tell us what happened, Myrna," Shandra hesitantly took a

few steps forward, but then stopped and returned to stand next to the throne.

"He hurt me down here," said the girl still sobbing and placing her hand on her groin, where her dress was torn in a few places, and several red dots around them now acquired a grave new meaning.

Shandra paled but held her stance.

"Who did this?" she asked.

"Him," Myrna pointed to a bald man in his fifties, sweating in his uncomfortably large body in the left flank of the hall.

"She's a little bitch!" he exclaimed. "She seduced me!"

A murmur passed through the crowd again, louder this time. Myrna carried on crying, hiding her face in her hands. Shandra grew even paler and leant on the side of the throne. I began to regret placing this burden on her, but it was too late to intervene.

"What do you have to say in your defence?" she whispered, but her words were distinctly heard.

"I'm the victim here!" exclaimed the man. "You may ask priest Kyaal. I am a pious and respectable citizen. She seduced me!"

Several angry shouts erupted from behind the crowd, so I decided to step in and give Shandra a helping hand. I remained seated but raised my hand, silencing everybody.

"Any witnesses?" I asked and received a grateful glance from Shandra.

A woman came forward.

"We dragged that animal from her with his pants around his ankles, my Lord," she said. "He's been on trial seven times in the temple. Each time we had caught him in the act, and each time he was proclaimed innocent by the temple! My daughter is still serving a sentence there, my Lord. She was only a six-year-old – how could she seduce a grown man?"

"And who are you?" I asked.

"I am Ritva," she said bowing. "I bake your bread, my Lord."

"Any more witnesses?"

A murmur ran through the crowd again as several more men and women stepped forward.

"I am Breden, my Lord," said one of the men. "He hurt my boy too. I am not afraid of the gods to tell you this. The temple just let him go and sentenced my son instead to serve as a medium."

I glanced at Shandra. She stood firmly, simply clenching the edge of the throne with her white fingers.

"We have heard enough," I announced, but I had already placed the responsibility on Shandra, there was no way back. "Now Lady Shandra will decide on the punishment for this man as his guilt is clear and has been well witnessed."

"It can only be death!" whispered Shandra and her quiet words echoed through the hall.

"I am a respectable citizen!" the man was sweating like a pig. "I will not be judged by the witch!"

"No one dares to speak to Lady Shandra like that! You are no longer a citizen," I said, standing up. "This verdict is final and will be carried out today in my name."

Suddenly Shandra broke from where she stood, rushed down the aisle, leaving the crowd behind and disappeared through the door.

"It will be done right now!" I said taking a few more moments to observe the man loudly protesting, as he was seized and dragged away, then I stormed after Shandra, initially doing my best to maintain my formal appearance and not break into a run. I was worried about her. It was silly of me to have placed this trial on her. I thought it would just be another simple case of theft, but instead, it had scratched and opened her old wounds. I could do nothing more but to regret.

The crowd was grim and silent as I passed. Myrna stopped sobbing, and my ears turned deaf to the cries and shouts of the sentenced man.

Back in the corridor, I stood still for a few heartbeats but couldn't hear even the distant echoes of Shandra's footsteps. I decided to check her room first.

The room was empty. I closed the door and rushed through the endless corridors and galleries of the castle, searching for her, stopping to listen, then searching again. I didn't try to call out to her. I was sure she wouldn't answer.

Long uncomfortable minutes stretched into an hour, squeezing my heart with the deadly fear of losing her. Suddenly she seemed much more important than my limp body next to the lion on another plane of reality.

I bumped into Carwyn who asked if I wished to attend the execution. I just shook my head and went on, not saying a word.

"She is in the northern back garden," said Carwyn as I walked on.

I thanked him and hurried there, almost sprinting through the long corridors and halls. I didn't care if anybody saw me nor if anybody questioned my sanity. My heart was restlessly rushing me forward.

I had never been in that part of the castle before, but Carwyn said it was northward, and when my wandering brought me into a long narrow corridor dimly lit by occasional arrow slits heading upwards with a set of stairs every twenty paces, I ran as fast as I could as if my life depended on it.

It ended abruptly on the second floor of the gallery facing the mountain, and I stopped, clutching the balustrade, breathless.

The northern garden was placed on an inclined slope of the mountain with black and grey rocks scattered among groups of dark green coniferous shrubs. It was surrounded by an elegant two-storey gallery with two high-peaked towers on the eastern and western sides, housing staircases. My statue made of black marble was at the centre of the garden with a small pond covered in scarlet waterlilies in front of it.

Shandra was sitting on a rock next to the pond with her shoulders sagging and her face buried in her hands.

"Shandra!" I called her, still breathless.

She raised her wet eyes to me. At the same moment, I heard a shuffle on my right – a barely audible sound as if a piece of silk had suddenly dropped on the ground. Before I had any chance to react, blue hands flashed around my neck and blue breasts pressed against my chest.

"I love you, Kyleb!" the blue lips sought my mouth as I still looked at the frightened Shandra. She sprang to her feet, ready to run away.

"I love you, Kyleb, with all my heart!" screamed Saqia as I pushed her away. "Don't do this to me!"

"Get dressed and go away!" I hissed through my teeth, dashing left towards the western tower.

A few steps later, I glanced at the garden where Shandra was hurrying away on a narrow cobblestone path heading east.

"Shandra, wait!"

She shuddered but stopped. I didn't glance back at Saqia, slipping into the narrow staircase and going down.

I found Shandra at the same spot in the middle of the

cobblestone path. She was crying.

"Why..." I began, but she shook her head, pushing my hand away.

I stood silently next to her. My heart ached, but there was no way I could comfort her, and I patiently waited until she had stopped crying and calmed down.

"Sorry," she said finally. "There's no need for you to look at my tears, sir. I hope you enjoyed the entertainment."

"Saqia means nothing to me," I told her. "I've never touched her, nor have I any desire to do so. I'll send her back to my sister Keely today if that would make you feel better."

"You may do as you please, sir," she said, wiping her tears away. "You are the Lord."

She flinched when I took her hand, and that felt like a strike of a dagger through my heart. *Damn!* We were slipping back to the beginning, but I was seriously determined to do whatever was necessary to win her back.

"Please, Shandra, just give me another chance," I whispered. "I will be patient."

She remained silent, and I couldn't decide if this was a good or bad sign.

"Why were you crying?" the question was stupid.

"Another man dies because of me," she explained without looking at me.

"It's not your fault, don't blame yourself in any way. He well deserved that fate," I said, still holding her hand. "You did everything right."

"But now I have to live with it," she told me looking away. "His blood is on my hands!"

She withdrew her hand and rubbed her palms against her gown as if trying to wipe them clean. Then she began crying again. I stood next to her, afraid to touch even the little finger on her left hand, afraid to scare her away.

"Life is cruel..." the attempt to comfort her was clumsy, and she stopped me.

"Please," she said with her face still buried in her palms. "Leave me alone..."

I stood still, hesitating. My soul ached and yearned to remain with her, to comfort her somehow. But she just carried on crying and shaking her head, and my feet, stiff as wood, carried me away.

I don't remember how I got back into my chambers. I went out onto the balcony just in time to catch a glimpse of the head of the former respectful citizen departing from his shoulders and the headless body slumping onto the ground. The image of the streaming blood passed through my mind without hitting my soul. My gaze was empty with the image of Shandra crying still etched in my mind.

"Wait! Stop that!!! Hold on!" a distant cry broke through my consciousness from the left, and I noticed the bulky figure of priest Kyaal running down the street.

The priest was waving his hands insanely, adjusting his pink wig as he rushed forward as fast as he could. I could only imagine how enormous this task was for his fat physique. He was sweating profusely with large dark spots on his robes streaming down from his chest and armpits.

"Wait!"

Then the priest realised at last that he was too late to change anything as the crowd of onlookers began to dissipate. He stopped in the middle of the street to catch his breath. The priest's face was crimson red – whether from anger or strenuous activity, was not clear from the distance.

He stood still for a few moments with his mouth agape and looked at the headless body in the dust, and then fixed his gaze on me on the balcony. A nervous smile crossed his lips, and he resumed his journey at a slightly slower pace, this time heading towards the castle entrance.

I needed to find the right words of reassurance for Shandra. I needed to calm my mind before facing the banshee. I desperately needed some solutions, but instead, problems were multiplying like rabbits.

I returned to my chambers. The clash with Kyaal seemed

inevitable, and I cursed angrily, realising that I couldn't just send him away. I was longing for some quietness but would have to deal with his whining. I must do that quickly and get rid of him. The temple must realise that its dominance was over.

The distant turmoil in the corridor grew closer and stopped at my door. I sat down at the table facing the entrance. The chaos and shouts calmed down, and somebody tapped on the door politely.

I maintained the silence still falsely hoping that they would change their mind. Carwyn popped in several moments later feeling, of course, quite embarrassed.

"Sorry to disturb you, my Lord," he said, stopping at the door. "The priest is demanding an immediate audience."

"I know," I said grimly. "Let him in."

Priest Kyaal broke in without waiting for an invitation, anxious, with his wig still sliding down his head and large wet stains under his armpits.

"Apologies for my appearance," he said, watching as Carwyn left. "I came as fast as I could but, apparently, not fast enough."

I kept on staring at him silently. This made him nervous and gave me a slight sadistic satisfaction. I didn't offer him a seat.

"Why have you killed poor Eamonn?" he moaned as soon as the door had closed behind Carwyn. "He was the best-paying client! It's bad for business."

"He was judged and sentenced," I observed calmly. "We found him guilty."

"Sweet tits of Maralyn!" he exclaimed. "When did you begin to hold trials?"

"I should have done it long ago," I remained while Kyaal was increasingly nervous.

He took a few steps closer, leaning over the table.

"Remember, dear Prince, that you are in the same boat as well," he licked his dry lips, but I didn't bother to offer him a drink. "All I have to do is spread the news of your part in the venture, and the crowd will gather under your balcony in no time!"

Was he threatening me? I made sure my poker face did not fail me this time.

"Go ahead," I responded, keeping the same boring intonation. "We'll see which one they crucify first!"

He moaned, stepping a few feet back, realising that his threats had made no impression upon me.

"Why? Why are you doing this?" his voice was now trembling. "Where or how have I failed you? You have your capital clean of thieves, without crime, without prisons. And you have a steady income for your treasury. The scheme was perfect! What suddenly went wrong?"

I didn't feel the need to explain anything.

"I hope you understand," he hissed through his teeth. "If you kill the hens who lay the golden eggs, then there will be no golden eggs!"

"I'm aware of the consequences," I stated flatly. "I wish to stick to income that comes from a more moral source."

His slumped body suddenly became straight.

"What could be immoral in religion?" he asked in a high-pitched voice.

"The religion itself," I told him.

Kyaal seemed to shudder as if from a sudden blast of cold wind. He hadn't expected such heresy.

"Has the holy church of Rhey offered you a better deal?" he seemed heartbroken. "Name it! I'm sure I could beat it!"

I shook my head.

"Was it the temple of Wayresh?" the priest demanded to know.

"No," I shook my head again.

He took off his pink wig and started to wipe his heavily perspiring forehead. The conversation was boring. The mere presence of Kyaal in my chambers was disturbing enough, and I wanted to end it as soon as possible.

"I will not let you torture my people again," I said quietly but firmly. "You and the temple of Qu'mun will be stripped of everything, and the right to hold the trials was just the beginning."

"You can't do this!" he exclaimed, turning pale at first, then bright red.

"Who will stop me?"

"People need something to believe," he groaned. "They need to worship something. It will be easier for you to rule them in the name of god. Why are you rejecting this? I was so efficient…"

"You've done enough," I said. "You may leave now and pack your things."

"Are you turning your back at Qu'mun?" he asked and then added after some hesitation. "The Serpent will eat your liver for such heresy."

"I have seen the white serpent recently," I added a wicked smile accompanied my words. "It didn't seem to be very aggressive or show any desire for my liver."

"Don't try to convince me that Qu'mun has blessed you…" he added a small hint of poorly hidden irony in his voice. "That's why you're getting rid of me? I've served you well, but maybe I could try harder? May I point out that it was your orders that I carried out?"

"It is not for you to judge me," I said. "Get out!"

"Please," he clumsily lowered his massive body to his knees. "I am old. Let me finish my days in the temple. I don't ask much. Just don't exile me. Please…"

A sense of guilt suddenly sneaked into my righteous stance. I knew the Bloody Prince hadn't been that white and shiny. My predecessor's dirty mind and dangerous actions must also be blamed for whatever the priest did in the temple. I couldn't just forget that. Damn! But I was unwilling to relent. On the other hand, I saw no harm if he was to spend his last days in the temple. I felt powerful and secure.

"You may stay," I told him. "But on one condition."

"Name it!"

"You will release all of your mediums today, and you will end this disgusting praying practice. No exceptions," I placed my hand firmly on the table. "Or I will crush you like a bug if you disobey."

"I'll do that! I will!"

"Go now!"

"Thank you, thank you so much… Let the Dark spare you, my Lord," Kyaal hesitantly approached the table again, seeking to kiss my hand, but my grim face didn't encourage any further contact.

He just bowed and retreated, leaving the bitter odour of his sweat filling the hall. Kyaal placed his wig back on his bald head before opening the door, cast one more dramatic glance in my direction and left.

For several long heartbeats, I just enjoyed the silence. Then grim thoughts and suppressed fears threatened to drown me again.

I stood up and went back to the balcony, where the sticky stink of the priest's sweat couldn't follow me. The sun was setting, painting mountain tops in pink and orange. Only the Gothic towers of the temple stood like a bloody red splinter against the dark green body of the mountain.

The evening was approaching. The time for the transfer was approaching. But I wasn't yet ready to meet the banshee.

I went out to check on Shandra. Her room was still empty. I decided against peeking into the backyard garden again. She needed her moments of privacy.

I met Carwyn in the corridor.

"Have you seen Lady Shandra?" I asked him.

"No, my Lord," he said. "Do you want me to search for her?"

"No," I said. "Let her do things at her own pace."

"Where do you wish to have dinner served?" asked Carwyn.

"Bring it to my room," I said with little thought. "But make it light."

"As you wish, my Lord," Carwyn bowed and left.

I paced my room, preparing to return to the cage next to the lion until my dinner arrived. It was light, as I had requested – just a few pieces of ham, cheese, a fresh bun, a few apples and a bottle of red wine.

I couldn't get rid of the overwhelming fear which filled my

bones. It was almost time. I was unable to eat, just poured myself a generous glass of wine, downed it and then went to bed. Black shadows of fear slipped in there with me, keeping me company under the covers, then lulled me into sleep, clutching my heart with their cold grip. The last thing I heard was the remote song of a nightingale from a dark bush beyond the castle wall.

Rick and John were sitting in front of me, leaning their backs against each other. The night was over and early morning mists slid down the mountain slopes, promising a beautiful and clear day.

"How are things going?" I asked, sitting up.

"Quietly," said John.

"At least, we've got some fresh air now," said Rick.

"Not forgetting the divine odour of rotting meat," mumbled John bitterly.

Everything was fine. We had survived the night.

"Have you found the answer?" asked Rick. "Do you know how to kill the creature?"

I shook my head.

"My source doesn't have such knowledge," I said sadly. "It might be indestructible."

"We're doomed…" started to wail John. "We're going to die

here!”

“That’s quite possible,” I agreed with him. “That friend did offer a possible solution, but I don’t think I like it very much.”

“What is it?” asked both Rick and John almost in unison.

“To tame the creature,” I said shrugging. “I don’t like how it sounds, but I have no other ideas.”

“This is crazy!” exclaimed John. “This is absolute madness!”

Vivid demonstrations provided by the ruthless creature were plentiful, scattered across the vast field.

“This is crazy. This is crazy…” John kept on whispering, and I sensed a rising panic in his voice. “This is complete madness...”

“I’ve never heard of a tame banshee,” said Rick. “Not even in the wildest of rumours.”

“But Morvarid has found some way to deal with the banshee,” I reminded them. “I see no other option.”

“It’s complete madness,” John kept on whispering.

“Do you have any idea how to do it?” asked Rick.

“My source of information wasn’t that specific,” I shook my head. “Sorry…”

The morning was quiet and peaceful. Too quiet. Then I noticed that the lion wasn't moving. His tongue lolled out of his gaping mouth, and his eyes gazed blankly at nothingness.

“When did this happen?” I asked, pointing at the dead beast.

“We didn't even notice,” said Rick. “It was too dark.”

We stood up and went closer, keeping our hands away from the bars. The lion's tail was sticking through the bars outside the cage – that's how the banshee had got him. And that was the route for it to leave the cage as well.

"Oh, god," moaned John. "That was so close… And you're thinking of making friends with that monster? You might have been more successful at that with a hungry lion. He just hasn't lived long enough for you to try."

"I don't think it's entirely hopeless," said Rick. "Even the wildest animals can be trained. You just need tremendous patience and plenty of time…"

"I can be patient," I responded. "But I think we are tight on time. With no food and no water here I don't think we'll be able to survive for very long."

"We can eat the tiger," proposed John. "It's still fresh… And we can put the lion to use as well. Meat is just meat."

The idea was repulsive, but I was afraid that we might be forced to try it.

"I don't think we should mess with the creature, guys," John placed his ginger head between Rick and me as we still faced the lion.

"Do you have a better idea?" I asked.

"What about waiting until somebody passes our way?" he asked. "We could shout to attract attention."

"And have a few more corpses around?" I asked him. "Don't forget that we are somewhere quite remote, somewhere in the mountains, and it may be weeks before anybody wanders by. Let me remind you again – no food and no water. How long can we stay like this? And one more thing – we're about to meet someone who has taken the trouble to capture us. Care to wait and see who did that?"

"Don't argue," Rick tried to calm us down. "Let's hear what your plan is. How could you train the banshee?"

"And who told you this nonsense?" John's voice was still pitched on high.

"I can't disclose the source of my information. Believe me, it's been tested more than once and proved to be reliable," I said to John and added to Rick. "I've been told that banshees could be tamed and kept as pets. I hate the idea, but we have no other way other than just to try to it."

"It's absolute madness..." mumbled John.

"I know, it is," I admitted. "But do we have any better options?"

"But how?"

"I haven't figured it out yet," I admitted. "I'll need to think on the go..."

"That's a very comforting attitude," observed John with increasing nervousness.

"I'm sorry," I said. "It's all I've got."

"Not too much..." remarked Rick as well.

"Whatever you do with that thing," said John. "Keep me out of this."

"How are you planning to avoid that?" asked Rick him. "If the banshee is in the cage, we all would be affected equally."

"Just give me as much space as possible," I told them. "I'll do my best not to put either of you in any danger."

"Will you be able to handle the banshee if it gets in?" asked John.

"I've caught it once," I replied. "I might be successful again."

"But may I remind you," said John. "That this time you lack that the protection of foil. It's all been left in the hands of the dead clown out there!"

"Guys, please, calm down," Rick laid his hands on both of us. "We're not enemies. Let's give it a try seeing as we have no other options at the moment."

"Fine," said John. "I'll say my prayers in advance!"

"Whatever suits you," Rick even managed a smile and then added, addressing me. "Just try to keep it out of the cage."

"I have no desire to die either," I told them. "I'll be careful."

"It's pointless arguing," agreed John finally. "Just try to keep it away from us."

"I will," I promised.

Hours passed as we stood close to the bars searching for any sign of the banshee, seeing nothing. Several crows landed to feast on the free meat scattered plentifully across the field. The sound of an occasional passing car reached us from a great distance, but not a single vehicle passed the quarry within visibility.

"Maybe it won't come back..." said John. "Maybe it's just gone?"

"Then we need to rely on the very remote possibility of being found," I replied, continuing to search the horizon. "Not to mention that we might see our captors first. Or die of dehydration."

"There is no way I can persuade you, I see. Sorry, guys, but I feel deadly tired after last night," John retreated to the back of the cage. "I'd like to see my wife for maybe one last time."

"Go ahead," said Rick. "Take a nap. Just don't get close to the bars."

Rick and I kept on looking around. The scenery seemed peaceful – we grew so used to the bloody presence of the marred bodies that we started to ignore them, only noticing flowers, butterflies and small birds.

Soon the cage filled with John's snoring. It was annoying and loud enough to wake the dead lion. Then, from the peripheral view of my left eye, I noticed a slight movement. The lion *was* moving!

I punched Rick with my elbow silently indicating the predator.

"Maybe, he's not dead..." I whispered.

Rick shook his head, vigorously. I followed where his finger was pointing. There was a tiny transparent tentacle sticking out of the lion's paw. The banshee!

I pushed Rick aside, behind me, and lowered myself onto my knees. The lion carcass froze and stopped moving as well.

I was desperate. All would be lost if the banshee slipped away. I quickly reached into the lion's cage and dragged its tail inside, next to the body. My Ring flashed me a warning, and I retracted my hand as fast as I could.

"Why?" asked Rick.

"Now it has to stay in the cage too," I said. "We'll be certain about where it is, at least."

The lion started to rise from the floor.

"I hope you haven't angered it again," whispered Rick.

The snoring from the back of the cage stopped.

"What the hell!" John asked and cursed loudly. "Why have you done that?"

"It was already there," I said, not looking at the redhead. "I just cut off its route of retreat. Now we know where it is."

"Good!" suddenly, John agreed with me. "Now we know that it's not outside. Let's get out of here!"

"How?" Rick crushed John's enthusiasm with a single word.

The key was still in the breast pocket of the corpse that lay several yards away from the cage. It still seemed hopeless.

The lion's body was now levitating several feet above the ground, making slow circles around the perimeter of its cage.

"What will you do now?" asked Rick.

"No idea," I shrugged. "Let's wait until it calms down."

We sat on the floor, now safely leaning against the bars next to the dead tiger. The flying lion was mesmerising. However, the pace seemed to be increasing.

"It doesn't appear to be calming down," observed John.

"It looks rather fierce," said Rick. "I don't think we're at a safe distance here."

The lion's head now became the centre of the strange vortex that raged in the neighbouring cage while its butt flew around the perimeter at increasing speed with its tail hitting the bars of the cage. A peculiar drumming sound was clearly audible, echoing from the mountain slopes, and all this wild cacophony gradually increased in pitch and loudness.

"I hope this will attract someone's attention," said John.

"I think both of you better hide behind me," I whispered. "I'll try to organise a shield."

I didn't have to repeat that instruction twice. They gathered behind my shoulders. I extended my will into the Ring and raised a shield between me and the banshee. It was energy consuming; I knew from my trip with Hel. I just hoped this creepy performance wouldn't last too long.

The deafening vibrating cacophony ceased abruptly as the lion's body began to disintegrate in the air. Pieces of skin, bone, flesh and gut sprayed around like bloody confetti while the head continued to spin in the middle of the cage at an even higher velocity. I raised the invisible shield just in time to stop a diabolical shower of the lion's entrails. A few more minutes, and it was over. The bloody lion's head bumped on the floor in the middle of the cage with a loud bang and became motionless.

"Is it still there?" asked Rick.

I saw his point. The banshee could have escaped along with the bloody shower as it passed through the bars.

"Let's hope so," I said.

"Do you think it could have escaped?" John's voice sounded desperate.

I dropped the shield and stood up. Our cage was still clean, but the neighbouring enclosure was thickly scattered with the lion's guts and fragments of bone. Blood was slowly dripping from the bars where the tail had hit them. *Had the banshee escaped?*

The lion's head was facing me as I approached the bars – lifeless and motionless.

"Is it still there?" asked John.

"I'm not sure," I said, staring at all the mess.

Slowly, the cheerful twittering of the birds returned, followed by the low humming of flies. Nobody and nothing else moved.

"Is it still there?" John nervously repeated his question.

"It might have gone," said Rick.

"Let's wait and see," I said, standing in front of the bloody lion's head. "We're still alive…"

"That won't be for long if it's slipped into our cage," John stood up looking around. "You might last longer with your protection, but we're doomed – Rick and me, both of us."

"We're all still alive," I repeated. "Let's stay close. I'll do my best to protect us all as far as I can."

"You might be too slow," said John. "Sorry, no offence. But that thing is lightning fast! Could you hold that shield permanently for as long as we're here?"

"It might not last until the evening," I explained not looking back. "It consumes a lot of energy, and I won't be able to do anything after the Ring's exhausted."

"I see…" John's voice reflected his poorly hidden disappointment.

For some time, we stood in the middle of the cage, silently observing the lion's head. Clouds of flies had already gathered around it, attracted by the banquet of rotting meat. Nothing moved in the neighbouring cage.

"We are idiots," announced John. "We're staring at an empty

cage. It's gone! Now it's waiting for us outside!"

"We can't be sure," said Rick.

"It's gone! It's gone!" notes of fear and desperation were bare in the voice of John. "Our heads will be spinning like that in no time!"

"Shut up!" I attempted to silence him.

"If you think it's gone, it's not in our cage," Rick's words voiced the first rational thought since we had witnessed that dreadful twister of lion flesh. "If you think it's outside, then look around outside. Maybe you'll spot it."

"Great idea!" John patted his hand on Rick's shoulder. "Great idea..."

"Just keep away from the bars!" I warned him.

"Don't worry," he mumbled, turning his back to us.

The better part of an hour passed as we watched a thick cloud of flies feasting on the pieces of meat. Suddenly a low rumbling noise erupted like thunder. We jumped, looking around. Nothing moved.

"Sorry, guys," it was John. "My butt couldn't hold it in anymore."

"I hope that was wind only?" Rick managed a smile of relief.

"Don't worry. You won't have to live with my shit!" John laughed nervously.

"It wouldn't make a big difference," I observed. "This stink can't get worse even with your shit."

The brief light-heartedness eased the tension a little, but it didn't remove the danger. Soon we grew silent again and carried on looking, waving away angry flies which strangely insisted on attacking us despite all those corpses lying around.

We stared until our feet began to ache as the sun slowly climbed in the sky and reached its zenith somewhere above our heads. The heat, the buzzing of flies and the smell of death around us put me into some sort of trance. Still, we achieved nothing, apart from being alive.

"I think we can safely sit down," said John finally. "My feet won't hold me up any longer."

"If it's not there," said Rick. "It can strike from any direction. We're not safe in any case. Let's sit down. We're exhausting our energies."

We retreated to the darkest corner of our cage, next to the dead tiger and sat on the floor. The buzz of flies followed us there like a dark cloud.

"Any idea what to do next?" asked John. "Any crazy ideas?"

I shook my head.

"Wait for somebody to find us and pray for good luck," said Rick.

It was getting hot. A piece of cloth covering the cage from above provided us with some shade, but the lack of wind soon turned our cell into a slow cooking oven.

Streams of hot air swirled around, blurring the vision. It looked like wind, but it didn't fool our brains with its mere illusion. My gaze through half-closed eyes was still fixed on the lion's head, and sometimes it seemed that the hot streams were moving its mane as well. Illusion... just illusion? *Really?* I sprang to my feet.

"What?" mumbled John.

"Shut up!" Rick was rising to his feet as well.

The lion's mane *was* rising and moving in a mesmerising swaying movement like the snakes on the head of Medusa.

"It's here..." whispered Rick.

I heard John gasp behind me. Suddenly the head sprang from its resting place and rushed forward in a parabolic trajectory to attack us but just banged into the metal bars and bounced back like a ball. We jumped away, shielding our eyes with our hands, but nothing else happened.

"Bloody hell!" John started to shout and cursed. "Are you still thinking you can tame that thing?"

"I'm not sure," I said, my eyes still fixed on the lion's head which was now slowly parading around the cage in mid-air.

The banshee didn't make any further attempt to attack us, so we sat down, leaning on the far wall of the cage. The lion's head circled methodically inside its prison with the mane now fully outstretched. It made no sound.

"It's caged, and it's tested its boundaries," observed Rick. "That's the sign of certain intelligence."

"I'm happy as long as that intelligent thing stays on the other side of the bars," said John quickly. "Let's keep it that way."

I had no objections this time. It was safer.

"Could we use some other known Sleeper to get us out?" I asked. "The banshee is in the cage, and it would be safe to approach us. And we know where to find the key."

"I don't know any other Sleepers," Rick shook his head.

"Me neither," I said. "What about your Asian guys, John?"

He frowned, still following the moving banshee.

"Well, I could try to ask, but it might be difficult if they're already on assignment," he said. "I don't know where they are."

"Assignment?"

"It's nothing personal," John squeezed a shy smile. "It's only business. But I'll ask them if they could help us somehow."

The day was coming to an end, and thick waves of heat were soon replaced by streams of chilly air sliding down the slopes of the mountains.

"What shall we do next?" asked Rick.

"I'm sorry," I said. "But I'll need a full night's sleep tonight as well. I've some urgent matters to attend to, and I'll try to find another solution for the banshee."

"You're the boss," said John. "We'll take it in turns then. But I may need the better part of the night if we want to count on any outside help."

"You sleep first," said Rick. "I've nothing in particular to do."

"I'll make sure nobody disturbs you," I promised.

"Great," he smiled. "I was counting on that."

The banshee was still marching around the cage, but it didn't make any further attempts to break through the bars.

"Keep an eye on it," I said to Rick. "But let me sleep unless there's a life or death situation. It might be dangerous to wake me up while I'm on the other side."

"I will," Rick said, leaning on the wall next to the tiger's body.

John was already snoring. I envied his ability to get through almost instantly, regardless of the situation. It wasn't the most straightforward task for me to get to sleep feeling such tension and with the loud gurgles from John's mouth next to my ear.

I don't know how much time passed while I waited to dream. It happened suddenly.

Somebody touched my shoulder. I raised my head, making Carwyn jump away.

"What happened?"

"Sorry, my Lord, for disturbing your sleep," he began to apologise. "I think you should know first – Lady Shandra has gone…"

"Are you sure?" I asked in disbelief, sitting up.

"She wasn't in her room. We've checked several times," he shook his head unhappily. "And we can't find her anywhere in the castle."

"Maybe she's somewhere in the city?"

"That will be difficult to find out," said Carwyn. "Would you like us to try?"

"Yes," I said, sitting up. "Respect her wishes though, please, if she doesn't want to be disturbed – let it be. I just want to know that she's all right."

He left, and for some time, I heard him in the corridor, issuing commands. Then everything grew quiet again.

Why? Why was this happening? Was it my entire fault that she had decided to leave? She hadn't said goodbye; she hadn't left me with even a kiss. Or was she still crying somewhere?

Carwyn returned and asked me where I wanted my breakfast. Food was the least of my worries, so I dismissed him and got dressed slowly.

Shandra's disappearance had knocked me off track. I paced my chambers, unable to gather my thoughts and worries in order with only sadness drowning my soul. Shandra was gone. Everything else seemed trivial and unimportant.

I went onto the balcony, letting the cold morning air chill my face. That didn't help either. My soul still ached.

Suddenly I felt somebody's arms around my shoulders and a light kiss on my neck. Shandra… Carwyn had been wrong!

I turned around and smiled. She smiled back at me, but it wasn't Shandra. Saqia looked at me with her pale blue, almost white, eyes which were set deep into her handsome blue face.

"I couldn't sleep, my Lord," she said, attempting one more kiss. "I missed you so…"

She was dressed in a long crimson gown, skin-tight on top and loose at the bottom, entirely covering her hips, legs and toes with intricate embroidery.

"I thought you went back to Porlock after yesterday," I said gently pushing her away from me.

"How could I? I belong to you, my Lord," she smiled again. "Care for some morning joy? I am still your gift."

"No, Saqia," I tried to restrain my growing embarrassment and to sound as polite as I could. "I accepted you in the castle, but not for this."

"What was your intention then, my Lord?" she was still smiling. "I hoped it was lust and pleasure?"

"I must admit that at first I just didn't want to make Keely unhappy because she was doing her best to impress me," I said watching the smile fade from Saqia's face. "I hated the thought that humans can be passed around as gifts, but I couldn't refuse my sister. I decided to break the cycle and let you live in my house, but I had nothing else in mind. I am not holding you here, and I would be happy if you left Chadrack and went wherever you wanted to."

"Don't you think I'm attractive?" she asked, looking at me.

"Do you like to be passed around like a gift?" I parried her with the question, ignoring her lusty glances.

Her face turned pink, and I couldn't guess if this change represented pallor or redness for a blue-skin.

"I am *your* gift, my Lord," she said through her now pursed lips. "I am yours to be used and to serve for your pleasure – that was the only intention of Princes Keely. I'm sorry if I have bothered you at an unfortunate time."

"It might have been Keely's intentions, but she didn't consult me before making such a gift," I said with a bitter embarrassment now leaking through my words. "I have no intention of regarding you as a tool for my pleasure. I'm sorry if this does not satisfy your lust. I had nothing to do with my sister's decision."

"Princess Keely will kill me if she finds out that you didn't like my services," she attempted a nervous smile.

"Keely won't find out," I said firmly. "I'll tell her that I was delighted with her gift. You may leave now."

She took a step towards the exit but hesitantly stopped as if changing her mind.

"I'd like to ask you about that other woman, my Lord," she said a voice that cracked. "Is she capable of satisfying you better? You can't even imagine what you are turning down..."

"I don't care to find out," I said, annoyed by the conversation already.

"Fine…" she whispered.

Saqia stood for a few seconds in front of me, motionless. Then she raised her right arm. Rays of the morning sun playfully glistened on her bracelet. Or was it only a bracelet? It took me a moment too long to focus on her fist and realise that she was holding a small dagger – a neatly decorated woman's weapon.

The first strike hissed through the air, half an inch from my face. I jumped back instinctively. She continued to advance towards me with the maddening gaze of her almost white eyes fixed upon my face. I was unarmed. All I could do was to retreat until my back touched the far side of the balcony. Now she smiled viciously.

"Why are you doing this?" I asked, desperately searching for another way to retreat.

"You are weak, Prince Kyleb," she hissed. "You are not the man everybody used to know. You are not the one from the songs and legends! You are weak! Even a woman can make you tremble!"

A few more near misses of the dagger parted the air in front of my face again. I jumped to my right, trying to avoid the mad woman, but she kept on advancing.

"Why?" I couldn't believe this was happening. "Did Keely ordered you to kill me?"

"You are weak!" she hissed through her teeth, striking out again, and this time managing to scratch my shoulder. "I know who you are!"

The wound wasn't deep, just a surface scratch, but it was now distracting me. This was going too far. What did she know? I couldn't believe that my personality was so different from my predecessor and so noticeable. This statement was too dangerous to be ignored.

"You're mad, woman!" I managed to parry her advance with one more minor scratch to my thigh. "You are wrong, and you know nothing!"

She chuckled and placed the dagger in her other hand.

"You are weak!" she screamed. "Even a woman can overpower you with just her left hand!"

My position now wasn't favourable – the sun was shining directly into my eyes so I couldn't see her clearly. I retreated to the other side of the balcony.

"You are not Prince Kyleb," she now looked like a mad blue monster in a dark crimson gown. "You are only a mere demon of the night, stealing his body! You are a thief!"

She hissed in front of me, as her dagger passed from one side to another, luckily only hitting thin air. I quickly glanced around when she stumbled on her long gown, allowing me a short breathing space. I couldn't find anything handy on the balcony to use for my defence. All I could do was continue to retreat.

Our fight hadn't gone unnoticed. I heard a few cries from the yard but had no time to have a look.

"You are a coward!" she raised her gown exposing her blue calves, the dagger still in her left hand as she attacked me again. "Stop whining and fight me back!"

"You are utterly wrong, woman!" I made certain my voice was heard in the yard. "You are mad! Why must we fight?"

"Because you are cowardly night demon!" she stumbled on her gown again and raised it higher to keep it away from her feet, but now it was too difficult for her to advance, attack and keep her robes in place at the same time. "I will cut you loose!"

She glanced down, trying to get a better grip of the gown. This was the perfect moment for me to attack, and I jumped forward. I grabbed her left wrist and squeezed it as hard as I could in the hope that she would drop the dagger. Saqia screamed but still held the blade.

"Coward! Coward!" she slapped my back with her free hand, letting her gown go.

I tried to avoid her sharp dagger, which was already covered with my blood and kept on squeezing her arm. Her wrist grew stiff, and I hoped that I would be able to slap the dagger out with one blow. She resisted all my moves, fighting, screaming and punching my back like a mad lioness.

I dragged her to the edge of the balcony and attempted to hit her hand on the rail. Then my right foot slipped on her gown, and I fell on the floor, painfully hitting my right shoulder.

I raised my head in a split of a second, shielding it with my left hand and instinctively waiting for another strike. It didn't come. Then I realised that Saqia was falling too, losing her balance and slipping over the rail of the balcony. I tried to grab the edge of her gown, but I was one moment too late – she was gone screaming her lungs out, then abruptly silent as she hit the ground.

It had become a peaceful morning again when I stood up. Saqia was lying on her back with her white eyes wide open. A red streak of blood slowly leaked from the left corner of her mouth. The skin-tight top of her crimson gown was torn in several places with bare ribs protruding through the garment. Her fingers were still jerking and clenching into fists, but she was already dead.

Jaegers stood around the convulsing Saqia with their crossbows pointing at her. Moments later, she became still.

"Take her away," I ordered still breathing heavily. "And burn her as our traditions dictate."

I didn't look at how my order was being carried out. I shut my eyes tightly, trying to whisk away the nightmare. I didn't understand one bit of what was going on. First, Seisyll with his weird requests and threats. Now, this… Why couldn't everybody just leave me alone? What kind of game was Keely playing with me? She had asked for an alliance and left Saqia behind to spy on me or to kill me? Rage rushed into my head, and I clenched the railing of the balcony just to calm down. I had sufficiently big problems on the other side of reality. Why did I need this nonsense? I turned around as I heard footsteps hurrying behind me. It was Carwyn.

"What happened, my Lord?" he asked, rushing closer. "We heard some trouble."

"Yes," I said, gesturing over the balcony. "There was some trouble indeed, but the troublemaker is no longer with us."

Carwyn stopped abruptly.

"Are you hurt, my Lord?" he asked. "You're bleeding…"

"It's only a few scratches," I shook my head. "It's nothing to worry about."

"Do you want me to fetch you a healer?"

"No, I'll be all right," I shook my head. "But I'll need some warm water and new robes."

"I will bring those at once," said Carwyn and rushed away.

I went inside. Dark anger boiling and surged in huge waves inside me. I had trusted my sister Keely. Why had she done this to me? Saqia was a strange woman, and I had always kept her at a distance. Had Keely ordered her lusty advances? What would have happened if I had allowed her to become close? Would Keely then have gained access to some of my secrets? I was sure that Saqia was just a mere pawn in my sister's game. Or had she acted on her own? It was irrelevant now if it had been her own game. But I still had to find out Keely's part in it.

Carwyn hurried in bringing a bowl of water, fresh robes, and a few bandages. He'd thought of everything.

"Thank you, Carwyn," I waited as he placed everything on the table.

"Will you need any help with your wounds, my Lord?" asked

Carwyn.

"No, I can handle it..."

He left without saying another word.

I stripped and inspected my wounds first. Both were just superficial scratches, not worth even bandaging. I washed them with warm water, waited until the bleeding stopped and then washed them again. I dressed frowning as the scratches hurt slightly. Then I began to pity my dehydrated body on the other plane of reality and decided against starving myself here, but I would have to get food for myself now.

My wounds just ached numbly; it was my heart that was bleeding. Shandra was gone, and now fear for her gripped my soul in a deadly grip. This place wasn't safe to wander alone with ghouls plaguing Chadrack from the south and the Mordakans probably still lurking somewhere in the woods. She was gone, and it was if she had vanished forever. Had Seisyll kidnapped her? Maybe she was lost somewhere in the intertwining streets of the empty capital?

These unsettling thoughts returned with each step I took down the familiar corridor on my way to the kitchen. I stopped myself from rushing around the castle, searching for her. I was sure that Carwyn had organised this much more efficiently. Suddenly a large part of my soul imploded and shrank out of existence, leaving a gaping and aching hole.

I must find her, or I would never feel complete again – that was the thought that continued to buzz around my head. A selfish thought. But the most important thing was to be sure that she was safe and well.

I passed several corridors and staircases with my mood descending into depression with every single step. I knew I must fight it back, but I seemed unable to. I felt almost crushed by it as I neared the kitchen and almost turned away seconds before I reached it, willing to allow myself starve to death in that stinking cage without her, rather than put a few crumbs in my mouth. But then I remembered Rick and John – both were depending on me. Without my Ring, they had no chances against the rage of the banshee, and it was because of me that they were in the cage in the first place. I was the one who had peeved the banshee to the point of boiling. It was entirely my fault, and now I had to find a way out.

Why had I forced Shandra to go through that trial? If only I could go back and undo it…

I spooked the cook, a woman in her fifties, as I burst into the kitchen as dark as a storm cloud. She paid her respects as I came closer and sat down.

"I need to eat," I said blandly. "Something simple."

They didn't have any coffee here, but I would have traded a horse for a cup of that dark hot brew. Instead, she placed a plate of some ham and cheese, a basket with freshly baked bread and a bottle of wine. I ate everything, not looking around, not tasting and not enjoying, just stuffing my stomach like a cooped up goose, preparing my liver for some weird pâté.

Wine helped everything down.

I thanked her and stood up when Carwyn came in with a very concerned look. My heart slid down into my heels, skipping several beats. Was she still alive?

"What?" I did my best not to sound rude.

"We haven't found her, my Lord," he said. "One of the guards let the Lady Shandra through the gate yesterday evening. She could be anywhere by now..."

Suddenly I felt weak at the knees and grabbed the table for support. Why had she left me?

Carwyn rushed to help me, but before he reached me that generous breakfast refused to be turned into a pâté and splashed out of my stomach! A few more spasms and everything calmed down. I lowered myself onto the chair that Carwyn had offered me for support.

"You've poisoned him!" he barked at the poor cook. "You'll be hanged for it!"

"No," I said. "She's done nothing wrong. The food was great. Leave her alone."

"Would you like to see a healer, my Lord?" Carwyn offered me a towel to wipe my mouth.

"No," I shook my head. "Just get me a glass of water!"

"Quick!" he turned to the cook. "You heard our Lord!"

The water was cold and soothed my burning mouth, but it couldn't extinguish the fire within which was tormenting my soul. I needed some time to grieve alone.

I thanked the cook and Carwyn and left the kitchen. A dark mood followed my footsteps like a shadow of doom snapping at my heels. I went forward without choosing any direction like a puppet. I met several men and women on my way but passed them with unseeing eyes. *She had left me. She had left me...*

Why had I been so stupid? Why couldn't I have told her how much she meant to me, how much I loved her? What kind of spell had been cast upon my tongue so that it became wooden when it was most needed?

I wasn't even aware how I had left the castle, crossed several gardens and empty intertwined streets and was now slowly crawling uphill following a small sandy path under the dark shadow of firs. I had left the city on my right. My problems kept running ahead of me and nagging me annoyingly – *fool, cripple, idiot!* Why hadn't I told her?

The path squeezed between two large black rocks, carried on down beneath a hanging cliff and emerged on the other side in a wide clearing which seemed familiar. I took a few more steps forward and found myself in front of the Grave of the Silent.

The giant's palm high above the city looked like the perfect place to sit down and think about the love that had gone, allow myself to grieve, wallow in a swamp of self-pity but perhaps plant some seeds of hope.

It was futile, but I hoped that she would return. She may just need some time to fight her own demons.

I climbed a few steps carved in the wrist of the giant palm and froze.

The Grave of the Silent was soaking in blood. Several dozens of bodies had been randomly dumped there – children, young men and women, naked or half-naked, with their throats cut wide open. All were dead.

It was a hellish abattoir of extreme cruelty, and I instantly recognised who was responsible – the priest had got rid of his mediums. Some even had short prayers carved into their skin!

I clenched my fists in desperation, but it was too late to cry for them. They silently called for revenge.

I don't know how much time passed as I stood on the palm of a giant facing the display of death in front of me when my senses finally returned, and blood rushed to my head. I must avenge them!

I reached into my Ring, looking for some cataclysm or disaster, which could wipe the temple from the face of the mountain. The options were plentiful – earthquake, landslide, avalanche. I could even open a small volcano under the temple! Then I stopped and allowed my boiling blood to cool. None of the options was good – my city lay below the temple. I instantly knew that whatever attempt I made to destroy my enemy, the consequences would be grave with countless more innocent lives sacrificed because of my rage as citizens slowly returned from their enforced exile.

I needed to fry Kyaal only. But not now.

My own heartache suddenly seemed selfish and pitiful. My wounded soul still bled, but I must forget my own pain in view of all those dead children and youngsters lying in front of me.

I began my slow task around the Grave, laying every single body comfortably, looking into their faces, scorched with pain and horror, closing their unseeing eyes and praying for them, swearing to avenge this atrocity.

It was well into the afternoon when I finished my task, and all the dead had been visited, touched, comforted and mourned. Then I returned to the castle.

"What?" Carwyn couldn't believe what I told him.

"He killed every medium in the temple and dumped them at the same spot," I said. "First, they need a proper burial, and then we'll decide how to punish Kyaal. Their blood is calling for justice."

"Yes, my Lord," said Carwyn. "We'll make a pyre for everyone there."

"Please, do it," I said. "I'll be in my room. I don't wish to be disturbed."

"I will place guards at your door, my Lord," said the old man.

"Thank you, Carwyn," I thanked him. "Is Bedwyr around?"

"Not yet, my Lord," he said. "He might be back in two or three days."

"I'll see him then," I said, disappearing into my chambers.

I closed the door behind me and leant on it for a few minutes, listening to the fading sound of distant footsteps in the corridor and finally letting my emotions to release and tears to run down my face.

I felt lonely and bereft. I could find plenty of good reasons to feel that way, but all I could do was to blame myself for everything.

Why was this happening to me?

I was unable to move any further. I just slid down onto the floor, cursed and cried loudly as hot tears ran down my cheeks. I didn't care what people would think about this. Half an hour later, I was exhausted. I was lying flat on the floor, my tears already dried, but still unable to move. The cold from the floor crept into my body, filling every cell with a chill. I did not have the strength to stand up.

Nobody bothered me, as I had ordered. I didn't hear any noise outside my door.

Then I cried a little again, now more out of self-pity than desperation. I would have my revenge! And I would find my love… I would… Wherever she was.

Later in the evening, I calmed myself down at last. My soul still ached, and now, although I did not yet have a plan, I did have the determination.

I rose from the floor and crawled into bed. I didn't even bother to get undressed.

An unbearable stink hit me first. Then I opened my eyes.

Rick was sitting next to me, leaning on the tiger's cage. John was still snoring at the back of the cage. We'd made it through the night!

"Where's the banshee?" I whispered.

Rick indicated with his eyes. The lion's skull had been stripped of its mane with bones protruding through the patchy skin, but it was still on the other side of the bars.

"You look very tired," observed Rick quietly. "What happened in Chadrack?"

"A lot of things..."

I told him the short version of the story – about the bodies I had found in the Grave of Silent.

"I think war with the temple is coming," I said. "I can't let this go unpunished."

"Then that war might get civil," Rick sighed. "Sorry to point this out, but priest Kyaal has a lot of supporters around."

"I need to crush that worm regardless of anything," I told him firmly. "I just haven't decided how."

"Then you need an ultimate weapon," observed Rick. "A weapon which could target a single man unexpectedly."

"What weapon?"

He silently pointed to the lion's skull resting on the floor in the neighbouring cage.

"Do you think it could be done?" I asked, unsure if I even wanted to try it.

"I've seen wolves and bears eating out the hands of a man and obeying commands, doing crazy things when ordered despite their instincts," he said. "Why can't that be done with a banshee? Do you know anything that could be attractive to this creature?"

"Hawa said they feed on energy..."

"That monster?"

I nodded. Rick shrugged.

"Then try it," he said. "But make it quick. Let's not wake John up."

I moved closer to the bars and sat down just a few feet away from the banshee. The head hadn't moved. For several minutes I just sat staring at the repulsive remnants of the big cat with my deadliest fear inside.

Then I reached into my Ring and tried to visualise a single

drop of purple water from the Well – a source of pure energy. Here we go! The purple drop appeared on the Ring, and I put it on my left index finger. With my right hand, I grabbed the nearest bar of my cage, exposing the Master of Destiny, ready to strike at the first instance.

I wasn't sure what to do next, so I put the purple drop between me and the banshee and quickly withdrew my hand. A few minutes passed without any movement.

Then Rick gasped behind me as the sparkling tentacle appeared from the lion's mouth, sensing the offered dainty from a distance.

The banshee leaked through the lion's nostrils like a silver stream and carefully closed around the sparkling drop, acquiring the form of a small cloud with tiny tentacles as it did so.

The scene extended into several minutes, accompanied by John's loud snoring. I kept my hand on the bar trying to force the images of twisting bodies and the sound of breaking bones from my head.

Finally, the banshee put its tentacles around the offering and sucked it dry. For some time, we were able to trace the purple ink stain travelling within the moving appendage. Then it dissipated.

"Don't scare it," Rick whispered. "Try that again."

We did our best to move as little as possible as John slept peacefully in the far corner of the cage.

The banshee had retracted its tentacles and was now hovering a few feet above the cage floor.

"I think I'm more scared than it is," I whispered, keeping my eyes fixed on the creature.

"Don't be fooled," said Rick. "Wild things usually attack because they're scared."

I was sure that the banshee was inspecting us intensely, although it was hard to believe that the cloud of mist could have some form of consciousness.

I slowly retrieved my hand with the Ring, and produced another purple drop which I put on my index finger, extended it through the bars and placed it in the same spot as the previous one.

The banshee retreated a few feet as I moved but didn't attempt to hide back inside the skull. We waited.

As the purple drop sparkled in the morning sun, it was too great a temptation for the banshee to resist. It lowered itself down and engulfed the offering. Then it returned to the same spot above the ground, waiting.

"What next?" I asked.

"Try to feed it from your hand," said Rick. "It needs to get used to you."

"Are you sure it's safe?"

"I'm sure it isn't," he shrugged. "It's a leap of faith for both of you."

"Are you sure I have to do this?"

"Sorry," Rick sighed. "There's no way around this – either you trust each other and get along, or you both remain on the wild side and in distrust."

I placed another purple drop on my finger and slowly extended it through the bars. It felt like I was attempting to feed a roaring tiger with my bare hand. The banshee retreated several feet away and hovered at a distance without trying to approach me.

"What next?" I whispered.

"Be patient…"

Several minutes passed. Finally, the temptation for the banshee was too great to resist, and the offering was so easy to get. The sparkling cloud produced a few tiny tentacles and slowly closed on my hand.

My heart was pounding insanely, but I forced myself to remain motionless.

The tentacles touched my skin. The sensation was weird, like touching a soft rod with static electricity. It felt like thousands of tiny needles were touching my skin but not yet piercing it.

Soon another purple stain was travelling into the sparkling cloud. The banshee retrieved its tentacles as soon as the drop left my finger.

“Do you think that's enough?” I whispered to Rick.

“I'll be damned! Never even imagined that! Try one more,” he whispered back. “What will you call that thing?”

“Never thought of that – let's call her Morag. But do we make it clear to it that she’s called Morag?”

“Why do you think it's female?”

I wasn’t sure how to explain.

“I don't know. It is easier for me to believe she is a female, and I don’t think it makes any difference to the creature.”

“I don't know how intelligent they are. Try to give her whatever you’ve given her again and speak the name at the same time,” suggested Rick. “She might be able to associate her name with the reward.”

I produced another drop and extended it to the banshee on my finger.

“Morag... Morag...” I slowly whispered in a low voice. “Morag... Morag... Morag...”

“Morag...” the banshee suddenly replied.

Her voice hissed like a snake. I didn't expect that and instantly withdrew my hand. The sparkling cloud retreated as well, partially hiding in the lion's head.

“Did you hear that?” I asked Rick.

“You’re on the right path,” whispered Rick over my shoulder. “Just keep going.”

I extended my finger again.

"Come, Morag! Come closer..."

The mist slowly leaked from the skull again.

"Morag..." she said approaching. "Morag..."

She touched my finger, and the drop of energy disappeared into her transparent body again.

I couldn't resist and touched her again. She didn't withdraw.

"She seems to like you," whispered Rick.

"What the hell?!" a sudden roar bellowed through the cage.

Morag shivered and slipped into my hand. I closed my eyes, expecting the sound of crushing bones at any moment, but nothing happened. My palm only grew numb.

"Stop shouting," whispered Rick.

We had been so busy with the banshee that we hadn't noticed the absence of snoring. John had woken up and was now desperately pressing his big body against the far wall of the cage.

It was too late for any regrets. The banshee was inside me!

My legs grew too weak to stand, and I had to sit down on the floor.

"Morag! Come out, please! Morag..." I gently stroked my numb hand.

"Morag..." hissed my palm.

"I'll be damned!" said John. "I can't believe it..."

"Be quiet," Rick cut him short firmly. "You're frightening

her..."

"Morag, come out, please..." I almost begged the bodiless creature.

"Morag..." came the answer.

"Try that purple thing," suggested Rick.

Why not? I put a drop on the ground and placed my hand next to it.

"Morag..." hissed my palm and the tiny tentacles protruded through my skin.

"Here! Good girl Morag..." I tried to sound encouraging, not frightened.

She slowly emerged from my palm and floated to the delicious spot. I sighed a relief.

"Morag!" the banshee hissed sucking the energy.

She rose from the ground and was now hovering like a bright cloud in the middle of our cage.

"Now what?" John was pale, pressing his back against the bars. "You've got it into our cage. What's next? We all die?"

"I don't know," I admitted.

Morag elongated her body into a strand of mist and produced tentacles that gently probed my face. Then she switched to Rick.

"Could you take that thing out of here?" Johns' voice sounded desperate as he realised it was his turn to be probed.

"Just close your eyes and stay still," said Rick. "She's curious, not angry."

"Why do you think it's female?" John's face was now red, and he was breathing heavily with drops of perspiration on his forehead.

"Does it make any difference to you?" I asked him. "Please, just don't make any sudden movements... We don't want her to become angry."

The banshee extended her bright tentacles and touched John's eyelids, cheeks, lips.

"Morag," I called her gently.

She immediately withdrew from John and turned back to me.

"Shoot me if I ever agree to help you with your quests again," said John.

I wouldn't ever help him either, but of course, I didn't tell him that. He might be unaware of his wife's precious gift and Saqia's attempt to murder me.

Rick began laughing. Soon we all were giggling. Morag just hovered above us, seemingly calm.

"Ok, we're alive and friends with the banshee," said John when we had calmed down again. "How do we get out of this damned cage?"

"Well, the key's in the pocket of that corpse," I indicated the body several yards away. "Any ideas on how to get it?"

"We have no rope and no hook," said Rick.

“Maybe your banshee can get it?” asked John.

“I don't think she could carry metal objects,” I remarked. “It's against her ethereal nature.”

“Morag...” hissed the banshee landing on my shoulder.

“What if,” said Rick. “If we could somehow trick her into bringing us that corpse? We could take the key out of his pocket ourselves...”

“Crazy idea,” said John.

“Why not try it?” I said. “We've nothing to lose. She can lift bodies. We saw that yesterday.”

“Do you know how to train a banshee?” asked Rick.

“No,” I shook my head. “But I once trained a dog although that was a very long time ago to tell you the truth...”

“Okay,” said Rick. “Where do we start?”

“We need a small body part,” I said.

“I am not cutting off any part of my body, so don't count on me,” replied John immediately.

“Don't be ridiculous. Do you still have that knife?” I asked.

“Yes.”

“Then could you cut me a piece of the tiger?”

“Which piece would you like?” asked John calmer now.

“Anything small... The ear would be ok...”

John got up on his feet. Morag partially submerged herself into my shoulder, but I calmed her with my hand.

John reached through the iron bars and grabbed the tail of the tiger. The animal was too heavy to move, so Rick stood up to lend a helping hand.

Morag appeared to be curious, producing a dozen tiny tentacles and extending them to the working men, but she preferred her body to stay on my shoulder.

A few minutes later, they presented me with the bloodied and stinking ear of the tiger.

"Here we go, Morag," I said, holding the ear for her to inspect.

She wasn't very interested or anxious. Then I produced a small purple drop and placed it in the ear, which immediately attracted her attention. Then I tossed it across the cage.

"Fetch it, Morag! Bring it to me!" I hoped she could understand me.

The banshee rushed forward, quickly absorbed the energy drop, and then she returned to me happily humming and leaving the ear behind.

"Get it, Morag. Bring that to me, and I will give you more..." I tried to persuade her.

She stopped mid-way.

"Bring it to me, Morag! Bring it!" I tried it again.

"Morag..." she hissed hovering. "Bring..."

"Yes, Morag, bring it!"

Hesitantly, the banshee returned to the tiger's ear and lowered her tentacles onto it.

"Good girl, Morag! Bring it!" I did my best to encourage her.

The ear levitated a few feet upwards and landed in my extended palm.

"Good Morag!" I fed her another purple drop and tossed the ear again. "Bring it, Morag!"

This time, everything happened more quickly. Morag soon understood my intentions and happily brought the ear back to me, each time being rewarded with a purple delicacy.

"Let's try to toss it outside the cage," said Rick.

"Ok, let's try..." I agreed. "Morag, bring it!"

I tossed the tiger's ear outside the wagon within clear visibility. The banshee approached the cage wall and stopped in hesitation. I went closer and let the creature use my hand to penetrate the cage. A sigh of relief reached me from the back of the cage where John was still was holding the tiger's tail.

A few seconds later, the banshee hovered just outside the cage, extending her tentacles in all directions, and then rushed forward. Soon the ear was in my palm, followed by a reward for Morag.

Time passed as we continued to play. Each time I tried to cast the ear as far as possible and into different locations of the field. Several times it landed on a corpse, but each time only the ear floated back in our direction.

It was already well into the afternoon. I became exhausted.

"Maybe we should try something else?" suggested John.

Why not?

I dropped the bloody ear on the cage floor behind me.

"Morag, bring me that man!" I pointed to the corpse of the fake policeman with the key.

The banshee hovered in front of me in the form of a sparkling ball but didn't move.

I repeated my request several times.

"Morag, bring that man..." hissed the banshee finally and shot into the field scattered with corpses and body parts.

I couldn't see what she was doing in the fading light of the early evening, but soon a ghostly figure was floating towards us.

"Good progress, but the wrong corpse," observed Rick as the fancily dressed blue-faced acrobat stopped in front of us – the lower trunk and both legs were missing, and the far end of his bowel was somewhere in the tall grass.

"Morag, bring that man..." hissed the acrobat.

"Good, girl," a reward still had to follow.

The corpse collapsed on the ground as soon as I put a drop of energy on my finger. Let's try again.

Soon the lifeless bodies of the magician, another acrobat, the clown and the strongman were piled in front of us accompanied by the increasing stench of rotten flesh.

"We've spent the whole day achieving nothing, and now we've

got a very smelly night ahead of us with this pile of decaying corpses," complained John.

"We're making progress," I said, not looking at him. "We'll be able to get out as soon as she brings the right corpse. Let's keep trying..."

The bearded woman was piled on next, then two fake police officers.

"Learning is a complicated thing," observed John. "I would have lost my patience long ago if not for this cage..."

He stopped his tirade in mid-sentence when the most desired corpse moved and slowly levitated into the air a few feet above the ground.

"I'll grab his belt, you go through his pockets," said John to Rick. "You take care of your pet," he added for me.

"Good Morag, good girl!" I said as soon as John had grabbed the corpse's belt.

The banshee slipped through John's body into the cage and happily landed on my shoulder.

"Shit!" cursed John but didn't release his grip.

I fed the banshee with a large portion of energy, and soon she was humming happily like a giant transparent bumblebee.

Rick pulled everything out of the dead man's pockets – a wallet, watch and finally – the key!

"Check everything," said John. "It might be the wrong key. We won't be able to reach him again if I let it go."

Rick fished out three more keys from his pockets, and one more was on a chain around his neck!

"Finished?" asked John.

Rick nodded, and the body in police uniform landed on other corpses just next to the cage.

The first key we tried unlocked the cage. Finally, we were free!

"Let's get out of here as fast as we can," mumbled John stepping out.

No one argued.

"But leave that thing behind, please," he indicated the banshee sitting on my shoulder.

"No," I protested. "I somehow feel responsible for her now. And she might be quite handy, just a little bit slow..."

Our car was still where we'd left it. We hopped in quickly, and John started the engine.

"We won't be able to get all the way back to Vienna before dusk," I said stroking Morag on my shoulder. "How about finding a hotel?"

"That's fine with me," Rick liked the idea. "I need a good shower..."

"But I won't sleep in the same room as your pet," said John, addressing me.

I consulted the map. A small motel next to the road was only a few miles away, but it took us away from Vienna. Nobody complained. It was getting dark, and we needed some rest.

"Will it be far enough away?" I asked.

"It doesn't matter now since you've got the killing tool now," observed John. "I just need a good night's sleep and a pleasant day with my wife in Rehen."

"Fair enough..." I agreed.

The motel was small but neat and clean. We took two rooms. Rick decided to stay with me.

"It's better to sleep with the banshee rather than that horrible snoring," he said when we were left alone.

"Guess you're right," I smiled.

Rick took a long shower. I watched TV. Morag drifted around the room in the form of a cloud and then landed on my shoulder as I prepared for the night. I still felt chills from her touch, but she seemed quite comfortable where she was.

"Morag…" she gently hissed in my ear.

I fed her another drop of energy as Rick emerged from the shower.

"Back to civilisation at last," he exclaimed smiling widely. "Thank you for bothering to rescue me."

"There's nothing to thank me for," I said. "I'm certain you would do the same for me."

"I'm not that influential, and I doubt if my efforts would

extend into another country," he shrugged still smiling. "I owe you my life."

"Come to see me in my room first thing in the morning. We need to discuss how to proceed with the temple," I said and asked him casually. "Which bed would you like to take?"

"It doesn't matter to me."

"Then I'll take the one next to the window," I said undressing.

Rick slipped into his bed. Morag eerily followed me under my covers, keeping her place on my left shoulder. I was too tired to object.

Angry cries from beyond the window sneaked into my dream, tearing it apart and woke my consciousness. I sprang out of bed. What the hell was going on?

The morning was grey with dense clouds, but it wasn't raining. I quickly dressed and ran into Carwyn carrying the usual bowl of water and towels into my chambers.

"What's going on?" I asked.

"I don't know, my Lord," he looked frightened. "The crowd has gathered from everywhere. They're demanding your appearance. I'm not sure if it's safe."

"I guess we have no other choice," I rushed to the balcony. "You stay inside."

Angry people carrying torches flooded the yard in front of the balcony and the neighbouring streets. Shouts reverberated, echoing from the dark rocks of the tall city walls but I couldn't make out the words. Guards – too few of them – gathered around the entrance in a desperate attempt to defend the castle. Then somebody spotted me on the balcony.

"It's him!" screamed a woman pointing at me.

I backed a few steps away as the crowd started to roar. Why were they doing this?

"Heretic! Heretic!" one of the voices sounded strangely familiar.

Then I spotted priest Kyaal in his pink wig and a dark red gown making angry faces in the front row of the crowd. Obie was holding a torch right behind his back with a victorious smile beaming from that androgynous face. The situation instantly became clear.

"What do you want?" I asked as loud as I could.

The angry cries subsided as Kyaal raised his hand and took a few steps forward.

"You killed the mediums in the temple," he stated this as a fact. "These people are grieving for their children, and now they demand an answer – why?"

"That is a lie!" I felt deeply offended by this false accusation. "You killed them!"

"How can you blame me?" he raised the staff he was holding in his hand, decorated with a white serpent. "I am the priest!"

A wave of affirmative murmuring sped through the crowd.

"The blood of those children is on your hands, and you know

it!" my voice was firm, but my heart trembled. "How can you blame this on me when you are responsible for it yourself! It was your hand that carved psalms on their backs! It was your hand that cut their throats. It was all your doing!"

"We've caught your men trying to burn their bodies and to hide your crime," said the priest. "What other proof do you need?"

The crowd spat forward several men – tied, beaten and bruised.

"These are your men?" Kyaal pointed at them with his staff. "Aren't they?"

I didn't know the men, but I was sure Carwyn had sent them on my order.

"Release them," I said. "They are innocent. They were trying to make a decent pyre for the deceased. The mediums were dead long before then!"

"How do you know this?" his question was followed by several angry cries from the crowd. "Because you killed them!"

"I found them dead already!" I was bursting with anger. "You sliced their throats! You carved words of prayer on their bodies! You did this!"

"I am only a humble priest of Qu'mun," he allowed himself a wicked smile, turning his back to the crowd. "How could I perform such an atrocity?"

The situation slowly heated to boiling point. It was clearly either him or me. He knew he was wrongly blaming me, he knew the truth, but I was unable to prove this to the crowd. It all seemed so awry.

"Qu'mun turned you down!" the priest was perspiring heavily, but the well-trained voice was as hard as steel. "We don't want a heretic on our throne! The Serpent turned his back on you, and he will eat your liver in hell!"

"It is you who will burn in hell!" my voice trembled slightly. "The blood of those innocents is on your hands!"

Kyaal just laughed loudly in response, shaking his staff.

"You wouldn't dare to strike your people with those lightning bolts, would you, Bloody Prince?" he asked, laughing.

Several rocks passed inches from my head, hitting the wall and then a flaming torch flew in a graceful arch and landed on the balcony. Luckily, nothing flammable was there. I needed to do something fast, or they might smash my head with a stone! It was him or me! I needed to resolve this, no time for thinking, no time for doubting... regrets would come later.

"My Lord, it's too dangerous," said Carwyn behind me. "The crowd is becoming out of control."

I looked at priest Kyaal. He was standing in front of the crowd with his fist raised high, threatening me with flames and promising hell for my followers.

"You're lying!" I roared at the top of my lungs.

The crowd roared back. More stones and torches flew in my direction, some hitting the wall behind me, some falling short in front of the balcony.

"It is too dangerous, my Lord!" I could clearly hear the whisper of Carwyn through the cacophony of the raging crowd. "We could defend the castle for a few days until Bedwyr shows up with your army. Please, come inside!"

The priest raised his staff, still grinning widely.

"Let's kill the heretic!" he shrieked in a high falsetto shaking the staff.

The crowd roared, and more rocks and torches landed on the balcony. Everything was slipping out of control, and I realised that the time for talking was over. My words meant nothing to the crowd. I had to do something, to resolve this explosive situation immediately – it would be too late if I waited five more minutes. And I had only one chance, no time for retrials. Kyaal was orchestrating this, but I couldn't use the Master of Destiny to create a cataclysm over the crowd to remove him – that would be like killing a fly with a cannon with extensive collateral damage. I needed a more precise weapon.

"Morag…" whispered my left shoulder offering a solution.

One of us must die – either Kyaal or me.

"You'll pay for your crimes!" I cried out to the fat priest.

He just laughed at my words.

"Morag," I whispered, pointing at Kyaal's pink wig dancing in front of the raging crowd. "Bring me that man..."

I didn't feel nor see the moment the banshee slipped away. I was still pointing at him, and the priest carried on laughing while the crowd continued to rage and shout obscenities while rocks were landing closer to me each time although none had achieved a direct hit so far.

"Let's kill the heretic!" screamed Kyaal again, pointing his staff at me.

A handful of jaegers were trying to hold the entrance to the castle, shielding themselves from the shower of rocks with buckets and planks. Some of them already had their faces bloodied. The situation indeed seemed hopeless.

"It's very dangerous, my Lord," whispered Carwyn behind me. "Please, come back inside. Maybe we could hold the castle for a few days until the army returns."

Kyaal's hand that was holding the white staff high above the crowd stopped shaking and froze. The rage of the crowd slowly subsided as everybody waited for a speech or sermon, or whatever he used to say to encourage his henchmen. Kyaal didn't change his pose, nor did he say a word although a wide grin remained frozen on his face. Then, unexpectedly, his fingers detached from his right palm and the staff fell on the cobblestones.

"My Lord…" whispered Carwyn again. "Please, come back inside…"

"That won't be necessary," I whispered back, keeping my eyes on Kyaal.

The massive body of the priest slowly lifted into the air with his bleeding hand still held high and that silly expression unchanged on his face. The crowd jumped back as the priest's left hand detached from his body and dropped onto the ground next to the staff. Dark blood burst from his wounds, and women began to scream, dashing away as fast as they could. The men maintained their stance for only a few seconds longer and then backed away with expressions of horror scorched upon their faces.

I kept my eyes on the priest's face. Kyaal still was alive as his large eyes were slowly blinking, but his mouth didn't emit a sound. He was lifted a few more yards and then froze in mid-air, still away from the balcony. Then bloody chunks of meat which once had been his legs gushed out of his gown.

The crowd gasped, and chaos instantly ensued in every direction. From a distance, it resembled a disturbed nest of hornets as Kyaal's henchmen dashed out of the yard in all directions. Screams and shouts quickly rose to their peak and then soon scattered among the side streets and faded.

Kyaal floated closer. His eyes looked at me, begging for death.

"This is for all crimes you have committed Kyaal," I said calmly extending my hand with a purple drop on my finger. "Come to me, Morag."

The bloodied body dropped to the ground as the banshee slipped back into my palm, absorbing the drop on her way. Only then did my eyes fix on a lonely figure in the middle of the yard, standing next to Kyaal's bloodied left hand with a flaming torch still held high. I said nothing as Obie picked the white staff up with a trembling hand and then slowly turned around and went away. The Kyaal's riot was over.

Carwyn was paper-white when I turned around to face him.

"I'm sorry, we failed you, my Lord," he said, looking at my feet. "We were unable to protect you."

"It's not your fault, Carwyn," I told him. "I should have dealt with this long ago."

"What would you like us to do with the priest?" he asked, raising his eyes.

"Toss him somewhere in the woods for the wild animals to gobble up," I said quietly. "He doesn't deserve sacred flames for the crimes he did. Just get him away from here."

"It will be as you wish, my Lord," Carwyn bowed. "Where would you like to have your breakfast?"

"Bring it to my room, please," I said. I was too agitated even to think about food, but I couldn't allow Carwyn's sense of guilt to grow any further – this riot wasn't his fault, and he wouldn't have been able to do anything about it.

He left at once.

My eyes slipped over piles of rocks and flaming torches, and I went inside never casting a second glance at Kyaal's body, spread out on the cobblestones in a pool of blood.

I sat down at the table, feeling empty. The twisted priest had got what he truly deserved, but some part of my soul was now dead too. It was clear that nothing would ever be the same.

"I am a killer," I whispered, and the thought frightened me.

I rubbed my palms on my robes in a desperate attempt to clean them, but they still felt sticky as if from priest's blood. There was nothing there – I looked, but the sensation was dreadful. I had the power to manage things without resorting to that level of violence, but I had failed. The righteous mask I tried to put on my face slipped and failed every time the frightening thought jolted through my brain – *I am a killer!*

It was quiet outside now, but the cries of the raging crowd still rang in my ears. I knew I had done the right thing, but that knowledge didn't save me from horrible self-torture. It was a heinous way to find out how Shandra had felt about sentencing a man to death, under the burden of the murder she had committed herself. I was glad that she was away from all this turmoil and hadn't witnessed Kyaal's death, but then I suddenly felt lonely and abandoned.

Where was she? Was Shandra safe? Those questions seemed much more important than Kyaal's coup and his failed attempt to kill me. I had survived. I must find Shandra. She might be unwilling to come back or to see me again, but at least I'd know that she was okay.

Carwyn rushed in, carrying a basket with my breakfast. He silently placed everything on the table and stood aside.

"Is there anything else you wish, my Lord?" he asked.

"No, Carwyn, thank you," I told him quietly.

He bowed and left. I stared blankly at the freshly baked bread, pieces of juicy ham, cheese, fruit and pies in front of me but my stomach refused to take anything. I stood up, taking a bottle of wine to drown my sorrow. I didn't need company, just a quiet, lonely corner where I could sit in silence, fixing my gaze on the horizon and organising my thoughts. The corridor was empty, and I turned right making my way down the staircase and into the maze of galleries, alleys and gardens heading north. There was no wall at the northern side of the city as only impassable mountains held the defence there. Chadrack had never been attacked from the north. People here believed that gods had planted those mountains at the beginning of time, and nothing but wastelands were beyond them. They were probably right.

I felt a small relief leaving the castle behind. My route took me uphill through the woods, winding between pines, firs and dark boulders. The sunlight dispersed through the fine needles of the green canopy above me, and the path was rocky with patches of dark brown moss. I travelled absentmindedly, placing my feet – one in front of another, not paying attention to where they were carrying me. An hour later, I emerged from the woods, and my nose was the first to tell me where I was. An unmistakable stench of death was there with a massive pyre built on top of a cliff which was hanging high above the capital like the palm of a giant – the Grave of the Silent.

My order to carry out the funeral with dignity wasn't completed. Probably Kyaal had interrupted Carwyn's men before they lit the pyre they had built to release the souls of the dead to the Road of Gods.

I looked at the firewood and at the mutilated bodies of the young and all the regrets I had felt for killing Kyaal faded away with the wind. The man was pure evil, and those souls in front of me could rest in peace at last – they had been avenged.

All I had to do now was to light the pyre and let them go.

Of course, I had no lighters or matches, nor I had any idea how they lit a fire in Rehen. I envied my sister Hel her knowledge in Ring magic – she would have lit up the firewood in a blink of an eye. I had no idea how to do this, or my Sapphire lacked the ability. I reached into the Ring and brought out the blue sphere before my eyes – I could create a small volcano with a little effort or a thunderbolt. Both could light the firewood, but both could be disastrous and lacked dignity for the deceased. I cursed, dropping the sphere. I needed a different approach.

The pyre was huge, maybe twenty feet high, with the corpses carefully lined across the top. I walked around it, touching the firewood, as dry as gunpowder. All I needed was a good primer and a spark. I lacked both.

I could find something dry in the woods, something suitable to catch alight and keep it alive until it transferred to the lined logs. But I still had no idea how to create that flame in the first place.

I went to the woods collecting every piece of flammable material I could lay my hands on – I couldn't find much though – everything had probably already been put in the centre of the pyre. When I finally returned to the cliff, I had a plan.

I took my dagger and dug it deep into the firewood at the base of the pyre stuffing the dry moss, some dry branches and pieces of bark around it. It wasn't much, and I placed a few green branches of pine with leaking sticky resin on top. Then I recalled the blue sphere of destiny from my Ring again. This time I wiped out lightning and eruptions but poured the pure energy on my dagger, skipping all the magic. The metal heated quickly, and soon it was shining like the sun, igniting the few primers I had.

The firewood began smoking and, a few minutes later, I smiled, welcoming a shy flame. It was all I needed.

I stepped back, looking at the spreading flames and sat down on a flat boulder a dozen paces away.

When the flames had engulfed bodies lined on top of the pyre, I raised the bottle of wine to my lips and took a sip. *Farewell, boys and girls, sons and daughters of Chadrack – I didn't know you alive, but your death was both cruel and meaningless. I will cry for you. I recall the faces of each one of you when I found you here last time. I said my goodbyes on that day, but your killer interrupted the funeral the same way he had interrupted your lives. Now you have been avenged. Rest in peace in your paradise, young boys and girls. I will make sure no one will ever make anybody walk your road of suffering.*

Farewell…

I took another sip of the blood-red wine and looked at the flames consuming the firewood and the bodies placed on top of it. I was sure the pyre would be clearly visible from the whole capital, but the city still was empty, and those few who had already returned from the forced exile would not dare to join me and mourn.

The sun had climbed to its zenith and then begun to slip down to the west as I continued to sit on the rock in the shade of a pine tree looking at the pyre. The flames shot up and then dropped down along with the sun until only a pile of hot embers remained glowing in the wind at the place where the dead youths had been placed to rest. My soul now felt empty. My bottle of wine had been emptied long before that, and I tossed it away.

I didn't move when the evening began spreading its dark wings across the world. I looked at the embers. They grew dark as the day slowly died around me. They became as dark as the empty capital below the Grave of the Silent and then later they became as dark as the forests outside the city walls. The youths killed by Kyaal were gone.

Later in the evening, I stretched down on the soft moss and looked at the bright Wyr'na – the ringed giant – in the dark velvet sky. I thought of my beautiful Shandra. *Where are you, my love? Will I meet you again?*

A faint shooting star high above in the night sky was my answer. I couldn't make out if it were for hope or for a farewell.

Then I closed my eyes and prepared my mind to transfer back to Europe where a journey back to London awaited me.

Afterword

You have just read a story from the Sleeper Chronicles series and may wonder which book will take you deeper into the world of the Sleepers. It's a difficult question, and the advice is not as straightforward as it may seem. The Sleeper Chronicles are a non-linear series where the story in book B doesn't necessarily follow the story in book A and book C doesn't precede the story in book D. Each main character tells his own story as a piece of a jigsaw puzzle. That piece may be as short as a short story or may grow into several books. Still, not one single piece can reveal the picture of the whole universe, but more details emerge when those pieces are added together.

The stories are listed on the webpage sleeperchronicles.com – in no particular order. It's up to you to decide which piece of the puzzle to pick up next.

Ray Zdan

Printed in Poland
by Amazon Fulfillment
Poland Sp. z o.o., Wrocław

63501029R00263

THE FINAL

JUMPS GUIDE

2016/2017

GRANT COPSON & LEE LEWIS

Published by The Final Flight Publications LLP
Written by Grant Copson

ISBN – 978-1-68419-643-2

THE FINAL FLIGHT JUMPS GUIDE 2016/2017

The Final Flight Publications LLP.
158, Homefield Road, Sileby, Loughborough, Leicestershire. LE12 7TQ.
Email: thefinalflightpublications@outlook.com
Website: www.thefinalflightpublications.co.uk
Twitter: @thefinalflight1

Printed by H&H REEDS PRINTERS.
Southend Road, Penrith,
Cumbria, CA11 8JH.

MAIN FRONT COVER IMAGE: **BLOW BY BLOW** (Katie Walsh) wins the Grade 1 AtTheRaces.com Champion INH Flat Race.

BACK COVER IMAGE: **AMY DEANS** photographed at Oliver Sherwood's Rhonehurst Stables (Upper Lambourn)

Cover photographs supplied by Dan Heap Photography (Front Cover) and Michael Harris (Back Cover).

THE FINAL FLIGHT PUBLICATIONS LLP

IN ASSOCIATION WITH

TOM MALONE BLOODSTOCK

CONTENTS

INTRODUCTION

The National Hunt season rarely fails to disappoint, with horses returning season after season to lock horns with old rivals as well as facing the task of conquering the new generation of rising stars. However, the 2015/2016 jumps season really did have it all; the crowning of a new Champion Jockey, a Trainers' Championship that went down to the wire, as well as witnessing numerous breathtaking equine accomplishments along the way.

The launch of the first edition of The Final Flight Jumps Guide meant that it was a memorable campaign on a personal level, but it was Sprinter Sacre returning to his imperious best that stands out as the Oscar-winning performance. His stunning display to regain the Queen Mother Champion Chase crown meant that he was once again the gold medallist of the two-mile chasing division and the post-race atmosphere categorised the 2016 festival as my greatest ever. On top of nurturing Sprinter Sacre back to top form, the master of Seven Barrows, Nicky Henderson, also managed to prepare My Tent Or Yours and Bobs Worth perfectly to peak at the festival, where both ran fine races in defeat in the Champion Hurdle and World Hurdle respectively. In addition to the aforementioned horses, Henderson struck with one final masterstroke when Simonsig, the talented but injury-prone grey, ran the race of his life to finish a close third in the Grade 1 Punchestown Champion Chase. Arguably Henderson does not have the same fire power as when winning his third Champion Trainers' title in 2012/2013, but he remains one of the most patient, attentive and talented members of the training ranks and Lambourn's king pin will be hoping that his current crop of youngsters can fire him back to the big time once more.

Paul Nicholls landed his tenth Trainers' title when wearing down his Irish counterpart, Willie Mullins, on a brilliant season finale at Sandown Park. The day was not without controversy though as once the title was out of his grasp, Mullins withdrew his star mare Vroum Vroum Mag and understandably there were plenty of disgruntled racegoers following the twelfth hour tannoy announcement. However, that decision was justified when Vroum Vroum Mag, described as the super-super sub, tenaciously landed the Punchestown Champion Hurdle the following week. Mullins will have returned home licking his wounds and contemplating what might have been, but he is sure to return even more determined to gain revenge on Nicholls and in the form of Douvan, he has another potential heavyweight of the National Hunt game. I predict that he will send over even more runners this time around, with a raid of Cheltenham's November meeting a likely starting point. His attempt to conquer the UK as well as Ireland is fascinating and will again add another dimension to our much-loved winter pass time.

While on the subject of the headmaster of Closutton, Mullins will be well aware that Gordon Elliott is breathing down his neck, with his County Meath-based training operation going from strength-to-strength. He is already heavily supported by Michael O'Leary's Gigginstown House Stud amongst others and there will be no surprise if he can get even closer this term. In talented youngster Jack Kennedy, Elliott has a jockey whom I believe can go right to the top and their partnership will continue to blossom this season. The yard's Grade 1-winning No More Heroes who lost his life at Cheltenham will be sorely missed, but Elliott has plenty of budding young stars in his care who are capable of filling the void this time around, including one of this year's 'Top Prospects', Death Duty.

Although Joseph O'Brien was not the official trainer of the Triumph Hurdle winner Ivanovich Gorbatov, the former classic-winning jockey was responsible for his preparation along with a lot, if not all, of his father's other runners under National Hunt rules. Taking into account his background, I predict that he will be a force to be reckoned with over the next few years. Similarly to the now ex-National Hunt trainer John Ferguson, O'Brien will receive cast-offs from a powerful flat operation, in this case the all-conquering Coolmore. It will also be extremely exciting to see multiple Champion Sire Galileo have more runners over obstacles. Though, I am also confident that O'Brien will have a number of horses with stout jumping pedigrees running in the famous green and gold hoops of JP McManus and that sort of financial backing should not be ignored.

Dan Skelton is arguably the most progressive member of the UK training ranks and his partnership with his brother Harry proved successful on the big stage when the pair landed the County Hurdle with Superb Story at last season's Cheltenham Festival. With the number of horses trained at his Warwickshire base increasing significantly, Bridget Andrews' contribution in the jockey ranks will prove even more important this season. Team Skelton will be hoping for more of the same during the 2016/2017 campaign and it is significant that Nicholls sees his former assistant as a real threat to his crown in years to come.

Richard Johnson gained a much deserved first Jockeys' Championship last season and he duly received a warm reception when collecting his trophy at Sandown. His long-term association with Phillip Hobbs was rewarded on numerous occasions including four wins aboard the progressive Village Vic. The loyalty and commitment that he has showed the Minehead handler over the last sixteen years sums up his personality perfectly – a truly genuine and professional man. Assuming that he avoids injury, I expect Johnson to add many more Jockeys' titles to his collection and trainers both sides of the Irish Sea will once again be scrambling to secure his services in the saddle.

In the last week of July, the world of horse racing lost one of its greatest friends as the brilliant amateur rider John Thomas McNamara passed away. McNamara was left severely paralysed after a fall at the 2013 Cheltenham Festival aboard the Jonjo O'Neill-trained Galaxy Rock and his courage in the last three and a bit years of his life was a testament to the great man himself. The tributes poured in from his weighing room colleagues amongst many others as the news filtered through and it was clear for all to see that McNamara, who was taken far too young at the age of 41, leaves a lasting legacy – one that he truly deserves. He will be missed by many, none more so than his wife Caroline and his three young children, Dylan, Harry and Olivia and as racing enthusiasts, it is important to remember those who have been cruelly taken from us, as well as continuing to embrace the sport we love as if they were still with us – something I am sure McNamara would wish for.

Onto this year's publication and it again highlights 40 'Top Prospects', a selection of horses that are predicted to be ahead of the handicapper, as well as a round-up of horses that have passed through the public sales in Lee Lewis' section, 'The Sales Ring'.

New to The Final Flight Jumps Guide this year are the following sections; 'Tom Malone Bloodstock' where Tom highlights some of his most notable purchases, 'Pitterson's Paddock Picks', 'Jockey's Stable Stars' which includes the views of the aforementioned Champion Jockey Richard Johnson, 'Pedigree Pointers' and a must read two-part Q&A in what I hope is the ultimate guide to the current National Hunt season.

A big thank you to my business partner Lee Lewis as well as my good friend Eoin Joy for their assistance with this publication. I would also would like to thank all of this year's contributors; Mike Cattermole, Ken Pitterson, Tom Malone, Richard Johnson, Lizzie Kelly, Tom Scudamore, Derek O'Connor, Luke Elder, Emmet Kennedy, Paul Jones (you can view his website at www.pauljoneshorseracing.com), Harry Drew, Maddy Playle and Ross Moynihan for their efforts. In addition, our regular website bloggers Liam Hedgecock and Adam Morgan as well as photographers, Dan Heap and Michael Harris have been an important part of the team – their efforts are also much appreciated.

Last but not least, many thanks to you for buying this publication and I hope that you find it a useful source of information.

Grant Copson.

Author of The Final Flight Jumps Guide

FOREWORD BY MIKE CATTERMOLE

Racecourse commentator & At The Races Presenter

I have to hand it to Grant Copson, I really do. Meeting him for the first time on a quiet evening at Wolverhampton just a couple of years ago, I had been highly impressed with his knowledge and enthusiasm for our great sport. But it went a little further than that. All Grant wanted to do was to observe horses, study them close and closer still and then commit his impressions and predictions to paper - for a living! My initial thoughts were that he would soon get over that fantasy and find something "grown-up" to do, just as I should have done a few years ago. But I could not have been more wrong.

Clearly Grant's initial passion had become an obsession and that meant only one course of action. Even so, who would have thought that it would take him such a short time to get out there and found The Final Flight Publications with his great friend, the equally enthusiastic Lee Lewis.

Grant has already impressed a lot of people with his bright and knowledgeable essays and his racing judgement. He gets the game. He also knows a good horse when he sees one and there is no coincidence that Willie Mullins' Blow By Blow has been chosen as his front cover horse for this publication.

I do hope you enjoy reading Grant's latest publication as much as he has clearly had in putting it all together. There will be plenty of winners in there from a young man who absolutely adores his racing. I wish him and Lee all the very best with their future editions of The Final Flight Jumps Guide as well as their newest publication, 'Following The Flat', which is due out in 2017.

Mike.

THE 40 TOP PROSPECTS FOR 2016/2017

BACARDYS (FR) *(5-y-o b g)*

Coastal Path - Oasice (FR) (Robin Des Champs (FR))
TRAINER: Willie Mullins
OWNER: Shanakiel Racing Syndicate
FORM FIGURES: F1/131-3

THE FINAL FLIGHT ANALYSIS:

One of Willie Mullins' leading bumper horses last season was Bacardys, a son of high-class stayer Coastal Path. Although his sire is not renowned for his top-class jumpers, Coastal Path is a half-brother to the well-known National Hunt sire Martaline. Putting pedigree to one side, this five-year-old gelding had an ultra-consistent season in bumpers including when he gamely fought off his stablemate Battleford in the Grade 2 Aintree Bumper at the three-day Grand National meeting. After falling on his debut in a point-to-point at Rathmorrissey, Bacardys made amends at the next time of asking when decisively landing a four-year-old maiden at Quakerstown. Held in the highest regard by his point-to-point handler Pat Doyle, he switched to Mullins' Closutton operation following his nine length romp and justified favouritism in what is often an above average Leopardstown bumper in December. After suffering interference, he showed a good attitude to get on top of Grotesque in the closing stages and justified his lofty reputation from the pointing sphere. Thrown in at the deep end on his second start for Ireland's premier jumps trainer, Bacardys contested the Grade 1 Weatherbys Champion Bumper and if his previous point and bumper victories hadn't already proved that he was well above average, his staying on third at Cheltenham certainly did. His penultimate start was in the aforementioned Grade 2 at Aintree where he put his Cheltenham experience to good use. He travelled smoothly into contention under Patrick Mullins before using his stamina to record a hard fought half a length victory, reversing the form with his Cheltenham conquerors. His final start was at the Punchestown Festival in the Grade 1 Champion INH Flat Race, where he found only fellow 'Top Prospect' Blow By Blow and the 2015 Champion Bumper hero Moon Racer too strong.

It takes a certain type of horse to run with credit in all three of the Grade 1 bumpers in the spring and Bacardys achieved this rare feat in 2016. There is no doubt that he is tough and has a natural will to win. He also possesses plenty of class which added to his genuine nature is a recipe for success, one that is sure to prove fruitful this season. He has the right attributes to develop into a leading staying novice hurdler and under the careful tuition of Mullins, he has the best possible chance of fulfilling his undoubted potential. It was unusual that Faugheen took the Grade 3 Liberty Insurance Novice Hurdle at Limerick over three miles en route to winning the Grade 1 Neptune Investment Management Novices' Hurdle at Cheltenham. However, it would be far less peculiar if Bacardys is to put his Grade 1 Albert Bartlett Novices' Hurdle credentials to the test in that race this time around. Though, horses contesting the Albert Bartlett have often never tried three miles before Cheltenham, so it would be no surprise if he races exclusively between two miles and two and a half miles prior to the spring festivals.

BADEN (FR) *(5-y-o gr g)*

Martaline – Ma Sonate (USA) (Val De L´Orne (FR))

TRAINER: Nicky Henderson

OWNER: Triermore Stud

FORM FIGURES: 125-3

THE FINAL FLIGHT ANALYSIS:

After winning his only start in Irish point-to-points when in the care of Ronald O'Leary, Baden was purchased for £160,000 in May 2015 to join Nicky Henderson. By Martaline, who is the sire of last seasons' runaway Betfair Hurdle winner Agrapart amongst others including Cheltenham Festival winners Dynaste and Very Wood, this grey gelding ran credibly on two of his three outings last season. He arrived in the UK with a good reputation, although it was rumoured by experts in the pointing sphere that he was more of a long-term prospect rather than a top-class novice hurdler. Taking those comments into account, his debut at Cheltenham in December was quite pleasing and although he was not fluent at a number of his obstacles, he was still in contention jumping the last before finishing second, four and a half lengths behind North Hill Harvey. Henderson opted for the Grade 2 Neptune Investment Management Novices Hurdle back at Prestbury Park on Festival Trials Day next, again demonstrating the regard in which this five-year-old is held in by his handler. After jumping much better and travelling well into the straight, he got very tired after the last and weakened into a remote fifth. It was no surprise that Baden was given time to recover after his second start on energy-sapping heavy ground and having clearly benefiting from the break, he showed plenty of promise to finish third in the Louis Fitzgerald Hotel Hurdle at the Punchestown Festival. He certainly appreciated the drying ground on that occasion, travelling supremely well and was actually the last to be asked a serious question. Although he failed to match the talented winner Woodland Opera on the run-in, this was his best effort to date.

A novice chasing campaign is very much on his agenda this season and considering that he showed improvement when racing on better ground, his connections will want to get on with his career over the larger obstacles sooner rather than later. When visiting Seven Barrows recently, various members of Henderson's staff were particularly fond of Baden and although he is currently only rated 135 as a hurdler, it is expected that he can significantly improve on that when his attentions are switched to chasing. The fact that he is only five, connections might be tempted to run him in an early season handicap hurdle. The handicap hurdle at Haydock in November over two miles and three furlongs which was won by More Of That in 2013, ahead of the Henderson-trained Blue Fashion, could be on his radar if connections opt to stick to timber. However, with chasing almost certain to be his chosen route, the Grade 2 Fuller's London Pride Novices' Chase at Newbury's Hennessy meeting is a likely target, a race won by Henderson with The Market Man (2008), Punchestowns (2009) and Bobs Worth (2011) in recent years.

BAGS GROOVE (IRE) *(5-y-o b g)*

Oscar (IRE) – Golden Moment (IRE) (Roselier (FR))

TRAINER: Harry Fry

OWNER: Michael Pescod

FORM FIGURES: 212-

THE FINAL FLIGHT ANALYSIS:

This five-year-old son of Oscar out of an unraced Roselier mare is arguably unlucky not to be unbeaten. Three runs in bumpers yielded two seconds either side of a win, but the bare form figures do not tell the full story. In each of his three races, Bags Groove was the last horse off the bridle and in each race he hit the front at some stage. His debut came in what looked a decent Ascot bumper over two miles on good-to-soft ground. After racing enthusiastically, this long striding gelding hit the front still on the bridle before being caught inside the final furlong by the useful Criq Rock – a horse highly thought of and took his chance in the Champion Bumper at the Cheltenham Festival. Bags Groove's inexperience was obvious to even an untrained eye and until the very closing stages, it seemed as if he would hold on for a debut success. It is also worth noting that the pair pulled fourteen lengths clear of the third horse which is usually a sign of two useful prospects and I certainly believe that this was the case on that occasion. His second start was over a shorter trip of one mile and five furlongs and it was noticeable how much Harry Fry's charge had improved physically for his debut run. Aside from winning and beating some well-regarded sorts with ease, the most impressive aspect of his performance was the manner in which he hit the front so easily before recording a comfortable success. The stylish performance on his second start at Huntingdon prompted Harry Fry to let his classy individual take his chance in Newbury's DBS Spring Sales Bumper – a race that was subsequently his final start of the season. Stepping back up in trip, Bags Groove raced in third place behind a farcical pace the whole way around. Turning into the home straight, he moved up behind the two leaders travelling powerfully and his rider Noel Fehily took him to the front, seemingly still travelling with plenty of enthusiasm. However, the more stoutly bred Sam's Adventure battled back to get the better of Bags Groove by the narrowest of margins.

Based on his three runs to date, it seems logical to assume that Bags Groove will be kept to the minimum trip for the duration of his novice hurdling campaign. With his low to the ground action, it also must be considered that this son of Oscar will almost certainly be seen to best effect on good ground – something that was obvious from his performances in bumpers. With few horses boasting the same level of bumper form and even less having the ability to create the visual impression that Bags Groove has, he is expected to make a smooth transition to obstacles. An obvious approach would be taking in a maiden hurdle which he should do with ease before a crack at something like the Grade 2 Kennel Gate Novices' Hurdle – a race run over two miles at Ascot in December. Although his talented handler will no doubt have his eye on a spring campaign where he will appreciate the better ground, another possible target is the two mile contest that opens the card at Kempton on Boxing Day. While it is not a graded race, it is often contested by top-class horses, a theory again proven when last year's winner Altior followed up in the Grade 1 Supreme Novices' Hurdle. Bags Groove is an exciting recruit to the jumping ranks and I eagerly await his hurdling debut.

BALLYOPTIC (IRE) *(6-y-o b g)*

Old Vic – Lambourne Lace (IRE) (Un Desperado (FR))

TRAINER: Nigel Twiston-Davies

OWNER: Mills & Mason Partnership

FORM FIGURES: 31F/225111-

THE FINAL FLIGHT ANALYSIS:

Blaklion and Ballyandy gave trainer Nigel Twiston-Davies a memorable Ladies' Day at last season's Cheltenham Festival, winning the Grade 1 RSA Novices' Chase and the Grade 1 Champion Bumper respectively, and he will be hoping for more of the same with Ballyoptic, a potential star of the staying hurdling ranks. Similarly to the aforementioned Blaklion, Ballyoptic had multiple starts in the point-to-point sphere but that was no concern to Twiston-Davies as he spotted plenty of potential in this son of Old Vic. His previous handler Ian Ferguson, who once had top-class performer Simonsig in his care, decided to run Ballyoptic in the INH Flat Race at Down Royal on Boxing Day where he finished fifth behind the smart mare Avellino and it was that performance that led to him being sold to his current connections. Since joining Grange Hill Stables he has remained unbeaten, firstly in a novice hurdle at Ffos Las defeating the useful Potters Corner by three and a quarter lengths. The heavy ground and long run-in ultimately played to the strengths of Ballyoptic on that occasion but it was a pleasing hurdling debut regardless in what looked a decent novice contest. He justified favouritism at Uttoxeter in an ordinary novice hurdle on his next start, defying a penalty and clearing away to record a visually impressive ten length success. This victory was enough for Twiston-Davies to let him take his chance in the Grade 1 Sefton Novices' Hurdle where he relished his first try over three miles under rules. He dug extremely deep to get the better of the strong-travelling Bellshill by a neck, a result which capped off a superb spring campaign for his trainer.

With Ballyoptic being an ex-point winner there was no surprise to see him show marked improvement over the extended three miles at Aintree. The manner in which he travelled into the race was particularly pleasing and the fact that he has already proved that he handles better ground bodes well for his prospects as a staying hurdler this season. His long-term future ultimately lies over the larger obstacles but given that the staying hurdling division is wide open, he deserves a crack at races such as the Grade 2 Long Distance Hurdle at Newbury, the Grade 1 Long Walk Hurdle at Ascot and ultimately the Grade 1 Ryanair World Hurdle at next year's Cheltenham Festival. Superstar staying hurdler Thistlecrack was included in last season's 'Top Prospects', so it is now a case of assessing whether lightning can strike twice.

Twiston Davies and his team will be certainly hoping so and the trainers' post-race comments couldn't have been more bullish - ***"Thistlecrack won this race a year ago, so if we can follow in his footsteps even slightly it'll be good, let's hope he can go right to the top".***

BIG MEADOW (IRE) *(5-y-o br g)*

Marienbard (IRE) – Lakyle Lady (IRE) (Bob Back (USA))

TRAINER: Neil King

OWNER: Peter Beadles

FORM FIGURES: 112-

THE FINAL FLIGHT ANALYSIS:

Jamie Codd was successful at the 2016 Cheltenham Festival aboard the Gordon Elliott-trained Cause Of Causes, but it was Big Meadow who provided him with his first win of the 2015/2016 point-to-point season when he won a heavy ground 4-year-old maiden at Maralin. After kicking for home of the final bend, he was pressurised by Reigning Supreme approaching the last, but a brilliant jump put the race to bed and his two length success earned him a rating of 93+. After his impressive debut between the flags, he was subject to plenty of interest when sent to Tattersalls November sales at Cheltenham and the hammer fell at £85,000, selling to Neil King. After he was given time to acclimatise to his new surroundings, his attentions were switched to bumpers and he was sent off as the third favourite in the County Marquees Maiden National Hunt Flat Race at Chepstow in February. He was ridden confidently for the duration of the contest, including when he breezed into contention turning for home and very quickly brushed aside what looked a decent bumper field (runner-up won since). After what can only be described as a visually impressive debut, Big Meadow was expected to defy a penalty at Uttoxeter on Midlands Grand National Day but he was unable to complete the double, bumping into a smart David Pipe newcomer, Mr Big Shot. Though the winner is clearly talented, Big Meadow failed to travel with the same fluency that he showed in both his sole point and his bumper debut, perhaps indicating that this wasn't his true running. In addition to this, it was a tough ask to give 7lb to an equally promising horse and taking everything into account, his second appearance was still full of promise. The fourth that day, Stowaway Magic, has since won a Warwick novice hurdle giving the form a nice boost and it is anticipated that Big Meadow will make a smooth transition to the novice hurdling ranks this winter.

All three of his runs to date have come on soft or heavy ground and that is unsurprising looking at his running style; a rounded action often implies that a horse is going to enjoy some cut in the ground. Big Meadow showed that he has plenty of stamina when winning his Irish point and with that in mind, it is pleasing that he was able to score in such taking fashion over two miles on his bumper debut. He is likely to slip under the radar given his connections, but he has an awful lot of natural ability and he rates as a lovely long-term prospect. He is guaranteed to have learned plenty from his final outing last season and although he is regarded as a chasing prospect, he can make an impact in the hurdling division this season. He proved he has the aptitude to compete over the minimum distance, though he is most likely to start his jumping career over intermediate trips with the potential of stepping up to three miles as the season progresses. King boasted a good strike rate over timber last season (22% of his runners won with a level stakes profit of £28.56) and he will be hoping that Big Meadow can lead the charge to better that impressive record this season.

BLOW BY BLOW (IRE) *(5-y-o ch g)*

Robin Des Champs (FR) – Shean Rose (IRE) (Roselier (FR))

TRAINER: Willie Mullins

OWNER: Gigginstown House Stud

FORM FIGURES: 211-1

THE FINAL FLIGHT ANALYSIS:

Ireland's Champion Trainer Willie Mullins has won the Champion Bumper at Cheltenham no less than eight times, most recently with Briar Hill in 2013. However, it was the Punchestown equivalent that he landed with Blow By Blow, a scopey son of Robin Des Champs. Since finishing a close second behind the Noel Meade-trained Tamlough Boy on his debut, he has remained unbeaten in the bumper sphere which included wins at Navan in February and at Fairyhouse a month later. It was the defeat of another of this season's Top Prospects Death Duty at the latter venue that really sparked public interest in this €130,000 Goffs purchase. Slightly out-paced some way out, Patrick Mullins remained patient and when the leader was able to give no more he stayed on strongly, stretching right away to record a comfortable one and three quarter length success. On his last start, the Grade 1 AtTheRaces.com Champion INH Flat Race at Punchestown, Blow By Blow was given an enterprising ride from the front by Katie Walsh fighting off the challenge the 2015 Champion Bumper hero Moon Racer, displaying a much-loved never-say-die attitude to score by three quarters of a length. Although the late defects of Castello Sforza and Battleford weakened the contest on paper, I believe that this race, the only Grade 1 bumper in the Irish calendar, had plenty of depth to it and is certain to be a race full of terrific jumping prospects for the future.

As obvious as it may be, it is a huge positive that that this gorgeous big horse who is improving rapidly with each race, was capable of winning a championship race over the minimum distance and that is encouraging when assessing his potential as a jumper. When interviewed following his Fairyhouse victory Mullins described him as ***"a real chasing type"*** and based on his way of going and his physical presence, one would describe him as a future Gold Cup horse. Having said that, he oozes class and I expect him to reach a similar level of form once sent hurdling. He proved throughout the 2015/2016 campaign that he is extremely versatile by winning small-field races on soft ground to the eleven-strong Champion bumper on his final outing. Judged on his achievements in bumpers, the 2017 Cheltenham Festival should be very much on his agenda and if pushed at this early stage, the Grade 1 Neptune Novices' Hurdle would be the chosen race, with the Grade 1 Albert Bartlett Novices' Hurdle the other alternative – a conundrum sure to be discussed all season long.

However, it is worth noting that Mullins has won the last three renewals of the Grade 1 Lawlor's Hotel Novice Hurdle over two and a half miles at Naas and there is every possibility that Blow By Blow can bring the trophy back to Closutton for a fourth consecutive year.

CAPELAND (FR) *(4-y-o b g)*

Poliglote – Neiland (FR) (Cyborg (FR))

TRAINER: Paul Nicholls

OWNER: Mrs Kathy Stuart

FORM FIGURES: 11-

THE FINAL FLIGHT ANALYSIS:

A half-brother to hurdle and chase winner Urano, Capeland made a winning start to his career when overcoming greenness to land a bumper at Le Lion D'Angers in May 2015 for French handler Alan Couetil before being sold privately and joining Paul Nicholls' Ditcheat operation. Although Nicholls won his tenth Trainers' title on a captivating final day of the jumps season at Sandown in April, there was a stage of the season when his runners were not firing on all cylinders. It is therefore noteworthy that Capeland recorded victory during this lean spell on his sole start for his new connections when landing a four-year-old only bumper at Cheltenham in January, a race won by The New One in back in 2012. The race was run over slightly further than officially advertised (1m6f 61 yards) and the fact that he needed every yard as he stayed on strongly to collar the leader Jam Session late on showed that he will have no problem when tackling a longer trip in the future.

Poliglote has sired some very useful jumping prospects for Nicholls in recent years including Graded winners Hinterland, Wonderful Charm and Far West and he will be hoping that this four-year-old can achieve similar heights when switching to obstacles this season. Given that he has only raced once in the UK, it would be no surprise to see him return to the venue of his debut success for the two mile and half a furlong 4-6-year-old Standard Open National Hunt Flat Race at the Showcase meeting in October. However, given that his stable rarely waste too much time in that sphere, an imminent switch to the hurdling division is predicted.

Nicholls often targets his novice hurdlers at Taunton and Wincanton so don't be surprised to see him make his hurdling debut at either venue. Similarly to a lot of his trainers' inmates, the vibes would suggest that he is more of a long-term prospect but winning a novice hurdle between two miles and two and a half miles should be a formality. Although the race he won at Cheltenham looked an average renewal, he created a good visual impression that day and with the scope to progress further over a trip and once jumping a hurdle, he can take pretty high-rank. Assuming that he achieves what is expected of him early on in the season, the Grade 2 Neptune Novices' Hurdle on Cheltenham's Trials Day is a potential target, especially as he already boasts the all-important course form.

CATWELLS (FR) *(3-y-o b g)*

Irish Wells – Cathelie (Sleeping Car)
TRAINER: Willie Mullins
OWNER: Mrs S. Ricci
FORM FIGURES: 1-

THE FINAL FLIGHT ANALYSIS:

Leading owner Rich Ricci has invested significant amounts of money into National Hunt racing over the last few years, though even he would admit that being associated with household names such as Faugheen, Annie Power, Vautour and Douvan is a dream come true. His relationship with Willie Mullins has blossomed over time and it is fair to say that Ricci's superstars have cemented Mullins' position as Ireland's leading trainer.

The pair have once again been busy buying new recruits from France – something you can read more about in this year's appendix on page 108 – and in three-year-old hurdler Catwells, it is hoped that they may have acquired a top-class juvenile for the 2016/2017 campaign. This son of Irish Wells won on his only start in his native France, a three-year-old hurdle over an extended two miles at Nancy. The gelding showed clear signs of inexperience throughout the contest, racing enthusiastically in the early stages and not entirely convincing in the jumping department – especially at the final flight of hurdles. Taking this into consideration, the manner in which Catwells quickened away from his rivals to record a five lengths success was even more impressive. He is a physically imposing individual - very much like last year's 'Top Prospect' Zubayr who won the Grade 2 Adonis at Kempton in February – and looks to have the scope to improve significantly for his debut outing. Although he clearly will make a chaser one day, it is expected that he will run in juvenile hurdles this season, particularly given that he isn't a novice having won at the end of last season (most juvenile hurdles are restricted to the horse's age and are not novice events).

It is notable that there has been a lot of activity during the spring and summer with agents purchasing juvenile hurdlers from France, with a vast number of them now being housed with either Mullins or Paul Nicholls. Mullins and Ricci were doubly represented in the Triumph Hurdle in 2015 by Dicosimo and Kalkir before their Let's Dance finished fourth in last year's renewal and it is expected that Catwells has been acquired with that race in mind. Let's Dance performed creditably in three Grade 1's last season, namely the Spring Juvenile Hurdle, the aforementioned Triumph Hurdle and the Champion Four-Year-Old Hurdle at Punchestown and there is no reason why their new recruit will not follow a similar route. Mullins will be hoping so as he attempts to add to his sole victory in the Triumph Hurdle after Scolardy was successful in 2002.

CLONDAW CRACKER (IRE) *(5-y-o b g)*

Court Cave (IRE) – Twelve Pence (IRE) (Bob Back (USA))
TRAINER: Neil Mulholland
OWNER: Roger Brookhouse
FORM FIGURES: 11-

THE FINAL FLIGHT ANALYSIS:

This five-year-old son of Court Cave is a half-brother to point-to-point winner Farfields and he made a winning start to life in that sphere when successful in a four-year-old maiden at Glenbane last November. He was two and a half lengths clear of the well-fancied Bel Sas (2/1f) and with that rival winning a bumper and a hurdle since, the form looks solid. Clondaw Cracker showed plenty of speed on that occasion, picking up in good style before the last and his natural ability was there for all to see. He was subsequently sent to the Tattersalls Ireland sales at Cheltenham in December where leading owner Roger Brookhouse secured him for £120,000. Clondaw Cracker made his bumper debut for his new handler Neil Mulholland at Warwick in April and after showing such a nice turn of foot when winning between the flags, it was no surprise to see him make a winning debut. He beat two well-fancied horses on that occasion, namely Asum (Dan Skelton) and Brio Conti (Paul Nicholls) with the latter boosting the form by winning on his next start at Stratford and it is expected that this bumper will be a good guide to plenty of future winners. After being well positioned throughout, Clondaw Cracker showed an excellent attitude to see of his two closest rivals by a narrow margin – a trait that will certainly aid him when switched to the novice hurdling division this season.

A winner on yielding ground on his sole start in point-to-points and good ground on his bumper debut, it is anticipated that Clondaw Cracker will be best suited to good or good-to-soft ground, though connections will hope that he proves himself to be versatile in that respect. Mulholland's Shantou Village (also a former point-to-pointer) had an excellent season in novice hurdles before it was ended prematurely after he cut himself in the Grade 1 Albert Bartlett Novices' Hurdle at the Cheltneham Festival and Mulholland will be hoping for better luck this season with that particular horse. If Clondaw Cracker can show a similar level of ability this time around then his connections may opt to follow a similar route – a novice hurdle at one of the lower profile tracks before being stepped-up in class. Whether he will be physically and mentally ready for a gruelling race like the Albert Bartlett remains to be seen and with that in mind intermediate trips at the spring festivals are far from ruled out at this early stage. Described by his stable as ***"a real straightforward and genuine sort"***, this gelding has a bright future as a jumper and although he will pay his way over timber, his long-term future ultimately lies over the larger obstacles.

CLOUDY DREAM (IRE) *(6-y-o gr g)*

Cloudings (IRE) – Run Away Dream (IRE) (Acceglio)
TRAINER: Malcolm Jefferson
OWNER: Trevor Hemmings
FORM FIGURES: 31/13112-

THE FINAL FLIGHT ANALYSIS:

Cloudy Dream is a gorgeous grey who cost a bargain £16,000 as an unraced three-year-old. He has already paid his way with his career earnings amassing to more than double that figure and with him being a horse with the scope to improve further, it is predicted that he will continue to be profitable to follow this season. After winning two of his three starts in bumpers, he made considerable improvement from his hurdling debut at Hexham to win his next two starts at Doncaster and Market Rasen respectively. However, it was his final start of last season that was most eye-catching after he finished strongly to be second in the Scottish Champion Hurdle – a race run over two miles which is a distance that is sure to prove inadequate for this son of Cloudings in the future. With only the final obstacle to jump at Ayr, there was a wall of horses ahead of him and his finishing position is a testament to his temperament, natural ability and perhaps most notably that he has plenty of stamina – a trait that will be a real asset this season. Having treated his hurdles with little respect throughout the contest, it was really taking how he still managed to hit top gear in the home straight, passing all but one of his rivals, just failing to get the better of the Dan Skelton-trained Ch'Tibello.

As is often the case with Trevor Hemmings-owned horses, this gelding was purchased with all of the leading staying chases in mind and there is no doubt that jump racing's most famous race, the Grand National, will be his owner's long-term aim. With that in mind, it is hardly surprising that Cloudy Dream is a fine stamp of a horse who still has plenty of growing to do and he looks the type to excel over fences. Looking at his physique, it would be a real surprise if Jefferson pursues a second season over hurdles, especially as this gelding has often showed a lack of respect to hurdles. It is expected that novice chases between two and a half and three miles will suit Cloudy Dream this season and even though he won at Market Rasen on soft ground, he has looked a better horse on a sounder surface. Although good ground shouldn't be a must when switched to fences, the manner in which he bounced off the ground at Ayr (good-to-soft) clearly proved that he handles spring ground and that coupled with his stout pedigree means that he can show his best form at next year's major spring festivals.

He has already showed a liking to Doncaster and a return to that venue for the two mile and three furlong novices' chase in December looks like a perfect starting point – the same card where fellow 'Top Prospect' Winter Escape made his hurdling debut last season. If all goes to plan with Cloudy Dream, it would be no surprise if he was up to contesting Grade 1 races in the spring, with one of Aintree's novice chases a more realistic end of season target than a similar event at the Cheltenham Festival.

CRACK MOME (FR) *(4-y-o ch g)*

Spanish Moon (USA) – Peche Mome (FR) (April Night (FR))

TRAINER: Willie Mullins

OWNER: Andrea & Graham Wylie

FORM FIGURES: 1-

THE FINAL FLIGHT ANALYSIS:

Leading owners Andrea and Graham Wylie has been associated with some high-class horses in recent times, the majority of them trained by Irish Champion Trainer Willie Mullins, and Crack Mome is another to add to that list. Out of Peche Mome who won twice in AQPS flat races in France, this private purchase is held in high-regard by his new connections and he rates as an exciting recruit to the Irish jumping scene.

Crack Mome made his one and only start in an AQPS flat race in the French provinces last May where after being settled in midfield, he quickened up in good style to record a three length success. Upon hitting the front inside the final furlong, the then three-year-old showed signs of greenness before he showed his rivals a clean pair of heels to win comfortably. It was particularly pleasing how Crack Mome handled the heavy ground on his debut, proving that winter conditions won't be an inconvenience and that is a big plus given that Ireland is renowned for having wet winters.

From a source close to the Wylies, I am led to believe that Crack Mome sits high on their horses to follow list and it is expected that he will announce himself as a leading novice hurdler for Mullins' Closutton operation this season. Nichols Canyon, who is also trained by Mullins for the Wylies, was a multiple Grade 1-winning novice hurdler two seasons ago, with his career over obstacles beginning with a maiden hurdle win at Cork. It is likely that this scopey gelding will follow a similar path by winning a maiden or novice hurdle before stepping up in class in due course. The aforementioned Nichols Canyon was a classy ex-Flat recruit with plenty of racing experience and it is fair to expect the once-raced Crack Mome to be more of a long-term prospect. Having said that, Mullins has dominated the Grade 1 Supreme Novices' Hurdle with three Rich Ricci-owned youngsters and maybe, just maybe, it will be the Wylies turn in 2017.

DEATH DUTY (IRE) *(5-y-o b g)*

Shantou (USA) – Midnight Gift (IRE) (Presenting)

TRAINER: Gordon Elliott

OWNER: Gigginstown House Stud

FORM FIGURES: 13/112-

THE FINAL FLIGHT ANALYSIS:

Gigginstown House Stud once again have a formidable novice hurdling squad this season and the Gordon Elliott-trained Death Duty achieved more than enough in bumpers last season to earn his place in this season's 'Top Prospects'. Since winning his sole point for Pat Doyle, which was notably 'Jumps Guide' contributor Derek O'Connor's 1000th winner between the flags, this five-year-old son of Shantou made a pleasing bumper debut to finish third at Fairyhouse in the 2015 renewal of the Tattersalls Ireland George Mernagh Memorial Sales Bumper. Always held in the highest regard by his handler, there was little surprise to see Death Duty justify favouritism on his second start under rules, quickening away impressively to record a facile sixteen length success in the Daily Mirror (Pro/Am) Flat Race at Down Royal in October. The Listed 'Future Champions' INH Flat Race at Navan in December was his next assignment and this race goes down as a battle between two staying chasers of the future. Our Duke pressurised Death Duty inside the final furlong but it was the latter who got the better of the Jessica Harrington-trained gelding, recording a gutsy half a length success to add to his Down Royal romp. He showed a really admirable attitude on that occasion and given that his trainer describes him as, ***"not really a bumper horse"***, it was particularly pleasing to see him record back-to-back victories in a race that his stablemate and Cheltenham Gold Cup hero Don Cossack won in 2012. Sent off the even money favourite for his final start of the season, Death Duty found only the subsequent Punchestown Champion Bumper winner Blow By Blow too strong and in hindsight, this is arguably the pick of his form. After settling beautifully in the hands of Nina Carberry, the pair attempted to make all, kicking for home turning into the straight and was simply unable to match the eventual winners turn of foot inside the final two furlongs. Given that his trainer had already voiced his concerns about this sort of contest suiting his horse, Death Duty lost nothing in defeat on this occasion.

In terms of his running style, Death Duty has similarities to the ill-fated No More Heroes who himself was a useful novice hurdler before announcing himself as one of the leading novice chasers last winter. With an imminent switch to the hurdling ranks predicted, Elliott will be hoping that this gelding can reach similar heights as a novice hurdler during the 2016/2017 campaign. Although it is predicted that three miles will be his optimum in the future, this long-striding individual has plenty of class and should waste no time in winning a maiden or novice hurdle over a much shorter trip. Gigginstown and Elliott struck with the aforementioned No More Heroes in the Grade 2 Navan Novices' Hurdle in 2014, lowering the colours of Willie Mullins' Shaneshill in the process and it is likely that Death Duty will contest that race this time around. Although he doesn't necessarily appear the type to contest a Cheltenham Festival race as a novice hurdler, the Grade 1 Daily Mirror Novices' Hurdle at the Punchestown Festival is a feasible end of season target, where he will have to prove his ability to handle quicker ground conditions.

ESPOIR DE TEILLEE (FR) *(4-y-o b g)*

Martaline – Belle De Lyphard (FR) (Lyphard´s Wish (FR)

OWNER: Roger Brookhouse

FORM FIGURES: F

THE FINAL FLIGHT ANALYSIS:

An unusual inclusion in this season's 'Top Prospects' in that he has yet to complete a race, is the Roger Brookhouse-owned Espoir De Teillee. After losing his much-loved 2011 Champion Bumper winner Cheltenian when he broke down in the Grade 3 Swinton Hurdle, Brookhouse will be hoping for a change of fortunes this time around with his new purchase. This stunning looking gelding is a brother to French hurdle winner Venus De Teillee as well as a half-brother to French chase winner Air De Teillee. His dam was also a chase winner in her native France, so Espoir De Teillee certainly hails from a nice jumping family. He comes highly recommended to me from leading Irish point-to-point rider Derek O' Connor (read his horses to follow on page 86) and this son of Martaline is one to follow for this season and beyond.

He made his only start in a strong four-year-old maiden at Athlacca in May where he travelled supremely well, taking up the running after jumping the fourth last. After showing a useful turn of foot to put the race to bed between the final two fences, he fell at the final fence and ultimately threw away the chance to record what would have been one of the most taking performances of the season. Brookhouse was clearly impressed by this four-year-old's debut effort and he stumped up a huge sum of £220,000 at Goffs in May to secure his services.

Espoir De Teillee may lack form substance compared to the majority of this season's 'Top Prospects', but he more than made up for that by the visual impression that he created on his sole start between the flags. Based on that, he looks a high-class prospect now switched to rules and has the potential to go to the very top of the game. Although I wait in eager anticipation to see him make his hurdling debut, the natural ability he showed to quicken away from the strong field at Athlacca was outstanding, so a two-mile bumper looks well within his grasp. Regardless of where he starts his campaign, he is a horse with real star quality about him and his future looks very, very bright indeed.

GIVE ME A COPPER (IRE) *(6-y-o ch g)*

Presenting – Copper Supreme (IRE) (Supreme Leader)

TRAINER: Paul Nicholls

OWNER: Done, Ferguson, Kyle, Mason & Wood

FORM FIGURES: 11-

THE FINAL FLIGHT ANALYSIS:

After speaking to Tom Malone over the summer, it was simply impossible to exclude Give Me A Copper from this section. Being a brother to bumper, hurdle and chase winner Presenting Copper as well as a half-brother to other winners including Copper Bleu and Cloudy Copper, this 6-year-old is certainly bred to make his mark as a jumper. Based on the positive vibes surrounding him and the deep impression that he made on his two starts to date, he has the potential to become the best of his dams' offspring. This well-related son of Presenting won his only start in point-to-points last May at Athlacca by an easy eight lengths and following that, he was understandably high on Malone's wish list. However, after failing a veterinary inspection for a minor problem, he remained in the care of owner, breeder and trainer, Donal Coffey. He made his rules debut in an INH Flat Race over two miles and three furlongs at Cork near the end of March where he made light work of defeating the Willie Mullins-trained Classic Place by six and a half lengths. Even on heavy ground which wasn't certain to suit based his pedigree, Give Me A Copper travelled beautifully throughout and showed a superb turn of foot inside the final two furlongs to put the race to bed within a matter of strides. After making a winning start to his rules career, Coffey sent Give Me A Copper to the Goffs UK HIT Aintree Sales and the hammer fell at £270,000, of course signed for by Malone.

Visually Give Me A Copper couldn't have been more striking in his two starts to date and those performances alone warrant his inclusion in this section. In addition to his achievements on the track, Coffey has had plenty of good horses in his care and therefore his post-race comments have to be taken very seriously – ***"He´s the best horse we´ve ever had. He´s a right horse and will be better on better ground. We´d sell anything if we got enough but if he isn´t sold, we´ll keep him for the Gold Cup! He´s a horse who will definitely run in it some year"***. With Malone, who has proved himself as one of the leading bloodstock agents over the last few years (read his section on page 71), being equally upbeat about this gelding, Give Me A Copper is definitely one to follow. He will now continue his career under the watchful eye of Champion Trainer Paul Nicholls for owners Done, Ferguson, Kyle, Mason & Wood and although he has been acquired with chasing in mind, he can make an impression on the novice hurdling division this season. He has passed every test with flying colours to date and he has the sort of star quality that is familiarly associated to Nicholls' Ditcheat operation. The likes of Kauto Star, Master Minded and Big Buck's have been responsible for flying the Grade 1 flag in recent times and those connected to Give Me A Copper will be hoping that their exciting youngster can compete at the highest level in the coming seasons.

GO LONG (IRE) *(6-y-o b g)*

Hurricane Run (IRE) – Monumental Gesture (IRE) (Head For Heights)

TRAINER: Evan Williams

OWNER: Mr & Mrs William Rucker

FORM FIGURES: 23/12-

THE FINAL FLIGHT ANALYSIS:

The Ruckers have been associated with some high-class staying chasers in recent years including Hennessy Gold Cup and Grade 2 Charlie Hall winner State Of Play and Grand National runner-up Cappa Bleu – both trained by Evan Williams. One of the Ruckers' and Williams' brightest young prospects is Go Long, a thrice-raced six-year-old under rules. He makes plenty of appeal on paper being a half-brother to the very smart Wichita Lineman and top-class bumper and hurdle winner Rhinestone Cowboy. After finishing second to a high-class rival in his sole point, Go Long made his rules debut in a heavy ground bumper at Warwick in March 2015 – a race that at the time looked a decent contest and the runner-up has since won twice over hurdles for Dan Skelton (winner hasn't ran since). The ground was blamed by his connections for his twenty nine length defeat that day and he justified his early promise when scoring in a two-mile novice hurdle at Doncaster, beating subsequent Supreme Novices' Hurdle fifth Charbel by three and a quarter lengths (Go Long was in receipt of 7lb on that occasion). Although he jumped out to his right at times, he showed significant improvement from his bumper debut at Warwick and it is worth noting that this, the second division of the novices' hurdles on the card, was run at a significantly quicker time than the first. On the back of his successful hurdling debut he was sent off a warm order for his second start, again at the Town Moor venue, but failed to carry a 7lb penalty for his earlier victory over a three furlong longer trip. Though, taking into account his penalty, his runner-up effort behind the useful Wade Harper was far from a disgrace and he emerged as a horse with the potential to continue improving.

Having not run since finishing runner-up in that second Doncaster novices' hurdle, Williams' inmate remains an unexposed individual and based on his pedigree and collateral form lines, the 2016/2017 season should be a profitable one for his supporters. The fact that he is only rated 134 and that he is yet to race beyond two and a half miles, connections may be tempted to aim him at a handicap hurdle over a longer trip – something like the Listed Handicap Hurdle over three miles at Cheltenham's November meeting could be ideal. However, it would be no surprise to see Go Long switched to the novice chasing ranks where the novice handicap chase route could be particularly rewarding. It is important to consider that his best performance last season came on good ground where he clearly appreciated the sounder surface and he is best watched on anything worse than good-to-soft. King's Odyssey had a similar profile to Go Long when embarking on a chasing campaign last season and he more than paid his way in handicap chases with wins at Wincanton (100/30) and Cheltenham (8/1). With plenty of reasons to believe that Go Long will be an even better chaser, it is that sphere where he is predicted to show vast improvement in when the time comes, though this extremely likeable six-year-old is one to follow under either code.

IBIS DU RHEU (FR) *(5-y-o b g)*

Blue Bresil (FR) – Dona Du Rheu (FR) (Dom Pasquini (FR))

TRAINER: Paul Nicholls

OWNER: John Hales

FORM FIGURES: 21/64/23518-

THE FINAL FLIGHT ANALYSIS:

The expectation of having a celebrated older sibling can often be a burden, one that many fail to overcome – take Black Sam Bellamy as an example who was a Group 1 winner in his own right but always lived (and still does as a stallion) in the shadow of his brother Galileo. Though, after Saphir Du Rheu was disappointing last term, one expects that Ibis Du Rheu will surpass the achievements of his older sibling and gain deserved recognition for his own achievements on the track. Since arriving from France as a juvenile hurdler, he has been a work in progress. After being convincingly beaten on his two starts in four-year-old only contests, this gelding took a big step forward on his return to action last season, just failing to get to Royal Guardsman by a neck. Supporting a hood and tongue tie combination for the first time, Ibis Du Rheu settled nicely at the rear of the field in the early stages. After jumping competently throughout the contest, he was squeezed along by Sam Twiston-Davies when the tempo increased and he was gaining on the eventual winner all the way to the line. He showed a similar level of form when third to the progressive hurdler Yala Enki in the Lanzarote Hurdle at Kempton in January before performing below par in a Grade 3 at Sandown a month later. On the back of his Sandown flop, his trainer Paul Nicholls remained confident in this five-year-old's ability, letting him take his chance in the Martin Pipe Conditional Jockeys' Handicap Hurdle at the Cheltenham Festival. That decision was justified when Ibis Du Rheu stayed on strongly to deny Imperial Cup winner Flying Angel by one and a quarter lengths. It was the first time that Nicholls' charge had faced ground quicker than soft and along with a stiffer test of stamina, this appeared to bring out significant improvement. A long season and a speedier track were two contributing factors for being unable to repeat his Cheltenham heroics at Aintree three weeks later and taking that into account, his poor run is easily forgiven.

Ibis Du Rheu's lack of consistency is a concern as he embarks on a novice chasing campaign but he has a huge amount of ability and he has always been regarded as a long-term chasing prospect since arriving on these shores. His victory at last season's Cheltenham Festival demonstrated that he has a willing attitude as well as stamina to burn and those are two attributes that will serve him well in the staying chase division. Nicholls has won three of the last ten renewals of the Grade 2 Worcester Novices' Chase at Newbury and was represented by third-placed Port Melon last season. The Champion Trainer has a strong team of novice chasers and with that in mind, this race could prove to be a perfect mid-season target, particularly as it is predicted that Ibis Du Rheu will be stepped-up to three miles sooner rather than later. Assuming that things go to plan over the larger obstacles, the Grade 1 RSA Novices' Chase is likely to be the end of season target. His owner John Hales has long been searching for a Cheltenham Gold Cup winner and he will be hoping that Ibis Du Rheu can announce himself as a live contender for the 2018 renewal.

INVITATION ONLY (IRE) *(5-y-o b g)*

Flemensfirth (USA) – Norabelle (FR) (Alamo Bay (USA))

TRAINER: Willie Mullins

OWNER: Andrea & Graham Wylie

FORM FIGURES: **1**/1-1

THE FINAL FLIGHT ANALYSIS:

Invitation Only provided Sean Doyle with his first four-year-old winner of the 2014/2015 point-to-point season and following his faultless display, he was subsequently sold privately to the Wylies to continue his career at Willie Mullins' all-conquering Closutton stables. Running in the colours of the Monbeg syndicate, who notably sold seven lots at Cheltenham's Tattersalls Sales in May for just short of €1 million, this gelding created a deep impression on his sole start between the flags. He jumped imperiously throughout, particularly at the third last where he ultimately put the race to bed, and his professional performance that day showed the nice blend of speed and stamina that he has already put to good use in his two starts under rules. "Can this Invitation Only keep going?" was the line from the point-to-point commentator with two to jump, quite ironic given that this five-year-old is thought of as a future staying chaser. After his likeable debut and taking into account his new connections, there was no surprise that Invitation Only was sent off the odds-on favourite for his rules debut – the Navan Race Members (Pro/Am) INH Flat Race in March. Patrick Mullins made all of the running aboard this son of Flemensfirth and although he didn't break any records with his early fractions, when Invitation Only was asked to go and win his race, he did just that, knuckling down well to record an impressive seven length victory. His second and final assignment of last season was at the Punchestown Festival in the Kildare Post (C & G) INH Flat Race – a race connections won with multiple Grade 1-winning novice hurdler Yorkhill in 2015. Again sent into an early lead, a tactic that is not believed to be essential, he travelled with ease throughout. Although he was asked a serious question to fend off the challenge of Blast Of Koeman, he was merely idling in the closing stages and his one and a quarter length success can be described as comfortable.

Invitation Only raced freely on his bumper debut at Navan, but after settling much better on his latest start, he can be ridden more patiently when switched to hurdling. The Navan and Punchestown races were run at an ordinary gallop, so he clearly has a decent turn of foot. Conversely, the visual impression implied that he is more of a staying prospect and significant improvement is expected when he tackles trips between two and a half and three miles as a hurdler. The physically imposing Invitation Only is a long-term prospect and rates as an exciting staying chaser when the time comes. It is predicted that he will prove himself as a star performer in that sphere, but with his career figures reading 111, Mullins et al will be looking to preserve that unbeaten record as he joins the novice hurdling ranks. Once again Ireland's Champion Trainer has a powerful team of budding young hurdlers and in this highly-regarded bay, he has another potential Grade 1 performer. Described as ***"a winter horse"*** by his handler, it is likely that Invitation Only will follow the same route as Bellshill by carrying the Wylies famous black and beige silks to victory in a maiden hurdle before taking a step-up in class and trip during the winter months.

JENKINS (IRE) *(4-y-o b g)*

Azamour (IRE) – Aladiyna (IRE) (Indian Danehill (IRE))
TRAINER: Nicky Henderson
OWNER: Pump & Plant Services Ltd
FORM FIGURES: 1-2

THE FINAL FLIGHT ANALYSIS:

Occasionally the only way to describe a performance is breathtaking; your pulse begins to race and you feel that you have witnessed the birth of a star. Jenkins made his racecourse debut in the West Berkshire Racing Club Standard Open National Hunt Flat Race on the final day of Newbury's National Hunt season and that is exactly the impression that he created. As a son of Azamour, this four-year-old has a flat pedigree so there was no surprise that he showed a brilliant turn of foot and as described during the commentary that day, "this horse would not be out of place in a flat race". Having said that, his unraced dam Aladiyna is a half-sister to hurdle winners Alaivan and Alarazi and on the back of his debut performance there is every reason to believe that this gelding has a really bright future when his attentions are switched to jumping. Travelling effortlessly in the hands of David Bass, Jenkins entered the straight with only five behind but once his rider asked him to quicken, he cut through the pack like a knife through butter and he drew readily away from the highly-regarded Cash Again to record a bloodless success. Following his runaway victory his trainer Nicky Henderson commented, ***"I'm trying to get a Land Rover out of these guys"***, highlighting the Goffs Land Rover Sales Bumper as his next target and he was sent off a hot favourite (8/11) to follow-up his page-turning debut. He was ridden more prominently at Punchestown under leading amateur rider Patrick Mullins, racing enthusiastically in the early stages. His rider kicked for home turning in and looked like going on to record another impressive display before getting caught close home by Robert Tyner's Coeur De Lion. Although he squandered his unbeaten record on only his second start, Jenkins lost little in defeat, especially taking into account how keen he was in the early stages and the fact that he appeared to get lonely after being in front for so long. In addition, the winner is clearly more of a staying type and it was stamina that allowed him to get the better of his speedier rival on this occasion.

Jenkins brought up a half century of winners for Bass when winning at Newbury and it is hoped that the pair will once again team up this season as he embarks on a novice hurdling campaign. The turn of foot that he showed on both of his starts to date demonstrate that he will be suited to two mile novice hurdles and due to his keen-going nature, it is anticipated that strongly run races will suit. Henderson has dominated the two mile Introductory Hurdle on Newbury's Challow Hurdle Card, with Premier Bond last season landing a fifth straight success for his trainer and it is likely that Jenkins could be his representative this time around. The race has been won by some very smart horses in recent years including 2012 Champion Hurdle winner Rock On Ruby and Jenkins has the potential to take that contest before competing at Grade 1 level at the Spring festivals. Although the Supreme Novices' Hurdle is perhaps the most likely target, with a guaranteed strong early gallop it can often become a test of stamina and the Neptune Novices' Hurdle might be a race that suits him better.

JUDGEMENT DAY (IRE) *(4-y-o b g)*

Martaline – Gaye Moscow (IRE) (Moscow Society (USA)

TRAINER: Willie Mullins

FORM FIGURES: 1-

THE FINAL FLIGHT ANALYSIS:

This four-year-old is a really nice horse who made a winning debut at Liscarroll in March – a track that Derek O'Connor describes as, ***"one of our better point-to-point tracks in which the maidens are often contested by promising horses"***. Judgement Day, the well-backed favourite on the day moved well throughout the contest and made good headway approaching the fence where the Gigginstown-owned Morgan, who subsequently ran well in a Fairyhouse bumper later that month, was still going well before unseating his rider. Although it is difficult to assess how Morgan would have fared had he stood up, Judgement Day created a good impression, winning in quite taking fashion. The fact that he showed signs of greenness when running wide on the bend before the final fence is a sign that this son of Martaline still has plenty to learn and he ultimately has scope to be much better with that experience under his belt. Although the form is yet to be put to the test under rules, a positive to take from the race is that the form has been subsequently franked with two point winners emerging (The Two Amigos – sixth and Getabird – ran out).

Courtesy of winning his point debut, Judgement Day was sent to the Goffs UK sales at Aintree in April where he attracted plenty of interest before Harold Kirk signed a cheque for £145,000 to secure him – Kirk was clearly equally as impressed with his three length victory at Liscarroll. He will now continue his career at Closutton with Ireland's Champion Trainer Willie Mullins and he couldn't be in better hands to excel under rules – Mullins boasted a 39% strike rate with his bumper runners last season.

Judgement Day's long-term potential is undoubted and he rates as a really exciting jumper when the time comes. However, O'Connor describes Judgement Day as, "***a really likeable individual, who has a high cruising speed and a decent turn of foot"*** – high praise indeed for a rider who has ridden over 1,000 winners between the flags – and those attributes should ensure he wins a bumper before switching to obstacles. His inclusion in his trainer's Champion Bumper squad is a decision for a later date, but with Mullins' ex-point-to-pointer Battleford going mightily close in last season's renewal, the race is certainly one where stayers of the future excel in and Judgement Day is a youngster with significant untapped potential.

LUCKY PASS (FR) *(5-y-o ch g)*

Ultimately Lucky (IRE) – Fuela Pass (FR) (Astarabad (USA))
TRAINER: Willie Mullins
OWNER: Gigginstown House Stud
FORM FIGURES: 1/11-

THE FINAL FLIGHT ANALYSIS:

After winning his sole point-to-to-point start at Loughanmore where he had his now stablemate and smart bumper performer Battleford held when that rival departed at the final fence, Lucky Pass was sold for £140,000 to Harold Kirk at Cheltenham's 2015 Brightwells Sales. He was sent off the 2/1 joint favourite for his new connections in a Fairyhouse INH Flat Race at Fairyhouse in November 2015 and although easy to back in the market, he made a winning debut, beating subsequent dual bumper winner Avellino by one and a half lengths. The form of that race has worked out particularly well with the third and fourth also winning bumpers since and therefore it is no surprise that Lucky Pass was able to back his debut success up with a win in the Ryanair Flat Race at Leopardstown's four-day Christmas Festival – a race won in recent years by Outlander (2012), Value At Risk (2013) and Vigil (2014). He beat First Figaro by a comfortable three and three quarter lengths on that occasion and with that rival subsequently finishing five and a half lengths behind Ballyandy in the Champion Bumper on his next start, the form looks respectable. This five-year-old chestnut gelding showed a professional attitude, idling when arguably hitting the front too early and ultimately had far too much class for his four opponents on the day.

Although one might expect an ex-point winner to be destined to make their mark in the chasing ranks, Lucky Pass is quite unique in that he has certain attributes that should help him excel as a hurdler, one being that he has the ability to quicken off a slow gallop. On his bumper debut at Fairyhouse he showed enough gears to assume that it is perfectly feasible to start him off over the minimum distance as a novice hurdler and step him up in trip in due course. In terms of his ideal ground conditions, his three wins to date (one point-to-point and two bumpers) have come when there is cut in the ground and his way of going would certainly suggest that he is at home on a softer surface. However, until he is tested on ground with good in the going description, it is foolish to rule out him being equally as effective. He should make light work of shedding his maiden tag over timber but it is predicted that his connections will want to examine his ability at a higher level sooner rather than later. Given that Michael O'Leary isn't keen on the Champion Bumper, it is no surprise that he left what looks to be one of his brightest prospects of the future at home and there is no reason why he will not make the trip over to the Cheltenham Festival in 2017. In the interim, the Grade 1 Future Champion Novices' Hurdle over two miles at Leopardstown in December is likely to come under serious consideration, a race that Gigginstown House Stud and Willie Mullins have been strongly represented in recently.

MOUNT MEWS (IRE) *(5-y-o b g)*

Presenting (IRE) – Kneeland Lass (IRE) (Bob Back (USA))
TRAINER: Malcolm Jefferson
OWNER: Trevor Hemmings
FORM FIGURES: 1-1

THE FINAL FLIGHT ANALYSIS:

If you backed every horse trained by North Yorkshire handler Malcolm Jefferson last season then you would have been in profit to a level stake and in the form of the Trevor Hemmings-owned Mount Mews, he has a potentially very smart novice hurdler to go to war with this season. This Presenting gelding, out of Kneeland Lass who is a sister to Hemmings high-class but ill-fated chaser Burton Port, quickened up in good style to land a Market Rasen bumper in April, two and a half lengths ahead of Ben Pauling's well-regarded Bally Gilbert. He was niggled along entering the home straight, but he responded well to jockey Henry Brooke's urgings and showed his rivals a clean pair of heels inside the final furlong to record quite a taking debut victory. In addition to the visual impression that Mount Mews created on this occasion, it is also worth noting that a significant number of Presenting's progeny prefer quicker ground conditions than what he encountered here (soft, good to soft in places) and that offers plenty of promise that he will handle a winter hurdling campaign. This five-year-old gelding followed up his Market Rasen success when scoring by ten lengths in a Kelso bumper a month later under a penalty. He hit the front plenty early enough but was kept up to his work on the run-in and was worth more than the eventual winning margin. This race was arguably not as strong as he faced on his debut, but he clearly handled the better ground (officially good) and given time to mature over the summer months, this sizeable individual has the scope to improve plenty.

Jefferson was dealt a hammer blow at the beginning of last season when Cyrus Darius was ruled out for the season but with his return imminent along with the prospect of Mount Mews switching to the novice hurdling division, he has a lot to look forward to. Attaglance won the Martin Pipe Conditional Jockeys' Handicap Hurdle for this yard four years ago and it is hoped that this unbeaten gelding can take him to similar heights in the near future. Judged on his confirmation, he is a chasing type which is unsurprising given that his owner is often associated with staying chasers. It is worth noting that Hemmings has had two of his horses finish second in the EBF Final at Sandown in recent years; Many Clouds in 2013 and Great Try in 2015 and although it may just be coincidence, it is perfectly possible that Mount Mews could attempt to make it third time lucky for his popular owner. Having not contested any of the championship bumpers, this gelding remains completely unexposed and an unknown quantity is what many racing fans get excited about.

ONE TRACK MIND (IRE) *(6-y-o b g)*

Flemensfirth (USA) – Lady Petit (IRE) (Beneficial)
TRAINER: Warren Greatrex
OWNER: Andy Weller
FORM FIGURES: 1/1U41/512-1-

THE FINAL FLIGHT ANALYSIS:

Lambourn based trainer Warren Greatrex had his best season in 2015/2016 recording fifty three winners, two better than the previous season. He could not have wished for a better start to the current campaign with One Track Mind giving him, jockey Gavin Sheehan and owner Andy Weller a day to remember, claiming the Grade 1 Ladbrokes Champion Stayers Hurdle at the Punchestown Festival. This good looking son of Flemensfirth has always been highly thought of by his talented handler and even going back to his bumper debut at Wetherby in 2014 in which he won by a comfortable six lengths Greatrex told the Racing Post, ***"He is an archetypal future staying chaser"***. Having recorded two wins from four starts as a novice hurdler which included a respectable fourth in the Grade 1 Challow Novices' Hurdle at Newbury, he reappeared last season in a two mile and seven furlong handicap hurdle at Cheltenham's International meeting. Sent off the 11/4 favourite, he still held every chance jumping the last but got tired on the run-in to eventually finish fifth. He took advantage of a drop in class when winning a two and a half miles handicap hurdle at Newbury in late December and although it was a workmanlike display, he was putting in his best work at the finish. There was no surprise to see him step back up in trip for the Grade 2 Rendlesham Hurdle in what was his penultimate start of the 2015/2016 campaign and after only finding the consistent and mud-loving Reve De Sivola too good in attritional conditions, that was a superb effort in what was by far his toughest assignment of his career. Immediately after the race, Greatrex made it clear that Punchestown was the plan and he executed it perfectly, recording a second Grade 1 prize in the staying hurdling division following Cole Harden's 2015 Ladbrokes World Hurdle heroics. One Track Mind repelled the challenge of the smart mare Jennies Jewel by two and a quarter lengths with the Ryanair World Hurdle runner-up Alpha Des Obeaux a yawning eight lengths further back and although the form of this race is likely to be scrutinised, this was a professional and impressive display.

On looks alone, this sizeable individual is built to jump a fence and he is expected to be a smart recruit to the novice chase ranks in the autumn. Still relatively lightly raced, there is every chance that One Track Mind will progress again this season and announce himself as one of the leading contenders for the Grade 1 RSA Novices' Chase at the 2017 Cheltenham Festival. The novice chasing division, particularly the stayers, doesn't look as deep as previous years and therefore if you are an ante-post punter, the 16/1 that is currently available is worth taking. The Grade 2 Rising Stars Novices' Chase run at Wincanton over two and a half miles is a feasible mid-season target, where the likely soft ground conditions will bring his stamina into play.

O O SEVEN (IRE) *(6-y-o b g)*

Flemensfirth (USA) – Kestral Heights (IRE) (Eagle Eyed (USA))
TRAINER: Nicky Henderson
OWNER: Triermore Stud
FORM FIGURES: 120/11218-2

THE FINAL FLIGHT ANALYSIS:

This well put together six-year-old by Flemensfirth out of two-time winner Kestral Heights cost a tidy €130,000 as an unraced three-year-old. He duly justified his price tag by proving himself as a high-class bumper horse in the 2014/2015 season before again showing up well over hurdles last season for the master of Seven Barrows, Nicky Henderson. A winner of four out of the nine races that he has contested, it is worth noting that four of his defeats came in Grade 1 company – firstly when a 40/1 shot in the 2015 Champion Bumper and twice behind high-class novice hurdler Yorkhill last season. As with a lot of Flemensfirth's offspring, this good looking sort looks sure to be suited by longer trips and a switch to fences this time around. During a fruitful novice hurdling campaign, O O Seven was a winner of three of his six starts with all three of his defeats coming in Grade 1 races. His most impressive performance was arguably when scoring in the recognised Albert Bartlett trial over an extended two miles and seven furlongs at Musselburgh. Despite making a few mistakes at a number of his obstacles, he travelled with zest throughout and stayed on strongly after the last to record a well-deserved victory – beating the subsequent Albert Bartlett runner-up Fagan by three quarters of a length. It was interesting after a taking success at Musselburgh that that Henderson and his team decided to drop him back two furlongs to contest the Grade 1 Neptune Investment Management Novices' Hurdle at the Cheltenham Festival. To say the race didn't go to plan at Cheltenham would be an understatement, with O O Seven being badly hampered and losing any chance of challenging at the business end of the contest. His second placed effort behind Jer's Girl at the Punchestown Festival was a creditable run given that he had to give away plenty of weight to a progressive filly and was also likely to be feeling the effects of a hard season on what was his final start.

The imposing O O Seven is the type that will improve for a switch to the larger obstacles where he rates as an exciting novice chasing prospect. His physique and likeable attitude is reminiscent of Captain Conan – also trained by Nicky Henderson for owners Triermore Stud – who often dwarfed his opposition too. With his aptitude for longer trips confirmed with that good run at Musselburgh, his connections should have plenty of options this season which is predicted to be where O O Seven will really come of age. The Grade 1 Kauto Star Novices' Chase (formerly known as the Feltham) over three miles on Kempton's Boxing Day fixture looks like an ideal race for a horse who's best performances have come on flat tracks when there is slight ease in the ground which are conditions that you would expect to find at Kempton in the depths of winter. Although Grade 1 races will certainly be on his agenda when switched to the chasing ranks, O O Seven will be capable of running in some of the top handicap races, though big-field, strongly-run races may come a season too soon for a gelding that has still showed signs of inexperience at times. The fact that has ran below par on two visits to Prestbury Park, it is quite possible that O O Seven will bypass the Cheltenham Festival, with a preference to either Aintree or Punchestown – both of which are meetings that Henderson likes to target.

OUTSPOKEN (IRE) *(4-y-o b g)*

Galileo (IRE) – Riskaverse (USA) (Dynaformer (USA))

TRAINER: Joseph O'Brien

OWNER: JP McManus

FORM FIGURES: 2-

THE FINAL FLIGHT ANALYSIS:

As mentioned in my introduction, the rise of Joseph O'Brien as a trainer, Galileo as a National Hunt sire, along with the support of leading owner JP McManus is a recipe for success. Purely coincidence, totally by accident or maybe even fate, Outspoken is an really nice prospect for the aforementioned trio and he rates as a potentially top-class individual in the novice hurdling division this season. A fifth foal out of US Grade 1-winning mare Riskaverse, Outspoken is well-related being a brother to Group 3 winner Say as well as being closely related to useful hurdler and chaser Saddler's Risk. It is slightly unusual in the fact that he appears in this section as a second-season novice hurdler after only one run in a three-year-old maiden hurdle at Fairyhouse last term. Though, he did show plenty of promise that day and but for a mistake at the last, there is every chance that he would have got the better of the subsequent Grade 1-placed Allblak Des Places. Following his very promising hurdling debut, it was no surprise that his connections saved his novice status with a view to this season and it is expected that their patience will pay dividends. Judged on his debut over timber, his jumping technique clearly needs some attention but he travelled like a good horse throughout the contest and he is more than capable of translating his high flat rating (101) to this sphere.

Outspoken will return this season with a tall reputation and taking that into account, he is likely to be a warm order for a maiden or novice hurdle in the autumn. Having said that, the competition across the Irish Sea is particularly strong at present with the dominant Willie Mullins and Gordon Elliott providing stiff opposition for their contemporaries. This lightly raced four-year-old gelding is thought of as a graded performer, with connections already highlighting the Grade 1 Supreme Novices' Hurdle as a long-term target and he certainly has the speed to cope with races over the minimum distance. In addition to this, there is also reason to believe that he will be just as effective over two and a half miles which opens up plenty of possible targets prior to and including the spring festivals. Aidan O'Brien recorded back-to-back victories in the Grade 1 Royal Bond Novice Hurdle with Thats My Man (1995) and the mighty Istabraq (1996) and it is possible that O'Brien junior will send Outspoken, who is certain to be one of his leading lights this season, for that same Fairyhouse Grade 1. Since being established in 1994, the Royal Bond has been an excellent pointer to future stars, yielding four individual Champion Hurdle winners (Istabraq, Hardy Eustace, Hurricane Fly and Jezki) as well as two Champion Chasers (dual winner Moscow Flyer and Newmill). Therefore if Outspoken is successful in this race, it is likely to be on the way to bigger and better things.

PETIT MOUCHOIR (FR) *(5-y-o gr g)*

Al Namix (FR) – Arnette (FR) (Denham Red (FR))
TRAINER: Willie Mullins
OWNER: Gigginstown House Stud
FORM FIGURES: 1/113482-2

THE FINAL FLIGHT ANALYSIS:

The progressive Petit Mouchoir is the only horse to retain his place in this season's 'Top Prospects' after a consistent but slightly unfortunate first season over obstacles and it is hoped that he will repay that loyalty with a productive 2016/2017 campaign. This son of Al Namix ran with the choke out on his hurdling debut but the fact that he was still able to score by a comfortable three lengths, albeit against weak opposition, was evidence that he had a good deal of ability. He stepped up considerably on his second start to finish a close third in the Grade 1 Future Champion Novices' Hurdle at Leopardstown, again racing keenly before staying on well to get within two lengths of the ill-fated Long Dog. Having performed so well with such little experience, a bold show was expected in the Grade 1 Deliotte Novices' Hurdle but he ran no sort of race, finishing a well-beaten fourth of five. He was far from disgraced in Grade 1 Supreme Novices' Hurdle at the Cheltenham Festival where he showed signs of inexperience throughout and was ultimately not ready for that sort of test at such an early stage of his career. Sent off an unfancied 40/1 in the Grade 1 Top Novices' Hurdle at Aintree, Petit Mouchoir ran a spectacular race, serving it up to the much more fancied Buveur D'Air in the straight, only to be denied close home by a quarter of a length. David Mullins was allowed to dictate the pace from an early stage and this keen going sort appeared to enjoy being ridden more positively. Similar tactics were employed on his final start at Punchestown in the Grade 1 Champion Novices' Hurdle, where he travelled well in the hands of Bryan Cooper, looking all over the winner Don't Touch It, before not quite having the speed to quicken with the eventual winner.

It is fair to assume that a tough spring campaign took its toll on Petit Mouchoir and that was probably what prevented him from recording a much-deserved Grade 1 success at the end of last season. The ever present hood was removed for his final two outings and it will be interesting to see whether or not connections decide to re-apply that aid. He has always been considered a horse that will be suited by two and a half miles, so his achievements over the minimum distance last season were somewhat extraordinary. It is predicted that Willie Mullins will send this grey gelding chasing and if that is the case, he rates as one of the most exciting recruits to that sphere this season. He clearly needs to learn how to relax if he is to fulfil his full potential but the level of form that he has showed without doing everything right is promising and it is only a matter of time before he records a victory at the highest level. He is capable of winning at the Cheltenham Festival in 2017 and although predicting Mullins' train of thought is practically impossible, the Grade 1 JLT Novices' Chase is the most likely target.

POLITOLOGUE (FR) *(5-y-o gr g)*

Poliglote – Scarlet Row (FR) (Turgeon (USA))
TRAINER: Paul Nicholls
OWNER: John Hales
FORM FIGURES: 21U210-

THE FINAL FLIGHT ANALYSIS:

After scoring in a four-year-old hurdle at Auteuil, Politologue was sold privately to John Hales, adding to his long list of smart French recruits. Hales has a long association with Champion Trainer Paul Nicholls and the pair tasted Cheltenham Festival success as recently as last season with another potential star of the chasing ranks, the aforementioned Ibis Du Rheu. Politologue, a five-year-old son of Poliglote, who has also sired top-class chaser Don Poli, was in the process of running a good race on debut at Cheltenham when unshipping Sam Twiston-Davies. After travelling like a good horse throughout the contest, he ducked out for no apparent reason, leaving his rider no chance of keeping the partnership intact. Clearly held in high-regard by his handler, he was then set a tough assignment to contest the Grade 1 Challow Novices' Hurdle on only his second start in Britain. Again he cruised into contention, looking a threat to Barters Hill who was unbeaten at the time, but he was unable to get to the hind quarters of that rival and eventually finished a twelve length second. Politologue was far from disgraced at the highest level on that occasion and there was no surprise that he took advantage of a drop in class at Exeter on his next start, opening his account on these shores in facile fashion. On the back of his demolition job at Exeter, he was subject to significant support for the Grade 3 Coral Cup at the Cheltenham Festival and it was extremely disappointing to see him finish well-beaten. Nevertheless, I am certain that this wasn't his true running. This was by far the fastest ground conditions that he had encountered and it is possible that he needs cut in the ground to perform to is best. In addition to this, a lack of cover throughout was a significant negative at Cheltenham and a couple of jumping errors which are often associated with novice hurdlers in big field handicaps, all but ended his chances.

Both Hales and Nicholls have independently described this grey gelding as a fine chasing prospect and although his season ended on a low note, he still rates as an extremely exciting recruit to the larger obstacles. His experience in the Coral Cup will no doubt stand him in good stead during his career over fences and his way of going should mean that he will be suited by races run at a genuine gallop. As previously mentioned, he has already showed a liking to both soft and heavy ground, so it would be wise to assume that his connections will plot a winter campaign. Nicholls' As De Mee bumped into More Of That in the two and a half mile Steel Plate And Sections Novices' Chase at Cheltenham's November meeting last season and it is possible that Politologue can go one better in the 2016 renewal. Looking longer term, the Punchestown Festival, where ease in the ground is more likely than both Cheltenham and Aintree, is almost certain to be the most suitable of the three spring festivals. The Grade 1 Growise Champion Novice chase over an extended three miles is a plausible option at this early stage, with a step-up to three miles sure to suit.

PROTEK DES FLOS (FR) *(4-y-o b g)*

Protektor (GER) – Flore De Chantenay (FR) (Smadoun (FR))
TRAINER: Nicky Henderson
OWNER: JP McManus
FORM FIGURES: 2112-

THE FINAL FLIGHT ANALYSIS:

Twice-raced in France as a three-year-old, once on the level and the other in a Listed Hurdle when runner-up at Auteuil, Protek Des Flos made a winning British debut for his new connections at Cheltenham on Festival Trials Day at the end of January. Described by Nicky Henderson as ***"a horse who doesn't show anything at home"***, this son of Protektor saved his best efforts for the track, landing the Grade 2 JCB Triumph Hurdle Trial on debut beating the well-regarded Paul Nicholls-trained Clan Des Obeaux. After being ridden patiently throughout by Noel Fehily, Protek Des Flos came from a long way back to stay on in taking fashion, springing a 25-1 surprise. After leaving the impression that he would be most effective over longer trips in the future, his Triumph Hurdle credentials were being questioned by many following his Cheltenham success, but he made no mistake in following up at long odds-on in a Sandown novices' hurdle less than a month later. On that occasion he again showed a liking to the testing underfoot conditions, again taking time to get going, but ultimately winning with a fair bit in hand. This race – a race that can only be described as an ordinary novice event – told us little more about the ability of this gelding and after showing signs of immaturity along with the likelihood of facing a sounder surface for the first time in his career, connections decided to swerve last season's Cheltenham Festival. Though, Protek Des Flos did have one final start of last season in the Prix Virelan back in his native France and in finishing a close second to Saint Goustan Blue who has won twice since, he lost nothing in defeat.

Protek Des Flos is a really likeable individual and judged on his three starts to date, he looks like playing a leading role over longer trips this winter. Having contested all of his races over obstacles on very soft or heavy ground, he clearly handles deep ground better than most and like the much-loved Reve De Sivola, he will be able to collect plenty of prizes on rain-softened ground throughout his career. His connections obviously didn't fancy him for his British debut which is hardly surprising given that he is such a sizeable individual and it is expected that he will have improved physically after a summer at grass. With that in mind, his two wins on these shores which came against some high-quality rivals (particularly at Cheltenham) should be taken very seriously and with him having the scope to be even better this season, he is one to follow. He is current rated 137 by the official handicapper and that mark will give his connections the option of running in a handicap before he is asked to step-up in class against his elders. The Grade 3 Fixed Brush Handicap Hurdle which takes place at Haydock in November is highlighted as a target for Protek Des Flos, a race that has been won by some very good horses since its inception in 2005 including; Diamond Harry (2009), Grand Crus (2010) and Dynaste (2011). His progression will no doubt dictate his other targets throughout the year, but the Grade 1 Long Walk Hurdle (Ascot in December) and the Grade 2 Cleeve Hurdle (Cheltenham in January) ought to come under serious consideration for a horse who I rate as a very exciting young hurdler.

ROBIN ROE (IRE) *(5-y-o b g)*

Robin Des Champs (FR) – Talktothetail (IRE) (Flemensfirth (USA)

TRAINER: Dan Skelton

OWNER: Mrs Barbara Hester

FORM FIGURES: 2/11-

THE FINAL FLIGHT ANALYSIS:

Dan Skelton, the former assistant to Champion Trainer Paul Nicholls, has made a bright start since embarking on his own training career which has already included a number of graded winners. Last season, only his third with a trainers' licence, Skelton surpassed the £1,000,000 mark for the first time which is an impressive achievement for somebody so young. With a stable full of equine talent, there is no surprise that a number of horses in his care feature in this publication – the first being point-to-point and bumper winner Robin Roe. After finishing a two length runner-up on his debut between the flags at Loughbrickland, he went one better on his next start, recording a half a length success over subsequent bumper winner Laser Light. The third that day, Minella Beau, has since won a four-year-old maiden and with the front pair a distance clear of the remainder, the form looks rock solid. Having been withdrawn from the Tattersalls Ireland Sales at Cheltenham in December (sold privately), Skelton set this son of Robin Des Champs an eighteen runner bumper at Warwick as his first assignment under rules. Sent off the 11/4 favourite, this five-year-old won a shade cosily in the hands of Harry Skelton, beating Kim Bailey's Royal Supremo by one and a half lengths. There is no doubt that Robin Roe was worth more than the eventual winning margin after idling upon hitting the front and he created a very good impression – it is advised that there will be plenty of winners to come out of that race. After winning with what looked a fair amount up his sleeve, it was reported that this gelding was under consideration for the Aintree bumper which shows the sort of regard that he is held in. However, connections decided that the one run was enough for his first season under rules and he was subsequently put away with a view to this season.

It can be fully expected that Robin Roe will be switched to hurdling and he certainly has the natural ability to excel over timber. He seems to have a nice blend of speed and stamina which will allow him to start out over two miles with the potential to step up in trip as the season progresses. One of Skelton's leading lights in the novice hurdling division last season was Welsh Shadow and it is possible that Robin Roe will follow a similar route this time around. The Bathwick Tyres-sponsored Plymouth Novices' Hurdle run at Exeter in early November is a feasible starting point – a race where Welsh Shadow bumped into the smart Yanworth, with the EBF Final winner Barney Dwan back in third. The Grade 2 Dovecote Novices' Hurdle, won in 2015 by fellow 'Top Prospect' Winter Escape, is another race which is sure to suit Robin Roe before a likely assault on the spring festivals. Having raced on a variety of ground (heavy, yielding-to-soft and good), he seems to be pretty versatile but I would be reluctant to see him contest too many races on really testing ground at such an early stage of his career. Being a point-to-point winner his connections have the added anticipation of his prospects over the larger obstacles in the future, but his future over hurdles in the short-term looks equally as exciting.

SAMCRO (IRE) *(4-y-o ch g)*

Germany (USA) – Dun Dun (IRE) (Saddlers´ Hall (IRE))

TRAINER: Gordon Elliott

OWNER: Gigginstown House Stud

FORM FIGURES: 1-

THE FINAL FLIGHT ANALYSIS:

Germany, a top-class middle distance colt, is probably best known by jumps fans as the sire of Champion Hurdle winner Faugheen. Though, it is also worth noting that he was also responsible for 2008 Supreme Novices' Hurdle winner Captain Cee Bee. Although he died as a twenty two-year-old, his son Samcro, a winner of his sole start in point-to-points, is a really promising individual and one who is definitely worthy of his place in this year's 'Top Prospects'.

In the care of Colin Bowe in the pointing sphere, this four-year-old made his debut at Monksgrange in early April where after being sent off a well-backed favourite, he made a winning start. He travelled with ease throughout the contest, handling the testing underfoot conditions particularly well to score by a cosy one length over Elegant Escape. The front pair were twenty lengths clear of the remainder and Samcro showed a really likeable attitude to keep finding more as the runner-up tested his metal on the run-in. Elegant Escape who was trained by Gordon Elliott at that point has since been purchased for €150,000 to join Colin Tizzard (read more about him on page 62) and the regard in which Elliott held his charge was backed up when he paid £335,000 for Samcro at Goffs in April. After briefly speaking to Derek O'Connor about this gelding he stated, ***"He cost an awful lot of money up at Aintree due to a lot of competition for him, but Gordon held the horse he beat in fair regard and he more than backed that up by signing for this fella". "He was visually impressive on his debut, particularly given that the ground was so desperate and I think he's a nice long-term prospect"***.

The race that Samcro contested on his debut looked a race of the highest order and it is expected that both he and Elegant Escape have bright futures under rules. However, it is Samcro that earned his place in this section with what I describe as a tenacious success and now in the care of one of Ireland's leading National Hunt trainers, he can go right to the top. He clearly handles winter ground after showing the ability to plough through the mud at Monksgrange, but I hope he will prove to be versatile in terms of ground conditions. He has the natural ability to win over the minimum distance, but I expect he will prove himself most effective over intermediate trips as a jumper. He is likely to gain valuable experience in a bumper before being switched to hurdles and his new connections will be excited about what the future holds for their four-year-old. Elliott and Gigginstown's Death Duty won the Daily Mirror-sponsored bumper at Down Royal in late October by a wide margin and that might be a nice starting point for Samcro to begin his career under rules.

SAVOY COURT (IRE) *(5-y-o b g)*

Robin Des Champs (FR) – North Star Poly (IRE) (Presenting))
TRAINER: Warren Greatrex
OWNER: Mrs T Brown
FORM FIGURES: 41-

THE FINAL FLIGHT ANALYSIS:

Warren Greatrex is renowned for nurturing young talent and does particularly well with his bumper runners, operating at an average strike rate of 30% over the last three seasons in that sphere. With that in mind, it is worth noting that he described Savoy Court as ***"a bumper horse with the potential to be a top class performer"*** when I caught up with him during the close season. A half-brother to hurdle and chase winner Audacious Plan (Old Vic), this five-year old gelding made a promising debut at Exeter when fourth of twelve in a good ground bumper. Ridden handily throughout, he had to be pushed along at the half way stage but responded well to his jockeys' urgings to remain in contention turning into the straight. Although he didn't travel with the same fluency as some of his rivals on this occasion, he showed a willing attitude to stay on stoutly in the closing stages and finished just one length behind the winner in a four-way bunched finish. With the benefit of hindsight, that bumper was certainly above average. The race had yielded four subsequent winners prior to Savoy Court making it five; recording a smooth success in a Ffos Las bumper at the back end of last season. Greatrex's stable jockey Gavin Sheehan was again in the saddle and he took full advantage of a soft lead, steadily increasing the tempo as the race progressed. The eventual runner-up Tommy Rapper looked a huge danger upon approaching the straight but Savoy Court found plenty in front and registered a comfortable two length victory, more than fulfilling the promise of his debut effort. Although the form of the race is yet to be put to the test, the front pair were seventeen lengths clear of the remainder and visually that was a dominant display from this good looking son of Robin Des Champs.

Savoy Court is far from the finished article physically, with plenty of growing still to do to fill out his huge frame. With that considered, there is no surprise that he was given plenty of time between his two runs and it is anticipated that his connections will reap the rewards for their patience in the future. An embryonic chaser, he is not certain to fulfil his enormous potential at the highest level in the novice hurdling division but he is potentially very exciting and is definitely a long-term prospect to follow. He has already proved that he is a high-class animal, so shedding his maiden tag over hurdles should be a formality. Being such a sizeable individual, it is also likely that he will be more effective when there is give in the ground so a winter campaign should suit. Greatrex's stable star Cole Harden won at Fontwell and Newbury before finishing down the field in the Grade 1 Neptune Novices' Hurdle at the Cheltenham Festival during his novice hurdling campaign and Savoy Court is capable of scaling similar heights this time around.

SILVERHOW (IRE) *(5-y-o br g)*

Yeats (IRE) – Monte Solaro (IRE) (Key Of Luck (USA))
TRAINER: Nicky Henderson
OWNER: Mrs Patricia Pugh
FORM FIGURES: 2-3

THE FINAL FLIGHT ANALYSIS:

Nicky Henderson and Mrs Patricia Pugh teamed up with Altior, who remained unbeaten over hurdles last season culminating in Supreme Novices' Hurdle success at the Cheltenham Festival, and they will be hoping that this son of Yeats can establish himself as a useful novice during the 2016/2017 campaign. Silverhow, a brother to the aforementioned Altior has showed plenty of promise in both of his starts in bumpers to date. This five-year-old started his career at Huntingdon at the beginning of 2016 in a bumper over an extended one mile and five furlongs. Sent off at an unfancied 16/1 (Henderson was also represented by the well-supported Thomas Campbell), he settled well in the hands of Peter Carberry. After being on the heels of the leaders for most of the journey, Silverhow appeared to lack a change of pace compared to his rivals when the field turned for home. Though, he continued to make progress under Carberry, staying on gallantly to finish a never nearer second to the impressive winner Bags Grove. Promisingly, Bags Grove gave the form a significant boost when running a fine race under a penalty at Newbury to finish second and in addition the fifth, seventh and eighth have all won races since – a further enhancement of the form. After such a pleasing debut, there was no surprise to see Silverhow sent off favourite for a Stratford bumper in May and although he was only able to finish third, he again showed that he has plenty of ability. Judging by the manner in which he stayed on at Huntingdon, his connections were right to step him up to two miles on his second start but after over-racing throughout the early stages, he made life hard work for Nico de Boinville. After racing so keenly, it was thrilling to see him finish his race off so strongly once more and was beaten less than three lengths by the equally promising pair of Brio Conti and Whats Not To Like.

Although Silverhow failed to scale the same heights as Altior in the bumper sphere (he won his debut before finishing third and sixth in Listed and Grade 1 races), Henderson's charge has undoubted potential when switched to the hurdling ranks this season. After seeing him in the flesh at Seven Barrows, he has a lovely temperament which immediately draws your attention to him and with the scope to progress further over obstacles, he should pay his way in novice hurdles. The fact that he failed to register a win in bumpers should not be held against him, but he may slip under the radar compared to some of his stablemates for that reason. Once he learns how to settle, I have no doubt that intermediate trips will be well within his range and it is over that trip that he is predicted to excel over. Henderson has a particularly strong crop of novice chasers this season – a code which this gelding may well excel at in the future – but the inexperienced Silverhow can once again prove why Henderson has such a splendid record at nurturing young talent to fulfil their potential.

SOMEDAY *(4-y-o b g)*

Black Sam Bellamy (IRE) – Like Manner (Teenoso (USA))

TRAINER: Mrs John Harrington

OWNER: Howard Spooner

FORM FIGURES: 2

THE FINAL FLIGHT ANALYSIS:

In 1991, Oh So Risky carried the crazy quilt silks of The Oh So Risky Partnership to victory in the Triumph Hurdle before he finished second to Sheikh Mohammed's Royal Gait in the following season's Champion Hurdle. In 2008, entrepreneur Howard Spooner paid £24,000 at a sporting memorabilia auction to have the famous multi-coloured silks registered in his name and Spooner has had big race success since with his Chasing Cars winning a valuable handicap chase at Punchestown in 2010.

Someday, a Jessica Harrington-trained and Spooner-owned four-year-old, created a very good impression when making his debut at the Punchestown Festival in April where he finished a close second to Willie Mullins' Cilaos Emery. Having been similarly placed to the winner with just over a half a mile to race, Someday wasn't good enough to go with him, but stayed on in tremendous style. The front pair pulled over six lengths clear of the remainder and there is no doubt that they both looking exciting prospects. Though, it was Someday who left a lasting impression, especially taking into account that he also encountered traffic problems prior to turning into the home straight.

On the back of his debut performance, Harrington's gelding is a sure fire winner of a bumper if that is the chosen route to begin his autumn/winter campaign. However, this son of Black Sam Bellamy is an exciting stayer in the making and it is anticipated that he will only be able to realise his true potential when tackling a longer trip over hurdles. A sizeable individual, Someday has the scope to improve plenty for a summer at grass and although he has already proved that he has a decent engine, he will need time to fill out his frame. Don't Touch It, Sandymount Duke and Woodland Opera are three horses that roll off the tongue when Harrington's name is mentioned with regards to horses to look forward to this season. However, in my opinion, Someday is right up there with the aforementioned trio and I wait in eager anticipation to see his attentions switched to jumping.

STOWAWAY FOREVER (IRE) *(4-y-o gr g)*

Stowaway – Forever Bubbles (IRE) (Roselier (FR))

TRAINER: Philip Dempsey

OWNER: Denis Cusack

FORM FIGURES: 1-

THE FINAL FLIGHT ANALYSIS:

Altior ended the recent Mullins, Walsh and Ricci domination in last season's Grade 1 Supreme Novices' Hurdle, with Champagne Fever landing the first leg of a spectacular hat-trick back in 2013. Stowaway Forever, a full-brother to the dual Cheltenham Festival-winning Champagne Fever, made a winning start on his debut outing at Loughbrickland in April – creating a good visual impression to score by three lengths. This good looker jumped into the lead at the fourth-last and although Wonderoftheworld was able to go with him for a long way, that pair quickened right away from their rivals. They bypassed what would usually be the final fence which is located at the top of the tight bend turning into the straight and once Jamie Codd asked his mount to go and win his race, Stowaway Forever readily drew clear and the winning margin didn't do his authoritative display justice. His impressive success earned him a rating of 93++ which is a particularly high rating in Irish point-to-points, so although the form of the race is yet to be put to the test, that goes a fair way to justifying that it was a serious performance.

Taking into account that he was a good winner of his sole point and his outstanding pedigree, it was quite surprising that the connections of Stowaway Forever didn't send him to the sales as there would have been plenty of interested parties. He would have been almost certain to make a large sum in the ring and having gone unsold for €72,000 in June 2015, potential buyers that day will now be ruing a missed opportunity. However, the fact that he is going to remain in training with Philip Dempsey for his owner Denis Cusack tells you the regard in which this four-year-old is held in and he is definitely one to follow this season, be that in bumpers or over hurdles.

Although he looks a lovely long-term prospect, he showed a nice cruising speed as well as an impressive turn of foot on his sole start so he looks to have all the right attributes to win a bumper if that is the chosen route. With his dam being from a family of smart staying jumpers it is not a forgone conclusion that Stowaway Forever will be unable to be effective over longer trips in the future, even though his older sibling Champagne Fever has fallen short over three miles – albeit at the very highest level. Naas, Navan and Kilbeggan are located close to Dempsey's County Kildare base and it is likely that Stowaway Forever's debut under rules may come at one of those venues – a date for your diary and one that I am eagerly awaiting.

STRETCHINGTHETRUTH (IRE) *(5-y-o b g)*

Gold Well – Maryanndoyle (IRE) (Turtle Island (IRE))

TRAINER: Noel Meade

OWNER: JP McManus

FORM FIGURES: 1-1

THE FINAL FLIGHT ANALYSIS:

Leading National Hunt owner JP McManus had a memorable 2016 Punchestown Festival, recording a total of ten victories. He arguably saved the best till last as the Noel Meade-trained Stretchingthetruth created a deep impression to land the concluding Pro/Am INH Flat Race. This son of Gold Well made a successful start to his career when he narrowly held on to win on his sole point-to-point start at Dromahane in November for his former handler Nicky Stokes. Having looked in command between the last two fences, he had to dig very deep to deny Royal Supremo in a pulverising finish between the two Stokes-trained four-year-olds. The front pair were twelve lengths clear of the third Poetic Rhythm and the fact that Royal Supremo has form figures of 211 since switching to rules (now trained by Kim Bailey), the form of this race is working out particularly well. Taking into account that the runner-up had given the form a significant boost and that Stretchingthetruth had subsequently joined leading connections following his win between the flags, it was no surprise to see him sent off as the hot favourite for his bumper debut (13/8). Ridden with plenty of confidence throughout by Nina Carberry, this five-year-old absolutely cantered into contention as long-time leader Rathnure Rebel came back to the field and the manner in which he made a mockery of this twenty three-runner field was tantalising. With Rathnure Rebel tearing off in front from the outset, Stretchingthetruth showed that he possesses a high cruising speed and Carberry didn't have to ask him a single question to go and win his race. Though as the race was run at a genuine gallop, he also gave the impression that he has plenty of stamina to power clear and record a six and a half-length success.

Stretchingthetruth is a real improver, something that you are always looking for when highlighting horses to follow, and the professional display that he put in on his rules debut also showed signs of maturity. After scraping home over three miles in his point-to-point, one may have concluded that he would appreciate a drop back in trip but given that he showed plenty of speed when winning over the minimum trip at Punchestown, he is sure to prove versatile in terms of his optimum distance over obstacles. Winning a maiden hurdle will be a formality for this gelding and last year's fiercely contested two-mile maiden at Gowran Park in November - which McManus' Punchestown Festival Grade 1 winner Don't Touch It finished second in - is a likely starting point. Described as ***"a nice horse for hurdling"*** by his handler Meade, Stretchingthetruth joins a strong squad of McManus-owned jumpers, rating as one of the most exciting novice hurdlers across the Irish Sea and looks a graded winner in waiting in that sphere.

SUTTON PLACE (IRE) *(5-y-o b g)*

Mahler – Glebe Beauty (IRE) (Good Thyne (USA)

TRAINER: Gordon Elliott

OWNER: JP McManus

FORM FIGURES: 3111-

THE FINAL FLIGHT ANALYSIS:

This five-year-old is a gorgeous looking son of Mahler and after a profitable first season over hurdles, this fine stamp of a horse has enormous potential when switched to the novice chasing ranks this season. A half-brother to bumper and hurdle winner Allez Encore, the Gordon Elliott-trained Sutton Place made his racecourse debut in a twenty eight-runner maiden hurdle at Navan on heavy ground. Although he finished third behind another JP McManus-owned horse in Anibale Fly, he made eye-catching headway up the home straight, leaving the impression that he possessed plenty of natural ability. Although his debut effort was incredibly promising for the future, one has to be pleasantly surprised that he remained unbeaten in his next three starts, culminating in a Grade 2 success at Fairyhouse on his latest start. Having looked to have strengthened up considerably from his debut, there was no surprise to see him land a Fairyhouse bumper with real authority on his second start – Elliott has followed this route with similar types in the past. Having landed prohibitive odds on that occasion, the team at Cullentra decided to let Sutton Place take his chance in the Listed Kingsfurze Novice Hurdle, a race run over two miles at Naas in early March. They were richly rewarded for what was quite a bold move on only his third start, with Sutton Place scoring in taking fashion by six and a half lengths, beating what looked a small but select field. His final start came in the aforementioned Grade 2 contest, the Rathbarry & Glenview Studs Novice Hurdle which is run over two miles at Fairyhouse's prestigious Easter festival. After running out an easy winner on his previous two runs, Sutton Place showed that he has guts and determination to match his raw ability by recording a hard fought success. Although his half a length victory over the re-opposing Royal Caviar was not as impressive as his Fairyhouse win, the fact that he showed a likeable attitude is another tick in the box and with the front pair pulling ten lengths clear of the Edward Harty-trained Moon Over Germany, this looks a strong piece of form.

It was noticeable that this scopey individual often dwarfed his opposition last season and the fact that he showed vast signs of maturity with each run, he rates as an exciting novice chaser. Having won on both yielding-to-soft and heavy ground, this sizeable individual is clearly versatile with regards to underfoot conditions which will make campaigning him during the winter months much easier. However, looking at his rounded action, it is logical to assume that he is likely to be most suited to races when there is a slight ease in the ground. After running exclusively over the minimum distance, Sutton Place has scope to improve plenty when tackling longer trips and races over two and a half miles over fences ought to come under consideration. A race that looks to be tailor made for Sutton Place is the Grade 1 Drinmore Novice Chase which is run over two and a half miles at Fairyhouse in November – a course that Sutton Place has already showed a liking to. Elliott won that Grade 1 with the ill-fated No More Heroes in 2015 and if Sutton Place can give him back-to-back victories then the sky really is the limit for him as a steeplechaser.

TOUCH KICK (IRE) *(5-y-o b g)*

Presenting – Bay Pearl (FR) (Broadway Flyer (USA))
TRAINER: Paul Nicholls
OWNER: Trevor Hemmings
FORM FIGURES: 1-

THE FINAL FLIGHT ANALYSIS:

The aforementioned Mount Mews is a novice hurdler trained in the North for owner Trevor Hemmings to get excited about, though he should be equally as enthusiastic about the prospects of Touch Kick who is trained at Ditcheat by the Champion Trainer, Paul Nicholls. This five-year-old son of Presenting made a winning debut at the beginning of April when landing the first division of the 'Newcomers' bumper – Nicholls, Hemmings and Sam Twiston-Davies also won the second division with another promising sort, Winningtry. The race was run a good gallop with eventual runner-up G For Ginger and Major Davis vying for the lead throughout the first half of the race and plenty of the others happy to take a backseat in the early stages. Twiston-Davies' mount settled well and he kept him covered up until making what was eventually a winning move to close up on the leaders entering the straight. Touch Kick hit the front between what would normally be the final flight of hurdles and although he idled up the run-in, he won in the style of a horse with serious potential. The fact that he had a good look around in front was most definitely a sign of his inexperience rather than him being ungenuine. Nicholls' post-race comments backed this up when saying, ***"He´s got a good attitude and can only improve. It´s the first time he´s been on grass and there will be plenty more to come".***

Touch Kick won what will probably work out to be an ordinary bumper, but it is sometimes the visual impression that counts and I believe that there are a few reasons why this gelding is the type to continue to improve. Firstly, he is by Presenting and a good percentage of his offspring show their best form on decent ground – Touch Kick won on soft ground at Wincanton, meaning that he is likely to be versatile in terms of underfoot conditions. The fact that he is a half-brother to a winning pointer as well as the manner in which he ran on in what was a strongly run race suggests that he will appreciate a step-up in trip when switched to the hurdling ranks and this makes his debut effort even more noteworthy. The final, but perhaps most interesting thing to consider is that both Nicholls and Hemmings have a reputation for being associated with staying chasers and therefore when they team up with a bumper winner it is normally worth taking note. Although it is unlikely that this sizeable bay will prove himself as a top-class hurdler, there is no doubt that he has plenty of ability and he is a sure fire winner in the novice hurdling division. In a lot of ways he reminds me of Great Try – who unfortunately missed the whole of last season through injury – in that he won an average bumper but should go onto better things once switched to jumping. Akin to Great Try, Touch Kick's long-term future lies over fences and Nicholls et al will be relishing the prospect of sending him over the larger obstacles when the time comes.

TRIED AND TESTED (IRE) *(5-y-o b g)*

Beneficial – Shean Alainn (IRE) (Le Moss)

TRAINER: Jonjo O'Neill

OWNER: JP McManus

FORM FIGURES: 2-

THE FINAL FLIGHT ANALYSIS:

Tried And Tested is another young horse to represent the powerful JP McManus in this section and another who himself is extremely lightly raced. Trained by Jonjo O'Neill who has a long association with McManus, this son of Beneficial made his hurdling debut at Chepstow in a maiden hurdle over an extended two miles and three furlongs – this subsequently turned out to be his only start during the 2015/2016 season. A brother to RSA winner Cooldine as well as 145-rated staying chaser Fists Of Fury, an ordinary gallop over an intermediate trip at Chepstow was unlikely to play to his strengths. Held up throughout the early stages of the race, he made nice headway to be just behind the leaders on the long run between the fifth and fourth-last. Approaching the penultimate flight of hurdles, Richard Johnson started to get serious with Tried And Tested and although his response wasn't instant, he stayed on in eye-catching fashion to finish second, two and a quarter lengths behind high-class bumper performer Potters Corner. Granted, the winner was value for more than the winning margin suggests (eased down at the line), but this was a very pleasing debut and it offered something to build on. It was expected that this five-year-old would be capable of following up in a similar event next time out, but he didn't reappear. Though, over the summer his trainer confirmed to me that he met with a setback which prevented him from running again and his novice status remains intact for this season.

Still only a five-year-old, Tried And Tested's career is very much ahead of him and there is no doubt that this sizeable individual has plenty of raw ability. He looked unfurnished on his debut, jumping a number of his hurdles awkwardly and it is anticipated that he will have benefited from the time away from the racecourse. As a physical specimen, he has the scope to continue to improve with time and the 2016/2017 season could be where he really blossoms into something like the horse that I believe he has the potential to be.

Staying chases are where he is almost certain to showcase his talents, but his future over hurdles looks far from dull. Based on the little evidence available, he looks likely to appreciate a step up in trip this season and is expected to make his mark in the staying novice hurdling division. There are plenty of handicaps over an extended two and a half miles as well as three miles and these could come under consideration - assuming that O'Neill is able to get the required experience into him early on in the season. The maiden hurdle that this tall, handsome gelding contested was run on good ground, but based on his running style and physique, he could be even better when there is some give in the ground. Tried And Tested is one of the darkest members of this season's 'Top Prospects', but he is a youngster with significant promise and rates as an exciting long-term prospect.

WESTEND STORY (IRE) *(5-y-o b g)*

Westerner – Sarahall (IRE) (Saddlers´ Hall (IRE))
TRAINER: Philip Hobbs
OWNER: Mick Fitzgerald Racing Club
FORM FIGURES: FF/115-

THE FINAL FLIGHT ANALYSIS:

Following two falls in Irish point-to-points when in the care of Colin Bowe, Westend Story was subsequently acquired by the Mick Fitzgerald Racing Club. Described as ***"a very useful youngster with a big future"*** after his final fence departure on his debut between the flags, this son of Westerner wasted no time in getting off the mark for his new connections by cosily landing the same Huntingdon bumper that smart hurdler O O Seven won 12 months earlier. He settled nicely for Champion Jockey Richard Johnson and upon entering the straight, Johnson asked his mount to go and win his race. He readily drew clear inside the final two furlongs, recording a six length victory over his market rival Better Getalong, with the third a further eleven lengths back. After winning in the style of a useful prospect on debut, there was little surprise to see his connections keep him to bumpers and he was even more impressive when routing his four rivals in a heavy ground Exeter bumper two months later. Westend Story's victory gave Philip Hobbs a hat-trick in this race after Trickaway and Drumlee Sunset had won the two previous renewals and his eighteen length romp earned him a crack at the Grade 1 Weatherbys Champion Bumper. Considering that he faced much quicker ground conditions than in his four previous starts and that he came from a long way off the pace, his fifth-place finish in what looked a decent renewal of the festival bumper was extremely promising.

Westend Story will reappear this season as a novice hurdler with considerable potential and after shaping as if stamina will be the making of him over obstacles, he is one to keep on side in the staying hurdling division. On top of shaping as if a step-up in trip will suit, his sire Westerner, a high-class stayer and runner up in the Prix de l'Arc de Triomphe, is responsible for a number of useful staying prospects including Cole Harden, Gilgamboa and Wakanda and Westend Story has showed all the right signs to believe that he can add his name to that roll of honour. Having already proved that he handles a variety of different ground, a winter campaign with a view to the spring festivals will be ideal. His relaxed nature will ensure that he is able to see out the longer trips over hurdles, but considering that he had enough speed to win over two miles last season, he is likely to begin his hurdling career over intermediate trips. Hobbs also won the previously mentioned Exeter bumper with Fingal Bay in 2011 before he took the Grade 2 Persian War Novices' Hurdle on his hurdling debut, so don't be surprised if Westend Story's credentials as a hurdler are tested quite early on. Another race that might come under consideration for this gelding is the Grade 2 Albert Bartlett Novices' Hurdle (Registered as the Bristol Novices' Hurdle) at Cheltenham's International Hurdle meeting in December.

WINTER ESCAPE (IRE) *(5-y-o b g)*

Robin Des Pres (FR) — Saddleeruppat (IRE) (Saddlers´ Hall (IRE)
TRAINER: Alan King
OWNER: JP McManus
FORM FIGURES: 111-

THE FINAL FLIGHT ANALYSIS:

This five-year-old son of Robin Des Pres is undefeated in his three runs over hurdles, the third of which was a Grade 2 contest over the minimum two mile trip, a distance that may be short of what this strapping gelding needs to be seen to his best effect. While the bare form of his first two wins at Doncaster is nothing special, the manner in which he travelled throughout those respective races marked him as different quality to those in behind. The visual impression that he created on his second start at the Town Moor venue meant that he started at odds of 4/6 for what looked a good renewal of the Grade 2 Dovecote Novices' Hurdle. After jumping and travelling exuberantly over the first mile and a half, he did show signs of inexperience over the last three hurdles. Having said that, his rider Barry Geraghty only had to administer three reminders in order for the then twice-raced gelding to draw readily clear of his rivals, recording a comfortable length and a quarter success.

With all of Winter Escape's three wins coming on good-to-soft ground, it remains to be seen how this gelding will handle slower conditions. However, his dam won a Fairyhouse bumper on heavy ground and judging by his action, slower conditions should not pose a problem to this high-class individual. Connections are likely to consider whether to stay hurdling or to go novice chasing in the autumn, but that is a nice problem to have. This talented five-year-old jumps his hurdles as though he was made to jump fences, but with the greenness he showed over timber it may be a logical approach to gain further experience in that sphere before tackling the larger obstacles. Whichever discipline his connections opt for during the 2016/2017 campaign, Winter Escape has two key things in his favour – time on his side only being a five-year-old and plenty of scope for improvement.

If kept over hurdles, he looks an ideal type for a race like the Listed William Hill-sponsored Handicap Hurdle which is run at Ascot over two miles in November. It is worth noting that like a lot of big handicap hurdles, this race is often won by unexposed hurdlers and the roll of honour includes horses such as Nicky Henderson's Sign of a Victory who had a similar profile to Winter Escape at the time. A later target could be the Grade 3 Ladbroke Handicap Hurdle which is again over the minimum two mile trip at Ascot in December. Although his mark of 142 is tempting to run in a handicap, I am under no illusions that this gelding's ceiling is in that company and if he remains over timber then he should develop into a very smart second season hurdler as the season progresses. If sent chasing, connections could look at the two mile and three furlong novice chase at Exeter in early December - a race won in recent years by Saphir Du Rheu. A novice chase campaign will no doubt be geared around a crack at one of the Grade 1 novice chases in the spring and he would rate as one of the most exciting prospects to be sent chasing this year. There is no doubt that Winter Escape has an incredibly bright future and he is certainly a horse to keep on the right side of this winter and beyond.

WITHOUT LIMITES (FR) *(4-y-o gr g)*

Martaline – Sans Limites (FR) (Nikos)

TRAINER: Miss Elizabeth Doyle

OWNER: Goliath Syndicate

FORM FIGURES: 211-

THE FINAL FLIGHT ANALYSIS:

Without Limites is yet another son of Martaline to work his way into this section and this improving four-year-old showed a good level of form in bumpers last season. He made his debut in the middle of January at Leopardstown in a Pro/AM INH Flat Race where after showing plenty of promise, he was no match for the well-touted Aspen Colorado. With the experience under his belt, Without Limites made no mistake at the second time of asking, recording a twelve length success at Punchestown a month later. He only faced two rivals on that occasion and talented jockey Finny Maguire took the initiative and sent his mount into an early lead. He took them along plenty quick enough in the heavy ground and after giving him a breather in the last half-mile, Without Limites quickened up in the style of a good horse to simply bolt up. He again contested a small field event, again in heavy ground, but this time in a Listed bumper at Limerick in April – a race won in 2015 by last season's useful novice hurdler Charbel. Although there was little depth to the race for the level, Harry Fry's well-regarded Chalonnial was ridden to challenge the winner, but he had no answer to Elizabeth Doyle's gelding, eventually paying the price to finish a well-beaten third. Without Limites again showed that he handles what were atrocious conditions and his wide margin victory couldn't be described as anything other than impressive.

The fact that Without Limites is with relatively low profile connections will ensure that he is not sent off too short a price – particularly when he is stepped up in class to face Willie Mullins' or Gordon Elliott's battalions – but Doyle's charge should not be underestimated. By the manner in which he handled the heavy ground when winning his final two starts of last season, there are unlikely to be many horses that relish such conditions as much as this four-year-old and a winter campaign over hurdles should see him develop into a useful novice. Whether he can prove himself on better ground remains to be seen and he is perhaps best watched on ground without soft in the official going description. One thing that is certain is that he has an engine and is almost guaranteed to improve for a step up in trip once sent jumping. One has to admit that this gelding is hard to assess on the back of winning two small field events at odds-on, but he leaves the impression that he is a relentless galloper, one that will continue to improve with time and for that reason he deserves his place in this season's 'Top Prospects'. Intermediate trips are sure to be his forte and the Grade 2 Novice Hurdle at Fairyhouse's Easter fixture is a possible end of season target if he proves himself to be up to that sort of level – a race Doyle was represented by her talented but ill-fated Le Vent D'Antan.

THE HANDICAPPERS FOR 2016/2017

This section is designed to highlight a number of horses who are predicted to be ahead of the handicapper. In last season's edition of The Final Flight Jumps Guide, this section included the likes of Sausalito Sunrise who progressed from a mark of 144 to 159, Cheltenham Festival winner Ibis Du Rheu (16/1 SP) and Cogry – a horse who was slightly unfortunate but is still potentially well handicapped for this season.

As per last season, I have compiled a list that is a mixture of hurdlers and chasers (some of the hurdlers may take the novice handicap chase route), as well as a combination of unexposed types and those with slightly more experience but who are expected to progress further.

AFFAIRE D'HONNEUR ***5-y-o-ch g*** **(Harry Whittington)**
Official Rating: 133
Predicted Rating: 142

Thrice-raced in the UK, Affaire D'Honneur created the impression in all of his starts on these shores that he has a good deal of ability. After finishing a close second behind the progressive Zulu Oscar on his British debut, this Harry Whittington inmate took a rise in class to contest the fiercely competitive Betfair hurdle. Having been strong in the market, his supporters were left aggrieved by the standing start – something his trainer later blamed for his slow beginning and his never nearer fourth placed finish. However, what he did show that day was that he was on a workable mark, putting in his best work at the finish. There was little surprise to see him sent off as the favourite for the Imperial Cup, where again he found himself a long way back in the field before finishing another creditable fourth.

Having paid €110,000 for Affaire D'Honneur last November, there is no doubt that his connections will be hoping for a return on investment this season. It is important to note that he retains his novice status having failed to win over hurdles to date, but it is in the valuable handicap hurdles where he is expected to make his mark. It is likely that he appreciates a bit of cut in the ground (quickest he has raced on to date is good-to-soft), so a winter campaign should be right up his street. Whittington enjoyed plenty of success in 2015/2016 including a Grade 1 victory at Aintree with the ill-fated Arzal. It will be much deserved were connections to gain compensation with this five-year-old chestnut – a horse who is predicted to fulfil his early promise this season.

ALOOMOMO ***6-y-o-b g*** **(Warren Greatrex)**
Official Rating: 130H / 140C
Predicted Rating: 138H / 148C

This French-bred is held in high-regard by his Lambourn handler, Warren Greatrex. Since making his chasing debut at Carlisle two seasons ago, Aloomomo has gradually progressed into a very useful chaser. Although he was slightly disappointing at the Cheltenham Festival when sent off the 3/1 favourite for the Listed Close Brothers Novices' Handicap Chase, he looks the type to continue to improve and looks set for a big season as a handicapper. The form of his back-to-back wins at Uttoxeter and Warwick were further supported with an impressive nine length victory up in grade at Newbury in November. After running extremely well over hurdles prior to the festival, Greatrex strongly fancied his charge for his end of season target, where he managed sixth behind Ian Williams' Ballyalton.

His sequence of wins in October and November came on rain softened ground and cut in the ground is thought of as a necessity for this six-year-old. Although the official going description at the festival was good-to-soft, he seemed to find things happening too quickly and he will have more to offer during the winter months. Many horses that have contested the previous season's novice handicap chase have also lined up in the two and a half mile handicap chase at Cheltenham's October meeting and this is a possible target for Aloomomo. Though, it must be tempting to run him in a handicap hurdle given that he is rated 10lb lower over timber.

ALWAYS LION *6-y-o-b g* (Ben Pauling)

Official Rating: 125
Predicted Rating: 137

Paul and Clare Rooney hit the headlines last season when removing all of their string from Donald McCain's Cheshire base – a real loss for the Northern jumping circuit. Always Lion, a member of the Rooney squad, was not one who was switched stables as he started his career in the care of his current trainer, Ben Pauling. A useful bumper horse in 2014/2015, this six-year-old embarked on a hurdling career with a good reputation and emerged with plenty of credit on both starts. He found Roll The Dough too strong on debut before opening his account at the second time of asking in an Introductory Hurdle at Ludlow.

Not sighted since, he will return to the track off a mark of 125 and that looks particularly lenient given that he has scope for significant improvement. A step-up in trip is expected to see Pauling's gelding in an even better light this season and if he remains over hurdles, he could be one to follow in the Pertemps handicap hurdle series. Though, he has the size to jump a fence and it wouldn't be a surprise to see his attentions switched to chasing, where he ought to be capable of winning a couple of novice handicap chases.

BAOULET DELAROQUE *5-y-o-b g* (Paul Nicholls)

Official Rating: 142
Predicted Rating: 149

It is anticipated that Champion Trainer Paul Nicholls may have some well handicapped horses in his stable and Baoulet Delaroque is one who appears to tick a lot of boxes. Since winning a Doncaster maiden hurdle in January, this five-year-old made rapid progress including two wins at Wincanton and Huntingdon before finishing a close fifth in the Coral Cup at the Cheltenham Festival. He blotted his copybook with a poor run at Aintree (pulled-up), but that can be forgiven following a quick turn around after Cheltenham.

The aforementioned form meant that his handicap mark rose from 124 to 142 last season, but he has the right profile to progress even further in 2016/2017. Importantly, his form proves that he handles all types of ground (won on heavy and good-to-soft) and that will make finding the right opportunity for him more straight forward. Similarly to Nicholls' Arpege D'Alene last season, there is a possibility that Baoulet Delaroque will go novice chasing in the autumn and he will be a smart recruit to that sphere. However, if that doesn't work out, there are endless possibilities for him over hurdles and he can continue on an upward curve.

BIG CHIEF BENNY ***5-y-o-ch g*** **(Alan King)**
Official Rating: 131
Predicted Rating: 141

A son of Beneficial that I cannot help but adore. He is certainly not the biggest, but he has a real desire to win and his attitude is once again going to be a real thorn in his opposition's side this season. In addition, his jumping is a real asset of his and that is a huge positive when contesting big field, strongly-run handicap hurdles. A horse who I described as babyish when running with credit in two of his three bumpers, Big Chief Benny started his hurdling career when third to Buveur D'Air and Wait For Me at Newbury in November. It is perhaps more significant that he had emphatic next-time-out winner Bun Doran (135) a further nineteen lengths behind in fourth – a really pleasing hurdling debut to say the least. A runner-up effort back at the same Berkshire venue and a maiden hurdle victory at Doncaster followed in successive months where his began to make his mark in the hurdling ranks, much to the delight of his connections. Highly tried at Ascot in February when far from disgraced, Alan King's five-year-old was back in the winners' enclosure with a gutsy head defeat of Beallandendall, this time at Chepstow.

Judged on that performance, one may argue that Big Chief Benny is in the handicappers grasp, but there are a few reasons why it is expected that he can progress again this time around. All of his form prior to his Chepstow victory had come on no better than good-to-soft ground and therefore it is predicted that a return to softer ground will do nothing but help. Secondly, he is yet to run in a handicap which can regularly prove harder for the handicapper to assess form – one explanation being that novice hurdles can often be run at a muddling pace. The last point is that Big Chief Benny has scope to take a marked step forward when tackling a longer trip. He is yet to race beyond two and half miles and given his running style, it is in the staying handicap hurdle division that he may be best suited.

BIGMARTRE ***5-y-o-b g*** **(Harry Whittington)**
Official Rating: 133
Predicted Rating: 142

Bigmartre is the second of Harry Whittington's horses to be included within this section and this five-year-old has a similar profile to the aforementioned Arzal. After springing a surprise on his British debut when a 20-1 victor, Bigmartre bumped into the useful Clondaw Cian on his next start before getting back into the winners' enclosure at Haydock in December, defeating the likeable Vintage Clouds. He returned to Haydock a month later, where a rise in class found him out as he finished fourth behind subsequent Grade 1-placed Its'afreebee. His final two starts of last season were in handicap hurdles at Fontwell and Aintree. His bold front running tactics found him out on the first occasion, folding once headed to finish third. He filled the same position at Aintree, this time ridden with more restraint and showing a good attitude to stay on in the closing stages.

With a switch to fences predicted, Whittington is likely to send Bigmartre to Newbury for the 0-140 Novices' Limited Handicap Chase at the Hennessy meeting – a race Arzal won on his chasing debut last season. It is likely that the galloping track will suit him down to the ground and if he is ridden aggressively, he may be hard to peg back. Due to the fact that Bigmartre is able to race off three pounds lower than Arzal, it is possible that he will be able to contest a few more races of this nature before stepping up in class. He shaped as if a longer trip wouldn't be a problem on his final start at Aintree and if that is the case, his connections will have plenty more avenues to explore. Richard Venn who operates as Whittington's bloodstock agent made the comment that he is a really nice type for soft ground and it is during the winter months where he is predicted to pay his way.

BOITE ***6-y-o-b g*** **(Warren Greatrex)**
Official Rating: 135
Predicted Rating: 142

This six-year-old son of Authorized was a useful Flat racer for Peter Chapple-Hyam prior to joining Warren Greatrex in 2015 to go jumping. After winning on his second start over hurdles at Stratford, he was highly tried at Ayr when eight lengths behind Different Gravey before a spell back on the Flat during the months of May, June and July. He only made two appearances over timber last season, finishing second to Gala Ball at Newbury in March and fourth in a competitive event at Aintree's Grand National meeting won by Ivan Grozny. Both of his two runs under National Hunt rules last season offered plenty of promise that he was still feasibly treated. A win back on the flat at Goodwood in June off 87 further enhanced his claims as a well handicapped horse when his attentions are switched back to hurdling and he is worth following in races between two miles and two and a half miles in that sphere.

Greatrex's greatest triumph to date came at Cheltenham when Cole Harden won the World Hurdle and it is predicted that Boite could contest the 0-140 conditional jockeys' handicap hurdle at Cheltenham's October meeting – a race won by subsequent Greatwood and International Hurdle winner Old Guard. There are umpteen other suitable races for this six-year-old and if he is campaigned carefully, he has the potential to run up a sequence. By assessing his form Boite appears to handle any type of ground, though being from a good Flat family, he is unlikely to appreciate extremely testing conditions.

BRAAVOS ***5-y-o-br g*** **(Philip Hobbs)**
Official Rating: 130
Predicted Rating: 140+

Mrs Diana Whateley has been involved with some fantastic horses down the years including Captain Chris and Menorah. Her famous colours were carried to victory in last season's Coral Cup by Diamond King and it is expected that her lightly raced Braavos can progress into a high-class handicap hurdler this season. This son of Presenting's most notable piece of form was when he bumped into Betfair Hurdle winner Agrapart at Aintree in December on only his second start over timber. That form looks particularly strong now with Flying Angel (rated 144) five lengths back in third, subsequently landing the Imperial Cup in the spring. A disappointing run at Uttoxeter in March came between two victories on vastly different ground at Exeter (heavy) and Perth (good), thus showing his versatility to different ground conditions. He lost nothing in defeat when five lengths behind Starchitect at Newton Abbot in May, with that rival boasting some solid form in top handicap hurdles and he looks sure to continue to improve this season.

Rock The Kasbah, also trained by Hobbs for Whateley, started his second season over timber in the Grade 3 Totepool Silver Trophy Handicap Hurdle at Chepstow from a mark of 131 and it is likely that this five-year-old will take a similar route. Rock The Kasbah found only Court Minstrel too good on his seasonal reappearance before landing back-to-back victories at Haydock and Ascot, ending the season rated 150. If Braavos can show anything like the same sort of progress then following him will be very profitable.

FREE EXPRESSION ***7-y-o-b g*** **(Gordon Elliott)**
Official Rating: 142
Predicted Rating: 150

A high-class hurdler during the 2014/2015 season, Free Expression was expected to contest the spring festivals before he met a setback after his third in the Grade 1 Lawlor's Hotel Novice Hurdle and was ruled out for the remainder of the season. He returned in November in a beginners chase at Punchestown where he jumped superbly, losing nothing but the race when a close second behind the useful Outlander. A third-placed effort behind the talented No More Heroes came later that month before he put in a laboured display to finish third to Outlander again, this time at Limerick. Although it is a slight concern that Free Expression failed to make it to the racecourse after his Limerick defeat, it is most likely that his connections decided to preserve his novice status over fences with a view to this season.

This son of Germany, who has sired Cheltenham Festival winners Faugheen and Captain Cee Bee, has always looked a chaser and it is in that sphere which he is expected to excel in this season. It is difficult to predict JP McManus-owned handicappers as they are often plotted carefully and have one or two intended targets in which they are certain to be primed for. Though, judged on his three starts over fences, an official rating of 142 looks workable and he definitely has one or two big prizes in him. It would be no surprise if Gordon Elliott decides to aim his talented seven-year-old at the Paddy Power Chase at Leopardstown's Christmas fixture – a race that owner JP McManus has won with Colbert Station (2012) and Minella Foru (2015) in recent years.

MESSIRE DES OBEAUX ***4-y-o-b g*** **(Alan King)**
Official Rating: 128
Predicted Rating: 138+

Silviniaco Conti has given the Potensis Bloodstock team some fantastic days out over the last few seasons, and although it is understood that only he and Zarkandar will remain in their ownership over jumps, I believe that some of their younger horses that have been sold over the summer have serious potential including four-year-old Messire

Des Obeaux. This brother to smart hurdler and chaser Bouvreuil, has only had two starts in the UK to date, finishing third at Haydock on his British debut before running a creditable race to be seventh in the Fred Winter Handicap Hurdle. He caught the eye at Haydock after travelling easily for a long way before showing signs of inexperience and he again moved well at Cheltenham before fading in the closing stages, notably only beaten around ten lengths behind the winner Diego Du Charmil.

Still a maiden over hurdles, it anticipated that this lightly raced gelding will put his experience to good use in a novice hurdle before switching to handicaps. He has plenty of size about him so should progress over time and given that he is in excellent hands, he looks set to make a big impression in handicap hurdles this season. His easy way of going will give his connections plenty of options in terms of trip but it is predicted that he is most likely to excel in races over intermediate distances. Messire Des Obeaux is an extremely likeable individual both as a physical specimen and according to the form book. Taking that into account, this horse has the potential to improve at least ten pounds, if not more, during the 2016/2017 campaign. The Lanzarote Handicap Hurdle over two miles and five furlongs at Kempton in January would seem a logical stepping stone to the spring festivals for this talented youngster, a race won by the five-year-old Saphir Du Rheu in 2014.

NED STARK ***8-y-o-b g*** **(Gordon Elliott)**
Official Rating: 133
Predicted Rating: 141

Many of you will begin reading this profile thinking "Ned Stark, it seems like he has been well handicapped forever" and I completely understand that point of view. However, there are two key reasons why he deserves his place in this section. Firstly, he has moved yards – Oliver Murphy signed a cheque worth £70,000 for this eight-year-old at Goffs in May on behalf of Gordon Elliott. There is no doubt that Alan King is an excellent trainer, but it is anticipated that a change of scenery will do this gelding the world of good. The second is that he has been running over three miles and having watched his races over and over again, it is predicted that he may be suited to a drop back to around two and a half miles.

A Grade 2 winner over fences in January 2015, Ned Stark has failed to win since but he has been fancied for some of the most competitive handicap chases including last season's Hennessy Gold Cup. On that occasion he travelled up smoothly before fading to finish fifth behind his then stablemate Smad Place. Arguably the ground (soft) may have gone against him that day but he ultimately failed to see out the trip, thus justifying concerns about his stamina. After two disappointing efforts between December and February, he showed up much better on what was his final start for King when second to Benvolio at Newbury. Though, even on the better ground, he was outstayed by the Paul Nicholls-trained winner once more leaving the impression that he will be most effective at intermediate trips for his new connections.

There are plenty of races in the Irish calendar that ought to suit Ned Stark including a two mile and six furlong handicap chase at Punchestown in December (won last year by Sumos Novios) and a two mile and five furlong race at Leopardstown in January (won in 2015 by Empire Of Dirt). Colm Murphy's Empire Of Dirt followed up in the Grade 3 Brown Advisory & Merriebelle Stable Plate at the Cheltenham Festival and that is a feasible end of season target for Ned Stark, where the likely drying ground conditions will enhance his claims further.

PADGE ***7-y-o-b g*** **(Evan Williams)**
Official Rating: 143
Predicted Rating: 151

This seven-year-old looks set for a big season in the handicap ranks assuming that he is switched back to fences after a frustrating chasing campaign last term. He gave subsequent handicap chase winner Voix D'Eau weight and a beating on his chasing debut at Ascot in October – at the time creating the impression that he was a smart recruit to the chasing ranks. After failing to complete on his next two starts, Padge was switched back to hurdling and contested a Pertemps Series Qualifier at Exeter where he was third behind the Grade 1 Albert Bartlett Novices' Hurdle winner Unowhatimeanharry. Evan Williams allowed his charge to take his chance in the Pertemps Final at the Cheltenham Festival just over a month later, but he failed to fire with the stiff three miles appearing to stretch his stamina.

This sizeable gelding has always been thought of as a chaser by his handler and he remains a horse with untapped potential. His sporting owners, Mr and Mrs William Rucker have been associated with some exceptional chasers in recent years and they will be hoping that Padge can scale similar heights this season.

Described by Williams as ***"a horse with a big engine but backward in his mind"***, this scopey son of Flemensfirth is the sort of horse that will continue to improve over time and it is quite possible that he will return to the venue of his chase debut success for a crack at the Bet365-sponsored handicap chase – a race run over two miles and five furlongs in January. Though, the Grade 3 Caspian Caviar Gold Cup at Cheltenham in December is also likely to be on his radar in what is predicted to be a profitable campaign.

SOUTHFIELD ROYALE ***6-y-o-b g*** **(Neil Mulholland)**
Official Rating: 147
Predicted Rating: 154+

It is often reported that horses by Presenting appreciate better ground but Southfield Royale is quite the opposite – he seems to revel in the soft ground conditions that are regularly on offer during the winter months. Having won two of his three novice chases prior to Christmas, Neil Mulholland's charge ran an excellent race to finish second to Tea For Two in the Grade 1 Kauto Star Novices' Chase at Kempton. He was subsequently sent off the 5/1 favourite for the National Hunt Chase over four gruelling miles at the Cheltenham Festival, where his respectable fourth place can be upgraded based on the fact that he didn't get home after racing freely early on. His final start of the 2015/2016 campaign, a disappointing run at the Punchestown Festival, can be forgiven with a long season to blame.

Southfield Royale will begin life in the handicap ranks off what is likely to be deemed a relatively tough opening mark. However, granted his optimum conditions – anywhere between three and three and a half miles on a galloping track – he has the scope to take a good step forward this season and compete in some of the top-class staying handicap chases. It is worth noting that Mulholland ran The Druids Nephew in the Grade 3 Murphy Group Handicap Chase at Cheltenham's November meeting in 2014 where he bumped into the well-handicapped Sam Winner (coincidently Sam Winner won off 147) and there is every possibility that Southfield Royale will represent Conkwell Grange Stables this time around. It should be expected to see this progressive six-year-old boasting entries in races such as the Hennessy Gold Cup, Welsh National and perhaps even the Grand National, where connections will be praying for April showers to enhance his chances of landing one of National Hunt racing's most coveted prize.

THE FRESH PRINCE ***6-y-o-b g*** **(Oliver Sherwood)**
Official Rating: 120
Predicted Rating: 133+

The Trevor Hemmings-owned Many Clouds gave Oliver Sherwood a memorable day in 2015 when his stalwart performer landed the Grand National – recording a third success in the race for Hemmings following Hedgehunter (2005) and Ballabriggs (2011). Perhaps best known for owning Preston North End Football Club, British businessman Hemmings is often associated with horses who have significant size and scope and therefore unsurprisingly they often fulfil their potential over the larger obstacles. The Fresh Prince, a six-year-old son of Robin Des Pres, is exactly that. Having won at the second time of asking between the flags, he was sold for £35,000 to Highflyer Bloodstock on behalf of Sherwood. He wasted little time in bumpers (just one run), before taking two runs over timber to start to fulfil the potential that he showed in point-to-points. On his penultimate start he finished two and a quarter lengths behind the Paul Nicholls-trained Alcala – a horse who has run creditably in handicap hurdles from a higher official rating. A win on his final start showed the sort of progress that he has made since switching to the hurdling ranks and although he showed signs of inexperience in the closing stages, he recorded a comfortable seven length success.

An embryonic chaser, The Fresh Prince is expected to have his attentions switched to the larger obstacles this season. He has a progressive profile and having only raced beyond two miles and one furlong under rules once, he has plenty of scope to improve further when he tackles a longer trip. The fact that he was due to take part in the fiercely competitive EBF Final at Sandown before being balloted out by one tells you that Sherwood believes his youngster is mature enough for sort of race – a huge positive when considering him for races at the spring festivals. He should waste little time in shedding his maiden tag over fences, with the novice handicap chase route looking likely taking into account that he can run off his hurdles mark of 120. Although it is a long way off, The Fresh Prince shapes as though a stamina test will suit and he may just end up being a candidate for the 0-140 Novice Handicap Chase at the 2017 Cheltenham Festival.

THOMAS BROWN ***7-y-o-b g*** **(Harry Fry)**
Official Rating: 137
Predicted Rating: 146

Similarly to Dan Skelton, Harry Fry's rise in the training ranks has been nothing short of impressive and in the form of Thomas Brown, he looks to have a potentially smart staying chaser on his hands. A dual winner in point-to-points, this seven-year-old bumper and hurdles winner had a satisfactory season over the larger obstacles last season, winning two of his six starts. However, it is well worth noting that his last three runs were in handicaps – a particularly tough task for such an inexperienced horse. He was sent off as favourite for his handicap debut in the Grade 3 BetBright Chase at Kempton, where after being caught behind, he parted company with his rider Noel Fehily before he was asked a serious question. He contested the Close Brothers Novices' Handicap Chase at the Cheltenham Festival on his next start – a race which is always a fiercely competitive affair – and he was far from disgraced finishing seventh behind Ballyalton. It is likely that the two and half miles on that occasion was too sharp for Fry's charge and the ground conditions (good-to-soft) were certainly quick enough. Akin to his handicap debut, his jumping lacked fluency on his final start of last season where he was well beaten at Aintree in a Listed event. One has to be slightly disappointed in his Aintree display, but it should be considered that in each of his three seasons under rules his form has tailed off in the spring and he may be one to catch fresh (won first time out in the last two seasons).

He will begin this season from a mark of 137, five pounds lower than his official rating over hurdles. Given the regard that he has always been held in by his connections and the fact that he has the physique to make an even better chaser, Thomas Brown looks a certain winner of a handicap chase or two during the 2016/2017 campaign. There is a chance that he may lock horns with the aforementioned Southfield Royale in the Grade 3 at Cheltenham, but it is also a distinct possibility that he may contest the Grade 3 Sodexo Gold Cup at Ascot – the venue that he made his chasing debut at almost twelve months earlier.

TWO TAFFS ***6-y-o-b g*** **(Dan Skelton)**
Official Rating: 138
Predicted Rating: 147

A gorgeous son of Flemensfirth, Two Taffs is a strong travelling six-year-old who is definitely going in the right direction. He created a deep impression on his debut two seasons ago when winning a Market Rasen bumper in fine style. He began last season with two narrow defeats in novice hurdles at Bangor and Kempton before he left punters scratching their heads when he was only third after being sent off as favourite for his handicap debut at Kempton. Given a break by his shrewd handler Dan Skelton, Two Taffs was well-supported for the EBF Final at Sandown where although he finished fourth, he met with trouble in running and therefore emerged with plenty of credit. He fulfilled that promise when shedding his maiden tag with a three length win in a decent contest at Ayr. After again travelling smoothly, he didn't find as much as expected once he hit the front and that is probably the reason Harry Skelton had been cautious about taking him to the front too early in his previous runs. Though, he is still lightly raced and it was him showing signs of greenness rather than him having temperament issues.

Although Two Taffs is a fine big horse, it is hoped that he will continue his progress over hurdles this season where he has the potential to take a significant rise in the ratings. His current mark of 138 will allow Skelton to find him plenty of opportunities, most likely in the higher class handicap hurdles. He appeared to show improvement when stepped up to two and a half miles last season and it is predicted that he will need at least this sort of trip to fulfil his undoubted natural ability.

Skelton was represented by Value At Risk in the Grade 3 Holloway's Handicap Hurdle at Ascot in January and that race over an extended two miles and three furlongs may prove an ideal race for Two Taffs this time around. A step up to three miles is certainly not ruled out with his easy way of going a definite plus when contesting races over even further. If he does prove effective in the staying hurdling division, don't be surprised if Skelton ensures that he is qualified for the Pertemps handicap hurdle series which culminates in the final at the Cheltenham Festival.

VALHALLA ***6-y-o-b g*** **(Colin Tizzard)**
Official Rating: 132
Predicted Rating: 139+

Valhalla, a six-year-old son of Scorpion, won a point-to-point in the same colours as useful chaser and now multiple point winner Sydney Paget when sent off as the 6/4 favourite. Having contested three races between two miles and two miles and five furlongs under rules, Colin Tizzard's gelding relished the step up in trip when scoring convincingly at Exeter in March on what was his final start of last season. After staying on strongly at Kempton over two miles on his penultimate start, it was no surprise to see this horse running over almost three miles at Exeter and it is that trip which he looks set to make his mark this season.

He has been raised ten pounds for his latest victory but given that he has a progressive profile, he should be able to cope with this and continue his steady rise up the hurdling ranks. It is worth noting that Valhalla appreciated the better ground in his sole point and at both Kempton and Exeter whereas he seemed to get stuck in the mud when racing on soft ground in his first two starts over timber. Taking that into account, Tizzard may opt to run his gelding in a couple of handicaps in the autumn before giving him a break with the spring campaign in mind. Another win over timber will likely see him reach a mark around 140 and that will allow his connections to consider races such as the Grade 3 handicap hurdle over three miles at Aintree's Grand National festival.

WALKING IN THE AIR ***6-y-o-b g*** **(Dan Skelton)**
Official Rating: 129
Predicted Rating: 136+

Having won his sole point and bumper, Walking In The Air found life tough on his hurdling debut at Exeter when beaten a long way behind multiple hurdle winner Yala Enki. Sent off the well-backed 15/8 favourite, this son of Flemensfirth struggled to land a blow in testing conditions – a suitable explanation for his disappointing effort. His two runner-up efforts at Wetherby and Newbury were satisfactory, especially at the latter track where he bumped into the potentially smart Hell's Kitchen. He shed his maiden tag over timber at the end of March at Warwick when running away with a maiden hurdle, scoring by a very easy eleven lengths.

The fact that this six-year-old was sent off favourite for all of his starts over hurdles shows the regard that he is held in and it is expected that a switch to fences this season will bring out further improvement. He will have gained confidence after winning on his latest start and can build on that over the larger obstacles, beginning life in that sphere from a very workable mark of 129. Although his sole win last season came in an ordinary event, it is worth noting that he handled the quicker ground conditions well and judged on that performance, it may be that he doesn't want the ground too soft. His trainer made the following comments post-race, ***"That was spot on and Walking In The Air will go on his holiday now. He´s bumped into two right horses on his last two runs and he´s a nice prospect. He´ll go chasing next year. We´ll start in handicaps and build up"***.

WILLOWS SAVIOUR ***9-y-o-ch g*** **(Dan Skelton)**
Official Rating: 138
Predicted Rating: 144

Willows Saviour is the third Dan Skelton horse to be included in this section, justifying the strength in depth that he has and will continue to have at his Warwickshire base. After winning The Ladbroke at Ascot in December 2013, this now nine-year-old did not see a racecourse for almost two years before making a winning chase debut at Warwick last season. Following a positive comeback, he was set a stiff task by his handler when contesting the Grade 1 Henry VIII Novices' Chase on his next start – a race which was ultimately too tough an ask at that stage of his chasing career. He justified odds of 1/20 at Fakenham in February, producing some spectacular leaps on the way around, setting up a crack at the Listed Novice Handicap Chase on the opening day of the Cheltenham Festival. He failed to complete in that particular contest, but he was still in contention when falling at the second-last and given that the winner wasn't completely disgraced in Grade 1 company at Aintree on his next start, he looks feasibly treated off 138 (the same rating that he achieved over hurdles).

The novice handicap that he contested at Cheltenham is a race that I am particularly fond of when looking for handicap winners for the following season and given that Aloomomo and Thomas Brown are also included in this section, I expect last year's renewal to yield plenty of winners. Willows Saviour has a tendency to be keen in his races so he will need to learn to settle if he is to be fully effective over intermediate trips. Though the fact that he has previously shown enough speed to win over the minimum distance (both over hurdles and fences) opens up plenty of options for his connections this time around.

ZAMDY MAN ***7-y-o-b g*** **(Venetia Williams)**
Official Rating: 140
Predicted Rating: 149

When the rain arrives in the middle of winter – or in the summer if this year is anything to go by – there are not many better trainers than Venetia Williams and her Zamdy Man is a handicap chaser to follow this season. This useful hurdler, who most notably claimed the scalp of Un Temps Pour Tout in a Grade 2 event at Haydock, looks to have been carefully campaigned by his brilliant trainer with a view to this season in handicaps. After being beaten in his first two starts over fences, he was switched back to hurdles to contest two of the most competitive handicaps – the Grade 3 County and Grade 2 Scottish Champion Hurdle. Back over the larger obstacles on his latest outing, he showed a good attitude to get the better of The Saint James (another who was considered for this section) at Uttoxeter with the pair a good way clear of the remainder.

Although he is still to reproduce his strong hurdling form over fences, he has the physique to progress further as a chaser and is handily rated 140 which will allow him to run in a 0-140 handicap chase first time out. Williams won the Wixworth Handicap Chase, a 0-140 event at Ascot, with Tenor Nivernais last season and there is every chance that Zamdy Man could take his chance in this year's renewal. Alternatively, the BetVictor Gold Cup (formerly known as the Paddy Power Gold Cup) is a feasible target and if the likes of Bristol De Mai were to turn up, he would be allowed to race off a fairly low weight.

THE SALES RING

Lee Lewis has once again been spending hours on end watching what can only be described as shaky Irish point-to-point videos in the attempt to find the next stars to be sourced from between the flags. In addition to the pointers, this section includes some horses in training and French imports that have passed through the public sales. This section, penned by Lee, will hopefully give you a detailed insight into some of the brightest youngsters of the National Hunt game, similarly to last year where he highlighted multiple bumper winner Lucky Pass. He has highlighted his top five horses in terms of fulfilling their potential in the short-term with a star and those horses in particular should be followed during the 2016/2017 season.

BACH DE CLERMONT ***5-y-o-b g*** **(Evan Williams)**
Sales Price Tag: £170,000
Form Figures: 1-

Mr and Mrs William Rucker have invested a lot of money into National Hunt racing in recent years and they have added another expensive youngster to their team of horses with Bach De Clermont – a sole point winner who subsequently cost £170,000. A winner of his only start at Loughanmore in a race which previous winners roll of honour included Ted Veale, Definitly Red and more recently Shantou Village – a horse who served The Final Flight Jumps guide particularly well last season.

He ran in the colours of Nigel Baring that day which coincidently were also carried at the same track to victory by the unbeaten and aforementioned Lucky Pass. Bach De Clermont produced a very impressive display in a fast time beating Tyrrells Success, who has since enhanced the form by winning a Perth bumper by six lengths. The remainder of the field were a distance behind, normally a sign that you have witnessed two useful prospects. I predict that this French import will need some time to develop, but he could be a real exciting acquisition for his new connections in the long run.

BILLY BRONCO ***5-y-o-ch g*** **(Evan Williams)**
Sales Price Tag: £110,000
Form Figures: 1-

After making a winning debut in a bumper at Towcester for trainer Debra Hamer, this shock 20/1 victor was sent to the sales and Evan Williams paid £110,000 for this five-year-old. The runner-up that day was Fergal O'Brien's Pride Of Lecale who was sent off odds-on. He gives the form some substance as he was subsequently only beaten seven and a half lengths in the Grade 1 Weatherbys Champion Bumper.

Billy Bronco looks a sure fire winner over hurdles this winter and by the way he seemed to knuckle down and enjoy the testing ground on debut, I expect his handler to find him an opening at Chepstow or Ffos Las – two tracks where the ground can get very testing. Once sent over obstacles, it is predicted that this horse has the ability to develop into a nice handicapper for his new connections.

BLACK OP *5-y-o-br g*
Sales Price Tag: £210,000
Form Figures: 1-

This big imposing gelding recorded a win on debut at the back end of March at Loughanmore - the same track in which the owners' Champagne West made a winning debut at in 2012. He showed signs of inexperience throughout, racing keenly and making quite a few jumping errors. Though it must be considered that he was facing rivals who had some racecourse experience which means that his performance was worth upgrading. He was left clear at the last when his nearest pursuer came to grief, but he did have him held at the time and he went on to record a twenty five length success. He was subsequently sent to the Goffs sale at the Aintree's Grand National meeting and created quite a stir when the hammer finally fell at £210,000, signed for by Roger Brookhouse. Assuming that he is given time, this really likeable sort has the potential to be a 140 plus rated chaser, but he should be more than capable of paying his way over hurdles in the short-term.

BURREN LIFE ***4-y-o-b g*** **(Gordon Elliott)**
Sales Price Tag: £135,000
Form Figures: F-

The highly-regarded Burren Life made his debut in a maiden point at Belharbour in February. Considering the soft underfoot conditions, the race was run at genuine gallop and that saw three horse pull well clear of the remainder in the closing stages. This four-year-old gelding looked to have the race at his mercy when falling at the last – a real shame after he had jumped so well up until that point. Although he failed to complete on his only start between the flags, this son of Pelder attracted plenty of attention when taken to Cheltenham sales in February and the hammer fell at £135,000.

He looks the type to begin to pay back his price tag under rules pretty quickly and it is expected that his new trainer Gordon Elliott will opt to run him in a bumper to gain valuable experience before switching to the hurdling ranks. This beautiful looking individual will now carry the famous Gigginstown House Stud silks and if he can scale similar heights to their other ex-pointers such as Milsean, Death Duty and Lucky Pass then they will be absolutely delighted.

CARTER MCKAY ***5-y-o-gr g*** **(Willie Mullins) ☆**
Sales Price Tag: £160,000
Form Figures: 21-

Sheikh Fahad is a name usually associated with Flat racing, but with his Pearl Bloodstock operation formerly owning bumper winner Castello Sforza (now in the ownership of leading owner JP McManus) and Current Event who finished fourth in the Fox Hunters at Cheltenham, he seems to be really enjoying the winter game.

He has recently purchased winning point-to-pointer Carter McKay for £160,000 at the Goffs sale at Aintree and this promising young horse will now be in training with Willie Mullins. Heavily gambled when runner-up on his debut, he made amends a few months later when sent to Ballynoe – quickening up from the back of the last to record a decisive ten length success.

This son of the one of my favourite sires Martaline is a physically attractive specimen. He travels well in his races and is thought of as a horse to go to war with in bumpers when returning from a summer break. One thing is for sure, he certainly seems to possess all the right tools to succeed in that sphere as he has a lovely blend of speed and stamina. Carter McKay's long-term future may be over middle distances once sent hurdling, but it is not hard to envisage this handsome grey winning a bumper at one of Ireland's better courses before forming part of Mullins' Champion Bumper squad in March.

CESAR COLLONGES ***4-y-o-ch g*** **(Evan Williams)**
Sales Price Tag: £200,000
Form Figures: 1-

This four-year-old made his debut in a heavy ground maiden point at Kirkistown and despite there only being four runners, this could turn out to be an above average race – the race has a good record of producing nice prospects. Cesar Collonges was sent off the outsider of the quartet but he put in a very professional display, jumping exceptionally well for a horse with no previous racecourse experience and the manner in that he was able to quicken up to put the race to bed in a matter of strides was impressive.

Judged on his debut performance, this son of Fragrant Mix looks to have the required attributes that could take him to the top of the jumping game and that belief was justified when Evan Williams signed for this gelding for £200,000 on behalf of Mr and Mrs Rucker. The Ruckers have a fantastic record of horses being placed in the Grand National over the years and given that Cesar Collonges' dam is a half-sister to Paul Nicholls' Grand National winner Neptune Collonges, he should prove himself as a useful staying chaser.

CLAIMANTAKINFORGAN ***4-y-o-b g*** **(Nicky Henderson)**
Sales Price Tag: £110,000
Form Figures: S1-

Having slipped up early on when making his debut at Inch, this four-year-old son of Great Pretender was turned out five days later at Loughanmore on Easter Monday – a race which has been won by Different Gravey (2014) and the unbeaten Lucky Pass (2015) the last two years. Lucky Pass took the honours in a race which also saw Battleford, who placed in a Grade 1 bumper depart at the last so the form of that contest is working out particularly well. This year's race also looks likely to be a strong renewal with the third already boosting the form since and the fourth has been subsequently sold as an expensive store horse for Gigginstown. The ground was heavy that day, but the rain softened ground conditions didn't seem to worry Claimantakinforgan as he relished it – a positive when he is asked to tackle winter ground under rules.

Sold to highflyer for £110,000, he will be joining Nicky Henderson to continue his career at his Seven Barrows base. It is possible he could start off in a bumper before being switched to the novice hurdling division, where I believe he could develop into a useful 130+ performer.

ELEGANT ESCAPE ***4-y-o-b g*** **(Colin Tizzard)**
Sales Price Tag: €150,000
Form Figures: 2-

Gordon Elliott trained this four-year-old son of Dubai Destination when he made his debut at Monksgrange where he unfortunately bumped into the well-backed and highly-regarded Samcro – a horse who features in this year's 'Top Prospects'. However, there was no shame in that defeat as Samcro has since been purchased by Gordon Elliott for £335,000 thus showing the regard in which this horse was held in. Elegant Escape will be crossing the Irish Sea to settle into a new home at Colin Tizzard's Dorset base after being purchased on behalf of John Romans at Goffs in April. He showed a really likeable attitude to stay on well in bad ground and based on visual impressions, I predict that this race could turn out to be decent maiden. Tizzard had a remarkable 2015/2016 season with Cue Card and Thistlecrack stealing the headlines and this horse is one to look forward to as he has the ability to become a very useful hurdler.

FIRST DRIFT ***5-y-o-ch g*** **(Ben Case)**
Sales Price Tag: £45,000
Form Figures: 11-1

This is a horse who has already run twice under rules but I have included him in this section after he was sold for £45,000 at the Cheltenham Festival Sales. First Drift won his sole point at Kirkistown in good style when sent off the 9/4 favourite and was quickly sold and sent into training with Ben Case. This chestnut gelding was next seen in a bumper at Southwell which he won by three lengths before he followed up impressively at Worcester scoring by an eased down ten lengths. A half-brother to the 2011 Champion Bumper runner-up Destroyer Deployed, this strong travelling sort looks a lovely prospect to be going hurdling with this season and could prove a real bargain buy for connections.

GETABIRD ***4-y-o-b g*** **(Willie Mullins)**
Sales Price Tag: €200,000
Form Figures: O1-

Willie Mullins and Harold Kirk were very busy at the sales this year – something that we are all becoming accustomed to seeing – and the pair acquired a nice four-year-old called Getabird from Colin Bowes' stables for a tidy sum of €200,000.

As a youngster from the first crop of Getaway, this well-related gelding hails from the same family as Long Run, Libertine and JY Vole and has the bloodline to excel under rules. He failed to compete on his debut in what looked a competitive maiden and the winner Judgement Day (features in this year's 'Top Prospects') fetched a decent price at the sales (also to be trained by Mullins). Following his debut run, he made amends at Largy when running out an impressive four length winner, despite making a major error at the fourth last. His rider that day never panicked and Getabird was soon back on the bridle to ensure that he was involved with two to jump. He was well in touch and making a challenge at the last when his main rival Storm Home and it's difficult to have predicted the result of the race had he stood up. Though, the manner in which he was still able to score by four lengths despite being badly hampered by the faller was rather taking. This potentially smart four-year-old seems to have plenty of gears which will enable him to win a bumper in what looks likely to be another decent season for the yard in that sphere.

KING'S SOCKS ***4-y-o-b g*** **(David Pipe) ☆**
Sales Price Tag: €210,000
Form Figures: 21/42122-152

The partnership of Professor Caroline Tisdall & Bryan Drew tasted Cheltenham Festival success last season with their expensive French import Un Temps Pour Tout when he won the Business Solutions Handicap Chase and in the summer the pair purchased King's Socks, a son of 2000 Guineas winner King's Best, for €210,000 at Arqana in July.

A taking individual who likes to race prominently, he is already a winner over both hurdles and fences in his native France which means that he isn't a novice for the current campaign, but he does boast a decent level of form. The pick of his form includes finishing runner-up to the Paul Nicholls-trained Adrien Du Pont who is now rated 147 and filled the same spot behind Willie Mullins' top-class juvenile hurdler Footpad in the Grade 1 Prix Alain Du Breil at Auteuil on his latest start.

Due to him already winning under both codes, he will be more difficult to place in the UK than most French youngsters, but he joins what I describe as a handicap genius in David Pipe and he is certain to win more races now trained on this side of the Channel. Regardless of what handicap mark King's Socks is given, I feel that the master of Pond House will find a good opening for his new inmate and it is quite possible that top-class handicaps such as the Bet Victor Gold Cup (formerly the Paddy Power) and the December Gold Cup which are both run at Cheltenham in November and December respectively will be on his radar. In addition, it is also worth considering that Pipe may opt to run him over hurdles where it is anticipated that intermediate trips will suit. Although he has already raced ten times over obstacles, King's Socks rates as a very interesting and exciting type for this season and beyond and his new connections will be looking forward to getting going with him.

LE PREZIEN ***4-y-o-b g*** **(Paul Nicholls)**
Sales Price Tag: £290,000
Form Figures: 83/211212-

After being acquired privately from France by Highflyer Bloodstock on behalf of the Million In Mind Partnership, Le Prezien had a successful first season in the UK which included Grade 2 success in the Premier Kelso Hurdle in March. An excellent run behind Yorkhill in the Grade 1 Mersey Novices' Hurdle at Aintree further enhanced his form and made him a very interesting member of his owners' annual dispersal at the Goffs Horses In Training Sales which takes place at Doncaster.

The five-year-old subsequently topped that sales as the hammer fell at £290,000, signed for by Frank Berry on behalf of leading owner JP McManus. Following his impressive novice hurdling campaign which yielded three wins and two seconds, this son of Blue Bresil is expected to embark on a novice chasing campaign and he should excel in that sphere. He is quick, athletic and scopey and races between two and two and a half miles will be ideal for him over the larger obstacles.

LOUGH DERG SPIRIT ***4-y-o-b g*** **(Nicky Henderson)**
Sales Price Tag: £190,000
Form Figures: 3-1

Lough Derg Spirit made his debut in the aforementioned four-year-old maiden won by Claimantakinforgan at Loughanmore where he finished third, five lengths behind the impressive winner. He then took a good step forward to win under Jamie Codd at Athlacca, showing a professional attitude to win gamely.

This half-brother to winning hurdler and chaser Sizing Machine looks built for hurdling and looks set to make his mark over distances of two and a half miles plus. He will look to build on his promising start to his racing career under the watchful eye of Nicky Henderson and run in the colours of enthusiastic owners Stuart Parkin and Mike Grech. Parkin and Grech have had recent bumper success with former point-to-pointers River Wylde and Stowaway Magic and it is hoped that Lough Derg Spirit will be another successful purchase. It is worth mentioning that the same clients signed for Claimantakinforgan so 2016/2017 could be a particularly exciting year for them.

MAHARI ***3-y-o-b c*** **(Kerry Lee) ☆**
Sales Price Tag: €280,000
Form Figures: 6-1135 (flat form)

One of this year's contributors, Tom Malone, had huge success when buying Grade 2 Adonis Hurdle winner Zubayr from the Arqana sale last summer and he returned again this year to acquire Mahari, a son of King George winner Duke Of Marmalade. His sire had success last season with his son Superb Story winning the County Hurdle in good style and with Mahari sharing the same page as 1000 Guineas winner Miss France, you can see why they had to pay €280,000 for this 3-year-old colt.

In addition to his likeable pedigree, this scopey sort has shown some very useful form in France on a variety of different ground conditions which included him running up a sequence of four wins. On numerous occasions he has been at his best when being allowed to dictate the pace, bringing his stamina into play, and that is something that he will be able to use to his advantage over hurdles. It is likely that this ex-Andre Fabre inmate will gain valuable jumping experience at one of the trainer's favoured tracks which include Ludlow, Chepstow and Bangor before being upped in class. There is every possibility that this classy recruit to hurdling will be lined up for a crack at the Grade 1 Future Champions Juvenile Finale at Chepstow, where the likely slow ground conditions shouldn't be an inconvenience. It is worth noting that Mahari also has the size to jump a fence in the future – perhaps fairly unusual with him being an ex-Flat horse – and he remains one for connections to be very excited about for this season and beyond.

MINELLA WARRIOR *4-y-o-b g* **(Kim Bailey)**
Sales Price Tag: £190,000
Form Figures: 2

Owners Julia and David Martin tasted Cheltenham Festival success with Darna in 2015 and they have recently acquired Minella Warrior for £180,000, a promising son of well-known jumps sire King's Theatre. Just like Darna, Minella Warrior will be trained by Kim Bailey and he is a trainer who excels with chasers so should get the best out of this ex-pointer.

This four-year-old was runner-up in his sole point to a more experienced rival (Lough Derg Spirit) who has subsequently been sold for £190,000. The race looks particularly strong with the third boosting the form since with a win in point-to-points. Minella Warrior's dam is a half-sister to the high-class Menorah and it is expected that this physically imposing sort will make a smart chaser one day. Although he is perhaps not sharp enough to be winning bumpers, it is expected that he could still take a similar route to the aforementioned Darna by running in a few to gain valuable experience. With that in mind, he is probably one to follow once sent over obstacles between trips of two and a half and three miles.

MONBEG AQUADUDE *5-y-o-b g* **(Michael Scudamore)**
Sales Price Tag: £80,000
Form Figures: 1-

Michael Scudamore had great success with Monbeg Dude who won the Welsh National for him in 2013. Monbeg Aquadude, a five-year-old bay is now in the care of Scudamore and his new handler will be hoping for plenty of success with this winning pointer. Rockfield, the track which this gelding recorded his maiden success at, can be one that really favours a horse who needs a test of stamina and that certainly applies this son of Flemensfirth. There was a lot to like about his debut as he virtually made all, sustained a decent gallop throughout and jumped superbly. In addition, he gamely held off the challenge of Nicky Henderson's River Wylde who after subsequently scoring in a bumper by a wide margin at Warwick in May, gave the form a significant boost.

There is a feeling that this could have been one of the better maidens to be run at the back end of last year and with former winners including Eider Chase winner Portrait King and Harry Fry's useful novice American obliging in this race last year, it wouldn't be the first decent renewal. A big raw individual, Monbeg Aquadude is every inch a staying chaser in the making. Therefore, I advise that if he appears in a bumper or a two mile hurdle then he would be one to avoid. Though, in time he will certainly pay his way with longer trips and give under foot likely to help his cause. A long-term prospect, but most definitely a horse to follow.

MONBEG CHIT CHAT *5-y-o-b g* **(Willie Mullins) ☆**
Sales Price Tag: £200,000
Form Figures: 21-

The very successful Monbeg Syndicate appear to have found another gem, this time in the form of Monbeg Chit Chat. Following his point win at Lismore, he will now be in the care of Ireland's leading trainer, Willie Mullins. This son of Cheltenham Festival Champion Sire Kayf Tara proved very popular at Tattersalls Ireland Cheltenham sale and the hammer eventually fell at £200,000, going to Harold Kirk on behalf of Gigginstown.

Monbeg Chit Chat has come highly recommended to his new connections and it should be noted that this is only the second time that Kirk has purchased from the Doyle family - the other being 'Top Prospect' Invitation Only. It is also worth considering that both of his runs between the flags were on testing ground, so there will be no problem for him finding a suitable opening in a bumper in Ireland during the winter months. I predict that when his attentions are switched to hurdles, he will be most suited to intermediate distances. This classy sort is one with graded potential over obstacles and one thing is for sure, he is in the right hands to do just that.

PRODUCT OF LOVE *5-y-o-b g* **(Alan Fleming) ☆**
Sales Price Tag: £120,000 (Unsold)
Form Figures: 21-1

Although bidding reached a significant figure of £120,000 back in November at Cheltenham's Tattersalls sales, this gelding remained with vendor John Hanlon at the time, but was later purchased by Barry Connell and is now in training with Alan Fleming. Although Product Of Love is already a winner under rules, I could not exclude him from this section as I genuinely believe that he is a really lovely horse for the future.

This son of Fruits Of Love was runner-up on debut at Inchydoney but he soon went one better when winning a four-year-old maiden at Rathcannon and the form of that race was given a significant boost when Ballycrystal who was runner-up that day won next time out between the flags before landing a Doncaster bumper for his new handler, Brian Ellison. Described as 'very smart' by Fleming, this tall gelding went on to score in taking fashion in a bumper at Killarney, beating a field of eleven by sixteen lengths. He showed a real change of speed that day to quicken right away from his rivals and it is hard to describe his rules debut as anything less than impressive. At this stage he has only raced on good ground and I feel this really could be key to him and it is advised that he is best watched on winter ground. Though, on decent ground it is not hard to envisage this talented five-year-old being graded class over obstacles.

REDHOTFILLYPEPPERS *4-y-o-ch f* **(Willie Mullins)**
Sales Price Tag: £200,000
Form Figures: 1

This wonderfully named daughter of Robin Des Champs won as she pleased on debut at Necarne. She will be joining the embarrassment of talented race mares which include Apple's Jade, Annie Power and Vroum Vroum Mag at Closutton after Harold kirk purchased this four-year-old chestnut on behalf of Willie Mullins for £200,000 - a fee which equalled the previous record for a mare set the year before by Theatre Territory.

Her dam was unraced and is a half-sister to Shuil Na, who herself was the dam of Willie Mullins' Cheltenham Gold Cup runner-up On His Own. This sizeable filly recorded the fastest time of the day when winning her point-to-point and showed plenty of gears to quicken right away from the field to score by ten lengths. Redhotfillypeppers looks banker material for a mares' only bumper before she is upped in class. It is anticipated that races such as the Listed EBF Mares' bumper at Sandown in March and the Grade 2 Mares' bumper at Aintree's Grand National meeting are sure to come under consideration. I am excited about seeing this one and she is one to really look forward to.

REIGNING SUPREME *5-y-o-b g* (Nicky Henderson)
Sales Price Tag: £130,000
Form Figures: F2-

Although he failed to register a win between the flags, this five-year-old has showed some useful form in his two outings. After falling on debut behind another of my sales entries, Bach De Clermont, he reappeared two weeks later at Maralin. On that occasion he met 'Top Prospect' and subsequent bumper winner Big Meadow where they fought out a fascinating finish - the pair pulled 20 lengths clear of the remainder. On the back of a fine effort in defeat, Reigning Supreme was sent to the Tattersalls Ireland Cheltenham sales in November and he was snapped up by Highflyer Bloodstock on behalf of Michael Buckley for £130,000. One thing is for sure, he's bred for the job being by leading National Hunt sire Presenting and his dam being out of a maiden half-sister to Cheltenham Gold Cup winner and Grand National runner-up Garrisons Savannah. Although he is likely to take a bit of time to come to hand, this likeable sort is another with the ability to develop into a graded performer and is one to follow.

ROCK ON RIO *4-y-o-ch g* (Andrew McNamara)
Sales Price Tag: £75,000
Form Figures: 1

It was impressive and at the same time extremely rare that a son of sprinter Captain Rio was able to win a four-year-old maiden point, but this physically imposing gelding did just that when he created a good impression to win by three lengths on his debut at Tralee. His dam, Glory Days, has more of a jumping pedigree being a full sister to smart chaser Ghizao and one of her offspring Chatez has also won over hurdles for Alan King.

This big raw chestnut was settled in at the rear of the field in the early stages before cutting through the field to make a challenge with two to jump. After he quickened up well after the last, he won going away under Champion point-to-point rider Jamie Codd. He was subsequently purchased for £75,000 by the young up and coming trainer Andrew McNamara at Ascot in July and he looks a value purchase based on the visual impression that he created on his debut. His pedigree and the turn of foot that he showed between the flags tells me that Rock On Rio will be sharp enough to go and win a bumper, recouping some of his sales price tag back immediately. Being such a fine physical specimen, he shouldn't hang around in bumpers for too long and looks set to make his mark over obstacles as soon as this season.

THE ORGANIST ***5-y-o-b m*** **(Oliver Sherwood)**
Sales Price Tag: £260,000
Form Figures: 11121F-

Following the sale of Le Prezien at Goffs Horses In Training Sales at Doncaster, the Million In Mind Partnership struck again with their smart mare, The Organist, selling for £260,000. This five-year-old was also purchased by Frank Berry on behalf of JP McManus and it is excellent that she will remain in training with Oliver Sherwood who has done a magnificent job with her up to this point.

After winning four of her first five starts, The Organist had a Listed race at her mercy on her final start before taking a heavy fall at the last. Fortunately she got up and she will return this season as a high-class mare that is capable of competing in all of the best Mares' only races prior to the spring festivals.

Currently rated 139, she will need to improve a fair bit to trouble the likes of Annie Power and Vroum Vroum Mag if they were to turn up in the Mares' Hurdle at the Cheltenham Festival, but races like the Listed Mares' Hurdle run at Warwick in February over two miles and five furlongs would be a feasible target.

THREE SWALLOWSNICK ***5-y-o-b m*** **(Willie Mullins)**
Sales Price Tag: £110,000
Form Figures: 11-

The third mare to appear on the list and another who has been purchased by Harold Kirk for Willie Mullins. After winning both of her starts in Irish points, she created a good enough impression to warrant Kirk to go to £110,000 at Tattersalls Cheltenham sale in March. Her second start at Durrow was the most impressive as it was a 'winner of one' race – these sort of contests are often filled with a number of promising individuals. She travelled strongly throughout as she had done on debut at Borris House and once asked to go win her race, she responded instantly and ultimately won in fine style.

She looks to possess a high cruising speed and is blessed with a natural turn of foot which is a plus when contesting bumpers and hurdle races over the minimum distance. This daughter of Westerner looks tailor made for the bumper ranks and connections' biggest problem will keeping her and the aforementioned Redhotfillypeppers apart once they are both stepped up in grade.

TIMEWAITSFORNOONE ***4-y-o-b g*** **(Alan Fleming)**
Sales Price Tag: £225,000
Form Figures: 21-

Timewaitsfornoone, another graduate from the highly-successful Colin Bowe ranks, finished runner-up to the well regarded Gigginstown-owned Hardline on debut in a point-to-point at Punchestown. With the race being run over what looked an inadequate trip of two and a half miles, it is also worth noting that the race was not run to suit and he seemed to be in need of a stiffer test. After his promising debut he reappeared seven days later at Tinahely and he again faced a Gigginstown representative, this time in the form of the Gordon Elliott-trained odds-on favourite Mind's Eye (Elliott won this same race with Alpha Des Obeaux in recent years). He created a good impression that day, quickening up well to record a one length success, with Mind's Eye filling the runner-up spot.

Following his win, he was then purchased by Barry Connell for £225,000 at Cheltenham in March and he will now continue his career with Alan Fleming. Timewaitsfornoone is a tough and genuine sort who looks to have the profile of a staying chaser of the future. Connell is renowned for being patient when it comes to his youngsters so this gelding will be given plenty of time to acclimatise to his new surroundings before hopefully giving his connections plenty of success. This good looking son of Oscar – who is also the sire of Connell's dual Grade 1-winning hurdler The Tullow Tank – may take time to show his full potential under rules but he is a horse with considerable promise and one to note for the future.

TOPOFTHEGAME ***4-y-o-ch g***
Sales Price Tag: £120,000
Form Figures: 1-

Topofthegame made his debut two days before Cheltenham Festival week and this tall son of Flemensfirth – who is related to the Grade 1-placed Artadoin Lad – created a huge impression by winning a small field maiden at Belclare, a race that back in 1999 was won by multiple Cheltenham Gold Cup winner Best Mate. Having been allowed to dictate the pace, this gelding set an average gallop and after barely seeing another rival, he went on to score by an impressive nine lengths. He looked a real natural at his fences and Highflyer Bloodstock were equally impressed as they signed a cheque for £120,000 to secure him. As often is the case with Irish point-to-points, only time will tell as to how good the race is, but he looks certain to make an impact on the UK bumper/hurdle scene this winter and is one for connections to look forward to.

OTHER NOTABLE SALES

Highflyer Bloodstock paid £100,000 for sole point winner *Reality Bites* at Tattersalls at Cheltenham in February and he will now be in the care of leading trainer Alan King. This five-year-old son of Mahler was sent off 4/5 favourite for his debut between the flags and he looks like a good long-term prospect for his new connections.

Brianstorm and *Vent D'Automne* finished first and second in a four-year-old point-to-point at Fairyhouse in April with the former coming out on top by six lengths. The winner was purchased by Rebecca Curtis at Goffs in April for £40,000, but what was most notable was that the runner-up was signed for by Harold Kirk on behalf of Willie Mullins for a significant sum of £100,000. Also in April, Denis Murphy sold a five year-old son of Milan called *An Siltean* to Highflyer Bloodstock. A winner of his sole point, he will now join Harry Fry and it is expected that he will start off in a bumper to gain valuable experience.

Highflyer also signed for a four-year-old by Oscar, *Oscar Mor*, who after being sent off favourite, he was successful on his only point-to-point start at Kirkistown on testing ground. One of this year's 'Top Prospects', Stowaway Forever was not sent to the sales and stays in house with Philip Dempsey. However, the horse who finished second behind him at Loughbrickland in April, *Wonderoftheworld*, was subsequently sold at Tattersalls at Cheltenham for £80,000, signed for by G H Bloodstock. Anthony Honeyball has a good record with his runners in bumpers and he paid £60,000 for Irish pointer *Tacenda* in April. After unseating on her debut at Inch, this daughter of Flemensfirth will likely go down the bumper route where she should be monitored closely. Evan Williams is renowned for acquiring ex-pointers and *Monbeg Oscar*, an easy winner of his only start, cost £90,000 and is another addition to his strong team of horses.

Super Follo, a four-year-old son of Enrique, won on his second start between the flags and was subsequently sent to Tattersalls at Cheltenham in May and Margaret O'Toole on behalf of Noel Meade paid £150,000 to secure his services. Another interesting purchase was *Drovers Lane* who is another new recruit to Curtis' stables. A winner of a point-to-point at Necarne in May, the hammer fell at £135,000 and this four-year-old son of Oscar is worth keeping an eye on in bumpers and novice hurdles. *Orchard Thieves* and *Trainwreck* met in a heavy ground four-year-old maiden at Durrow in February with the latter getting the better by half a length and the pair were twelve lengths clear of the remainder. The runner-up was sold for £115,000 to David Pipe a month later with Trainwreck going for significantly less at Doncaster (£78,000) to Gordon Elliott. Both horses showed potential on what was their only start to date and should pay their way under rules for their new connections.

In addition to acquiring Vent D'Automne, Mullins and Kirk were busy at Goffs in May and winning pointer *Calino D'Airy* cost the pair £150,000 and he will continue his career at Mullins' all-conquering Closutton operation. *Ravenhill Road*, a fifteen length winner of his sole point, is another notable youngster to be sold at Doncaster and this five-year-old who cost Phil Martin £100,000 looks a nice long-term prospect.

Faugheen's half-brother, *Telmadela*, went through the sales ring in July, selling for £20,000. Given that he took four attempts to get off the mark in point-to-points meant that his price tag was not a surprise, but the fact that he is out of the same dam as the brilliant Champion Hurdle winner, his rules debut will be eagerly anticipated by many. In addition to the aforementioned King's Socks, David Pipe also signed for *Maggie Fu Ma* at Arqana's July Sales for €210,000. Hailing from the same family as American wondermare Zenyatta, this three-year-old looks likely to make her mark over hurdles, with Pipe already stating that he will work back from Cheltenham with her. Also at the same sale, Guy Petit went to the same figure for *Ibleo* who is a son of Dick Turpin. He will be trained by Venetia Williams for the Bellamy Partnership who have had plenty of success including when their Emperor's Choice won the Welsh National. It would be unusual if Kirk and Mullins didn't have their say and the pair paid £75,000 for the promising Icario who is another interesting recruit for the Champion Trainer.

The Goffs UK August Sale took place in Doncaster and the Potensis dispersal was the highlight with high-quality mare *Jessber's Dream* topping the sales, signed for by Tom Malone for £190,000 on behalf of Ditcheat Thoroughbreds – a newly formed syndicate. Two other notable purchases were *Activial* who was sold to Neil Mulholland for £80,000 and the day's second-top lot *Crin Au Vent* (£120,000) who remains with Paul Nicholls.

TOM MALONE BLOODSTOCK

In 2009 ex-jockey Tom Malone started out as a bloodstock agent, plying his trade amongst the best in the industry, where 35 winners in his first season quickly progressed to a tally of 131 in 2011. The 272 winners that he recorded in 2015 was his best to date – a record that he is on course to beat again in 2016.

A combination of Tom's riding experience, knowledge of the thoroughbred and enthusiasm ensures that Tom Malone Bloodstock provides clients with a tailored, personal and professional bloodstock consultancy service.

Operating as one of the leading bloodstock agents, sourcing a number of top-class horses which include Grade 1 Queen Mother Champion Chase winner *Dodging Bullets*, the ill-fated Grade 1-winning *Brindisi Breeze* and Grade 2 Adonis Juvenile Hurdle winner *Zubayr*, I am delighted that Tom agreed to be part of this season's publication. During the close season Tom has been busy at the sales, buying plenty of new stock for leading connections, and he has kindly included some of his notable purchases in this section for our readers benefit.

This section includes a nice blend of bumper and hurdling types as well as long-term prospects. It is sure to produce plenty of winners this season and with a bit of luck, it may just unearth a real star of the National Hunt game.

ANCHOR MAN – 2012 *(Stowaway – False Note)*

This is a really nice four-year-old by Stowaway that I bought at Cheltenham in April for £55,000 and he has since joined Paul Nicholls for owner Peter Hordle. He was second in his sole point, a maiden that was held in high-regard by a lot of people and numerous horses have been sold for significant sums since – the winner has gone to David Pipe for £140,000 and the third made £80,000 at Aintree. He is not overly big but he is a really racy type and looks a good bumper and hurdles prospect for his new connections.

CASKO D'AIRY (FR) – 2012 *(Voix Du Nord – Quaska D'Airy)*

This is a horse that I have sourced from France for Jed Mason and Partners. He impressed me when winning a bumper on the all-weather in the provinces last August and subsequently had a break after. The manner of his debut victory and the fact that he is by a very good sire, I was interested in this four-year-old but ultimately needed to see him do a bit more before making a commitment. He put in a lovely performance for a youngster in Auteuil on his second start in March (the fact that his former handler took him to Paris proved that he also held him in high-regard). A private acquisition for his new connections, he remains a novice over hurdles and I look forward to following his career at Ditcheat.

CRACKING SMART – 2012 *(Great Pretender – Maya Du Frene)*

This is a four-year-old who I acquired privately in France and will be trained in Ireland by Gordon Elliott for Gigginstown House Stud. He is a beautiful big horse who fell at the last in a hurdle race in the French provinces, where he would have definitely been in the first two had he stood up. He caught my eye as a nice jumping prospect on that occasion, with plenty of scope for further improvement in the future. Being such a sizeable individual I do expect that he will be sent straight over hurdles for his new connections – perhaps a maiden or novice event around November time. He is from a decent family, with his half-sister winning four bumpers in France and he is definitely one to follow.

GIVE ME A COPPER (IRE) – 2010 *(Presenting – Copper Supreme)*

I genuinely think that this horse is a star. I had this horse bought as a five-year-old when he won his sole point but a little issue meant I couldn't get him straight away. He subsequently bolted up in his bumper, creating a deep impression and I signed for him for £270,000 at Goffs' Aintree sale in April on behalf of Jed Mason and Partners. He is from a very good family and has plenty of class, which he more than demonstrated when he galloped a good bumper field at Cork into the ground. Although he is a long-term prospect, he has the ability to go a long way over timber too and he is just the type of horse that Paul excels with. I believe he is a graded performer, ultimately a Cheltenham Gold Cup type and he fits into the bracket of 'could be anything'.

MAHARI – 2013 *(Duke Of Marmalade – Mission Secrete)*

This youngster is a three-year-old who I purchased at Arqana in July for £280,000 and I just had to purchase him after I fell in love with him in catalogue. The manner in which he showed himself capable of jumping out and galloping from the front tells me that he has the aptitude to be a nice jumper and now in the care of Kerry Lee, he is in good hands to excel under a new code. Andre Fabre told me that he came home sick after his last run when he was last of five runners so that can certainly be ignored. Although he has the right sort of profile to make a smart four-year-old hurdler, that is definitely not all that he is – he's a big, rangy sort who has the size to make a chaser one day. Having won four flat races on the bounce in France where he achieved a rating of 92, he proved that he is a classy sort and is an exciting recruit to the jumping sphere. I see little point in winning a low grade juvenile or novice with him as he is a horse who I anticipate to be even better in a years' time – a bit like Dodging Bullets in that respect.

SECRET INVESTOR – 2012 *(Kayf Tara – Silver Charmer)*

This lad put in a big performance when winning a hot four-year-old maiden at Athlacca in May where he achieved a nice rating of 91. Although he was booked for second before the speedier looking Espoir De Teillee fell at the last, he is a big backward type who is only going to improve with time. I was therefore delighted to secure him at Cheltenham Tattersalls sales in May for £175,000 and he will now continue his progression with Paul (Nicholls). Being by a Champion Sire in Kayf Tara, he has a nice jumping pedigree and he is the sort of horse that Paul has a very good record at getting the best out of. It is probably in two to three years' time before you this gelding's true potential, but he is worth taking note of and rates a decent long-term prospect.

SUMKINDOFKING (IRE) – 2010 *(King's Theatre – Shannon Rose)*

This five-year-old gelding is a lovely individual by top-class jumps sire King's Theatre. He showed plenty of improvement to win by nine lengths on his second start at Inch in March. He sat in fourth or fifth for a long way before sprinting away from what appeared a good quality field on the day. That certainly looks the case now with the form being boosted on numerous occasions (second, third, fourth and eighth have since won a point). Although he is not overly big, the way that he was able to quicken away on the bridle was particularly pleasing and this brother to the smart Minella Foru should make a smooth transition to life under rules. He has joined Tom George for owner Dave Fox and he is expected to start justifying his sales tag of £70,000 sooner rather than later.

WEALTH DES MOTTES – 2013 *(Silver Frost – Wavy)*

This is a horse who I also purchased privately for Jed Mason and partners from France. He won a three-year-old hurdle race first time out in July, travelling well before quickening away on the bridle to record a very impressive three and a half-length victory. He is by a young sire in Silver Frost and this fella looks like a proper juvenile hurdle prospect to me. He will also join Paul Nicholls and is sure to be a great addition to his team.

WHATDUHAVTOGET (IRE) – 2012 *(Presenting – Smooching)*

This daughter of Presenting has a nice pedigree being a half-sister to point winner Sizing Chile and she is a youngster who I am quite excited about. I bought this filly after she won a four-year-old maiden point at the first time of asking on the 20th February at Durrow. She looked a real star that day, galloping through the bottomless ground to record a one length victory. This big strong individual is one of the nicest fillies/mares that I have every bought and after joining Highclere to be trained by Dan Skelton, she looks to have a very bright future under rules.

PITTERSON'S PADDOCK PICKS

As a member of 'The Talent Spotters' for the Racing Post, Ken Pitterson is well-known for his expertise when it comes to the appearance of a racehorse, especially in the preliminaries prior to a race. Although Ken will openly admit that the form of any given horse is critical, he uses his experience to assess the physical well-being and there is no doubt that this is something that can assist you when considering the chances of a particular horse. Throughout the duration of the 2015/2016 campaign, Ken has collated a list of horses that, in his opinion, should be worth following in the 2016/2017 season.

ARKWRISHT (FR) – 2010 *(Lavirco – Latitude)*

If there is a bigger horse in training I have yet to see it because this fella fills the eye and I would hate for him to step on my toes. He came to Aintree on the back of winning a Grade 3 novice hurdle at Clonmel on heavy ground and looking at him this track was never going to play to his strengths - he ran an honourable seventh. When you look at this Gigginstown-owned six-year-old he has staying chaser stamped on his forehead and I am sure he will make a big impression when he tackles the big fences.

ASUM (GB) – 2011 *(Kayf Tara – Candy Creek)*

He was backed down to 5-2 favourite in a Warwick Bumper at the end of April and looking at the field he looked the class act. Held up off the pace he was set too much to do and was finishing like a rocket only to fail to get up on the line. Looking at him you can see he possesses a wonderful physique and he can only improve with a summer out at grass. He may have another run in a bumper, but he looks to have the qualities to make an impact throughout the winter.

BALLYHENRY (IRE) – 2010 *(Presenting – Afarka)*

Ben Pauling has always thought the world of this Presenting gelding and has always mentioned him in the same breath as Barters Hill. He won his first start in a bumper and backed that performance up by carrying a penalty to win his second start. However, after he was thrown in to the deep end on his first start over hurdles at Newbury at the Hennessy meeting, he was given two months off and produced a personal best by beating Grade 2 winner Label Des Obeaux at Kempton. When you look at him you can see he will come in to his own this season when he goes over fences.

BORN SURVIVOR (IRE) – 2011 *(King´s Theatre – Bob´s Flame)*

Some horses cost a fortune and you cannot see how they reached those sort of prices, but looking at this son of King's Theatre you can see why he cost a fair packet. He made his debut for the Skelton yard in a maiden hurdle at Warwick and he brushed aside a decent field. Always travelling comfortably he had to be shook up to stamp his authority. He started off a very short price favourite for a Grade 2 Leamington Hurdle, but he failed to make an impact. It was possibly a step too soon in his education, but I feel he will make a big impact this season.

CLAN DES OBEAUX (FR) – 2012 *(Kapgarde – Nausicaa Des Obeaux)*

He first impressed me when he contested a juvenile hurdle at Newbury in December and having cast my eyes over the eight runners, he looked a Premier League player against League 2 rivals. He confirmed that opinion oozing class to duly win by 21 lengths. He was beaten in his next two starts at Cheltenham and ran sixth in the Triumph, but looking at him you could see that he still had plenty of growing to do and was still on the weak side. I eagerly await his reappearance because I feel he has plenty to offer this winter.

GALA BALL (IRE) – 2010 *(Flemensfirth – Nuit Des Chartreux)*

This horse won a hat-trick of races throughout the winter and showed his quality each time. What I like about him is that he looks a thorough stayer and enjoys soft ground. He made great strides throughout the winter, but his physique always suggested that three miles and fences was going to bring out the best in him and I think he will come into his own this winter.

HELL'S KITCHEN (GB) – 2011 *(Robin Des Champs – Mille Et Une)*

I don't get soppy over horses but I will make an exception for this fella. I first saw him on a racetrack at Kempton and he looked a gorgeous type in the paddock, but was nowhere near fit. He showed a fair amount of ability, finishing third behind the highly-regarded Wait For Me. His next stop was a novice hurdle at Newbury on soft ground and I could see he had made significant improvement fitness wise and beat a fair sort in Walking In The Air. Harry Fry's five-year-old had his final start in a novice hurdle on good-to-soft ground, but you could see that he was hating the underfoot conditions and never looked happy jumping hurdles. His ideal requirements are soft ground and I look forward to seeing him because I think he will be something special.

MICKS LAD (IRE) – 2010 *(Beneficial – Floreen)*

The Radford's have owned some good horses over the years and hopefully Micks Lad will fill the void. He made his debut for Dan Skelton in the Huntingdon bumper and looking at him pre-race he was clearly a nice type, but was unfurnished. He was given time to learn as the race developed and I like the way he came in to the home straight full of running until his fitness gave out. I am sure he will be making an impact this winter.

NEW TO THIS TOWN (IRE) – 2011 *(Milan – Jade River)*

He came to the Cheltenham Festival strongly fancied after winning two bumpers on heavy ground. He looked the part and this big son of Milan possesses plenty of quality, but I think we did not see the best of him. This coming season his attention will be switched to hurdling and given his love for soft ground, I am sure he can go very far in his new discipline because physically he was one of the nicest types in the Champion Bumper.

OK CORRAL (IRE) – 2010 *(Mahler – Acoola)*

This JP McManus-owned gelding looked the real deal when winning his first bumper at Kempton in 2015 and he beat a decent line up on that occasion. His trainer skipped

Cheltenham and sent him over to Punchestown where he finished second to Yorkhill and behind him was Up For Review so we know he has a touch of class about him. Hopefully he will return with the same ability intact and I know the Henderson camp thought a great deal about him. I am sure he has developed over his time off and should have the make and shape to make a big impression over jumps.

PETER THE MAYO MAN (IRE) – 2010 *(Dylan Thomas – Mommkin)*

I was first taken by this chestnut gelding at Doncaster where he looked fairly straight and you could see he had plenty of filling out to do. As he walked around the parade ring you could see signs of immaturity and as the race started he made a number of mistakes on the way around. Once clearing the second last, he picked the bridle up to finish his race off particularly well. He was given one more run around Bangor and he performed with credit in fourth. This year we will see what he is made off and I am predicting a bright future.

VILLAGE MYSTIC (FR) – 2011 *(Saint Des Saints – Mistica)*

This horse ended up in Ireland having won a point-to-point in deepest Somerset and won a Leopardstown bumper in January. The word on track that afternoon was that he is one of the best bumper horses in Willie Mullins' yard and when I saw this gorgeous looking gelding I thought he looked quality from head to toe. Always up with the pace, he asserted and showed an impressive turn of foot to win as he liked. Interestingly the trainer never ran him again which hopefully has given him time to strengthen up over the summer months. He looked one of the most exciting youngsters I saw all winter and I eagerly await his next appearance.

WINTER ESCAPE (IRE) – 2011 *(Robin Des Pres – Saddleeruppat)*

Alan King adopted a softly, softly approach and he didn't run at any of the major festivals last season. He won all of his starts and what was noticeable was the way he could change gear after jumping the final flight. After his Kempton win the trainer was eager to go to Aintree, but instead he sent him out to grass. Given what he has shown, I could see him dining at the top table over hurdles this season, especially on good ground.

ZIPPLE BACK (IRE) – 2012 *(Sendawar – With Conviction)*

This four-year-old gelding had been working well on Alan's gallops and was fancied to run a very good race on his first start in a Huntingdon bumper. He showed immense promise, running well behind Bags Groove. His next assignment was a tough one because he was sent to Aintree to contest their Grade 2 Champion Bumper and looking at him compared to the rest you could see he was very immature. Given he has had two runs to gain experience he should have learned a great deal and he has the size and scope to show his qualities once switched to hurdling. He may need good or good-to-soft ground to be seen at his best.

JOCKEY'S STABLE STARS

The 2015/2016 season was record-breaking on many counts, but in terms of jockey's achievements it was most notable that Richard Johnson landed his first jockey's championship and Lizzie Kelly's victory aboard Tea For Two in the Grade 1 Kauto Star Novices' Chase was the first Grade 1 success over jumps for a female jockey on these shores.

That pair are joined in this section, 'Jockey's Stable Stars', by David Pipe's stable jockey Tom Scudamore and Ireland's star point-to-point rider, Derek O'Connor. The quartet have kindly put together a list of their own horses to follow for the upcoming campaign and these horses are well worth noting for the future.

RICHARD JOHNSON

BRAAVOS (GB) – 2011 *(Presenting – Tatanka)*

He is big baby but he is a horse that we have always liked. He was just a frame last season and I look forward to seeing how he has improved physically after a summer at grass. He is in the same ownership as Rock The Kasbah and Garde La Victoire who enjoyed profitable second seasons over hurdles and there is no reason to believe Braavos will not follow a similar route. A real winter horse, he will enjoy good-to-soft and soft ground and I feel that he is a horse with considerable potential for this season and beyond.

COPPER KAY (GB) – 2010 *(Kayf Tara – Presenting Copper)*

A super talented mare who has showed some really smart form in bumpers over the last two seasons. She will embark on a novice hurdling campaign this season and she could be a very high-class recruit to that sphere – especially against her own sex. She failed to sparkle like we know she can in the spring, but that was in good race and she is the type to improve for the switch to hurdling. The mares' hurdling programme is going from strength to strength and she is certainly the best mare by some way that I am likely to ride this season. She is a horse that I am really looking forward to riding again this season and one that sits high on my horses to follow list.

DRUMLEE SUNSET (IRE) – 2010 *(Royal Anthem – Be My Sunset)*

Although I didn't have a good experience on him at Cheltenham on his second start over hurdles last season, he is very honest and straightforward to ride. He showed a consistent level of form throughout his novice hurdling campaign, bumping into a number of good horses along the way and it was good for him to get his head in front on his penultimate start at Warwick. He was still quite immature last season and it is not unusual for horses that come from point-to-points to take a while to achieve their full potential under rules. He isn't a big horse but he's a very athletic type and should have no problem in jumping a fence in time. However, the fact the he is rated 133 means that races like the Grade 3 Silver Trophy at Chepstow will come under consideration with him.

DUKE DES CHAMPS (IRE) – 2010 *(Robin Des Champs – Ballycowan Lady)*

If I had to pick one horse for this season, Duke Des Champs would be the one that I would choose. I have loved him from the start when he won his bumper debut at Chepstow. He had a good time over hurdles last season, winning two of his six starts and filling the runner-up spot on another two other occasions. I feel that he had gone over the top at Ascot but the fact that he is still a big baby, I hope that he will return as a man after another summer at grass. He will go down the novice chasing route and I am really excited about him over fences as he was bought with that in mind. He fits the mould that Aiden (Murphy) often buys for Graham and Diana (Whateley) – a big staying chasing type. He has a lovely pedigree, he moves well and he is also pretty versatile in terms of underfoot conditions. He should take high-rank as a novice chaser.

GARDE LA VICTOIRE (FR) – 2009 *(Kapgarde – Next Victory)*

He didn't finish on a high last season after falling in Grade 1 races at both Cheltenham and Aintree but he showed when winning his first three starts over fences that he has a lot of talent. He has given us some very good days and he retains all of the ability that saw him win the Greatwood off top weight a couple of seasons ago. He jumped very well on the whole in his first season over the larger obstacles so that isn't something that worries me with this season in mind. I expect something like the Haldon Gold Cup or another valuable handicap like that will be on his early season agenda. He is versatile ground-wise, he has a fantastic attitude and I hope that he has his best days over fences ahead of him.

ONEFITZALL (IRE) – 2010 *(Indian Danehill – Company Credit)*

He's absolutely fine after last season and he certainly didn't run his race when he was last seen at Market Rasen. We were disappointed that he lost his unbeaten record at Leicester after he had created a good impression in his first two starts at Uttoxeter (bumper and novice hurdle). He has been back to Mick's (Fitzgerald) over the summer and the fact that he is a big baby, I hope that he will come back much stronger. He doesn't take his racing as well as some, but he is a real talented horse and I am looking forward to seeing what he can achieve this season.

ROCK THE KASBAH (IRE) – 2010 *(Shirocco – Impudent)*

This six-year-old is a typical example of a horse who needed a second season over hurdles and with his owners being so patient, there was no panic to send him chasing too early. That patience was rewarded after he won two valuable handicaps at Haydock and Ascot and although he ran below par at Cheltenham and Aintree in the spring, he remains a horse with considerable potential. He improved from a mark of 131 to 150 over timber last term and I hope he can continue on an upward curve this season when he is switched to the novice chasing ranks. He wouldn't want the ground rattling quick, but after he excelled at the early part of last season, he is pretty versatile ground-wise. He is a very honest individual and three miles over the larger obstacles will see him to really good effect.

SADDLERS ENCORE (IRE) – 2009 *(Presenting – Saddlers Leader)*

He came back after a layoff and ran a really promising race on Boxing Day where he wasn't beaten very far at Wincanton under Conor Smith. I was pleased to be back in the saddle when he won well at Sandown in a competitive Grade 3 and I have to admit, it was a tough choice between him and If In Doubt at Cheltenham. Hindsight is a wonderful thing and it is likely that the year off took more out of him than we first thought (the reason behind his disappointing efforts at Cheltenham and Aintree). He was bought to jump a fence and he will be joining the novice chase ranks this season. He is lightly raced and has scope to improve further over the larger obstacles. He has an unexposed sort profile for a seven-year-old and is one for some of the better staying handicap chases.

WESTEND STORY (IRE) – 2011 *(Westerner – Sarahall)*

This horse is a real likeable type and I was frustrated that we didn't get a clear run in the bumper at Cheltenham. I expect him to take to hurdling well and after being sourced from the pointing sphere, I think he will prove himself as a stayer in time. Trips between two and a half and three miles will most likely be his bag over hurdles but he has plenty of class and he may even start out over two miles at somewhere like Chepstow and Exeter if the ground is on the soft side. He's one to follow.

WISHFUL DREAMING (GB) – 2011 *(Alflora – Poussetiere Deux)*

He did really well as a bumper horse, but it is often hard to read those three and four-year-old bumpers. I can't hide the fact that we were all disappointed last year, though I will definitely give him the benefit of the doubt and as he's only five, he has plenty of time to bounce back. Although he didn't set the world alight in his two runs over hurdles last season, his opening mark of 117 could be lenient if he can show the ability that we believe he has. He is a jumping bred horse and I expect that he will continue to improve with time and further racecourse experience. He did have a little problem last season which prevented him from running again after his run at Wincanton, but it wasn't anything major. It is worth noting that his older brother Wishful Thinking was a slow burner (didn't make his debut in point-to-points until he was five) and I hope that is the case with this fella.

LIZZIE KELLY

ADMIRAL BARRATRY (FR) – 2013 *(Soldier of Fortune – Haskilclara)*

Admiral Barratry made an encouraging debut in a three-year-old hurdle over an extended two miles at Enghien where he finished second, only beaten two and a half lengths. He was a little green that day and allowed a kind ride as it was his first run. He will ultimately stay further and hopefully given his size and scope will take to fences in the future. We expect him to be very competitive in juvenile hurdles this coming season in whichever country he runs in, and with not only a popular sire in Soldier of Fortune but also a strong dam line, we look forward to seeing how he progresses.

AGRAPART (FR) – 2011 *(Martaline – Afragha)*

Agrapart has always been an interesting horse. Nick sourced him from the Arqana sales in France as a yearling and he was all legs, giving him a lovely long stride. He started his career on the flat in France and didn't waste much time in winning when successful over one and a half miles at Le Croise Laroche on his third start.

His hurdling career started at Worcester over two and a half miles and at Ffos Las over an extended one mile and seven furlongs, where he unfortunately pulled far too hard throughout both races and finished fifth and second respectively. It was with this mind that when I rode him at Aintree it was agreed that I would make an attempt to teach him to settle. He won emphatically, travelling like a demon, jumping well and nobody got close! He far from disgraced himself when third in the Grade 1 Tolworth Hurdle over the minimum distance finishing behind subsequent Cheltenham Festival winner Yorkhill and the useful O O Seven – proving that he was able to hold his own in top-class races even on ground that was probably too soft for him. The Betfair Hurdle was his next start and that was the perfect race for Agrapart – a race that Nick had in mind since the previous year – and he duly obliged winning in facile fashion by eleven lengths. Beaten just over ten lengths by Buveur D'Air in a Grade 1 at Aintree on his last start, everything just seemed to happen a bit too quickly for him.

Looking forward to this season, he is a horse with considerable potential and as he will stay further, he will have a whole host of options – including the possibility of a long distance flat race. He's got the heart of a lion and that will always stand him in good stead.

AUBUSSON (FR) – 2009 *(Ballingarry – Katioucha)*

This horse is absolute lamb and has a very special place in our family – if he were smaller he'd probably live in the house! Last season was a little stop start for him as he had a couple of injuries at home so we gave him plenty of time to recover. He did however manage to finish 2nd in the Grade 1 Grand Prix d'Automne and after only being beaten by the narrowest of margins by Thousand Stars, it rates as a remarkable run. He also notched up a victory on his chasing debut in a three mile novices chase at Uttoxeter where he won well beating a decent field by four and a half lengths on ground that was a little too soft for him.

He has returned to France twice since and has been placed in both a Grade 2 and another Grade 1, both of which were hugely competitive. As the time of writing, we are planning to return for the Grand Prix D'Automne. After that we are unsure whether or not Aubusson will return to chasing, but we feel he will stay further which that gives us plenty of options to consider this season and beyond.

COO STAR SIVOLA – 2012 (FR) ***(Assessor – Santorine)***

Coo Star is a big rangy son of Assessor who is very much similar in stamp to our faithful warrior Reve De Sivola. He only had three starts last season, but he kept good company on each occasion and each of his performances offered plenty of promise with a view to this season in which he remains a novice. He made a bold impression on his first run in the Grade 2 Triumph Hurdle Trial at Cheltenham in November, staying on well to finish second behind Wolf of Windlesham. The ground was far too soft for him in the Grade 1 Future Champions at Chepstow and he ultimately did well to pick up third and only be beaten just over ten lengths by Adrien Du Pont.

His run at the Cheltenham Festival absolutely delighted us and his strong finishing third, only beaten by a head and half a length, was a brilliant run. I think he will stay further in time and he will also be able to jump fences in the future. His plan is to run in the Grade 2 Persian War Novices' Hurdle at Chepstow first time out and we will go from there.

DAISY DE SIVOLA (FR) – 2013 ***(Assessor – Kerrana)***

Daisy De Sivola is a tough cookie which will help her enormously. The improvement she made between her first and second run was very encouraging. On her first run she showed signs of inexperience and finished well down the field in a Fillies' Only Listed race at Auteuil – eventually getting the hang of things in the last half a mile and staying on strongly. She recorded a well-deserved victory on her second run at Dieppe, beating Duena by one and a quarter lengths. She jumps very well and the French hurdles certainly suited her on that front. There is a good programme of races for mares over the winter in England, France and Ireland so there should be no problem finding her some good opportunities.

FLYING TIGER (IRE) – 2013 ***(Soldier of Fortune – Ma Preference)***

A striking looking gelding who was successful at the first time of asking at Compiegne over an extended two miles in a three-year-old hurdle. He very nearly followed that up with another victory just over a month later but was unfortunately beaten two inches for second. He was sourced by Nick at the Arqana sales for €38,000 and has a compelling pedigree with his dam Ma Preference being a Listed and Group 3 winner. At this stage, his future looks to be over hurdles in the UK and we are excited to see what he can achieve in some of the better races in that sphere.

TEA FOR TWO (GB) – 2009 ***(Kayf Tara – One for Me)***

To say that we learned a lot about Tea For Two last season would be an understatement. Initially, we had imagined that he would be suitable to step-up through the ranks, following on from his successes the previous season and be a contender for races such as the Long Walk and the World Hurdle. He started the 2015/2016 season in the Silver Trophy at Chepstow before running in the Fixed Brush at Haydock and although running relatively respectable races in both, he didn't show the same spark that he had showed in his races the previous year - his jumping wasn't as slick and he seemed under pressure.

Given his size and scope, it wasn't a difficult decision to send him chasing, even though we felt that it may be a year too early. However, he schooled very well under my brother, Chester, at home and we found a lovely race for him to make his debut at Exeter. He won impressively over two mile and three furlongs, beating a good yardstick in Calipto and that cemented our plans to continue chasing for the rest of the season. The idea to go for the Grade 1 Kauto Star Novices Chase (formerly the Feltham) was a slight risk given he hadn't run over three miles before. Though, we felt he would stay the longer trip and I was told to give him a patient ride to ensure he had plenty left, and as they say 'the rest is history'.

We were delighted with his run at Sandown next time out over shorter, where he travelled and jumped very well, but was just outpaced and hit the third last which certainly didn't help. After this run, we felt he had done enough for the season and given that he's a little fractious and gets stressed easily enough, we decided he deserved a holiday. I am incredibly excited about teaming up with him again this season and it is quite possible that we will find ourselves at Kempton on Boxing Day yet again, here's hoping.

TOM SCUDAMORE

CHAMPERS ON ICE (IRE) – 2010 *(Robin Des Champs – Miss Nova)*

He did nothing but improve last year, showing an improved level of form on every single run. Although we have always thought of him as a nice horse, he somewhat exceeded expectations over hurdles and his run in the Albert Bartlett was brilliant. It took longer for the penny to drop with him than some of our others but he is really exciting and I hope that he really comes of age this season. He should be a very high-class recruit to the novice chasing ranks and there is no reason to believe he can't run in some of the best novice races over fences.

CADEYRN (IRE) – 2012 *(Flemensfirth (USA) – Kapricia Speed)*

This gelding won his sole point by twenty five lengths and created a deep impression on that occasion. He has since joined my brother Michael and he's a nice youngster who is worth noting for the future. Whether it is this season or next that he starts fulfilling his potential remains to be seen, but he certainly has a decent level of ability and should pay his way.

JOT'EM DOWN (IRE) – 2011 *(Kalanisi (IRE) – Shuil A Hocht)*

He's a horse who came from pointing field before joining David Bridgewater. After a satisfactory start at Towcester, I rode him for the first time at Plumpton and I was quite impressed by his three length success. He ran in the Champion Bumper at Cheltenham after that where it all happened too quickly for him. He remains a really likeable individual and is a stayer of the future. I expect he will make his mark in staying hurdles this season and he is certainly one to follow over longer trips.

MOON RACER – 2009 *(Saffron Walden – Angel´s Folly)*

Moon Racer is so talented and of course we all would have hoped to see more of him at this stage of his career but David did a wonderful job to get him to Punchestown and his second behind Blow By Blow was a superb effort. He bumped into a good one that day and was perhaps a little unfortunate to lose his unbeaten record. I have schooled him a lot at home and he has pleased us in that respect. We simply ran out of time with him last year but he is a high-class individual and I expect him to make up for lost time. He is a very, very good horse and I can't wait to get back on him on a racecourse.

MR BIG SHOT – 2011 *(Flemensfirth (USA) – Une Etoile)*

This horse won quite spectacularly on his debut at Uttoxeter when scoring by eight lengths ahead of a nice horse of Neil King's. Although I didn't ride him that day he impressed me a lot after running two races in one. He appeared to be struggling but once the penny dropped he won in the manner of a very good horse. He is a big scopey type so although he quickened up well, he is certainly a long-term prospect. He is obviously open to plenty of improvement and I expect that we will take things slowly with him – perhaps a maiden or novice and then see where he goes from there.

SPEREDEK (FR) – 2011 *(Kapgarde (FR) – Sendamagic)*

I have won twice out of the three times that I have ridden this horse – firstly in a Carlisle bumper before winning a handicap hurdle at Exeter. Nigel Hawke does particularly well with this type of horse and he should continue to improve over time. He reminds me of Nigel's chaser Samingarry who reached a useful level over the larger obstacles and that may well be the case with this horse too. He needs a bit of cut in the ground to been seen to best effect so I expect he will perform at his best when the mud is flying in the depths of winter.

THISTLECRACK – 2008 *(Kayf Tara – Ardstown)*

Thistlecrack had an amazing time last season and proved himself as the leading staying hurdler with three Grade 1 victories including a memorable World Hurdle win. I am very lucky to be associated with such a talented horse and his progression last season was quite remarkable. I have no reason to believe that he won't be just as good over fences and Colin, Joe, John and Heather are understandably extremely excited about what the future holds. I haven't schooled him over fences yet but I know Joe will have done plenty of work with him and his chasing debut is a day I'm really looking forward to. There is no doubt that he is the best horse that I have ever sat on and the sky is the limit with him.

UN TEMPS POUR TOUT – 2009 *(Robin Des Champs – Rougedespoir)*

Un Temps Pour Tout has been a wonderful servant for Pond House over the years. Obviously it is always a thrill to ride a Cheltenham Festival winner but I was really pleased to ride him to win at last season's meeting as his connections are big supporters of David's yard. We have always thought of him as a high-class horse and with him being a Grade 1 winner over hurdles (French Champion Hurdle), we hope that he still has more to offer over fences. There are plenty of options for him over trips between two and a half and three miles with races such as the Bet Victor (formerly the Paddy Power) or the Hennessy likely to come under consideration. He has often been labelled as a mud lover, but he is pretty versatile with respect to underfoot conditions and that makes targeting races more straight forward too.

DEREK O'CONNOR

ARVICO BLEU (IRE) – 2012 *(Arvico – Sharifa)*

This is a horse that I think an awful lot of, in fact I believe he could be a Grade 1 performer. He has had two starts in points and he finished second on both occasions after looking the likely winner before not seeing out the three mile trip. This gelding is a big, tall individual who I can only describe as a fabulous jumper. Standing at seventeen hands, I believe that he was simply too immature to run over three miles at this stage of his career so the fact he showed the promise he did at Cragmore and Quakerstown was particularly pleasing. He is by the same sire as Arvika Ligeonniere who was a high-class two miler and I definitely think that this gelding will have the speed to run over the minimum distance. Being out of a King's Theatre dam, he is sure to appreciate the better ground and in my opinion, he is the best maiden in the Irish pointing scene. He joins Willie Mullins now and is one to get really excited about.

ASK NILE (IRE) – 2012 *(Ask – Spirit Of The Nile)*

This youngster is by a sire I really like – his progeny often have a great temperament and are intelligent which make them easy to work with both as a trainer and as a jockey. After he finished third on his debut (he needed the run that day), he improved considerably on his second outing where he put in a flawless display to pulverise his opposition. I am always looking for a horse that is progressing and this fella is certainly going the right way. The fact that he weakened at the line wouldn't worry me as this was a sign of inexperience and he is a gelding who may need a bit of time to really achieve his full potential. He has everything that I look for in a horse and has the potential to be a graded performer further down the line. He stays in training with his handler from the pointing sphere, Seamus Neville, and may just sneak under the radar a little.

ESPOIR DE TEILLEE (FR) – 2012 *(Martaline – Belle De Lyphard)*

This good looking son of Martaline has been acquired by Roger Brookhouse after falling with the race at his mercy in what I think was the strongest four-year-old maiden of the season. He showed plenty of speed on that occasion, jumping very well baring where he over jumped at the last and he was certainly in control at that stage. The way that he quickened away from his rivals between the final two obstacles was visually impressive and he clearly has a very good turn of foot. This was a really good performance, particularly taking into account the regard that I hold this race in and he is a real high-quality horse. As he has plenty of speed, winning a bumper should be a formality before switching to obstacles. He's exciting.

GOLDEN FLOWERPOWER (IRE) – 2012 *(King´s Theatre – Golden Flower)*

This four-year-old filly by King's Theatre is similar to Ask Nile in that she was beaten on her first run between the flags. She came on a good deal to win on her second start and put in a very professional performance. She has since won a bumper for the same trainer and Colin (Bowe) is exceptional with fillies and mares. I expect that she remain in his care and looks the perfect candidate for those black type mares' races which the programme for is getting better each season. I wouldn't be surprised to see her running early on in the season as her action and pedigree tells me that good ground will be key to her. A few runs early season followed by a spring campaign ought to suit her and I am looking forward to following her career under rules.

MONBEG WORLDWIDE (IRE) – 2012 *(Lucarno – Molly Duffy)*

This gelding won what is traditionally the first four-year-old maiden of the season and is often a competitive affair – Florida Pearl won this very race in 1996. Monbeg Worldwide put in a very polished performance on this occasion, galloping his rivals into submission, handling the testing underfoot conditions particularly well. He proved that jumping is a real asset of his and that along with his high cruising speed are two attributes that will serve him well under rules. He joins Willie Mullins and is rated as a certain winner of a bumper, with the Leopardstown bumper run over the festive period highlighted as a likely target – a race Mullins won last year with Bacardys.

SECRET INVESTOR (GB) – 2012 *(Kayf Tara – Silver Charmer)*

This horse picked up the pieces after Espoir De Teillee fell at Athlacca and has since been purchased for £175,000 to go to Paul Nicholls'. He was ridden positively throughout and showed real staying qualities to gallop all the way to the line. Although stamina is probably going to be his forte, he did show some nice speed by quickening after the last. Obviously he wouldn't have beaten Espoir De Teillee if he had stood up, but given that the race was run in a time 9 second quicker time than average on the day, I still regard this four-year-old as a serious long-term prospect and is one for your notebooks.

STORM HOME (IRE) – 2012 *(King´s Theatre – Miss Mayberry)*

Trainer Warren Ewing and leading jockey Barry Geraghty have a partnership where they buy store horses to win a point-to-point or bumper before selling them and that is almost certainly what they had in mind when sending Storm Home to Largy in April. He made the running that day, travelling and jumping well throughout and he was well in command when falling at the last. By a brilliant National Hunt sire in King's Theatre, he definitely wants some nice ground and based on his debut performance, I have no doubt that he can win a bumper before tackling middle distances over jumps. He is ultimately a chaser and will have a really bright future in that sphere when the time comes.

PEDIGREE POINTERS

In this section, I have listed ten National Hunt stallions (both established and upcoming) whose progeny are worth keeping an eye on. Admittedly, pedigree isn't everything, particularly in National Hunt racing, but it can often be a guide to what trip and ground a horse is going to be best suited to and I therefore hope that this section proves useful.

BLACK SAM BELLAMY (17-y-o b)
Sadler´s Wells (USA) — Urban Sea (USA) (Miswaki (USA))
Standing at Shade Oak Stud (GB) for €3,000
Top NH earner: The Giant Bolster (£372,438)

Best known for being a brother to champion sire Galileo, Black Sam Bellamy was a useful performer on the track as a three and four-year-old, including victory in the prestigious Group 1 Tattersalls Gold Cup. As a sire, this son of Urban Sea's most notable offspring is The Giant Bolster who has twice been placed in the Cheltenham Gold Cup. He is renowned for producing stock that develop over time and in the form of Sir Anthony Browne and Sam's Adventure, he will be represented by two talented individuals over hurdles this season.

Taking into account his beautiful bloodline, he has undoubtedly been a touch disappointing at stud (his highest rated flat horse reached an RPR of 116). Though it must be considered that he isn't being sent the same quality of broodmares that his more celebrated sibling is and at a mere €3,000, he represents excellent value for National Hunt breeders.

One to follow for 2016/2017: *SIR ANTHONY BROWNE*

CALIFET (18-y-o b)
Freedom Cry (GB) - Sally´s Room (FR) (Kendor (FR))
Standing at Boardsmill Stud (IRE) for €5,000
Top NH earner: Blue Dragon (£448,353)

A high-class performer on the track with a brilliant attitude, Califet has proved himself as a decent National Hunt stallion and he is responsible for Clarcam, Blue Dragon and Calipto amongst many others. His stock seem to have two key attributes when it comes to jumping; they are very athletic and also act on winter ground. He is also a stallion that often produces good-looking horses and it is expected that he will have a good season with Burlington Burt (novice hurdler with Warren Greatrex) and Adrien Du Pont (Paul Nicholls) likely to fly the flag at a decent level. The latter has already won at the highest level over timber last year when winning the Juvenile Finale at Chepstow and there is every chance that Califet's offspring can scale similar heights this time around.

One to follow for 2016/2017: *ADRIEN DU PONT*

FAME AND GLORY (10-y-o b)
Montjeu (IRE) - Gryada (GB) (Shirley Heights (GB))
Standing at Grange Stud (IRE) for €7,000

Fame And Glory had a fantastic racing career, yielding fourteen wins from his twenty five starts including Group 1 wins in the Irish Derby, Coronation Cup and Ascot Gold Cup and he is expected to produce top-class progeny now switched to the stallion ranks. It is reported that he is producing very well put together foals and with his first two-year-olds hitting the track in 2016, the future is exciting for the ex-Aidan O'Brien inmate. Taking into account that he was an excellent stayer himself and is by a brilliant sire in Montjeu (also stayed 12f), he could prove to be a very good National Hunt sire in years to come.

KAYF TARA (22-y-o b)
Sadler´s Wells (USA) – Colorspin (FR) (High Top (GB))
Standing at Overbury Stud (GB) for £5,000
Top NH earner: Thistlecrack (460,000)

As a son of Sadler's Wells, Kayf Tara hails from one of the most prolific bloodlines in recent history. A top-class stayer when representing the all-conquering Godolphin operation, Kayf Tara enjoyed plenty of success as a stallion last season, surpassing the £2,000,000 barrier for the first time. Although he's proven as one of Britain's leading National Hunt sires, it is worth noting that the majority of his most successful progeny have come in recent years and his leading earner Thistlecrack proved himself as a star of the staying hurdling division last term.

His stock are generally good looking and appear to get better with time which offers prospective buyers of his offspring all-important longevity. In addition, Kayf Tara is responsible for all types of horses – speedy two milers such as Identity Thief and Special Tiara as well as the aforementioned Thistlecrack and Blaklion who have showed significant improvement when tackling longer trips. He's an extraordinary sire and his sons and daughters will continue to win races at the very highest level.

One to follow for 2016/2017: *VALUE AT RISK*

MARTALINE (17-y-o gr)
Linamix (FR) – Coraline (GB) (Sadler's Wells (USA))
Standing at Haras De La Reboursiere Et De Montaigu (FR) for €10,000
Top NH earner: Dynaste (588,608)

A smart colt when trained by Andre Fabre, Martaline recorded a notable victory over fellow top-class jumps sire Westerner when successful in the Group 2 Prix Maurice De Nieuil at Maisons-laffitte in July 2003. Since switching to the stallion ranks, he has performed particularly well and last season he added the Betfair Hurdle to his already impressive CV as a sire, courtesy of runaway winner Agrapart.

Bred by Juddmonte farms, there is no surprise to see his offspring are catching the eye over obstacles and it is expected that he will continue to hit the headlines in the coming seasons. Plenty of trainers will be keen to get hold of some youngsters by him, especially when taking into account that his stock keep on improving and that they can go on all types of ground. It is worth looking out for the Martaline/Cadoudal nick (a nick is when a horse has the same sire and dam sire) as this has produced a number useful horses in recent years.

One to follow for 2016/2017: *CHEF D'OEUVRE*

MULTIPLEX (13-y-o b)
Danehill (USA) – Shirley Valentine (GB) (Shirley Heights (GB))
Standing at Mickley Stud (GB) for £2,750
Top NH earner: Out Sam (30,126)

Another who raced in the famous Khalid Abdullah colours, Multiplex was a winner between seven furlongs and a mile and his speed is something that he has clearly passed onto his progeny, boasting a useful strike rate with two-year-olds. Having said that, he is slowly making his mark as a jumps stallion, with his offspring often having plenty of size about them.

Given his exploits on the level, it is hardly surprising that Multiplex has proved himself capable of siring bumper winners, with the speed element proving a real asset. At a stud fee of £2,750 he is extremely good value for money and the fact that he is having a few Irish point-to-point winners will only continue to make him more popular in the National Hunt breeding industry.

One to follow for 2016/2017: *POSITIVELY DYLAN*

PRESENTING (24-y-o br)
Mtoto (GB) — D´Azy (GB) (Persian Bold (GB))
Standing at Glenview Stud (IRE) for a private fee
Top NH earner: Denman (£1,141,347)

Presenting, a top-class three-year-old over twelve furlongs, was represented by the ill-fated No More Heroes during the 2015/2016 campaign and as mentioned earlier, the loss of that particular horse will leave a huge hole to fill at Gordon Elliott's. As a sire he is often associated with horses who appreciate better ground and having been responsible for two Cheltenham Gold Cup winners in War Of Attrition and Denman, his stallion page understandably generates plenty of interest in the breeding industry. He gets a real nice type - sound and lovely-looking horses.

Being a multiple Champion Sire, Presenting is probably one of the more obvious stallions included in this section. However, given his remarkable record since switching to his second career, he has certainly earned his place. A couple of his most notable progeny currently in training are Grade 1 winning hurdler Yorkhill and also the aforementioned Southfield Royale (read about him on page 53). The fact that he is now a grand old age of twenty four, Presenting is unlikely to spend many more years at stud, but there is no doubt that it will be fun following his offspring while they last.

One to follow for 2016/2017: *YORKHILL*

ROBIN DES CHAMPS (19-y-o b)
Garde Royale (GB) – Relayeuse (FR) (Iron Duke (FR))
Standing at Glenview Stud (IRE) for a private fee
Top NH earner: Quevega (749,280)

Robin Des Champs, one of the best National Hunt sires in recent years, is very unusual in the fact that he didn't race on the Flat, but instead achieved a good level of form over hurdles in his native France. Trained by the brilliant Guillaume Macaire, Robin Des Champs won four of his five starts over hurdles before switching to the breeding ranks. He is renowned for producing sizeable individuals – Un Temps Pour Tout, Tombstone and Champers On Ice are fine examples of this – and with that in mind, you can expect his sons and daughters to improve with time and also excel over fences.

Given that his progeny include superstar mare Quevega, multiple Cheltenham Festival winner Vautour and Cheltenham Gold Cup runner-up Sir Des Champs, it is hardly surprising that this stallion proves very popular with bloodstock agents and with plenty of promising youngsters, he looks set for another successful season in 2016/2017.

One to follow for 2016/2017: *WOODLAND OPERA*

WESTERNER (17-y-o b)
Danehill (USA) — Walensee (GB) (Troy (GB))
Standing at Castle Hyde Stud (IRE) for €5,000
Top NH earner: Cole Harden (£292,479)

Multiple Group 1-winning stayer Westerner is an established sire I am very fond of. Although he has sired two-year-old winners, the majority of his success as a stallion has been over jumps. His sons Western Warhorse (Arkle), Cole Harden (World Hurdle) and Solar Impulse (Grand Annual) have recorded Cheltenham Festival victories and it is only a matter of time before another of his offspring perform on the biggest stage.

Grade 1 winners are what connections dream of and considering that this stallion is well-known for producing high-class individuals, it isn't a surprise to see his progeny extremely popular when offered at the various sales throughout the season. He generally produces horses that are tough, go on any type of ground and they have also showed aptitude over both hurdles and fences.

One to follow for 2016/2017: *HELLO GEORGE*

YEATS (15-y-o b)
Sadler´s Wells (USA) – Lyndonville (IRE) (Top Ville (IRE))
Standing at Castle Hyde Stud (IRE) for €7,500
Top NH earner: Capivari (£52,419)

Even the youngest of readers are likely to remember this exceptional stayer. The four-time Ascot Gold Cup winner, Yeats, is relatively new to the breeding ranks but has already showed plenty of promise in his second career. Hailing from a good family, he is expected to produce jumpers with speed and longevity – two attributes that will make his offspring popular. As a racehorse he had an admirable attitude, finding plenty under pressure to deny his rivals on numerous occasions. In any sport an individual with a good attitude can often outshine one with a touch more class and if Yeats can pass on his mental stability to his progeny then they will enjoy plenty of success over obstacles. The rise of Joseph O'Brien has been mentioned continuously throughout this publication and I am personally excited to see Yeats' youngsters representing the man who I deem to be one of National Hunt's most promising trainers.

One to follow for 2016/2017: *SHATTERED LOVE*

Q&A PART ONE

Part one of the new question and answer section brings together three respected industry professionals; William Hill broadcaster Luke Elder **(LE)**, the former author of the Cheltenham Festival Betting Guide, Paul Jones **(PJ)** and Emmet Kennedy **(EK)**, the host of the popular The Final Furlong Podcast. In this section we talk trainers and jockeys as well as a look at some of the most popular equine stars who are expected to return to action in the coming weeks and months.

Richard Johnson and Ruby Walsh are the current Champion Jockeys in the UK and Ireland respectively and barring injury they look likely to regain their crowns. Assuming that you agree, who do you expect to fill the runner-up spots in the two championships this season?

(LE) Sam Twiston-Davies is a jockey who gets a lot of unfair stick on social media, but one who is going from strength to strength in the saddle. The yard of Paul Nicholls haven't had the firepower of past seasons recently but with the likes of Aux Ptits Soins and older campaigners like Dodging Bullets, it won't be long before they are back. As for Ireland you'd think it will be a case of the usual pretenders like Paul Townend and Davy Russell that push Ruby, but my main wish is for Bryan Cooper to have a long run without injury after another bad fall at Galway.

(PJ) Sam Twiston-Davies looks in prime position to be the one to follow Richard Johnson home having made a good start over the summer but odds at the time of writing (mid-July) of 50/1 for the title look very big about Tom Scudamore should the defending champion suffer time away with injury. Given that Barry Geraghty will have many trips to Britain to ride for J P McManus then the owner's number two Mark Walsh will be picking up plenty of rides in Ireland for his boss as well as outside rides so I'd nominate him over Bryan Cooper and Paul Townend.

(EK) There are some seriously talented jockeys in the weighing room, but considering the fire power at their employers disposal, it's hard to look beyond the claims of Bryan Cooper in Ireland and Barry Geraghty in the UK. Gigginstown House Stud already have an established group of stars with some exciting prospects coming through, while JP has opened the cheque book to acquire some new talent, giving their respective talented stable jockeys a lot to be excited about for the new season.

While on the subject of jockeys, who do you think is the most exciting young talent in the saddle in both the UK and in Ireland?

(LE) I imagine young lads such as David Noonan and Tom Bellamy will dominate this question, and rightly so as they are fantastic young jockeys who will go far. But a couple of younger and more seasoned jockeys who are just gaining the recognition they deserve are Nick Scholfield and Josh Moore. The former of the two has really impressed me in the last couple of season. As understudy to Sam Twiston-Davies he may not get the best rides but he is a superb judge and will go anywhere for a winner. The same applies for Josh Moore (who will one day make a terrific trainer) after a fantastic season for his father and bigger yards such as Jonjo O'Neill. A Cheltenham Festival success still eludes him but he gave Ubak a sublime ride at Aintree and just shows that he has the superb horsemanship that is so prominent in the Moore family!

(PJ) Mark Walsh is top drawer material as is Sean Bowen. However, and although I wouldn't class him in the 'most exciting young talent in the saddle' category as he is beyond that, Aidan Coleman deserves a really big job and I hope to see him at Seven Barrows one day soon.

(EK) It's hardly splitting the atom to name a jockey who has won the biggest prize in racing, but David Mullins gave Rule The World an ice cold ride that belied his youth to win the Grand National. He also displayed great strength in the saddle when giving Nichols Canyon a brilliant front running ride in the Morgiana Hurdle to beat Faugheen. In the UK I've been impressed with Ryan Hatch who is making the most of the opportunities being giving to him by Nigel Twiston-Davies. Both young jockeys have displayed the skills to suggest they have very bright futures in racing.

Talking trainers and Dan Skelton has made a brilliant start to his career since leaving Ditcheat. Other than Skelton, can you highlight one trainer who, given more fire power, has the potential to be Champion Trainer in the future?

(LE) Dan Skelton is the obvious choice as you mention after passing the 100 winner marker last season. But I will be fascinated to see how Harry Whittington gets on this season after losing his stable star Arzal after winning his first Grade One. Still in the yard are Emerging Force and Affaire D'Honneur who will both make big splashes this upcoming season.

(PJ) Harry Fry is the best of the younger trainers for my money as I'm a strike rate and chasers-rather-than-hurdlers man. Fry's strike rate, especially with novice chasers, is outstanding. If he is considered already there now rather than in the 'younger trainers' category then I would nominate Harry Whittington as the emerging trainer to note who enjoyed a 23% strike rate from 93 runners last season and posted his first Grade 1 success with the ill-fated Arzal.

(EK) Both Paul Nicholls in the UK and Willie Mullins in Ireland have demonstrated that skill as a trainer isn't enough, you have to have the diplomatic skills to attract high-profile, big spending owners and keep them all happy. Joseph O'Brien is the obvious candidate to follow in their footsteps. The son of arguably the greatest trainer of his generation, he was himself a top-class jockey, who won some of the highest profile Flat races around the world. He has the advantage of excellent training facilities and has spent his whole life in racing. He also understands the pressures of working for high-profile owners. Having trained a Cheltenham Festival winner – albeit in his father's name – in his first season and with the backing of owner J. P. McManus – Joseph O'Brien is a Champion Trainer in waiting.

Now onto the horses and Sprinter Sacre had a fantastic 2015/2016 campaign but as he will be eleven at the turn of the year, do you think he is vulnerable to any of last season's novices? If yes, who is his most threatening rival in the two-mile division?

(LE) Douvan is the obvious and almost only answer to this question, he was simply awesome in all starts last season. In my opinion, his near flawless performance at Aintree was the best of those and he is an individual that excites massively. Of the others that will need to up their game, Traffic Fluide is a fragile but talented horse who we only saw once last season. That came behind Un De Sceaux at Ascot and for his first run out of novice company, I have the impression he was capable of much better before injury struck.

(PJ) Douvan is about as an obvious answer as you can get to that question. With the stable's Un De Sceaux having proven to be have been a little over-rated, it looks a nigh-on certainty that Douvan will be kept to two miles this season with the top prizes over longer distances to be attacked later in his career.

(EK) I thought Sprinter Sacre was a has-been who would be blown away by his younger rival Un De Sceaux last season, but I've learned my lesson and won't doubt him again. It will be tougher for him at eleven years of age, but it would be foolish to write him off.

However, in Douvan, he faces his toughest foe yet. He has been described by his owner Rich Ricci as the best horse he has owned, high praise indeed considering the talent he has. Douvan is a champion in the making. While they may not meet until Cheltenham, the thought of the old champion and the young pretender locking horns in the Tingle Creek is a hugely exciting prospect.

This time last year Faugheen was the unbeaten two-mile hurdler that everyone was talking about but after being on the sidelines since January, do you think he will be able to return to his best and regain his Champion Hurdle crown in 2017? If no, who do you predict will win this season's Champion Hurdle?

(LE) Yes, 100%. I have been a huge fan of Faugheen for the past few seasons and have often said he is the best since Istabraq (just don't tell Cathryn Fry I said that). His first minor hiccup came when missing the defence of his Champion Hurdle crown through injury which allowed us to see Annie Power in full glory. Despite rumours that Faugheen may step up in trip, Paddy Mullins has said he will follow the same campaign as normal this season which is ideal for me!

(PJ) I don't see any reason why Faugheen won't return as good as before as it wasn't a major injury that ruled him out of Cheltenham. It's a shame that it is unlikely that he and Annie Power will never meet being in the same ownership and as the mare is versatile (staying hurdling and chasing are also options), I have to think that Faugheen will be Rich Ricci's Champion Horse again with the mare being aimed at other leading prizes. I also suspect that Ricci wants Faugheen to end his career having toppled Night Nurse's record hurdles rating which has stood since 1977.

(EK) Willie Mullins sounds confident that Faugheen can return to his best, but he's had a history of injury problems as a younger horse and you would have to be concerned.

Apple's Jade put in an astonishing performance at Aintree and backed that up with another impressive display at Punchestown. Considering she is owned by Michael O'Leary, it would be surprising if she is not given a Champion Hurdle campaign. Stepping into open company will be much tougher, but she is already a three-time Grade 1 winner from only five starts. In my opinion, she is the most exciting two-mile hurdling prospect for the new season.

Willie Mullins and Rich Ricci upset plenty of people when sending Vautour to the Ryanair after owner Ricci said "he'll run in the Gold Cup or stay at home" at a preview evening prior to the festival. What was your take on this decision and if you owned Vautour would it be back to the Ryanair for more of the same or a crack at the Cheltenham Gold Cup?

(LE) I have long thought that the Ryanair is a much disrespected race and for little good reason. Cheltenham is mostly about prestige which a new race can find hard to gain, but without it we'd have horses unsuited to the Champion Chase or Gold Cup hindering chances for all. Now do I think Vautour should run in the Champion Chase or Gold Cup? Neither, if he were mine, Vautour would be winning the Ryanair year after year as the race is ideal for him. It wasn't Rich Ricci's best moment to say what he said at the Cheltenham preview, but plans change late on in the day and despite it leaving a sour taste in the mouth, he can do things like that. Also, it's not as if we haven't been gifted plenty of good words for his horses in the past few seasons!

(PJ) Having attended that very preview night and given the firmness in his voice when Ricci stated that view, it was embarrassing to him and for that reason I doubt that he enjoyed Vautour's Ryanair win as much as he should have done. We certainly know who makes the ultimate decision in the Mullins-Ricci relationship now if we didn't already unlike in the Gigginstown relationship with their trainers. I wouldn't hesitate at aiming Vautour at the King George first and then take a view - a cop out I know!

(EK) Having hosted Cheltenham Preview nights, I usually push the panel to get off the fence and tell us what they really think. The drink is flowing, there's a big crowd engaging in the banter and the panel feel free to speak openly. I have no doubt Rich Ricci genuinely thought they were going for Gold when he made that statement. That said, the decision to run Vautour in the Ryanair left a sour taste. However, I would be very reluctant to criticise Rich Ricci as some in the media have. He speaks so openly and enthusiastically about his horses, which is very refreshing when compared to many other owners who say so little, you would think they are clandestine operatives. A high-profile owner who is prepared to engage with the media and racing fans is very good for the sport.

For what it's worth, I think the Ryanair was the right race for him last season and he was sensational. On the back of that performance he deserves a crack at the Gold Cup and I would be very surprised if that's not his target this season. I have no fear of him getting the trip and quotes of 8/1 seem very fair.

Thistlecrack was a member of last year's Top 40 Prospects and he dominated the staying hurdling division culminating in a Cheltenham and Aintree double in the spring. It appears that a switch to fences is imminent and the 2017 Cheltenham Gold Cup is already being talked up as an end of season target. Would you stick to novice company with him and go the RSA route or attempt to re-create the epic 2015 renewal where Coneygree became the first novice to win the Gold Cup for more than 40 years?

(LE) Firstly, if Thistlecrack were mine he would stay over hurdles and try to emulate his 2015/16 season. However, I admire Colin Tizzard's sportsmanship and after the unbelievable job him and his team have done with Cue Card, who am I to begrudge his plans? It's always a grey area for me, for all that it was great to see Coneygree win the Gold Cup as a novice, it was far more upsetting and devastating to see Gloria Victis meet his end when doing the same thing years ago. Until we see Thistlecrack over fences in public, I shall reserve judgment, but in my mind novices should contest races against fellow novices.

(PJ) If he takes to chases as well as we expect he will then I'd go for the Gold Cup as if they wait another year then his first crack at the race would be as a ten-year-old and there has been no winner aged in double figures since Cool Dawn in 1998.

(EK) If Thistlecrack were mine I'd let him dominate the weak staying hurdle division and try to emulate the achievements of Big Bucks. But I can understand where the owners and Colin Tizzard are coming from. The Gold Cup is the prize every racing fan wants to win and there is no question that he has the ability to win it. If inexperience catches him out early in the season, they can revert back to the smaller obstacles and win another World Hurdle. He's a machine and his connections are right to aim for the stars.

Now a chance to dream, given the opportunity to be associated with any horse in training, who would it be and why?

(LE) Faugheen would be a dream but as nothing more than a racing fan it was unbelievable to see Sprinter Sacre back to his best last season. If any of us were ever to get a horse half as spectacular as the black aeroplane we would be lucky!

(PJ) I'd go with Apple's Jade. She was jaw-droppingly good when winning by forty one lengths at Aintree and then followed up in style at Punchestown. She's hugely exciting and could be absolutely anything and then I could breed from her when her career ends. It will be interesting to see what Willie Mullins (or more like Gigginstown given that they call the shots with their horses) elect to do with her this season.

(EK) Douvan. When you speak to Patrick Mullins and Rich Ricci the enthusiasm they have for the horse is infectious. Some of his performances on track have been sensational. He was a super novice hurdler and was an even better novice chaser. Already a dual festival winner, if he stays sound, there are some very exciting days ahead for the Walk In The Park gelding.

Finally, can you give the readers three horses to follow for this season – a bumper horse, a hurdler and a chaser?

(LE) Captain Moirette may not have won a race yet, but has shaped with potential on each start in the bumper sphere for Sue Smith. As a strapping big grey he won't be missed on the northern circuit but reminds me a lot of Blakemount who was a top novice hurdler for the yard a couple of seasons ago before injury struck.

Ubak is a horse who we haven't seen the best of, mostly through injury but still remains a horse with potential. If Gary Moore can nurse him back to full health then he will be a live outsider in the World Hurdle.

The last couple of seasons I would have given Djakadam, as much as I feel he deserves to win a Gold Cup I shall go elsewhere. It's only a matter of time before Gallant Oscar goes close in another big prize and from this far out I can see him going well in a Grand National. He was still swinging along under Mark Walsh last season before unseating at the 18th. If Tony Martin can campaign him well enough then he could be a horse for the biggest race of them all!

(PJ) It's hard to suggest a bumper horse as most of those from last season will be going hurdling but the bumper horse I took a real shine to last season was La Bague Au Roi on her victories at Aintree and Huntingdon so I am inclined to forgive her seventh in the Grade 2 at the Grand National Meeting.

Apple's Jade for reasons given above is the hurdler I'm most looking forward to seeing this season and, if she is as good as I think and Gigginstown go down the Champion Hurdle route, she will be very interesting receiving 7lb there.

Killultagh Vic's novice chasing season came to an end before the spring festivals so he has the look of a well handicapped horse if they want to start down that route but I'm convinced that he is a Grade 1 chaser in the making and could be interesting for something like the Ryanair.

(EK) I was very impressed with Invitation Only at the Punchestown Festival. He goes novice hurdling this season and could be an ideal type for the Neptune Novices Hurdle. He is highly thought of and is one to follow this season.

Bellshill has yet to perform at Cheltenham, but I think they ran him over the wrong trip in the Supreme. He goes novice chasing and has RSA Chase written all over him.

Finally, I'll stick with the Willie Mullins/Graham Wylie partnership and mention a horse that I became synonymous with on The Final Furlong Podcast last season, Black Hercules. A few eyebrows were raised when he lined up in the JLT Novices Chase, but he put in a taking display of jumping to win comfortably. Connections will have to decide between the Gold Cup and the Ryanair Chase, but if he makes the expected progress he can be a major player in open company staying chases this season.

Q&A PART TWO

Part two of the question and answer section includes three individuals who are well-known for sharing their views on horse racing via Twitter. The horse racing community on Social media is constantly growing, particularly on Facebook and Twitter and I am pleased to have caught up with Harry Drew **(HD)**, Ross Moynihan **(RM)** and Maddy Playle **(MP)** over the summer to discuss some of the rising stars of the jumping game, ante-post betting and the Cheltenham Festival.

There is no better place to start than Douvan who was sublime in all of his six starts over fences in an unbeaten novice chase campaign. He clearly has the ability to go to the very top, but over which distance would you campaign him?

(HD) With Un De Sceaux stepping up in trip for next season and Sprinter Sacre edging towards retirement, I can't see Willie Mullins changing Douvan's winning formula. He's the best two mile chaser in Britain and Ireland and the Champion Chase will be his to lose come next March. I understand people thinking he might be a Gold Cup horse but he's still only young and that avenue will always be open.

(RM) I see Douvan as a champion chaser in the making. He has so much natural speed. Stamina isn't exactly an issue either though, and it is fun to dream "What could be?" if he were campaigned with the likes of a King George in mind. From day one however Douvan has been leaving everything for dead, both at home and on the track, predominantly over two miles. He's clever at his obstacles, he's won a Supreme, he's won an Arkle, and I for one cannot wait to see him and Sprinter Sacre lock horns up the Cheltenham hill. Younger legs will prevail in my book!

(MP) I still have a few questions to ask Douvan, and over which trip he would ultimately like to be campaigned over is one of them. I did wonder how close Vaniteux would have got had he not unseated Nico De Boinville in the Arkle and I also question the quality of horses he has faced thus far. But, his jumping is his main asset, and I think that is what will allow him to tackle a longer trip. I certainly don't think he will always be an out and out two miler, but for this season at least, I think the likely aim will be over two miles in the Champion Chase. The Ryanair could also be an option over an additional five furlongs, but I wouldn't even entertain going for the Gold Cup at this stage. To go from winning an Arkle straight to the Gold Cup the next year is a mammoth task, and if anything, an unnecessary one. It would be hugely exciting were he to go that route and I'd praise connections for being bold, but there looks to be plenty of time for Douvan to tackle the two mile division first.

Supreme Novices' Hurdle winner Altior was the highest rated novice hurdler in the Anglo-Irish Classifications when they were announced back in May. If you owned this Nicky Henderson inmate would you be aiming him at the Champion Hurdle or switching to fences for a novice chasing campaign?

(HD) Altior has always looked like a chaser to me. Long stride length, big frame and a keen eye to attack his obstacles. If he ran in the Champion Hurdle next year he certainly wouldn't be disgraced, but I can't see this being his path considering his size and scope.

I'd personally put him straight over fences and the Arkle looks tailor made for him. He's going to be some horse.

(RM) I love this horse. I've loved him since day one actually, day one for me being the time we lumped on and got him beat in a bumper at Newbury at 6/4. He hasn't done too much losing since that day though, and looks a serious horse now who is only beginning to fulfil his potential. Much like Douvan, this lad is a horse I see as a two mile chaser going forward. Supreme winners have a nice record in the Arkle and I can see Altior enhancing this record going forward. He has options but if you have the choice of not racing against Faugheen and racing against Faugheen, you go with the former.

(MP) Funnily enough, my answer is I honestly do not know. Or rather, I don't mind. After Cheltenham I thought it would be great to see him against Faugheen and potentially a whole host of others, so why not give it a go before a season over fences? I'm always of the opinion if horses are high quality hurdlers, they should explore that avenue as much as they can before they go chasing. He will get the strong pace he needs in the Champion Hurdle, and there is always the option to step out of novice-company in what would be his first season over fences. However, I could understand if Henderson opted for what is now considered the more conventional route, as Altior is six years old now, the age he considers ideal to send a horse over fences. From what we've seen, Altior looks versatile, which in a way only complicates the problem. But, to coin a hugely overused phrase, he has always been considered a chaser, and therefore the main point in this argument may be if they go hurdling again, he may not take to fences with another year under his belt. Cole Harden will aim to disprove the theory this season, as he is set to go chasing, and of course Paul Nicholls's recent juggling of his juggernauts from hurdles to fences and back again has proved relatively fruitful. But, if the reports are correct, Altior has already been schooled over fences, so it seems the question has already answered itself.

Excluding the two aforementioned horses, is there another standout novice hurdler or novice chaser from last season that you are particularly excited about?

(HD) I'm obviously looking forward to seeing how our lads get on over their new obstacles and distances next season; but if I was to look forward to seeing one novice next year it would be Barters Hill going novice chasing. He's just an absolute bull of a horse with great size and ability. He looked a bit of a character at the start of last season but still managed to sweep aside decent opposition. It was most impressive that when it mattered, he rolled up his sleeves and out battled his rivals. I personally thought that two miles and five furlongs would have been far enough for him at Cheltenham, especially with his turn off foot but he still put in a fine display in the Albert Bartlett, falling on his sword finishing fourth. I can't wait to see him attack his fences with great enthusiasm this season and it wouldn't surprise me if he drops back to intermediate trips.

(RM) I'd say half of Willie Mullins' yard would be the answer here. Min still could be anything, and despite his hype bubble being popped at Cheltenham I doubt we've seen the best of him yet. Yorkhill is a serious horse who was given a masterclass of a ride by Ruby at Cheltenham. He has options now but I'd say the Arkle is calling his name. Outside of Willie's yard, I won't give up on Disko just yet. Noel Meade's grey has a bit of a reputation and despite coming sixth on his last start at Punchestown, I'd say he's a handy fella to have around and on side next season.

(MP) I'm not often one to follow the crowd, but in terms of novices moving forward, I'm intrigued by Apple's Jade. In recent years, particularly following the Peace And Co fiasco, the Triumph Hurdle is a race that has received plenty of criticism, with the four-year-olds being unable to progress against their elders. But, not for the first time, it may be a case of the amnesic racing fan, as the likes of Katchit, Zarkandar, and more recently the ill-fated Our Conor have proved they could make hay in the big time following their victories in the Triumph. I'm already a big fan of this year's race, as I think so many of those in behind will have high-profiled careers as chasers. Consul Du Thaix and Clan Des Obeaux both fit into that category and Footpad and Zubayr have already franked the form, showing great promise in the Grade 3 Prix Questerabad at Auteuil. Apple's Jade comes across as a speedier filly with more to give over the smaller obstacles, but equally she could excel over fences, too. Overall, it will be fascinating to see how her career works out.

In comparison to the Flat where there are numerous mid-week festivals, National Hunt racing has one main focus which is the Cheltenham Festival. Do you think that the 'jumps' season is geared too heavily around one week in March?

(HD) Not at all. I think it's fabulous how all the best horses are aimed for one special week. If you asked any owner where they would most like to win, I bet the answer would be the Cheltenham Festival.

(RM) Not really to be honest. I love everything about Cheltenham. I love the build-up, I love the event and I love talking about it all year before it happens again. While perhaps we are a tad guilty of binging on Cheltenham talk and focus, I'd rather have it this way than any other. It's a great week simply put, one that we should cherish, and not pick holes in.

(MP) I think it all depends on your personal perspective. As a jumps fan first and foremost, I see so many wonderful performances outside of the four days in March, and I think they are there, if one is intent on seeing them. Willie Mullins has made it clear he means business when it comes to winning the UK Trainer's Championship, and the increased ammunition that he is sending over can only be considered beneficial to the wider calendar. Even domestically, Colin Tizzard's bold campaigning of both Cue Card and Thistlecrack has meant jumps fans haven't had to go very long without seeing a superstar. I understand the frustration, as it appears the fashion these days is to target horses for Cheltenham and Cheltenham only. But in general, I think there is far too much pessimism regarding the targeting of Cheltenham. It's inevitable, and I'd suggest issues such as poor prize money in the North are far more significant. I think racing fans should embrace the great stories often only poorer weekday cards can provide.

While we are discussing the Cheltenham Festival, are you a fan of the current four day meeting? If no, would you change it back to the old format of three days or extend it to a five day fixture?

(HD) Four days is perfect in my opinion; a great mix of Grade 1 races and top-class handicaps. I am a believer in the saying if it isn't broken, don't fix it.

(RM) Four days does it for me. Five days I'm against, three days wouldn't satisfy me. While I can see the five day argument from a commercial point of view, I'd rather we didn't dilute the quality or the experience of the current arrangement. Plus, I don't think my wallet, liver or emotions could stretch to a fifth day!

(MP) As a relatively new fan to racing, I am unfamiliar with the three day meeting but from what I have experienced I think the four day festival is pretty good, as it gets me another day off work and college! I'm no industry expert, but I can understand wherever there is an opportunity to make money it will bc exploited, and I don't see any real fundamental issue with the way the Festival currently is. It is growing every year and an element of change is only natural given it's increasingly popularity. Although, I fear if the meeting was stretched to five days the quality of the racing could be compromised and the focus of the event could shift further towards those looking to have a drink and a day out, and away from satisfying the demands of the racing purists.

Now here is your time to shine, if you had to put your last £100 on one horse to win at next year's Cheltenham Festival, who would it be and for which race?

(HD) You could easily say Douvan for the Champion Chase as he's going to have another flawless season and he will go off favourite if everything goes to plan. But I am going to stick my neck out here and say Thistlecrack for the Cheltenham Gold Cup. From what I can gather from connections comments, he will bypass a novice campaign and go straight for big one and with him being nine next year, I can see why. He has to be the most improved horse I've ever seen and if he takes to fences, he will be pretty unstoppable.

(RM) Altior for the Arkle, I've convinced myself. He's generally second favourite behind Yorkhill at the time of writing, and 5/1 is out there. He's better than Yorkhill I'd say, and I doubt many are better than him.

(MP) In my mind, an admittedly dangerous place, Thistlecrack will win the Gold Cup if he lines up, without a doubt. However, if we're talking about my last £100, I'd be looking for a little more profit. I'm always one to take a risk, but at the same time I think 20/1 about Jezki for next year's World Hurdle is a shade insulting considering he has been one of Ireland's classiest hurdlers in recent years. And that takes some doing when you've got Hurricane Fly and Faugheen for company. I've always had a soft spot for Jessica Harrington's charge, and indeed the family he hails from, and he was simply outstanding when winning the Ladbrokes World Hurdle in 2015 before injury struck. The former Champion Hurdler has proved his aptitude for the three mile trip, and any horse that can out-battle Hurricane Fly after pulling ferociously for a circuit doesn't deserve to be 20/1.

Finally, can you give the readers three horses to follow for this season – a bumper horse, a hurdler and a chaser?

(HD) Starlight Court. This is a horse that came with a good reputation after travelling beautifully in his point-to-point only to fall at the last. He was going to win that day and Dan Skelton really liked the look of him so my Dad (Bryan Drew) decided to take a punt on him and bring him to England. On his debut he wasn't himself and scoped badly afterwards. Dan thinks the world off him and thinks he's going to be special. I am therefore really looking forward to seeing him over hurdles next season and hopefully he can transfer his fantastic work at home to the course.

Moon Racer. I could not be more confident about him winning this year if I tried; he's perfection. The way he came back from his long layoff was quite astonishing and with different riding tactics he would have won with a bit in hand. He jumps his hurdles well at home and with his novice status still intact, he has a lot of doors open for success. He's good enough to run in any race at the Cheltenham Festival and it wouldn't surprise me if he beats everything put in front of him this season.

Champers On Ice. He had a grand season last year winning twice and running cracking races behind better opposition on the day. He left his best performance till last at the festival and the step up to three miles really played to his strengths in the Albert Bartlett where he finished a creditable third. He was born to be a chaser and with his fabulous attitude, he can go right to the top of the staying chase division.

(RM) Ainsi Va La Vie. I have a share in her and she should make her debut in coming months and likely in a bumper. Would be worth keeping an eye on.

Jenkins of Nicky Henderson's is one to keep on side. He was beaten in the big bumper at Punchestown but was only worn down late having been in front by himself quite a long way out. He has a serious engine and will play quite a role in the coming season.

Altior won't be beaten much. Back Altior and keep backing him.

(MP) Jetstone. I confess I'm not hugely educated when it comes to spotting bumper horses, but I'm a big fan of Richard Pugh's 'Point To Point Review' on At The Races, and he highlighted Jetstone as a mare to follow after she won a three mile maiden at Dromahane at the end of May. She was bought for just €1,500 by Bernadette Murphy as a yearling, which now looks an absolute bargain. Being by Milan and out of a Presenting mare, she boasts a lovely National Hunt pedigree and no doubt there are more races to be won with her. She travelled smoothly on debut before making a small mistake three out, but showed her class to quicken best and put the race to bed with minimal fuss. She strikes me as a very athletic mare with a turn of foot, and hopefully she will be capable of running well in a few bumpers before going on to better things.

Blow By Blow. Besides the few I have already mentioned, I'm a huge fan of Blow By Blow as a hurdler to follow. He built on his second placing on debut to beat the highly touted Jett on his next start, who is a member of the aforementioned illustrious family of Jetson and Jezki and deserves to be followed in his own right. He then beat one of Gordon Elliot's reputable bumper horses in Death Duty at Fairyhouse, who will also prove to be a serious horse in years to come. He then surprised a few people at Punchestown with a commanding, heart-on-sleeve, pillar to post display where he truly lived up to his name and gave Katie Walsh her first Grade One winner. Perhaps the thing that draws me towards Blow By Blow is the fact that he has belied expectations and those expectations were sky high already. He was born to be old school National Hunt. He is a tall, raw five-year-old, and not, one would think, a precocious Champion Bumper winner, yet that is exactly what he has done. I think the Neptune would be a realistic target this season, and I wouldn't be surprised to see him lining up in a Gold Cup a few years down the line.

Richard Hobson is most know for finding and purchasing the likes of Sir Des Champs and the legendary Hurricane Fly, but he has recently turned his hand to training with great success. His Allysson Monterg is my chaser to follow, as he has only had five runs in his life, but has showed a huge amount of raw ability. Most of us first saw him when finishing a neck behind the highly touted Champers On Ice on New Years' Day at Cheltenham – he showed plenty of inexperience on that occasion – but it was clear to see the talent was there. He then won at Leicester before another promising run in the Albert Bartlett, where he finished sixth after being amongst the cut throat pace in an attritional race. For a big horse he jumps very neatly and with some more experience under his belt, as he is only a six-year-old, I think he will become a high quality staying chaser to follow.

National Hunt 10 To Follow
2016 - 2017
November 11th 2016 - April 29th 2017
Simply select 1 Star Hurdler, 1 Star Chaser,
2 Grade One Contenders & 6 Stable Stalwarts!
- Weekly Bonus Races &
Fantastic Monthly Prizes!
1 Entry: £5
3 Entries: £12
6 Entries: £21
12 Entries: £36
20 Entries: £50
18+
Follow us on Twitter:
@NH10toFollow
@Jimbo_JumpsMan
@george_weyham
Supporting the IJF

APPENDIX

This section of the publication includes a brief review of last season's 'Top Prospects' as well as looking at a number of other horses that have joined the UK or Irish National Hunt scene after being sold privately from France

Appendix A – 2015/2016 Top Prospects Review

Anibale Fly landed the Coral Handicap Hurdle at the Punchestown Festival at odds of 6/1 on his last start and now up to a handicap mark of 146, he will find life much tougher if he embarks on another season over timber. *Aux Ptits Soins* only had the one start last season and finished a well-beaten fifth behind Thistlecrack in the Ryanair World Hurdle. With chasing very much on his agenda now, he rates as a leading prospect and along with Politologue and Ibis Du Rheu, he forms John Hales' strong trio of novice chasers. *Bellshill* had a consistent season baring a disappointing effort at Cheltenham and his Grade 1 win at the Punchestown Festival for a second successive season sets him up for another profitable season – this time over the larger obstacles. Although he lost his unbeaten record at Cheltenham in the Grade 1 Albert Bartlett, *Barters Hill* lost nothing in defeat and he is another really high-quality horse that is predicted to join the novice chase ranks this season. Expensive ex-point-to-point recruit *Born Survivor* was purchased with chasing in mind and after a satisfactory season over timber, it is expected that he will begin to fulfil his potential this time around. *Champers On Ice* who ran a fantastic race to finish third in the Albert Bartlett has a very progressive profile and he was arguably one of the hardest of last year's 'Top Prospects' to leave out of this year's list. The strong travelling *Cultivator* was included as a novice hurdle prospect last term but he remained in bumpers, ultimately disappointing in the DBS Spring Sales Bumper at Newbury. He began his hurdling career in May when runner-up in a Kempton maiden hurdle and he could well return to that venue for the novices' hurdle in November that his trainer targeted on two consecutive occasions with West Wizard. It was a shame that *Disko* could only manage to have three starts over hurdles last season, but he still has a lot of untapped potential and he is a horse who I am excited to see make his seasonal reappearance. *Douvan* remained unbeaten over fences and as predicted in last year's publication, he landed the Racing Post Arkle with considerable ease. In my opinion, he remains the most exciting horse in training and the world is his oyster. *Great Try* and *Milsean* missed the whole of last season with injuries, but assuming that they have made a full recovery, they should both make a smooth transition to the novice chasing division. *Minella Rocco* may have been called a few names at the start of the season, but the well-related gelding delivered when it mattered and won the National Hunt Chase at the Cheltenham Festival under a brilliant Derek O'Connor ride. He will be hard to place this year, but ultimately looks a perfect Grand National type. 2015 Champion Bumper winner *Moon Racer* made his belated seasonal reappearance in the Punchestown equivalent in 2016 and with connections seemingly bullish about his prospects as a hurdler, he can compete at the highest level over timber this season. The now JP McManus-owned *Ok Corral* failed to make the track during the 2015/2016 campaign with what was described as 'niggly problems', but with his bumper form looking very strong, he should be followed now he is switched to obstacles. *Peace And Co* started last season as a live contender for the Champion Hurdle, though he flattered to deceive in all three of his starts and he is now on a revival mission to prove that he retains the ability that saw him win the previous season's Triumph Hurdle. *Shantou*

Village lost his unbeaten record when second to Yanworth at Cheltenham in January and subsequently ran below par at the festival two months' later, where connections reported that he sustained a cut during the race. However, that is not an injury that will cause him long-term damage and his attentions will be switched to fences in the autumn. In boxing terms, *Thistlecrack* is the current 'Heavyweight Champion of the World' after he recorded five straight victories culminating in World Hurdle glory at last season's festival. It is reported that he will embark on a novice chasing campaign this time around and I certainly can't remember many better hurdlers being switched to fences. *Tycoon Prince* is a horse who I have always had a soft spot for and although he failed to reach the heights expected of him over hurdles, his connections have always thought of him as a staying chaser and it is in that sphere where I expect him to excel. David Pipe and Tom Scudamore teamed up with *Un Temps Pour Tout* to win last season's Ultima Business Solutions Handicap Chase at Cheltenham – one of five of last year's 'Top Prospects' to win at the festival – and he should have another successful season over fences, with all the top handicaps coming under consideration for the son of Robin Des Champs. *Welsh Shadow's* first season over obstacles yielded two wins from six starts and given that he contested some of the best novice hurdles last term, he proved that he is a really talented individual. Whether he remains over hurdles for a crack at the staying hurdling division or embarks on a novice chase campaign, he remains a horse to keep on the right side of. High-class bumper horse *William Henry* was another who failed to make the racecourse last season and I understand that he had minor injury problems. He will hopefully return in the autumn and I still rate him as a young horse with the potential to go to the top of the jumping game. *Yanworth* and *Yorkhill* locked horns in the Grade 1 Neptune Novices' Hurdle at the Cheltenham Festival and it was the latter who came out on top, recording a one a three quarter length success. However, the pair are still closely matched in terms of natural ability and after Yorkhill showed mental frailties by pulling ferociously at Aintree, Yanworth is more reliable as a long-term prospect in my opinion. Last but certainly not least is Grade 2-winning juvenile *Zubayr*, who remains a youngster with plenty of talent and Paul Nicholls is one of the best at nurturing long-term prospects to make sure that they fulfil their potential.

Appendix B – Other Notable French Imports

Rich Ricci has sourced a number of his National Hunt stars from France in recent years including Douvan, Vautour and Min and he has again been busy acquiring what he hopes are his next crop of champions. Arguably his most well-known French import this time around is the current Supreme Novices' Hurdle favourite, *Senewalk*. By Walk In The Park, a sire who Ricci has had a lot of success in recent years with, this youngster won on his second start and looks to have a bright future as a jumper. *Game In The Park* is an unraced three-year-old also by Walk In The Park. He will either be targeted at juvenile hurdles similarly to his owner's Let's Dance, Dicosimo and Kalkir or put away for novice hurdles as a four and five-year-old next season. Another pair of three-year-olds who will be next seen in the famous pink and green spotted silks of Ricci are *Winter Soldier* and *Francin*. The former was runner-up on his sole start at Nantes on the Flat with the latter winning his final two starts under that same code. *Montalbano* is a year older and being a four-year-old, he is one for the novice hurdling division this season. He finished second to *Park Light* on his sole start over hurdles in a Listed contest at Auteuil in March and given that the winner gave the form a handsome boost by winning a second Listed race at the same venue on his next start, it is predicted that Montalbano will take high-rank.

Other purchases to join Mullins include *Meri Devie* (Andrea and Graham Wylie) who won on her second start on the flat before finishing seventh in the Group 1 Prix Saint-Alary on her latest outing. *Melon* who features high in the current market for the Supreme Novices' Hurdle is a four-year-old who won on his third start at Moulins and he appears to be held in high-regard by his new connections. Another one to note is *Timi Roli* who won his sole start on the flat last August and will carry the colours of George Creighton – colours that are widely associated with dual Champion Hurdle winner Hurricane Fly. Another of Mullins' flagbearers over the last two seasons has been Un De Sceaux and Chateau Conti, a thrice-raced four-year-old, will bear the same silks as the 2015 Arkle winner in novice hurdles this season.

Gigginstown House Stud are less often associated with French recruits but they have purchased three useful three-year-olds that are well worth following for this season and beyond. *Dinaria Des Obeaux* who won an AQPS race in the provinces on her sole start is a really likeable individual with a bright future over jumps. Similarly to Apple's Jade last season, she is likely to go down the juvenile hurdle route with her new connections working back from Cheltenham, Aintree or Punchestown. *Delphi Collonges* is another mare who won on the level on her second start at Nancy before subsequently finishing second and fifth on two starts over hurdles, the latest at Auteuil. Again, she is expected to run in juvenile or novice hurdles. Though given that the pair are both in the same ownership, it is likely that either Delphi Collonges or Dinaria Des Obeaux will stick to racing against their own sex. *Dakota Moirette* is a gelding by well-known jumps sire Voix Du Nord and he filled the runner-up spot on his only start on the Flat. Only beaten by a narrow margin on that occasion, this youngster is sure to improve for the switch to hurdling and is another exciting prospect to join Michael O'Leary's powerful operation.

Grade 1-winning chaser *Kotkikova* is arguably one of the most interesting recruits to the British National Hunt scene after she joined leading owner JP McManus. Also placed in a Grade 1 over timber, this daughter of Martaline will have plenty of options now trained in the UK and her new handler Nicky Henderson must be relishing the prospects of unleashing this smart mare on these shores.

Citrus is yet to get his head in front in eight starts on the level in France, but he has now been switched to the UK and will be in the care of David Pipe. He is likely to make an impact on the novice hurdling scene and it should only be a matter of time until he can register his first career victory.

Similarly to Mullins, Paul Nicholls has sourced some of his former stars from France and in the form of *Garo De Juilley* he may well have another high-class performer on his hands. This four-year-old gelding won his last four starts on the Flat and now trained at Ditcheat, it is certain that he will embark on a novice hurdling campaign. *Clo Sacre*, unraced in his native France, was acquired by Nicholls and has ran twice in English point-to-points for Jack Barber since. From the family of Sprinter Sacre, this gelding looks to be a lovely chasing prospect – the type of horse that Nicholls repeatedly excels with.

If numbers are what you go on then the AQPS flat race that was run in the French provinces last June is worth noting with no less than five of the thirteen runners now stabled in either the UK or Ireland. The race was won by *Crackdeloust* (Brian Ellison) by a length with the third *Chambord Du Lys* (Willie Mullins) showing real signs of promise.

The sixth (Calie Du Mesnil) and seventh (*Chateau Conti*) have also joined Ireland's Champion Trainer with the fourth (*Crin Au Vent*) now in the care of Mullins' British counterpart, Paul Nicholls.

INDEX

LIFE IS A
CONSTANT
EXCHANGE
OF
BEAUTY,
WISDOM
& GRAVY
THE FINAL
FURLONG